The Rights of Man and Fish

Dedicated to Sue, who makes it all worthwhile

The Rights of Man and Fish

Paul Halas

Illustrated by Pete Field

αn editions

AN Editions
aneditions.co.uk | editors@aneditions.com

Second edition.

British Library Cataloguing in Publication Data
A catalogue record for this book is available from the British Library

ISBN 978-1-7384023-4-2

CONTENTS

Preface

'*Bienvenue*, welcome.... So you're the reporter from *La Dépêche*.... You speak English? That's a relief.... Well, I've been here – what is it? Four? No, very nearly five years, and my French is still...a work in progress. And of course you want to know about the odd English writer who's been holed up here all this time.

'I'm guessing you haven't read my book? No? Not surprising really, since there hasn't been a French edition yet. Which means there's a bit of a story to tell. It may take a little time, and you'll no doubt end up saying I've been talking a load of *conneries* – rubbish. You're still interested? Gosh – it must be a very slow week for real news. Anyway—

'The book is about history...although it's been described as fantasy, a mishmash of misinformation...absolutely crazy, according to many. Ah, so you've read the reviews already. It's true, quite a few critics have said that, but actually that's pretty wide of the mark – I'd say it was a chronicle, an account of the stories behind the stories. You see what's really interesting about history isn't the bare facts – we all know them – but the back stories...what made historical events take place – that's what's so different about the book, and that's what got people so worked up. But first things first. Let's take a seat on *la terrasse*, and can I offer you a glass of rosé? It's from the local vineyard, and it's very nice – especially on a day like this.

'Where to begin? I pitched my first history article – *The Battle of Hastings: the true story* – to an online magazine called *The New Polymath*. They were very rude at first, asked if I even knew what the term meant, but then, surprise of surprises, someone there actually bothered reading it through to the end, and, even more surprisingly, decided to use it. And that was just the first surprise. One of the readers at a small publishers called Benham Kleber (maybe there was only one reader) saw the piece and thought there might be mileage in it. I think they were really desperate at the time, but they proposed that I wrote a book – a real one. Because the advance was so piddling – yes, I mean small, about enough for a trip to the supermarket – they offered me a decent deal apropos of royalties…and the rest, as they say, is history.

'People always ask me where my outrageous ideas come from, but they're actually factual accounts and, truth be told, I'm not the real narrator of the work – more an editor or agent or something like that I suppose. It's all in the book – as written – and that's where people have so much trouble with it. Many critics simply dismissed it as a Baron Munchausen-type fantasy, which I don't have a problem with as long as the books fly off the shelves. You're *still* interested? *Bien.*

'Once you know the whole story you'll understand why people have a problem taking it literally, and that's why I don't give interviews to the British press anymore. Why? Because they always think I'm taking the piss, *que je me fous de leurs gueules*…. And your average British hack doesn't have very much imagination.

'So I'm telling you, it all sounds pretty bizarre. I mean at first *I* didn't believe any of this stuff could be for real, but as for anyone else…. Well, you aren't going to believe me. But you're still up for it? Really? Then have another glass. Make yourself comfortable. That's right. This is going to take rather a long time, so I hope you've nothing else scheduled for the rest of the day. I just want to make one condition. You're going to find what I say absolutely outrageous. However mad it all sounds, I'm asking you not to stop me or butt in or we'll be here until next month. You interrupt me and this *tête à tête* is over, *compris*? Very well, if you're sitting comfortably let us begin—'

Chapter One

Coote Lake. In which Gisella makes a very dumb mistake and meets Mike

A Saturday afternoon in early July, six years ago. I'd cleaned my flat and done the shopping, and pitched up at a lovely secluded swim at Coote Lake for an overnight fishing session. Coote was a small gravel pit, a club water that not many people fished because it contained such a low head of carp and it had the reputation for being hard. As well as carp there were tench, roach, rudd, perch and pike, but not in great numbers and not particularly large. The club had other larger and more prolific lakes that the majority of its members preferred, which suited me just fine.

It was perfect. A very slight ripple blowing diagonally across the water towards me, a bank of reedmace to my left and a large bed of lily pads about fifty metres out to my right. Magic. I used to fish with only two rods, and anyway the club had a two-rod maximum rule on Coote, so it didn't take long to set up and cast out a couple of baits. Landing net, carp cradle and weighing sling in position, I erected my bivvie and unfolded my bed chair. The cooking stuff could come out later, when I fancied a brew. Now I could sit back and wait for Mr Carp.

I usually fished single baits, with a small dissolving mesh bag of micro fish pellets for a bit of extra attraction, simply because everyone else used to fire out a load of freebies that could easily over-feed the swim. My baits that day were all of three years old, from a half-empty tub of long discontinued boilies that I'd lost during my last house move. Old the boilies may have been, but they still smelled strongly of fenugreek and maple syrup – Vor-Tex, they were called, a classic bait in their day – so I reckoned they'd still be worth a try.

I guess fishing was my major haven of sanity. Not that I went in for it like many others – spending thousands, snapping up all the latest gear and faddy baits, a slave to the latest rigs, joining the most exclusive fishing syndicates, total tunnel vision, wrecking their marriages. Actually, my marriage had gone to shit without my fishing myself out of it. Anne said it was more that I didn't have any ambition, any get-up-and-go. That I lacked imagination, that I failed to thrill her anymore. That a follicly-challenged septic-tank salesman who collected old seaside postcards – and not even the smutty ones – evidently did thrill her didn't exactly help my mental well-being. In addition, the fact that I absolutely detested my job, that I detested pretty well every job I'd ever had, and you start to see why my weekly overnighters at Coote Lake were such a welcome escape. That, and reading history books – pretty well any history books actually – every night till I fell sleep, made up the positives in my life.

Of course people should have ambitions in life. After all, at that time I was still only in my mid-thirties, but all that corporate ladder stuff never seemed to be for me. It was as if the very first rung was way out of reach, and I couldn't be arsed to make the effort anyway. Maybe Anne was right. What did float my boat, what really did quicken the pulse, was the idea of catching Mrs Lopsided, a common carp of stunning proportions for such a modest lake. Mrs Lopsided was probably a myth, but the tiny handful of people who claimed to have spotted her (the biggest carp is usually a she) said she swam with an odd sideways list. They also said she weighed thirty-seven pounds, which puzzled me slightly because she'd never ever been caught. But it was all hearsay and rumour; every water has its own folklore and legends, and ninety-nine per cent of the time they're bullshit. So why did I fantasise about catching her? A reluctance to deal with the real world, perhaps….

As far as I could tell I had the lake to myself. Apparently its days were numbered. The whole area was down for development, into a new 'village', or yet another expansion of Springhampton more like – sod the green belt – and it was only being held up by a lively local protest group and the few councillors with any shred of integrity. A lake on the critically endangered list seemed to be putting the regulars off – but me, I was only too glad of the peace and quiet.

The droning of insects in the late afternoon heat was making me dozy, when the peace and quiet were rudely shattered by one of my bite alarms trilling. I almost fell off my bed chair and made contact with the culprit, which tried to dash for the reeds. I stopped it, as it wasn't that big. Then it suddenly bolted diagonally back across my swim and before I could regain all the slack line it embedded itself in the only weed bed in that part of the lake. Bloody typical! I applied steady pressure and slowly but surely a clump of the weed detached itself and I was able to winch it bit by bit into my landing net.

When extracted from the weed the tench – of course it was a tench – went 5lbs 10oz on the scales. I'd hoped it would make six, but five-ten was pretty respectable – especially for Coote. Never underestimate a tench; they fight dirty. It had proved one thing, though: the fish appeared quite willing to chomp three-year-old baits.

I slipped it gently back into the water, rebaited and cast out again. I was fishing both lines a few metres apart, in a slightly deeper gulley a little way short of the lily bed. Tight to the reedmace bank would've been a good spot too, but casting to the pads I'd be able to use a couple of poplars on the skyline as night-time markers for later on, when I'd be casting in the dark. It very seldom ever gets pitch black at night, and the silhouettes of trees make ideal points of reference, so you can put your baits where you're aiming to. Sort of, in my case.

That lovely drowsy feeling again. The gentle buzz of insects. Then the lengthening shadows and fading light, moths replacing damsel flies, bats replacing swallows. The mosquitoes didn't bother me. I reckon when you spend a lot of your time outside you get some kind of immunity to the little bastards. And then my mind turned to food – lunch was a long time ago.

I'd brought a tin of ravioli for my supper, supermarket own brand of course. Tell me it isn't exactly the same as the pricier bands.... Well, if it isn't I still bet no one can tell the difference. Strange how I never get bored of tinned ravioli, but truth be told the effects of the open air and ravenous hunger mean taste becomes somewhat secondary. The only problem with heating up my evening meal was the prospect of getting my arse off my bed-chair. Strange how inertia sets in, even when one could eat a horse.

Then, in a fraction of a second, I was on my feet. My right-hand bite alarm bleeped – once, twice. Then it was silent, though I could still see my line twitching slightly. It was probably a little roach or rudd pissing about with my bait, but there was just a chance the culprit was a crafty big fish trying to eject the bait without launching into a full-blooded run. Very gently I raised my rod – and felt something very solid. I wound down, and, fully expecting hell to break loose, had the odd sensation of not fighting a large angry fish, but pulling in what felt like a supermarket bag filled with rice pudding. While pumping the fish in, I slipped my landing net into the water in readiness to greet whatever it was I'd hooked. A big bream? Were there any bream in Coote? Then the fish, which by now I could tell was seriously big, knee-tremblingly big, decided to lend a hand. It swam straight towards me and right into the waiting net.

'Fuck me, it's Mrs Lopsided!' I gasped.

'I do detest that name,' said a distinctly female voice. It was the kind of voice you associate with a forty-Gitanes-a-day habit and jazz-singing in a Rive Gauche nightclub. The husky, slightly Gallic voice belonged to the carp. 'My name happens to be Gisella.'

Whatever I'd expected to happen, this wasn't it. There was absolutely no one around. It can only have been the carp that had spoken to me. My legs turned to blancmange, and I sat down on the grass.

'I've told you my name,' the carp peered at me from the net, which was still mostly submerged in the lake's margin. 'It would be polite to reciprocate.'

'Er, I'm…Mike…. Mike Apperley.' Remembering my name was a struggle.

'*Enchanté*,' said Gisella. 'Now, do close your mouth before a frog jumps into it.'

'But you can—'

'Bravo – humans have such a gift for stating the obvious. Now, before we go any further, can you get your bloody stupid hook out of my mouth?'

Hands shaking, I leant over the net and quickly obliged.

'While we're at it, you wouldn't happen to have a drop of the hard stuff with you?' said Gisella.

I shook my head. 'Afraid not. I could do with a stiff slug myself.'

'I'm only a social drinker, mind, but getting caught. It's not the most pleasant experience.'

'I can offer you coffee.' Gisella completely ignored that suggestion.

'I can't believe it,' she continued. 'I fell for a bog-standard shock rig. It's so bloody embarrassing. My eyes must be going, but I still feel like an utter tit. It was that Vor-Tex boilie that did it – that heavenly *mélange* of fenugreek and maple syrup – no one's used those for years and I guess I let my guard down. A single bait, though, sitting in the middle of nowhere all by itself. I need my head examined.'

'They'd been pushed to the back of a cupboard. I lost them way back. I was devastated when they stopped making them.'

'You're not the only one. In their heyday, anglers in the know fired in thousands of them – free grub for yours truly. I guess lots of carp here fell to those Vor-Tex boilies, time after time probably, but of course not *me*.'

'So you're an expert on rigs?'

'*Naturellement*, after so many years of having an entire A to Z of end tackle heaved into the lake, I bloody well should be. Plus fishermen are always prattling on about baits, tactics and rigs. You'd be surprised just how human voices travel under the water.'

'Then I guess there was never an ultimate rig that really impressed you? Surely some are better than others.'

'You know what? It may have gone out with free love and flares, but you probably couldn't improve on simple freelining with a balanced bait. Hang on! You're trying to tap me up for fishing tips, you cheeky arse!'

'Sorry, sorry. No offence.'

'And you can stop glancing at your weighing sling. A lady doesn't reveal her weight – even when she's a carp.'

'Excuse me, I wasn't thinking. It's just, I'm a little thrown here. It's not every day one gets to speak with a carp.'

'You should feel honoured.'

'What's it like being a…?'

'Look, I suppose I don't mind sticking around for a little chinwag, but how about you put me back in the water first?'

I hesitated. I didn't want our little chat to come to an end quite so quickly.

'Don't worry, I won't swim off. As it happens, I've missed intelligent conversation over the past few years. And believe me, compared to most of the anglers here, you appear to be moderately articulate.'

'You don't talk to the other fish?'

'Some, but it's not an edifying experience. They're all pretty monosyllabic, even the tench.'

'Really? I always say you should never underestimate a tench.'

'Quite so, they're resourceful enough. But they're no conversationalists; their topics don't extend much beyond whether they prefer white or red maggots. No, I hate to admit it, but there's much more to engage the mind above the water than below. Now, if you don't mind?'

I pushed the landing net out into slightly deeper water and, once free, Gisella flicked her tail and circled back to within inches of the lake's edge. It was very noticeable how much of a tilt she swam at.

'It's rude to stare. And yes, I suppose I am a bit lopsided.'

'Were you always?'

'Since I weighed half a pound or so. I was attacked by a certain predator called Mack the Pike, who damaged my lateral line – hence the slight problem with balance.'

'Mack the Pike. Hmm, very droll.'

'Well I never, an angler who knows his Kurt Weill. Actually, I *did* know him once, but that's completely by the by. You're right, the name's bullshit, but as a young *carpeau* in Normandy a thousand or so years ago I was attacked by a very uncouth pike.'

'*How* long ago?'

'Mouth, Mike. Frogs.'

'So you – you date back to the Norman Conquest?'

'A few years before it, actually.'

'And to cap it off, you can speak.'

'Getting on for fifty languages I should think, but I don't keep a tally. Human languages, that is.'

I sat back down on the grass and took deep breaths. This was quite a lot to take in. I'd dropped acid a couple times in my not very dissolute youth, but I didn't think this was a delayed reaction – my trips had never been anywhere near this weird. Until anything happened to prove the contrary, I had to accept I was having a chinwag with a carp. Quite an erudite carp it appeared. I had the impression she'd be just as at home in the *Quartier Latin* as a muddy pond.

'The next question you're going to ask is why? How? What caused me to be like this?'

I nodded.

'When I was a fingerling in some small river in our corner of Normandy – I never learned the name – the region was hit by multiple natural phenomena. Earthquakes, solar flares, aurora borealis, electrical storms. The river boiled like a witch's cauldron, and for a few instants I glowed like the brightest of celestial bodies.... You're not buying any of this crapola, are you?'

I shrugged my shoulders. It was hard to believe anything I was hearing, but I realised that not only was Gisella rather loquacious, she also had a penchant for taking the Mickey.

'Quite right. I actually haven't a clue why I'm like this – I guess I'm just a freak of nature.'

'A freak of nature from before the Norman Conquest – or so you say.'

'That part's true, carp's honour.'

'But this is...sensational. Mind-boggling. The things you must have lived through, the panoramic sweep of history you must have witnessed over the past millennium.'

'A lot of the time I was avoiding the limelight, keeping my head down under the lily pads so to speak. But yes, I've witnessed a few momentous events. Even taken part in one or two.'

I looked at Gisella expectantly.

'How long have you got?'

'All the time in the world. Until tomorrow teatime anyway. I never turn down a bit of history.'

'Then reel in your other line and make yourself a brew. This is going to be a long night.'

Chapter Two

1066 etc. How Gisella learns to speak, joins the Norman invasion and makes two very unlikely friends

Following my narrow squeak with Mack the Pike – okay, that nameless upstart of an obnoxious pike – I tried to keep to the parts of the river where it would be hard to ambush me, such as weed beds and sunken tree branches. But I was young and naïve, and the very next time there was an abundant hatch of yummy freshwater shrimps I broke cover and was promptly scooped up in someone's net.

The expected sharp crack on my cranium didn't happen. Instead I, and a motley collection of roach, bream and chub, were dumped into a wooden box, wedged in with sodden pondweed, and dragged overland to a new home: a small pond at the end of what I later learned was the kitchen garden belonging to a fortified manor house. The thing about being wrapped in wet pondweed is that you go into a state of suspended animation almost – it's amazing how long we carp can survive out of the water. Of course you have to be revived afterwards, usually with a dab of something strong on the tongue. In this case it was Calvados. I generally prefer Cognac or Armagnac, but Calvados is acceptable, especially if it's *hors d'age*. Now some historians would have you believe that drinking spirits only came into vogue during the thirteenth or fourteenth century, but of course that's hogwash. Crafty monks had perfected the art of distillation centuries earlier, and those in the know habitually bought or pillaged it according to their customs. But I digress.

Ideal, I thought, as I swam around the pond. I'd be safe here. Silly little carp – I soon learned my mistake.

The manor house's cook, a chap from the south called Ugolin, and a female servant called Fionne, frequently found their way down to the pond for secret trysts. With my sharp hearing I could make out every word they said – and before long I found I could understand all their whispered sweet nothings – not that they were all that riveting. Unlike my fellow fish, it turned out that I had a superb lateral line for languages.

(A minor digression here: for those who don't know, a fish's lateral line is a most wondrous organ. It detects minute variations in pressure, which enables us to hear very clearly, detect the distant movement of both predators and prey, and even forecast the weather. Forget the Met Office, those wonks have got nothing on us fish. For instance, we can foresee a storm several days in advance, although the fact that most fish are far too dim-witted to act on that information is a moot point. Also, while I'm rambling here, a word or two about our barbules, the dangly bits by the side of our mouths – in the carp and catfish families that is. No more jokes about bearded ladies, please. There isn't one I haven't heard. Our barbules detect chemicals in the water, in the most minuscule dilutions. In other words we can taste remotely, which leads us to food in very muddy water etc., although this wonderful gift is a double-edged sword when it comes to anglers' baits. *Très bien*, lecture over.)

What I did glean of interest, however, was that Ugolin was terribly homesick for his native Provence (as it's called nowadays), where the sun always shone, where winters were balmy and soft, and the air was scented with lavender and rosemary, where gentle breezes rusted the leaves in the olive groves, and the ponds and rivers were filled with great bronzed carp, and life was milk, honey and ambrosia. Of course, Ugolin was going to take Fionne away from all this, and they'd settle back down south and live happily ever after. I wished they'd take me with them. I'd already suffered two harsh Normandy winters in my short life and I didn't think much of them.

I also quickly learned that my new home was no safe haven after all. Periodically Ugolin would march down to the pond, giving the game away with his elephantine footfalls, cast in his net, and take away some of my companions for Count Roland's table. At the first *tremblement de terre* I quickly learned to shoot into the marginal weed and keep well out of trouble. The only other fish who learned to take evasive action was a tench – never underestimate a tench – although as a companion she was dull as ditchwater: worms, water snails and maggots, that was her conversational limit. Of course we'd ended up in a stew pond; the river would've been far safer after all.

History books will tell you that stew ponds didn't arrive in northern Europe until at least the thirteenth century. I can tell you that the epicurean Count Roland had one at the end of his kitchen garden in 1065. The count really liked his food, and that included pretty well everything that swam.

I also learned that Count Roland was the most important human thereabouts, and that a count counted for more than a cook, and a cook counted for more than a peasant. Humans appeared to love having a hierarchy, but it would take a few more centuries before I completely got the hang of their bizarre system. With fish, if you come across something bigger than you, you clear off out of its way because it may eat you – that's all you really need to know. Digression over.

The cook and his lady love weren't the only ones to tryst by the pond. The Countess Cunegonde, Roland's comely spouse, often snuck past the raspberry canes and artichokes to meet the gallant Baron Fredo, a splendidly moustachioed specimen whose muscles bulged from his tunic. Apparently Fredo had a reputation as a mighty warrior, and I suspected the females of the species saw something else in him too. Cunegonde would always cast aside her wimple for their illicit assignations, and what would follow made a very fascinating contrast to the way fish did it. It occurred to me that while a baron was apparently worth less than a count, the countess certainly didn't see it that way.

The months trundled by, the trysters trysted, and Ugolin periodically came to scoop out more unsuspecting fish. When stocks ran low, another batch was netted from the river and dumped into the stew pond with us. It's not as if the tench and I didn't try to warn them about the dangers of their new home, they just weren't very good at avoiding the net, and saving our own scales definitely came first for my red-eyed companion and me.

As the summer of 1066 waned, one couldn't avoid the talk of impending war against the Anglo-Saxons, even down in the stew pond. Something about a broken promise, and Guillaume le Bâtard going to seize King Harold's crown. It appeared kings were even more important than dukes, earls and barons, although in Harold's case probably not for long. The invasion became the main topic of conversation between Fredo and Cunegonde – once they'd seen to their more pressing needs. I listened avidly as one evening the conversation took a sinister turn.

'They say King Harold has a moustache as fine as mine,' said Fredo, eyes creased with displeasure, 'though as God is my witness I find that hard to believe.'

'Surely not,' said Cunegonde, adjusting her shift. 'The glory of your upper lip is celebrated throughout the Christian world, and from what I hear the Saxons are all weak-chinned and weedy.'

'When we come face to face I'll chop his head off,' said Fredo. 'Moustache and all. And if anyone else gives me any lip I'll chop theirs off too.'

'So it's true. It's really happening.'

'You must've noticed how many trees have vanished. Ships are being built, scores of ships. William the Bastard is completing his invasion fleet as we speak.'

'What if I lost you? I don't think I could bear that. Plus I'd be stuck here with my disgusting pig of a husband, with no hope of reprieve.'

'Ha, Count Roland the Roly-Poly won't be able to sidestep this shindig – he's managed to slip out of every scrap over the past decade, but William is keeping a beady eye on him now.'

'Maybe he'll meet a heroic death on the battlefield,' said Cunegonde wistfully.

'Oh, I don't think his chances of survival are very high. In fact, I'd rate them as absolutely zero, if you get my drift.'

'Just be careful,'

'It's the Anglo-Saxons who'll need to be careful. And a certain rotund Norman count. He'll never know what hit him.'

Over the next few days, I caught wind of much human activity. Evidently Count Roland was preparing to take his leave to join the invasion, and minions were sent scurrying hither and thither. Was I bothered? Not in the least. I knew the score, I was safe in my stew pond – or so I believed.

One morning a really fine figure of a man accompanied Ugolin to the pond. It was the count himself. I've always wondered at how humans rate big bulky fish as fine specimens, while they tend to mock people with the same characteristics. It doesn't make sense. It appeared that Count Roland was worried about what he'd get to eat across the Channel, and had made up his mind to take a few choice provisions with him.

'Such a shame you can't come along and cook for me,' said Roland.

'Only room for fighting men,' said Ugolin. 'I'm pretty good with a paring knife but useless with a sword.'

'And I'm supposed to go and chop people up? It's a nightmare. I can't fight. And I won't have you to cook for me.'

'Sire, after all the time you've spent cooking with me you're quite capable of producing the *hautest* of *haute cuisine.*'

'Ah, the millstone of a noble birth. I would've been far happier as a humble cook.'

Count Roland took no notice of Ugolin muttering under his breath. 'Tell me it's not true the rosbifs[1] eat boiled mutton,' he continued.

'Only the aristocracy get boiled mutton,' said the cook disdainfully. 'It's considered a delicacy. And they eat it with what they call *mint sauce* apparently.'

'With *sauce à la menthe*? Surely not!'

'Sadly true, sire.'

'*Quelle horreur*, such barbarians!'

'Mostly the people eat pottage, though. At least it's a step up from mud.'

'*Potage* you say? Things are looking up. Seasonal baby vegetables, good quality veal stock, chervil and sorrel, a dollop of truffle oil.'

'No, sire. Pottage. I know it sounds almost identical to *potage*, but in actual fact it couldn't be more different. It's just a slop of anything the livestock wouldn't touch, reheated day after day, sometimes with the judicious addition of a *soupçon* of mud.'

'Eek!'

'Indeed, sire. The problem is, there's not much in the way of provisions to take with you. William the Bastard's men requisitioned it all.'

'There must be some fish left in there.'

'You've had nearly all of them. There's just a tench and a carp of a couple of *livres* or so that always seem to avoid the net.'

'Then empty the bloody pond!'

Merde, I thought.

'I'll have the tench for my supper, and you can pack the carp up to take to England. Some fresh *carpe à la moutarde* should fortify me for the impending slaughter, even if I do have to cook it myself.'

After being scooped unceremoniously from the muddy pond bottom, I was parcelled up with sodden pondweed and shut in a wooden box. Over the next few days, I intermittently went into a state of suspended animation – or dozed if one prefers – and periods of awareness of people's voices. It appeared I was on *a ship*, although I didn't yet know what a ship was. Because the wind was wrong, the time spent on the ship was far longer than it should've been. At one point it tossed and pitched quite violently, and people complained of feeling ill and having to throw up. Myself, I tried to will myself to pass out again, because the feeling was most unpleasant. I felt quite green about the gills, and if there had been anything in my stomach I'm sure I would've puked up as well.... which would've made me the first fish in history to get a bout of seasickness.

Relief came in the form of near oblivion. There's only so much oxygen in wet pondweed, and my supply was running desperately short. I drifted in and out of consciousness, and when the lid was finally levered from my box I was barely alive. I could make out I was under some kind of covering – a tent, as it turned out – and although it was dark outside, within it a burning torch cast an eerie, flickering light. Count Roland, who didn't look any brighter than I felt, turned and poured himself a small goblet of…there was no mistaking the aroma, it was Calvados.

'Gimme a hit of that,' I managed to croak.

The count and I were both stunned. The count because a half-dead carp had just asked for a snifter, and me because up until that point I hadn't realised I could actually speak with humans. Necessity being the mother and all that, I suppose.

'Please,' I repeated. 'I'm gasping here.'

Count Roland emptied a slug of Calvados into my mouth, and I felt instant fire spread through my body. *That* was better.

'What magic is this?' Roland blinked. 'A carp that speaks to me. A carp that should be my supper. My last supper in all probability.'

'Sire,' I said. I thought it best to keep the right side of him. 'I'd really appreciate it if you'd consider not eating me.'

'But what about my supper? Everyone else has been into Pevensey and pillaged a halfway decent banquet, but I'm not very good at that kind of thing. My stomach's in knots and I need sustenance.'

I racked my brain. It looked as if the count's famous appetite was imminently going to override his sense of wonderment at the miracle of a talking carp. What did I have to bargain with? 'Tell you what – you save my skin and I'll save yours.'

The count's raised eyebrows indicated a nibble at the bait.

'I have information that can save your life,' I said. 'But first you must promise to take me to the nearest water.'

The count nodded cautiously. 'Well?'

'During the forthcoming battle Baron Fredo is aiming to chop your block off.'

'But the baron is a dear friend. He visits me quite regularly.'

'He visits the Lady Cunegonde far more regularly, if you get my drift.'

'What are you trying to tell me?'

'They seem to hit it off together. Quite a lot actually.'

'He's a handsome devil, I'll give him that. It's the moustache – big as a scrubbing brush – sends the *mademoiselles* doolally.'

'It's the *madames* I'd worry about – yours in particular. Can I spell it out any more plainly?'

'*Sacré bleu!*'

'He aims to do you in and run off with your missus.'

'My little *crêpe Suzette*.[2] All those trips into the garden. "*Ooh la la, I must go and tend my camellias again,*"… and she suffers such dreadful hay fever. It all makes sense now. *La salope!*'

'So? What we agreed? I'd really appreciate a little help. If there's a river nearby? A pond will do. I'm really suffocating rather badly here. Is there a ditch even?'

'Psychotic Saxons in front of me, homicidal Norman barons behind me, what chance do I stand?'

'The nearest puddle, please? I'm about to croak here.'

'Huh? Sure. No problem. I lost my appetite anyway.'

The count picked me up and, concealing me under his voluminous cape, made his way out of the tent and into the moonlit Norman encampment.

'Where are you off to, Roly-Poly?' called a jovial knight from where he and several companions sat around a blazing campfire. Glistening fat ran down his chin from the lamb leg he'd been gnawing. 'Got a secret assignation with some Saxon wench?'

Others joined in the merriment.

'Pevensey's the place, *mon ami!*'

'Plenty of good pillaging there, *and* the other!'

'Fourth hovel on the left, ask for Gwendryth.'

'But you'll have to join the queue.'

'No, look at the way he's holding his stomach, he's got the trots!'

'That's right,' panted Count Roland, bent over and clutching me under his cape, 'I'm desperate, which way do I go?'

'The bog's that way, keep going downhill, you can't miss it.'

The count carried on jogging and lurching down the slope, while I felt I was on the point of expiring. Soon the ground levelled out, however, and a swirling mist diffused the moonlight. The count's feet squelched through mud. From Roland's cape I saw that clumps of sedge grew here and there, along with banks of reedmace that bordered a network of shallow channels of silty water. The area was indeed a bog – and sanctuary for yours truly.

I luxuriated in the feeling of drawing water through my gills at long last, even if it was stagnant, murky stuff that had a distinctly dung-like niff to it. Then I remembered my saviour, who still stood at the bog's edge, trying to catch his breath.

'This might not be a bad place for you to lie low, sire,' I said. 'No disrespect, but I really don't fancy your chances against Baron Fredo.'

The count shook his head. 'I don't either. But if I sit out tomorrow's bloodbath I'll have William the Bastard on my case. He and every other Norman will turn the place upside down until they find me and mince me into *andouillettes*.[3] No, I'll have to pray some Saxon chops the baron's block off before he gets the chance to remove mine – though I still don't fancy my odds.'

I watched as the count trudged slowly away through the mist. Then I turned to explore my new English home. I hoped not all of this maze of drains and ditches was going to prove as shallow and smelly as the channel I'd been dumped in. But I soon realised that whichever channel I entered, the water was just as shallow and choked up as the one I'd left. If this was the best England had to offer, I was singularly unimpressed.

The next morning, I was still no nearer to finding my way out of my silty labyrinth, and I realised with a heavy heart that I'd managed to swim back to the very spot that the count had dropped me into. Then, unmistakably, I started to hear the sound of cries and screams and the clashing of metal from somewhere in the distance. Of course at that point I had no idea what a battle entailed, but afterwards I was able to piece together what happened – or at least some pretty vital elements of it.

King Harold (I'd by now twigged that a king was the ultimate head honcho, certainly more important than a count) and the Saxon army occupied the high ground on Senlac Hill, and as long as they maintained their position and their discipline, the Normans, having to attack up the gradient, would be at a disadvantage.

To his utter dismay, Count Roland was thrust into the first wave of Norman troops – on foot to boot, as horse riding was most certainly not his forte – to storm the Saxon positions. William the Bastard had been quite emphatic about Roland proving his courage in the vanguard of the attack – and Roland had been quite emphatic that his upset stomach was absolutely for real – at least on this occasion. But now squelchy chainmail was the least of Roland's worries, as he was carried along by the surge of human and horse flesh that charged towards the Saxon lines.

William the Bastard wasn't the only one keeping a close eye on Roland. Baron Fredo was keen to make sure that if his weighty adversary escaped the Saxon blades and arrows he wouldn't avoid his battle axe.

The first surge towards the Saxons' line of spears and shields stuttered, faltered and then ground to a complete halt. Arrows hissed here, there and everywhere like angry hornets. Knights and horses collapsed, infantry were dropping like flies. The fellow next to Roland was pierced in his throat, thigh and groin. Blood spurted in a multitude of directions. 'Keep advancing, you cowardly *blancmange!*' a mounted knight yelled at Roland. An arrow deflected from Roland's helmet and flew straight into the knight's still gaping mouth. That was it. Roland turned and ran.

Roland's retreat – at a speed no one thought him remotely capable of – didn't go unwitnessed. William the Bastard caught sight of his flight and swore he'd have the cowardly jellyfish minced into *hachis parmentier*.[4] Baron Fredo had also spotted his tactical withdrawal, and realised he's never have a better opportunity to eliminate his rival.

Roland wasn't the only one to turn and run. The first wave of attackers had been cut pretty much to ribbons, and those who still had all their limbs did what anyone with half a grain of sense would do: they dropped their weapons and fled. To the Saxons on the crest of the hill, it looked as if the entire Norman army had been put to flight, so, sensing a famous victory, they broke ranks and started to pour downhill in pursuit. After all, what self-respecting warrior can ever turn down the opportunity to skewer one's retreating foe in the back?

That, as any history book will tell you, can be a fatal mistake, and in the Battle of Senlac Hill it was no exception. The charging Saxons succeeded in chopping up nearly all the remnants of the first wave of Norman soldiers, but then they ran smack into the second wave. Who were made of far sterner stuff. In addition, they were attacked on either flank by reserve forces of Norman, Breton and Flemish troops, who decisively turned the tables on King Harold and his men. The fighting spread out over a wide area, but as the afternoon progressed it became increasingly certain that the Saxons were taking one hell of a beating. What of Count Roland in the meanwhile? Although he'd somehow succeeded in disappearing, he remained very much on William the Bastard's *to do* list. And Baron Fredo's.

Down in my bog the mist was closing in again, although I was still able to witness many individual skirmishes. I quickly learned that humans can be far more vicious than any pike; at least when one fish kills another it's almost always for food. All of a sudden, something very large came splashing through the water and collapsed next to me. It was Roland – utterly spent and very red in the face.

'Keep your head down and try and keep a low profile,' I hissed at him.

'But I'll…*pant!*…drown.'

'Then breathe through a hollow reed or something, just try to keep out of sight.'

Roland was still trying to break off a reed stem when a Norman archer emerged from the whiteness, chuckled that the Bastard would surely reward him richly for bagging this weighty prize, and drew an arrow from his quiver. He never got as far as firing it, however, because a retreating Saxon pikeman, while barely slowing his breakneck dash, delivered such a blow to the back of his neck that his head was nearly severed.

At last Roland seemed to be breathing comfortably under the foul, murky water. It was so shallow, however, that his ample stomach rose out of it like the back of a giant turtle – only in chainmail. I reckoned that if one didn't look too closely, his tum could be mistaken for a large rock.

Very close by, the final *dénouement* of the chaotic battle was taking place. King Harold, distinguished by a truly fine moustache, had managed to seek out William the Bastard, and was engaging him in single combat.

'It's over, Harold,' cried William, warding off a sword blow with his shield. 'Your men are routed, for God's sake accept you're vanquished!'

'Not so fast, you Norman toerag,' Harold countered in very respectable French. 'When your men see your head on a spike the day may yet be mine!'

Warding off blow after blow, William was forced back through the murk. Then, parrying yet another strike, William's sword shattered. The next flurry of blows reduced his shield to kindling. '*Putain!*' he cried, turning tail and running.

Hotly pursued by the triumphant Harold, William dashed through the lowland bog and towards one of its reedy channels. Not breaking his pace, he leapt onto the rock in its middle and away on the far bank. Only of course it wasn't a rock he'd leapt onto. Up reared Roland, clutching his gut and bellowing in pain. The next instant the speeding King Harold careered right into him, sending his sword spinning several feet away into the stagnant ooze.

'Shit, fuck, piss!' cried Harold, flat on his back in the mud. This he said in Old English, which for some reason I had no problem understanding. Then he reverted to his rather good French. 'The bastard's getting away!'

'Count Fredo,' groaned Roland, 'I'd know that moustache anywhere.'

'I'm King Harold, you stupid oaf,' Harold snorted as he sat up in the quagmire. 'And you just let the Bastard get away from me.'

'*I'm* Count Fredo,' boomed Fredo as he stepped out of the gloom, his battle axe poised for slaughter, but then he stood stock still. '*Mon dieu!*'

Like everyone in this little gathering, I was taken aback. There was absolutely nothing to choose between Harold and Fredo's magnificent, walrus-like moustaches. What's more, the overall resemblance between the two men was unmistakable.

'*Two* plump pigeons to pluck, the Bastard will reward me richly for this!' Fredo stepped forward again, axe raised. Harold scrabbled about in the mud for a sword that wasn't there, but only succeeded in grasping hold of the dead archer's ankle.

I realised action had to be taken. Being a carp, I suppose I should've been a neutral in what was a strictly human disagreement, but out of all the humans I'd so far come across, Fredo was the one I liked the least – by quite a long way. I heaved myself half up onto the bank.

'Hey, pondweed face,' I shouted. 'Keep your chopper to yourself, you oversized thug!'

Fredo froze in mid-action. His jaw dropped and his mouth worked silently. King Harold must've been equally shocked by the verbal intervention of a two-pound common carp, but his speed of thought was far faster than Fredo's, and he seized the opportunity to pick up the dead archer's bow, nock an arrow, and shoot his adversary in the eye before he could move a muscle.

In the crepuscular gloom we held a council of war, or a council of defeat more like. Harold now regretfully accepted that it was all over. His army had been routed – decimated – and if he were caught now it would be *his* head on a spike. The outlook was similarly grim for Roland. William the Bastard was definitely out for his blood, and he was well aware that he wouldn't last a day if he tried to slip back to Normandy.

'If they're after King Harold we should give them King Harold,' I said.

'Of all the—' Harold began to growl, but then a grin spread across his face. 'That musclebound cretin really does have a formidable moustache. Nearly as fine as mine. We have similar chainmail, and with a switch of cape, we could just get away with this.'

Thus, the Battle of Hastings, 14 October 1066, ended with victory for William the Bastard and an arrow in the eye for poor old Harold. Only it wasn't Harold.

After leaving the stiffening Fredo, now wearing Harold's cape and helmet, and his face ever so slightly mutilated to help muddy the waters further, we slipped away through the swampy low ground.

Travelling by night to avoid the triumphant Norman patrols, we headed north. I travelled wrapped in Frodo's wetted cape, and would stop for a breather every time we reached a pond, stream or horse trough.

Thanks to Harold's tuition it wasn't long before I was speaking fluent Early English, and it was around that time we decided I needed a name. Hitherto I'd just been known as Fish, which wasn't really very respectful for someone who'd saved his two companions' bacon.

'It should be a Norman name,' said Harold. 'Not that I've got much time for the Normans – present company excepted – but we should all respect our cultural identities – roots and all that.'

'The only two female names I know are Cunegonde and Fionne,' I said. 'Which probably aren't very appropriate.'

'Very delicately put,' said Roland. 'There was a serving wench called Gisella who I rather fancied. I never did anything about it though, because – ha-ha – I wanted to be faithful to Cunegonde. I kind of like the name though.'

'It's a very elegant name,' Harold agreed.

'Whatever,' I said. And that's how I became Gisella.

From time to time we stopped at friendly monasteries, where all three of us would be revived by some of the inmates' favourite tipple – usually brandy – and it was at one of these, inhabited by a humble order of monks that had taken a vow of hushed, respectful tones, whose gaunt abbey, cloisters and kitchen garden lay by the banks of the River Medway, that we eventually found a home. The friendly monks, Saxons all, appreciated the muscle lent by Harold, who was apt to put the fear of God into any Norman soldiers come to pilfer ecclesiastical goodies, and also Roland, who, apart from making himself a useful translator thanks to his native Norman French, soon proved he could make far more dainty dishes than porridge and pottage from the kitchen-garden produce.

I made a new home in the Medway, and greatly enjoyed Roland and Harold's discreet riverside visits and diverse, wide-ranging conversations. It was explained to me that kings were indeed more important than earls (which I'd already sussed, but I buttoned my lip), and earls more than churls etc., *ad infinitum*, and that someone no one ever got to see called God was the most important of all. I also learned that you became a king if you were born into a king's family, but you could also become a king by killing another king and stealing his kingship. Some people got to be kings just by killing loads and loads of people. Which was pretty much what William the Bastard had done. Clearly I was a very primitive fish, and the civilised ways of men (and women, they were apparently nearly as bad) were still beyond my comprehension.

I got to hear all the gossip about what the royals were up to, the bad behaviour of the new Norman aristocracy, and the shenanigans during visits by the nuns from the nearby nunnery. The abbess was quite smitten by Roland's *crème brûlée*[5] and they developed a very *intime* friendship, as did Harold with a lady bellringer of impressive stature. It was agreed that what happened behind the cloisters stayed behind the cloisters, as long as the rule of hushed, respectful tones was strictly observed.

Roland would bring me all kinds of appetising tidbits from the kitchens (Although nothing can quite match the flavours and

nutritional balance of modern carp baits such as Vor-Tex. Or brioche, for that matter. But brioche had yet to be invented), and I steadily gained weight. Within a decade I'd reached my present size, which I've maintained pretty much for nearly a thousand years. My two friends didn't fare so well. As the years rolled past they became grey and stooped and complained bitterly when they sat down and stood up. Then, one day, Roland was no longer there. Both Harold and I lamented his passing, but Harold survived his Norman friend by only a couple of years before he too was gathered by Father Time.

It appeared I didn't age. Most of my fellow fish lived but a handful of years before shuffling off this mortal coil. Carp are known for their longevity (although to the best of my knowledge I was the only carp in England at that point), living for thirty years and sometimes considerably longer, but I – I apparently defied nature. The decades trundled past, and I remained youthful and fit as a fiddle.

My existence was serene and largely untroubled – once, that was, I'd learnt how to deal with troublesome otters. Some humans find them cute, but we fish find them about as loveable as a fox in a hen house. One time, to my outrage, for I was far too big for it to make a meal of me, a vicious *salaud* of an otter set its sights on me, and, after a ferocious chase, cornered me by some sunken tree roots. What to do? 'Piss off!' I shouted at the top of my voice. The beast actually stopped in its tracks. It obviously found my human-like voice alarming. 'Fuck off!' I bellowed. 'Sling your hook! *Va t'en, sale bête!* Begone, foul creature!' It turned and fled as if a crowd of villagers with torches and pitchforks was after it, and thereafter if any otter as much as looked at me, a loud flood of invective inevitably saw it off.

There was no doubt that I missed human contact. Other fish were fine, great, but not what you'd call convivial company. No pike was big enough to trouble me, but they're abject brutes and notorious cannibals, and certainly not the kind of fellows I wanted to be seen with. (Actually, most of us fish are cannibals at some point in our life cycles, but let's gloss quickly over that.) Roach are shoal-followers, perch are headbangers, and chub are greedy and venal. Even tench, which should never be underestimated, are very poor conversationalists, as I believe I've already mentioned. No, I missed people and I missed chitchat, but I never felt sufficiently confident to make myself known to anyone who came down to the river's edge. There was always the risk that, fascinating discourse or not, I could be bopped on the head and shoved into a cooking pot.

So, I kept myself to myself and remained blithely unaware of events such as the assassination of Thomas Becket, the signing of the Magna Carta, and the advent of the various Crusades… As the decades trundled past I tried to think of ways to build bridges (ha – what a strange expression for a fish) with humans, but none occurred to me. There was no danger, however, of my losing my facility with English and French (Early English and Norman French if you want to be picky), I'm blessed with a wonderful memory and kept in practise by holding numerous conversations in my head. But *mon dieu*, they were boring!

Notes

[1] *Rosbifs.* A French corruption of "roast beef", used to describe the English. It can be affectionate or derogatory, depending on the context. Usually the latter, though.
[2] *Crêpes suzettes.* Pancakes, liberally doused in Grand Marinier orange flavoured liqueur.
[3] *Andouillettes.* A type of sausage made from the large intestine of pigs. It smells like it too. Not for the faint-hearted.
[4] *Hachis Parmentier.* French cottage pie. Sounds more exciting in French.
[5] *Crème brûlée.* Egg custard with a burnt sugar crust. Sounds far more exciting in French.

Chapter Three

Sir Ten Percent. How Gisella inadvertently messes up badly but helps create an outlaw legend

For over 200 years my universe revolved around the Medway. Two hindred mind-numbing years while the events of the world passed me by. From time to time, I tried to strike up conversations with bream or chub, but inevitably ended up depressed. There had to be some way of expanding my very limited universe, but I never felt close to finding it. At least time was on my side. I outlived nearly everything, even most trees, without showing the least sign of ageing.

I found a good source of food: the wheat that dropped through the cracks in the floorboards of a mill, near the tiny village of Yaxley. It was located on a wide bend in the infant river. The main channel actually ran beneath the mill, where a trapdoor led down to the water

and the millwheel mechanism, while a leat, leading from the watercourse a short distance upstream, powered the waterwheel itself. Generations of millers ran a tight ship, or mill rather, keeping the building immaculately clean, and forever sweeping up the debris of wheat chaff and grit from the querns (that's grinding stones to you and me), but they could never prevent a certain amount of grain from falling through the cracks and feeding yours truly.

There was another reason I found the mill a very passable spot to hang out. Almost immediately under its trapdoor, the river current had scoured out a large hollow beneath the flat stone area that housed the mill's workings – a hollow that was sufficiently large for me to hide in during times of need.

Following the curve of the river downstream stood a fortified manor house, the seat of the de Yaxley family, the landowners of Yaxley and thereabouts. The building had started life as little more than a single hall not long after the Norman Conquest, but over the next couple of hundred years it had been added to considerably. One of its walls abutted the river, while a tower, a courtyard, a fortified gatehouse and stables had been added to the original hall. That was as good as it got. Another century on and it was obvious that the de Yaxleys weren't that keen on manor-house maintenance: the tower's crenellations looked as if they could come crashing down during the next storm, while most of the walls were starting to crumble, especially the riverside section. The departure of the lord of the manor for the Crusades, and his replacement by his steward, the weaselly Hereward Scabb, only accelerated the process. Hereward spent the fifteen years of his master's absence making the local serfs' lives a complete misery, seizing nearly all their produce, and endlessly pursuing the local wenches claiming *droit de seigneur*, even although he wasn't a seigneur at all. It didn't take me long to work out that Hereward was an utter *merde* – a *salaud* in fact.

Most of the serfs whose lives Hereward made a misery lived in Yaxley, which lay at the far end of the river's wide bend, about a half mile upstream from the mill. I say most of the serfs, because life had become so hard during Hereward's tenure at Yaxley Manor, a band of them had fled into the depths of the surrounding Ashdown Forest and become footpads and brigands. Well, a small band. Six of them. And they weren't really that fierce. But I'm getting ahead of myself.

For generation after generation I enjoyed eavesdropping the villagers' conversation, both from the deep pool that lay below the rickety bridge a short distance from the village, and the shallow spot a hundred or so yards downstream, where the village women did their washing. Okay, the gossip about how unfair the tithes were, how the lord of the manor was a useless pillock, and who was tupping who, was less than scintillating, but it certainly beat my fellow fishes' inane blather about which kind of worms they preferred.

On a few occasions I was careless enough to be spotted, and of course there was a clamour to catch me – after all, I could've provided a meal to feed the entire village. All their efforts would come to naught, however, for they were always too slow to cast their nets anywhere near me, and I was far too nimble for them to bag me with spear or arrow. Each time they came after me I sped downstream in my lopsided fashion, and sought the sanctuary of my undercut refuge at the mill.

Eventually they stopped trying. I became an almost familiar sight, imaginatively named 'the big fish', and I passed into village folklore. I still didn't trust the locals enough to strike up any conversation, but it was reassuring to hear the villagers tell any visitors who caught a glimpse of me that they didn't hunt the big fish, for catching it would surely bring evil luck, maybe even carried a curse. Bless their superstitious souls.

The years swam by without many changes, each generation closely resembling the next. Even the Black Death, which scourged most of the rest of the country, passed Yaxley by, and while the living was easy, more and more I found myself missing the adventure I'd lived through when I first came to Merrie England. The lord of the manor's departure to chase the heathen horde from the Holy Land, and the *salaud* Hereward Scabb's promotion as his agent, would eventually satisfy that craving.

The not very large band of serfs-turned-brigands who preyed on passers-by on the highway would often pounce by a river bridge not far from the village, where a dissolute churchman, the hulking Friar Stack, leaning on his sturdy staff, would engage the victims in pleasant conversation for long enough for the robbers to sneak up and take them unawares. The pickings were never that great, the brigands were never confident enough to tackle the rich and the powerful, but they stole enough to keep the bibulous friar in ale and the villagers from starving.

One day a bearded traveller in his middle years, evidently well-fed yet plainly dressed, walking with the aid of a stout stick, found his path across the bridge blocked by the recumbent, snoring Friar Stack.

'I say, good fellow, if you have to sleep one off how about doing it elsewhere?'

'Grumph,' the friar answered.

From the pool below I watched the drama unfold.

'You're in my way. Please move.'

'Piss orff.'

'I've travelled a long way and I'm too tired for this sort of thing.' The newcomer gave the friar a prod with his stick. At this Friar Stack lumbered to his feet and brandished his staff, his face thunderous. The traveller was no ninety-seven-pound weakling, but he was dwarfed by the furious man of God.

'Do you know who I am?' stuttered the traveller.

'I don't care if you're King fucking John himself!'

'I'm your lord and master, Sir Rod—'

Sir Rod was unable to finish his sentence. A hefty blow from Friar Stack's staff caught him on the side of the head and sent him flying into the river, where I had to take swift evasive action to avoid becoming a second casualty.

Face-down and unconscious, the traveller was carried downstream. I swam after him and managed to prop his head up above the surface, so at least he could breathe, and guided him steadily down towards the shallows where the village women did the washing.

Meanwhile, back at the bridge, the brigand band had joined the friar, who was now starting to look a little bit contrite, not to mention hungover. 'I don't suppose he really was...?'

'Really was what?' said a lanky fellow known as Small Jack.

'I think he was trying to tell me he was Sir Rodney.'

'Sir Rodney died in the Crusades,' said another brigand.

'We don't know that for certain,' said yet another.

'Well, if that *was* Sir Rodney he's certainly dead now,' said another member of the band, who, on close inspection, turned out to be a woman. Like her companions, she wore a ragged tunic, leggings and a hood, which was pushed back. There were sticks and leaves in her hair. She glared pointedly at the reddening friar.

'Hadn't we better go and fish him out?' said Small Jack.

Having finally pushed the traveller up onto the shingly river shallows, I waited patiently for him to recover so that I could make my introduction and be showered with gratitude. I figured he'd be so thankful he'd be able to resist the urge to cook me, and I'd be able to have a first decent conversation for a couple of hundred years. Gasping, he struggled to open his eyes, but before we could exchange a single word, my plan was scotched by the noisy approach of what seemed to be the entire village of Yaxley. My nerve failed me. I may have become a part of their folklore, but even the remote possibility of ending up in their pottage cauldron sent me scudding into some nearby reedy water, a small distance downstream.

'Blimey,' groaned Sir Rodney, rubbing his head as he sat up in the water. 'That's some welcome home.'

'A thousand pardons, sire,' muttered Friar Stack. 'That last tankard of porter must've been off. And you did prod me with your stick.'

'You nearly brained me with yours,' said Sir Rodney, still looking groggy.

'It really is you?' said a village elder. 'When you left for the Crusades you were little more than a fresh-faced, callow youth.'

'Of course it's him, you silly old bat,' said an old woman. 'He may have stacked it on a bit but look at the squinty eyes, the bow-legs, the beard that doesn't hide the weak chin. He's every inch a de Yaxley.'

'What happened to you?' said the lady brigand. 'All the other Crusaders returned years ago, but you pissed off for fifteen years and left us to the tender mercies of that monster Hereward Scabb.'

'It's a long story, but not so unusual I suppose,' said Sir Rodney. 'For two years we crossed swords with the crafty Saracen, but little by little we lost our foothold in the Holy Land, and with great sadness the decision was made to cut our losses and head for home.

'Our voyage from Constantinople was beset by storms and attacks by pirates from the Barbary Coast, but at length we safely arrived in Venice, where we reprovisioned and then continued our trek over the inhospitable Alps, and thence into Burgundy. On the way I lost companion after companion, to the cold, to attacks by brigands, to sickness and malnutrition, until one night the remaining four of our number took shelter from a blizzard by a rocky bluff, and as all feeling left our bodies, we made our peace with God and awaited the inevitable.

'I awoke on a pallet of most luxurious straw, and was brought hot milk and honey and brioche to help me revive. Although I lost a little finger and three toes to frostbite, I was otherwise unharmed – unlike my companions, all of whom perished.

'As my strength returned my host made himself known to me. The chevalier Gaspard de Montfort (yes, it's a *very* big family, and Gaspard turned out to be a *very* minor member of it) made me most welcome at the Chateau Montrachet, overlooking the River Saône, where I was very well treated – but it was soon made clear to me that I wasn't going anywhere soon. I was de Montfort's prisoner.

'You may not know it, but hostage-taking is one of the age's growth industries. After every battle hostages are taken, and their ransoms do much to keep the economy afloat. The more noble the hostage the higher the price, and the fact that I was an unfortunate traveller rather than a prisoner of war cut no ice. A price was set for my release – insultingly low in my estimation – and I just had to sit and wait for some knight in shining armour to come along and bail me out.

'Years dragged by, but no one came to my rescue. In the meanwhile, my stay wasn't so unpleasant. The excellent *cygne-au-vin, escargots, boeuf bourguignon, cuisses de grenouilles, tartes aux pommes, charlotte aux poires, gâteaux aux griottes* and several *grands crus*[1] rather of took the sting out of captivity.

'It was there that I learned the art of shooting with the crossbow, just to keep the boredom at bay. It's really an ingenious weapon, and so much less demanding than drawing a longbow. Could I have shot my way to freedom? With a small army I could've I suppose, but what a way to repay *le chevalier* Gaspard's hospitality, eh?

'It eventually dawned on Gaspard that I hadn't been the wisest of investments – let's face it, he wasn't the sharpest of the de Monfort clan – and he decided that if someone just stepped forward to pay for my bed and board he'd be happy to let me go. However that, after nearly thirteen years, still amounted to a pretty penny.

'Just when I was despairing of ever leaving Burgundy, my bond was paid by one Guy of Huntspill, a merchant risen above his station and eager to elbow his way into the landed elite. En route home after purchasing spices in Venice, he'd been told of my predicament and offered to pay my debt to Comte Gaspard – with the understanding that I would repay him on my return to Kent, or forfeit my lands to him. Huntspill has the sort of face that frightens infants, but he's immensely proud of his long, wavy locks – which he evidently believes more than make up for all his other defects. But I wasn't going to let an unseemly merchant make me look a gift horse in the mouth. Fortunately for me I left all my affairs in the honest hands of the faithful Scabb, and the collective income from my estate should be sufficient to cover my debt.'

There was silence, except for a slight rustling from some nearby bushes that only I heard. I caught sight of the *salaud* Scabb slipping furtively away, and decided to try and keep an eye on what he was up to. Scabb's path along the track to Yaxley Manor was far more direct than my route around the wide bend in the river, but I had the current on my side, and I was still less than 300 years old and fit as a fiddle.

The villagers, meanwhile, filled Sir Rodney in on what a *faithful* steward Scabb had been during his absence, how he'd seized nine-tenths of the villagers' produce, rather than the one tenth the benevolent young de Yaxley had taken hitherto, how he'd lived a life of debauched luxury, and still managed to salt away a very tidy sum from the crops he appropriated, and how he'd seized the mill, from which he also filched a nice profit. It was rumoured that he had hidden at least fifty golden guineas down at the manor, in other words a fortune.

Skutch, the former miller, now aged and suffering horribly from gout, was especially bitter about being kicked out of the mill. He complained that the fellow Scabb had replaced him with was a numskull who didn't know the first thing about milling grain. Half the wheat ended up in the drink, and he kept the place like a pigsty – chaff, dust and quern grit forming heaps everywhere. It was downright dangerous, he added, that mixture could've gone bang any time, the idiot was lucky he hadn't blown himself sky-high already.

Sir Rodney declared they must waste no time in making their way to Yaxley Manor and recovering the pilfered golden guineas before Guy of Huntspill turned up, otherwise his estates would be in peril of being lost. Several of the villagers set off with him, determined to have their old master back in situ. Coughing up ten percent certainly beat being robbed of ninety percent, and they all fancied seeing Scabb get his comeuppance anyway.

I had just finished my race downstream when I saw the *salaud* Scabb take to a small boat and row along to the side of the riverside wall of the manor. There he stopped and reached just under the water, and placed a weighty silken purse in the wall where a stone was missing. The cunning hiding place couldn't be seen from above the surface, but of course I had a perfect view of what he was up to. I had a fair idea what was in that purse, and of course I'd learned just how much humans valued those shiny gold metal discs, and also that they represented what he'd stolen from the villagers, so as soon as he'd rowed away again I grabbed the purse's drawstring in my mouth and set off upstream with it, pulling it along after me. God it was heavy, but it would be worth all the effort to fuck up the *salaud* Scabb's nefarious plans, and I had a very secure hiding place for the gold in mind myself. No one else had a clue about my bolthole under the stone platform beneath the mill. Naturally, once Scabb had received his just desserts, I'd return the loot to its rightful owners and bask in adulation as the hero of the hour. And nobody cooks a hero.

It was then that my clever plan began to unravel. Accompanied by the brigands, Sir Rodney marched into Yaxley Manor and apprehended Hereward Scabb in the main hall. Scabb denied any knowledge of golden guineas, and swore by all that was holy that the slothful serfs of Yaxley had neglected their duties so badly, there wasn't a groat of profit to be shown. The hound is lying, the brigands exclaimed, the villagers had been worked to the bone. Sir Rodney grabbed Scabb by the throat, but before he could throttle any truth out him a clatter of armour and chainmail announced the arrival of several men-at-arms.

Guy of Huntspill, richly dressed in his merchant's robes, strolled into the hall. 'De Yaxley,' he exclaimed, bypassing any preliminaries, 'I trust you have the gold you owe me.'

'All in good time, good sir,' said Sir Rodney. 'I have business with this scurvy knave first.'

'Time is what you don't have. I trust you remember the terms and conditions of the document you signed at Chateau Montrachet, but if not, you're welcome to reacquaint yourself with them.' Huntspill thrust a parchment into Sir Rodney's hand.

Sir Rodney squinted at the document, but evidently could make little of it. 'The handwriting is ever so small, I can't make this out at all.'

'I'll recap then. It says that upon my return to England I undertake to pay Guy of Huntspill the sum of one hundred golden sovereigns, without delay or prevarication. Failure to do so will result in the forfeit of my property, lands and title.' All the while Huntspill twirled his dark, lustrous locks around his forefinger. His unconscious vanity was quite disturbing.

'One hundred sovereigns? That's outrageous! You only paid de Monfort fifty to set me free!'

'You should've read the small handwriting, dear boy. There are also all sorts of expenses to take into account. Transport costs, service charges, interest payments, insurance, depreciation. It all adds up, you know.'

'But you've got to give me time. Scabb's swiped all the estate's money. As soon as I get it back from him the money's yours.'

'Me, squire?' Scabb shrugged. 'Don't know what you're on about.'

'Anyone can tell this scurvy fellow is as honest as the day is long,' said Huntspill. 'No, this has to go down as prevarication, therefore Sir Rodney – or plain Rodney, as you are now – you are trespassing on my property, and I think your departure is now overdue.'

Faced by a group of severe-looking men-at-arms, Rodney and his companions chose discretion over valour and set off back towards the village.

Huntspill, meanwhile, turned to Scabb. 'Right, now you can cut the bullshit and tell me where the gold is.'

'Like I said,' Scabb put on his most innocent face. 'There's no gold. Nothing. The estate is destitute.'

'Let's go about this differently.' Two of the soldiers grabbed Scabb by either arm, a third unsheathed his sword. 'Apparently the human intestine is a full twenty-two-feet long. I've always wanted to put that to the test.'

'Wait! One moment. Now I think about it, I do have some recollection about some golden guineas. Must've slipped my mind.'

'No funny business, Scabb. Hand over the gold and you live. You'll continue as my steward because you obviously have quite a talent for screwing people, but screw with me and you'll be helping me measure out your disembowelled gut. Do I make myself clear?'

'Perfectly, sire!'

Scabb and one of the soldiers took to the rowing boat once more, while Huntspill and the rest of his men looked down from the ramparts. When Scabb found his submerged hole in the wall empty, he let out the most pitiful howl of anguish, nearly tipping the boat over.

'I warned you!' roared Huntspill.

'This is where I hid it, I swear it!'

'I think he's telling the truth, sire,' the soldier next to Scabb grimaced. 'The filthy varlet has soiled himself.'

'De Yaxley!' Huntspill hissed.

'It can only have been him,' said Scabb. 'He grew up here, knows every nook and cranny in the place. Who else could ferret out the best hidey-hole in the manor in such a short time?'

'Muster the men,' cried Huntspill. 'Raise a hue and cry![3] I will have de Yaxley, and I will have my sovereigns!'

Dusk was falling over the village as Rodney and the villagers gathered in one of the elder's hovels to try to figure out their next step, but no obvious strategy was forthcoming. Heads were still being scratched, and ideas such as storming the manor being dismissed, when the clank and clatter of approaching soldiers alerted the gathering to imminent danger. Rodney complained to his companions that he'd done nothing wrong and had a perfect right to be there, but when Huntspill's strident voice rang out, demanding the surrender of the outlaw de Yaxley or face the consequences, he had a swift change of heart.

The villagers said they'd delay the soldiers for as long as possible, while the band of brigands – minus Skutch the erstwhile miller, whose gout rendered him borderline immobile – said they'd lead Sir Rodney to safety.

Unfortunately, upon slipping past the backs of the village hovels, the fugitives found the river bridge and their path into the sanctuary of Ashdown Forest already blocked by soldiers. 'This way,' hissed Friar Stack, 'there's one place left to hide.'

In the meanwhile, I'd been blithely unaware of developments. Tired from all my swimming up and down the river, I'd rested up in the watercourse beneath the mill, and was alerted to the drama taking place on dry land only when the outlaws noisily led Sir Rodney into the mill.

Any notion of having gained a place of safety was quickly dispelled. Their flight had evidently been spotted, and now a throng of men-at-arms, carrying swords, spears and burning torches, preceded Scabb and Huntspill through the fields towards the mill.

From my watery spot beneath the floorboards, I could hear desperate voices. Sir Rodney and his companions were trapped like rats, the soldiers would be upon them within a minute or two, and they could never hold out against such a number of well-armed men. There was no escape! Obviously none of them knew about the mill's trapdoor.

'Through here,' I yelled at the top of my voice, 'the trapdoor by the giant quern, it's your only chance!'

They heard me. The trapdoor lifted open, and Sir Rodney and his companions speedily dropped through it. Friar Stack became momentarily stuck in the opening, but with an outlaw tugging either leg he was heaved through it, and landed painfully on the stone slab below. The trapdoor was pulled to, and I urged the fugitives jump in the river and follow me upstream.

Their shock at being rescued by *the big fish* was overridden by the need to save their skins, and I led a bedraggled procession up to a quiet stretch of water overhung with weeping willows – where several humans could remain well hidden from the surrounding countryside.

I gladly accepted the thanks of Sir Rodney and the brigands, and, being a bit carried away with the moment, boasted that I'd also found the stash of gold coins, and had them hidden in a very safe place. Of course I should've brought the purse with me, but in the heat of the moment I'd forgotten it. Hindsight is a very fine thing.

Back down at the mill, the torch-bearing soldiers succeeded in smashing in the door and streamed inside, followed by Huntspill. Along with the vengeful Scabb, they proceeded to search every corner of the dust-and-debris-filled building, and or course the inevitable followed. One of the chaff heaps was ignited by a thrusting torch, sparks flew, then the whole shebang went up in a flash of flame.

The count was four dead – including Scabb – and another half-dozen badly maimed. Guy of Huntspill escaped with minor burns and some really sore splinters (but he lost his eyebrows and all his lustrous hair, which never grew back, and resulted in his becoming crabbier and more unpleasant than ever).

I, meanwhile, made the decision that my immediate future lay well downstream of Yaxley. Trying to find the gold hidden at the mill would've been a futile gesture, because there was no longer a mill, just a pile of stony rubble. Naturally I felt I wasn't to blame for the loss of the stash of guineas – after all, it wasn't me who blew up the mill – but I could quite understand that Sir Rodney and the brigands might not see it that way. 'The big fish' with the odd French accent that had promised the gold and then failed to deliver? That seemed to me a short route to the pottage pot. No, for the next generation at least I'd stick to the Medway's lower reaches, with slow-witted bream for company.

Some have probably noticed a slight parallel between Rodney de Yaxley and Robin of Loxley. This is how minor passages of history get twisted into myths, and myths contorted into legends. Having become an outlaw – the furious Guy of Huntspill never forgave the loss of his lustrous crowning glory – Rodney joined the band of robbers, and continued the noble tradition of preying upon those too feeble to fight back. As for the village of Yaxley, it continued to die a slow death. Huntspill proved a worse squire than Scabb had been, and every year more serfs jumped ship until, within a decade, the settlement was no more than a collection of deserted and crumbling cob ruins. Rodney proved a decent shot with a crossbow, but in truth it was Friar Stack who played the lead role in separating travellers from their wealth.

As tales of the merry band of outlaws spread, Rodney became Robin, and, for reasons of levelling up, they were moved north to Nottinghamshire. The crossbow, a practical but prosaic weapon, became the Hearts of England longbow, and a scruffy group of brigands became a jocular band of social progressives. According to the popular version, anyway.

It was back to square one for me, however. I was still stuck in the Medway, with roach and eels for company. Sometimes I told myself that the next person I saw, I'd throw caution to the wind and go and speak to them. But then most times that person would turn out to be carrying a net or a fishing rod, and that would have an oddly sobering effect on me. So, it was back to being a fish; a frustrated fish, marking time.

Notes

[1]*Droit de seigneur.* A barbaric feudal custom that gave the lord of the manor the right to sleep with the bride of any of his dependants upon their nuptials. Some of the more enlightened lords waived this right, but plenty didn't.
[2] *Cygne-au-vin,* swan in red wine, preferably a Burgundy, a precursor of *coq au vin. Escargots*, snails. *Boef bourguignon*, beef in Burgundy. *Cuisses de grenouilles*, frogs' legs. *Tartes aux pommes*, apple tarts. *Charlotte au poires*, a boozy pear dessert with sponge fingers and lots of cream. *Gateaux aux griottes*, sour cherry cake. *Grand crus*, serious wines, obviously Burgundies.
[3]Hue and Cry. A quaint custom that dictates locals must take part in manhunts or face a very extreme form of asset-stripping.

Chapter Four

Writer's block. How Gisella helps a famous writer make a creative breakthrough, which gives birth to the major literary work of the late Medieval period

The decades continued to slip past, and I occupied myself by meandering up and down the Medway, between its swiftly flowing headwaters, where the strange tale of the talking fish had quickly faded from memory, and its sluggish lower reaches.

I missed intelligent conversation more than ever, and to be honest I would've settled for a chat about crop rotation or leather tanning for beginners, but I remained cautious about exposing myself to the human world, and contented myself with observing the changes of the seasons and the year-on-year transformation of my watery home. Those humans that don't spend their lives making sport with us fish have little idea how dramatically rivers and even lakes can change from one year to another. Floods shape watercourses, as do changes in vegetation, and where animals come to nest and burrow and feed and drink. In lakes and ponds, the varying winds determine the underwater currents, and the currents shape the underwater contours, creating new ridges and troughs and silt beds. Fishermen and fish know all that.

One of my frequent stopping places was by the Old Spotted Sow Inn, which lay by the river close to the wooden bridge at Yalding. The inn provided a constant source of food for us fish, because the innkeeper's wife, a formidable dreadnaught of a woman, was such a terrible cook that in order not to offend her – which would have been most *périlleux* – most guests would surreptitiously sneak out and pitch their dinners into the river. We were not so fussy. Charred pease pudding?[1] No problem. Overripe fish pie? I'm afraid to say it could be pretty good. Even Drusilla's cannonball-like bread rolls eventually softened in the water and made good eating.

Getting sufficient nourishment wasn't a problem, so at one point late in the late 1380s I started to wonder why I was losing weight, not feeling at all my old self. Could my venerable age have been catching up with me at long last? Was the grim reaper about to reel me in?

Fish are supposed to live purely for the present and be incapable of self-pity. Well, *merde*, that may be true for others but it isn't for me! I was not a happy carp.

It was a tench (what else?) that set me right. It wasn't old age that was sending me to piscatorial heaven; attached to my belly a lamprey was sucking the lifeblood out of me – a bloody great, record-breaking lamprey![1] Okay, maybe I'm exaggerating, but it was still a whopper, and it was still shortening my life to a matter of days. Naturally I went berserk. I leapt, I swam at a hundred miles per hour, I rubbed myself on the rocky river bottom and scoured myself against beds of razor mussels, but all to no avail. My parasitic passenger refused to let go.

At length, drained of my strength and drained of a good lot of my (yech) bodily nutrients, I drifted into the shallow water by the Spotted Cow's riverside lawn. There, a well-dressed, bearded gentleman of advanced years reached down and pulled me to the bank. I was too tired to resist, my one hope was that perhaps he'd find the lamprey more appetising than me.

Painstakingly he removed each hook-like tooth of the lamprey's revolting, sucker-like mouth from my stomach, leaving a sore and bloodied wound, but one that would doubtless heal before long. Calling it a godless abomination, my rescuer flung the lamprey into a dense patch of bankside undergrowth, then, to my immense relief, he slid me gently back into deeper water.

'Thanks, good sir.' Good manners overrode my natural sense of caution.

The gentleman recoiled so violently I was afraid I'd done him irreparable damage, but then, sitting back on his haunches, he recovered the power of speech. 'Great Gadfrey! What manner of miracle is this, a great fish that speaks?'

'Not a miracle sir, just a…phenomenon let's say.'

'But a speaking fish, and one that speaks with a slight Gallic lilt to boot. Surely that's the Devil's work? Is it not against nature?'

'No more than men that speak, whatever their accent. Do you go around calling men the Devil's work?'

'Some men for sure, but I suppose I take your point.'

'The wonders of nature, do you call them the Devil's work?'

'Hmm, then what about that loathsome thing that was trying to suck your insides out? Would you not call that a beast from depths of hell?'

'Not really. We all have to make a living. Just not on me preferably.'

'You're being remarkably philosophical about it I must say.' The gentleman scratched his beard pensively. 'I suppose that as God made all that's in the heavens and on the earth, he's got to carry the can for—'

Fascinated as I was by our conversation, a number of heavy vibrations emanating from the riverbank warned me of approaching men – several men, with heavy footfalls – so I swiftly slid away into some deeper water behind a bed of rushes, but not so far away that my lateral line was unable to hear voices as well as clodhopping.

My new friend gave every sign of discomfort at the arrival of several beefy men in leather breeches and tunics, armed with heavy cudgels. They had a sour demeanour, but not as sour as their leader, a tall, cadaverous individual, wearing a flowing black cape of some black silken material, and an oddly flamboyant chaperon-style hat. It was as if he was trying to dress down, but couldn't bear to dress cheaply.

'Well met, sirrah.' The cadaver's voice was oddly whiny for such a presence. 'I would have a quiet word with thee.'

'Bishop Runkem,' my friend answered. 'And in mufti too. To what do I owe the pleasure, your grace?'

'A few points to clarify, questions that need answering.'

My friend said nothing.

'Why, just for a start, do you sit idly by a river on the sabbath,' the cadaver whined gratingly, 'when any true Christian would be attending mass?'

'Isn't being on a pilgrimage enough? Is my devotion seriously to be doubted? To be honest I wearied of my fellow travellers, and sought a few moments of quiet reflection.'

'A trifle, a trifle. There are more important matters to consider. Such as your beating of a poor friar, a humble and goodly servant of God, in a London street in broad daylight, not ten days ago. You knocked out most of his teeth, and the wretched fellow is having to live on milk and porridge.'

'The blackguard got off lightly.'

'Explain yourself, sirrah,'

'I caught sight of him drunkenly cavorting with two ladies of pleasure by the entrance of the Codpiece and Placket Inn. When he recognised me, he tried to make out I was the one doing the cavorting, and demanded a full shiny crown for his silence. I merely declined his offer in a way he couldn't misconstrue.'

'There are witnesses to your assault.'

'Witnesses from the Codpiece and Placket, who I'm sure will say anything for of the price of a tankard or two of porter.'

'There are other charges. Far more serious than common assault.'

By this time my rescuer was looking seriously worried. Naturally I knew nothing about Bishop Runkem, but it was obvious that he wielded considerable power, and he got a real kick from doing so.

'You stand accused of being a Godless Lollard,[3] the worst kind of heretic.'

I'd never heard of a Lollard, but I got the impression that it wasn't a good thing to be at that moment.

'I'm no such thing. In fact, I'm not entirely sure what that even means!'

'He feigns innocence, ha!' The cadaver turned to his surly henchmen for dramatic effect, but with their granite faces they weren't ideal foils. 'A list of grievous misdeeds, sirrah, a shameful list, and topped by membership of a proscribed sect in league with the Devil!'

'What am I supposed to have done? I haven't signed up to anything sinister!'

'Do you deny you're a Wycliffian?[4] You want to see the scriptures set out in plain English? You people are worse than the Cathars,[5] worse even than the infidel horde that occupies the most holy of cities!'

'That's outrageous – I'm none of those things!'

'We'll see what song you sing after a few turns on the rack.'

'People say anything under torture, and well you know it.'

'Absolutely! Torture is the very foundation stone of our exalted legal system. Due process? Burden of proof? Pshaw! Namby-pamby stuff, we'd never get any confessions.' The cadaver was even more sinister when he showed amusement. 'However, there is a way this unpleasantness can be avoided. A way to make it all go away.'

'And that way wouldn't have anything to do with pounds, shillings and pence would it, Your Grace?'

'There's still work to be done on Southwark Cathedral.'

'And a certain bishop's palace, I'll wager,'

'Indeed. In which case the Heavenly Father may deign to look favourably on the miserable sins of—'

'So, let's get this straight: either I get my neck elongated by a couple of feet, or I end up out on the street.'

'I knew you were an intelligent man.'

I'd heard enough, his grace was obviously a bloody disgrace. Without understanding all the nuances of the scenario taking place on the riverbank, I knew my kindly friend was in serious trouble, and if I was to be of any help I had to act at once. I just hoped the black-clad cadaver was as capable of being freaked out as he was himself of freaking out others.

Keeping well hidden, I filled my gills and bellowed, 'Cease and desist, this good man is innocent!'

The leather-clad goons' stony faces now cracked into expressions of abject terror, but the bishop was merely shaken. 'What manner of trickery is this? A mystery interloper who sounds like a French strumpet? Identify yourself!'

Drat. Think, fish, think! 'I am this good fellow's guardian angel!'

That was embarrassing, I didn't even know his name. 'And he has done no wrong.'

'If you're his guardian angel then show yourself.'

My walnut-sized brain was under extreme pressure.

'Tremble, mortal, for I could rain thunderbolts upon you, I could smite you with earthquakes, whip up hurricanes to blow you all the way to the Devil's kingdom!'

The bishop was now looking seriously worried. His men had been reduced to gibbering wrecks. My friend just stood stock still, open-jawed.

'Were I to manifest myself your eyeballs would ignite at the very sight of me and you'd join the legions of the unseeing, so I am sending you a sign. A great fish, clad in golden scales, will leap before you!'

I was still weak and tired, but, best fin forward, I had to continue the show. I leapt high from the river and, while hovering in the air for a second, succeeded in spurting a mouthful of muddy water right into the bishop's face. My re-entry into the river soaked him from head to foot.

He cracked. The cadaver was beyond scared. He dropped to his knees and babbled that he'd been a bad bishop, a very bad bishop, and henceforth he'd confine himself to doing charitable works and get out of the neck extension-extortion racket for good. He called to his men to follow him, but his men were already nowhere to be seen. Dripping and hunched, he set off after them.

'Bravo,' my friend applauded as I reappeared at the water's edge. 'You probably committed half a dozen acts of blasphemy during that little performance, but I'm mightily thankful that you did.'

'*Pas de tout*, it's the best I could come up with on the spur of the moment. I'm a little puzzled as to what a Lollard is though.'

'I'm not exactly sure myself. No one has defined it that clearly, but I think the Lollards are a group of folk who think most people should be able to understand the scriptures. That Mass should be said in English instead of Latin – which of course practically no one can understand.'

'And that's a bad thing?'

'Shh! Anyway, as far as I can make out Lollards have come to mean anyone the Church disagrees with at any given time. But don't quote me on that.'

'Yoo-hoo!' a voice rang out.

I gently glided behind the rushes once more.

'There you be,' said a stout, middle-aged lady as she waddled towards the water's edge. She was well dressed, flamboyantly even, radiated good spirits and spoke with a broad-vowelled accent I was unfamiliar with, but later learned was West Country. 'Come on, Mr Chaucer, you've already missed Mass and now you'll be late for luncheon. You don't want to face the wrath of Mistress Drusilla, do you?'

'Perish the thought, Mistress Alyson, but my stomach's still not right after yesterday's offering.'

'It were a tad, er, unusual, come to think of it.'

'I've never eaten roast pike with crackling before – especially roast pike that *was* crackling. And if fortune smiles on me I never will again.'

Actually, very few of the guests had touched their roast pike. Not many of the fish in the river had fancied it either, save a few eels – they'll gobble up virtually anything.

'I'll get her to save a plate for you, Mr C – we don't want to start a rumpus, do we?'

'Thank you, mistress, I'll re-join the throng anon.'

We both watched as the West Country lady made her way back up the slope towards the inn.

'Nice woman, that Wife of Bath,' said Mr Chaucer, 'even if she tends to ramble on a bit. But fair play to her, widowed several times and runs a business all on her own. That's worthy of respect.'

'And there's others up there you're giving a wide berth to?'

'Several, and from all walks of life – from the humble to the noble, the ecclesiastical to the chivalrous. Why, there's a knight, a miller, a reeve, a clerk, a nun, a squire, a friar, pardoner…and Uncle Tom Cobbley and all. But the one thing they have in common is rabbiting on all the time. I can't hear myself think for all the tittle-tattle.'

'Sounds pleasant enough to me. It must help pass the time while you're travelling.'

'But I came on this pilgrimage[6] to clear my head, give myself space for a bit of divine inspiration.'

I was all lateral line.

'I'm a successful man,' Mr Chaucer continued, 'I've served in high office to three kings, aided military campaigns and been a diplomat, but first and foremost I consider myself a writer – a writer of poetry and a writer of prose…or so I supposed.

'I'm searching for inspiration for my *magnum opus*, the work by which I'll be remembered, a work to reach out to everyone, regardless of their station, but the spark has gone. I'm struggling. A classic case of writer's block. How does one such as me achieve the common touch? I've invented several new forms of poetry and penned tomes on philosophy, but when it comes to holding a simple conversation with a goodly soul such as the Wife of Bath I'm stumped – whereas she's quite relaxed chitchatting and swapping stories with anybody.

'Is there such a thing as literature for the masses? Decidedly yes, for on my travels in Italy, in Genoa and Florence, I met with great writers whose work spoke to the many. The great Petrarch, surely his ideas on enlightenment will change the way we live (or get him burnt at the stake). And then there's Giovanni Boccaccio and his *Decameron*. A work both sacred and profane, uplifting yet coarse and bawdy. A monumental achievement that speaks to everyone – a veritable blockbuster.'

'It sounds intriguing, though I haven't got around to learning to read yet. It's hard when you're a fish.'

'All human life is there. Mendacious merchants, courageous knights, gullible peasants, horny priests and insatiable abbesses. Would that I could find the voice of real people like Boccaccio.'

'I see your problem. You're a bit of a brainbox, aren't you.'

'That's not helpful.'

'Well stop me if you're not comfortable with this, but how about *borrowing* some common voices?'

'Ye-es?'

'Your fellow pilgrims, both the humble and the noble, tittle-tattling all the time. You know the saying, everybody has a story to tell? Get them to give you their stories. Note them down, make that your ground-breaking book. I bet you'll be spoilt for choice.'

'I don't know. It doesn't seem quite kosher to me.'

'Look, I'm sure they'd all be flattered to lend you a hand. And if you're still uncomfortable, change things around a bit. You know, creative licence. Cover your tracks. Just so no one can accuse you of nicking stuff.'

'No, sorry. It's out of the question. Totally unethical – I won't do it.'

'It was only a suggestion. But what do I know? I'm only a carp.'

'Well, I thank you, but the search for inspiration continues. And I thank you for saving my bacon with Bishop Runkem. Yours was an, um, inspired intervention.'

'Think nothing of it. I'm still sore from that bloody lamprey.'

'I bid you farewell, fair fish, I should re-join my companions. I'm sure a goodly portion of our lunch will soon be coming your way.'

I watched as Mr Chaucer made his way back up to the inn. There was a definite bounce in his step. I didn't agree with his squeamishness about using his fellow pilgrims' stories, but certainly admired him for sticking to his guns. You've got to admire *un type* with morals.

Notes

[1]Pease puddling. A savoury pudding made from split yellow peas, often flavoured with various spices and, if you're lucky, off-cuts of ham. A step up from pottage.

[2]Lampreys are jawless, eel-like creatures that have round, sucker-like mouths with circular bands of tiny teeth that latch onto their prey in order to suck their vital juices out of them. It's said that Henry I of England died after eating a surfeit of lampreys. Gisella wishes he'd eaten a few more of them before he was taken ill.

[3]Lollard. Prototype Protestant.

[4]Wycliffians. Followers of Sir John Wycliffe, who argued against the privilege of the clergy and advocated translating the Bible into language everyone could understand.

[5]Cathars. A singular offshoot of Catholicism that prospered for a while in Southern France. Among their beliefs was the notion of twin deities, both good and evil. The real Catholics didn't like them and killed nearly all of them.

[6]Pilgrimages to Canterbury, scene of the assassination of Thomas Becket, were all the thing for good Christians in the 15th Century. The route remains well-trodden to this day.

Chapter Five

La Pucelle. Gisella makes her way back to France and plays a major part in creating the nation's patron saint

After my brief encounter with Mr Chaucer it was back to the same old routine in muddy old Medway. Year after year after year of the same old grind. At least on the warmer days I could hang around outside the Old Spotted Cow and listen in on all the customers' conversations, but I still lacked the confidence to join in with any of them. One consolation was the ready source of food, still surreptitiously being tossed into the water on a regular basis, which I generally managed to get first dibs on before any of the bream, chub or eels.

But, to coin a modern-day expression, the Medway was doing my head in. Yalding was a boring backwater where absolutely nothing happened from year to year, bar discarded *basse cuisine* landing on your head three times a day, seatrout and salmon passing you by without as much as a good-day, and over-ambitious otters having to be dodged. Much of the chin-wagging at the inn centred on London, which was obviously the place to be if you wanted any pizzazz in your life – which I definitely did. I had two problems: one, I had no idea where London was, and two, no idea how to get there.

A chance conversation in the spring of 1428, between a cloth merchant and a knight at arms, set me in the right direction. Or what I assumed was the right direction. The road on their trip from London had been borderline impassable, a muddy nightmare, so they agreed that for the return leg they would stop at the Port of Rochester, on the Medway estuary, and catch a boat for the journey back west along the Thames to London. The mystery was solved. It was the bright lights of the capital for this lucky carp.

The farther downstream I swam, the brinier the water became. This was something I hadn't considered. Of course, carp are known as freshwater fish, not that I was aware of it at the time, and it was plain that the saltiness of the water was making me feel somewhat queasy. In fact, as I approached the port of Rochester I noticed lots of other differences in the water around me. For a start, twice a day the river current went backwards! Craziness – all the water flowing upstream! The waterweed was different, the shellfish were different. And the fish were different. For a start, for several miles back upstream, where the water wasn't salty at all, I'd been seeing large numbers of quicksilver grey mullet. But here at the port they teemed in their thousands. And there were flounders, odd flattened-out fish with their heads squished to one side, that looked like they'd been trodden on by an elephant. Shreds of past overheard conversations popped up in my head: I'd heard talk about the sea. Well, I was evidently

approaching it. The question was, could I survive in it?

It occurred to me that there were some fish that were quite at home in both sea- and freshwater, such as salmon and seatrout, but what struck me particularly were the grey mullet, who grazed up and down the river with the tides, oblivious to the salt content of the water they were swimming in. I asked one of them if there was a trick to their adaptability, but the only answer I could elicit was 'Like um whelks.' Not very helpful. Grey mullet are very speedy, attractive fish, but they make bream look bright.

The longer I dithered around the port, the more I tolerated the salty water. This was obviously the trick: acclimatisation. I was going to be fine heading into the seawater and finding my way up the Thames to London. Carp at sea may run contrary to everything people know about fish, but of course no other carp has ever been (ahem) intelligent enough to go about it properly. I was fine. Full of confidence I headed out of the Medway estuary and into the briny world of dogfish, cod and whiting. But, as they say, pride comes before a mishap.

Which way was west and which way was east? Hell, at that point I wasn't too clear on which was my right fin and which was my left. The direction of the current was no help at all, because, as I'd found out, tides are sneaky things that confound your expectations. My lateral line was giving me a red-light warning of a major storm brewing, but out in the expanse of the Thames estuary I didn't have a clue how to avoid it. I just went with my instinct and swam, and was soon engulfed by the most filthy tempest and massive storm surge.

Going with the flow can mean different things to humans and fish. I had little choice but to go with the flow, and after several days at sea I had to admit to myself that either I'd taken a wrong turn, or the distances involved were far greater than I'd anticipated.

Some fish, such as salmon, seem to have an inbuilt navigation system. Carp don't. I had zero idea about geography, and as far as I knew London could've lain in absolutely any direction. I was all at sea. But finally, after several very confused days, I could smell fresh water and mud, and found myself heading into a wide delta, then an enormous river estuary.

There were both seagoing ships and river barges on the watercourse, some sail- and others oar-powered, so I swam alongside one of the smaller barges to see if I could glean any information about my whereabouts. The crew members chatted freely among themselves as they rowed, but they were chatting in a language I'd never heard. Did Londoners have a dialect I was unfamiliar with, or had I taken even more of a wrong turn than I feared? There was only one thing for it – carry on swimming. The tides and currents were still confusing, but now I'd got the hang of heading into the less salty water I just had to ensure that I was travelling upriver.

After a couple more days the river split, and then it split again. Out of a mixture of frustration and curiosity, I headed into one of the smaller – but still considerable – tributaries, and continued my voyage. I was still hopeful that I'd reach London. After all, I hadn't heard of many other places.

I passed many different species of fish, some familiar from my centuries in the Medway, some not. Asp, something like a chub, but not as greedy, and barbel, musclebound torpedoes but mightily dim, were new to me, as were zander, rather brutish but no threat, and wels catfish, some of which were disconcertingly large and probably *were* a threat. I gave them a wide berth and carried on swimming.

Gradually the river changed in nature, as rivers do, from wide, sluggish breamy regions, to swifter roachy and barbelly stretches, and on upwards into tinkling and dancing headwaters, rather like the upper reaches of the Medway, where I'd made the very brief acquaintance of Rodney de Yaxley. One question remained uppermost in my mind: where the bloody hell was London?

After travelling for nearly two months, I decided the time had come for me to take a risk and ask someone for directions. Early summer was in full swing. The lilac was in blossom, swallows and swifts dipped and darted. It was a time of plenty, with the river almost bursting with tasty crayfish and freshwater shrimps and succulent crunchy water snails, but although the living would've been easy for the next few months, my heart was set on the big city. At a shallow section of river a teenage girl, who should've been busy with her basket of washing, was on her knees staring into space. She was a slight figure, with long, straw-coloured hair, a pasty complexion, a slightly beaky nose, and shoulders that looked perpetually hunched. She was utterly unremarkable except for her glazed eyes, which at that moment were peering into the ether. She didn't look at all threatening, so I plucked up my courage—

'Pardon me, young lady, could you—'

She let out a shriek, leapt backwards, tripped, hit her head on a rock, and then rolled forward again, coming to rest at the water's edge once more. She lay on her side, blood dripping from the side of her head onto the water-margin gravel.

'Oh merde.' That was not what I'd intended. At least she was still breathing, so she was evidently alive.

After I'd blown a couple mouthfuls of water into her face she started to come to. 'Sorry,' I muttered, 'I really didn't mean to startle you.'

'*Qu'est que vous dites?*' she blinked. '*Qui êtes vous?*'

It occurred to me that maybe I wasn't as close to London as I'd hoped. My French came back to me instantly, even though it was over 300 years since I'd spoken it – a bit like riding a bicycle, not that fish ride bicycles.

'I'm on my way to London, but I think I've got a bit lost.'

'London is in England is it not? It must be far away. We do not like the English, they steal our lands.' She had a little girl's voice.

Rather than launch into a political discourse with an adolescent who was still lying helplessly on the shingly water margin, I decided to keep my line of questioning very simple, such as *where were we?* The answer that we were on the banks of the Meuse, near the little village of Domrémy, wasn't very helpful, although of course I now know my travels had taken me through the North Sea, and across modern-day Holland and Belgium into northeast France, via the Rivers Rhine and Meuse.

Her name was Jeanne, Jeanne d'Arc, known thereabouts as *La Pucelle de Domrémy.*[1] She supposed that was because there weren't many girls of her age in Domrémy who were still *pucelles*. Her father and brothers worked on the land, while her sisters wove wool. She, however, had never got the hang of using a loom, or carding the wool, or doing the sewing, so she was just allowed to wander about and occasionally do the washing. Her father called her his special girl – his very precious girl.

'Are you feeling any better?' I asked. 'Do you think you can get up yet?'

She levered herself up onto one knee and attempted to stand, but then let out a cry, held her head in her hands, and sank back to her knees.

'My Lord!' she gasped.

An instant transformation had come over her. Her skin appeared to glow almost, and the blank eyes had become sharply focussed, like steel-cutting lasers. Now she rose to her feet, steady as the Statue of Liberty, seemingly taller and slender like a poplar, yet crackling with energy.

I was worried. A sharp blow to the noggin can have unpredictable consequences.

'I hear you,' she said, her voice clear, suddenly mature and commanding. 'Saint Michel, yes, I understand. And Saint Margaret the Virgin, Saint Catherine of Alexandria, I hear you too. The English and their allies the Burgundians must be driven from our shores.'

Her eyes were sharply fixed on something I couldn't see. I just hoped she'd snap out of it soon, and that no one would blame me.

'How is this to be achieved?' she asked, sounding a little more like her former self.

'I must entreat the dauphin[2] to give me an army to drive the invaders into the sea,' she went on, in a piercing voice.

'Is that all?' she whimpered. Then: 'I will vanquish our foes,' she stated forcefully. 'I will lead the dauphin to Reims where he will be crowned King Charles VII of France.'

'Can I really do all that?' asked the young girl of herself.

'I *will* do that,' declared the confident young woman.

A few seconds later Jeanne sat back down on the riverbank. A semblance of normality returned – the cries of a kestrel could be heard, a few hatching damselflies were ascending reedmace stalks, rising dace dimpled the water's surface.

'Are you all right?' I asked tentatively. 'At least you no longer seem freaked out by the sight of me.'

'I've just had the most wonderful vision, the heavens parted and I was visited by the most astounding, beautiful host of angels. I conversed with the Saints Michel, Margaret and Catherine, and am entrusted with Returning *la France* to the French. Compared to all that, having a natter with a fish, even a biggun like you, doesn't rate too highly on any scale of shocks.'

I was relieved to hear that. Naturally I wanted more information about where I was and what was going on, but Jeanne wasn't exactly a mine of information. She was able to give me her limited overview of the Hundred Years War,[3] except of course she didn't call it that: she called it something like *The War to Boot Out the Filthy English.*

Would life be better under a French king than an English one? I asked. She nodded vigorously. The men in her family would continue to work the plough until they dropped at an early age, and the women would continue to weave the cloth even as they lost their teeth and eyesight, but they'd be ploughing French soil and weaving French cloth. There was obviously something I was missing, so I didn't pursue that line of questioning. It was then that I decided that come what may, I had to find out more about the puzzling world I was living in. For 300 years I'd been drifting through life with no more purpose than a muddle-headed mullet afloat on an ebb tide. I was going to have to get myself a real education somehow.

With no great hope of a coherent answer, I asked Jeanne how one went about learning...stuff. To my surprise she answered that a priest at Nancy, which the family had visited one time to attend a fair, had spoken of receiving his training at a place called *la Sorbonne*, which was something called a university, in Paris – which was the capital of France, but currently in the hands of the accursed English and Burgundians. Apparently universities were places where you learn.

Well, I was going to have to visit this university in order to acquire some learning, and in order to do that I was going to have to find my way to Paris, which, after my attempts to reach London, probably represented a monumental task. One of my first areas of study would be geography. Of course, I wasn't so naïve as to think that I'd just turn up at the Sorbonne and people would fall over themselves to educate me. I'd find where erudite folk hung out near a river to chew the fat and listen in on their conversations. I was going to learn stuff by osmosis – which isn't a word I learned until much later.

Jeanne snapped me out of my reverie. 'Do you think I can do it? Is it possible for a mere girl – a maid – to carry out what I've been asked?'

I was none too keen on getting involved in what after all was a political dispute between humans, but this was sexual politics – a very different kettle of fish. 'Listen here,' I said in my sternest voice, 'a woman is just as good as a man, and sometimes far better. Don't sell yourself short. Look at us lady fish, we have to carry around hundreds of thousands of eggs before we spawn, while the men, it's one quick shake of the pelvic fins and they're done. Hubba hubba. You show 'em, girl!'

'I understand.' The commanding, steely Jeanne was back. I had a feeling charismatic Jeanne was there for the long haul. 'The fish is right. I, Jeanne d'Arc, am quite capable of leading armies. As your beatitudes command me, I will restore a French king to the throne.'

Jeanne was now buzzing with purpose. I didn't know what effect she'd have on the wider world, but charismatic Jeanne certainly brought some benefits to yours truly. To my surprise her family was quickly turned around into supporting her mission to offer her services to the Dauphin at Chinon, and she gladly agreed to help me on the first leg of my intended trip to Paris.

Such was her new-found magnetism, no one questioned her request for a wooden chest to be brought to the river, and filled with sopping pondweed for my comfort. Her father had told her that within a day's march from Domrémy her path crossed the infant River Marne, and the Marne led eventually to the Seine, and thence to Paris. Thus I endured the discomfort of another boxed-up journey, on the back of an oxcart this time, before receiving my very welcome shot of *eau de vie*[4] and being released into the Marne. Darkness was falling. Although we carp are more than capable of night swimming, I decided to rest up in the weir pool I'd been deposited in, so I could make a fresh start at sunrise.

Notes

[1]*Pucelle.* Virgin.
[2]*Dauphin.* French prince, first in line to the throne.
[3]During that period large areas of France were under English rule. The French considered the Hundred Years War a liberation struggle. The English thought the French were uppity.
[4]*Eau de vie.* Firewater. Spirits made from whatever is available, in this case very poor-quality plonk.

Chapter Six

La Vie Parisienne. How Gisella finds more friends, gains a university education, and begins a long and troubled relationship with river bridges

It was just as well I set off on my downstream journey in daylight, for the upper reaches of the Marne weren't easy to negotiate for such a fish as large as me. Many a trout and grayling scattered out of my way as I barrelled lopsidedly down with the current, not to mention the tiddlers such as minnows, stone loach and bullheads.

My directions were clear. All I had to do was carry on downstream until I reached Paris, which I was assured I'd be unable to miss, though no one had mentioned how far it was. On I sped, through rapids, glides and more sedate pools, scanning the banks for what I'd been assured was the epicentre of human civilisation. By the end of the day I'd passed countless hills, forests and cultivated fields, but the only signs of human habitation had been very occasional mud-and-straw hovels – which I didn't really think amounted to *the greatest city on Earth.* With a quarter moon rising, I sheltered under an overhanging willow, supped on an abundance of water snails – which would've been improved by some garlic and parsley butter, but what the hell – and recharged my batteries once more.

The next morning brought more of the same, the river growing bigger as more tributaries joined it, but after no more than a couple of hours I noticed the current was becoming stronger and stronger – uncomfortably strong. I was obviously approaching a weir, or waterfall, the size of which I hadn't yet encountered. I had a choice: head for the slack water close to the riverbank and go absolutely nowhere, or take a chance. I chose the latter.

The water churned and surged, frothy white, almost opaque. The rush of excess oxygen through my gills made me lightheaded, as if the turbulence of the water wasn't playing merry hell with my lateral line as it was. Okay, I thought, this was a *really* bad decision – but of course there was no turning back.

All of a sudden I was plunging vertically downwards, then, with a shock that juddered me from barbules to tail, I hit the foaming water below, and was dragged past rocks and boulders and over scrunching gravel, until at last the water slowed and I floated past streamer weed and water cabbages and even a couple of lily patches. Regaining my equilibrium, I tried to figure out how badly hurt I'd been. I was sore, very sore, but I didn't think I had any open wounds, nor had I even lost any scales. Scales schmales, you may say, but lost scales can lead to all sorts of infections. What's more they're an open invitation to unwanted hangers-on, such as leeches and my friends the lampreys.

I drifted gently downstream until at midday I reached a bankside *auberge*, a half-timbered building whose walls were part-clad with wisteria, where a group of travellers were enjoying pleasant sunshine, sitting at a trestle table with goblets of wine and plates of something that smelled rather delicious. I settled in close to the bank and enjoyed a good old listen.

The travellers turned out to be merchants, all in the wine trade. They'd been dealing with growers in nearby Épernay, very pleased with the business they'd conducted, and were presently going to make their way back to Paris. The fine white wine they'd purchased was to make the journey downriver by boat, but they were debating whether they themselves would travel by road, which was both uncomfortable and dangerous, or by river – which was also uncomfortable and dangerous. Tell me about it, I thought. Then the penny dropped. If a boat could make the journey, so could a large, resourceful carp. Perhaps I was really over the worst of the trip; all I'd have to do was keep to the boat lanes and I should be able to stay clear of any cataracts and waterfalls.

Sated with *daube de venaison*[1] and *pain perdu*[2] the merchants amused themselves by tearing up and throwing their uneaten bread into the river for the ducks. I amused myself by chasing off the ducks, who protested loudly, and eating the bread. I needed to fortify myself for the next leg of the journey.

The Marne was now better behaved as it meandered through vineyards and orchards, and passed smallholdings with a few scattered cows and pigs. Other tracts of countryside remained uncultivated, just scrubland and forest, with signs of human habitation few and far between. While some of the narrower sections of river were still fast flowing, mostly it was sedate and the going was easy. I let the current do all the work, and just corrected my course from time to time with a flick of my tail.

The river presented no more hazards until eventually it straightened and widened, and then joined forces with a much bigger river – the Seine. Here many of the higher banks were lined with timber huts built on stilts that looked like storks' legs. They all had protruding crane-like arms suspended over the water, which could be lowered and raised, beneath which dangled large rectangular nets. I was so transfixed trying to figure out what they were that I swam straight into one of them, and only realised my mistake when the two humans in the hut started to hoik the net out of the water.

With a furious surge and a great deal of splashing I bolted for freedom, and, to my immense relief, tore clean through the net. Either it had been made with small fry in mind, or it had simply weakened through neglect. Whichever, I was free, and shot out into midstream like a slightly tilted guided missile. The two fishermen were inconsolable. They'd learned their lesson about using a feeble net, and I'd learned my lesson about swimming near drop nets.

From there on downstream there was a steady build-up of houses on either bank of the river. They were simple dwellings, one to two storeys, of daub and wattle or half-timbered, well scattered, some with little plots of land, domesticated animals, vegetable plots, and fruit trees. But soon I passed what looked like fortified city walls, and within them there was a concentration of much finer buildings, many stone-built, and mostly three and even four storeys. I passed one small island, crammed with buildings, then approached another larger one, on which, standing in amongst houses both tall and grand, was an edifice that simply dwarfed them all, crowned by two magnificent square stone towers. Just as breath-taking, in my piscine estimation, were two of the city's three bridges, on which there were fine houses, three, four, even five storeys tall. A fourth

bridge was currently under construction, with two stone-built piers rising from the water to a crazy latticework of timbers, that had crept across between them. I subsequently learned that this was to be the second crossing between the Ile de la Cité and the Rive Gauche. As for the river itself, it was a main thoroughfare, crammed with boat traffic: passenger boats, cargo boats, fisherfolks' boats, posh people's pleasure boats, barges – nearly all oar-powered, as only short-masted vessels could pass beneath the bridges. This was most certainly a brave new world.

In some places the buildings rose vertically from the river, while elsewhere there were wharves and jetties and grassy areas that sloped down to the banks. And there were people. People in the streets, on the riverbanks, on boats, on the bridges, in the buildings, everywhere – I'd never seen so many. There was also a great deal of detritus from so many people. The chief way of getting rid of anything unwanted was evidently via the river, whether it was food waste, general rubbish, dead cats, dogs and murder victims, or of course the results of human bodily functions. You could dart towards what to all appearances was an appetising discarded *saucisse* bobbing in the water, only to find it was something rather disgusting.

First thing, I had to stop gawping like a stunned mullet. I didn't want to be a country bumpkin hayseed, or whatever the aquatic equivalent is. The city had its fair share of fisherfolk, and ending up as a trophy catch was definitely not on my agenda. I was going to keep a low profile, look, listen and learn.

It took me several days to get used to all the noise in the city: people arguing, shouted conversations, religious processions, horses clattering and donkeys braying, mobs chanting for blood, vendors hollering and loudest of all by far, the tolling bells of what I learned was Notre-Dame Cathedral. I soon found a quieter haven, however, towards the end of the Ile de la Cité, beyond the Palais du Roy's[3] garden walls, where the grassy ground fell gently away to the water's edge.

Close in, the water was reasonably deep, and afforded me shelter in the form of numerous large clumps of streamer weed. There people came down to the river to enjoy the relative quiet, picnic, carouse, chitchat and spend a few hours fishing. I found little to fear from these anglers, who seldom, if ever, caught anything. A half-dead worm impaled on a crude-looking hook, attached to a braided horsehair line almost as thick as a hawser, was unlikely to hoodwink the dimmest of fish, let alone me. I soon learned that these fisherfolk came out more for the fresh air and a bit of a social than in expectation of actually hooking anything.

I soon came to recognise the same faces coming down to the water's edge day after day. I was particularly interested by a particular group, young men who listened intently to a couple of older fellows: one rotund and jolly, who wore a simple black robe and was missing a neat circle of hair on the top of his head, the other a much taller, gaunt-looking chap, dressed in tattered leggings, a loose tunic and an odd, squashy hat with a tassel. They were occasionally joined by a third older fellow, more flamboyantly dressed, with a hat like a giant *cep* mushroom (or cowpat if one were less polite), a colourful baggy tunic and pointed shoes that were certainly too big for his feet. This chap, despite his sallow, whiskery face and unfortunate physique – he managed to have a willowy frame and a pot belly at the same time – clearly believed he was a divine gift to the fairer sex.

I quickly learned the two more soberly attired old chaps were from the Sorbonne, giving students extra tuition in divinity and the natural sciences respectively – I'd struck lucky, after only a couple of weeks! Father Flammarion hosted discussions about the Bible, and was keen to encourage his charges to ask questions and challenge established ideas, while Maître Cornelius Azimuth was far more orthodox in his teaching of *scientific facts*: things were as they were; all answers were to be found in the Good Book. Much of the conversation was in French, for although Paris was ruled by the English and the Burgundians, French was the native language of the Parisians, and anyone attending the Sorbonne was expected to be fluent. Latin figured strongly in the discourses as well, being the language of most serious religious study. I listened intently and soon began to pick it up. My excellent lateral line for languages has always been a boon.

Despite their differences in both approach and temperament, the two savants were very good friends. Most times, once the students had dispersed, they'd stay on a while and bicker and try to shoot down one another's ideas. Why did the sun rise in the east and set in the west? Father Flammarion would ask. 'Because God wills it,' Maître Azimuth would answer. 'So would someone pick it up in a barrow and lug it back round to the east in time for the morning again?' the old monk would grin. On and on they'd squabble, with the good Father generally in the more radical camp, and the so-called man of science much more conservative. They wrangled, but they never fell out.

The ageing popinjay who sometimes sought their company fancied himself as a latter-day troubadour, extolling the virtues of courtly love, and waxing lyrical about the latest damsel (his description) to have caught his eye. Flammarion and Cornelius regarded Claude de Gaillac with great affection, but ribbed him that troubadours and chivalrous love had been dead as mutton even before the Black Death. Although he was convinced that one day he would be recognised as the great poet of the age, his companions would always cut him off very abruptly when he launched into the latest of his poems. It wasn't just that his voice sounded like a glass cutter; in truth his poetry was absolutely excruciating.

One early evening in late August, after the students had taken their leave, and the three older men had discussed at some length whether Lazarus indeed been brought back to life by the Messiah or was simply very fast asleep, Father Flammarion turned to me. As ever, I'd been eavesdropping from the edge of the weed bed. 'What do you think, my scaly friend?' he smiled. 'It's obvious you can understand us; you listen in every time we come to the river.'

'I don't know what to say,' I answered. 'I'm a fish. Bible studies aren't exactly my forte.'

'And he speaks,' Father Flammarion clapped his hands together in delight. 'Or rather she speaks, for you have a quite delightful feminine voice.'

In contrast to the monk's elation, Cornelius Azimuth had grave misgivings about my *outing*. 'Indeed, the fish speaks, that gives much food for thought. For surely is not such a phenomenon grossly unnatural and therefore an affront to God?'

'A veritable aquatic sylph,' gasped Claude de Gaillac, 'with the voice of an angel – albeit a slightly husky one. How can this apparition be aught but the work of the Heavenly Father?'

Me? Voice of an angel? I've always reckoned I had the voice of chain-smoking cabaret artiste with a severe hangover, but I suppose I was still quite young then.

'God's mysteries and creations are infinite,' said Father Flammarion, 'and this fish is most certainly one of them. After all, birds can fly in the air, moles burrow under the earth, the bee sucks nectar from the flower and gives us honey.' The good father was off on one. 'How often do we hear that across the seas there are winged serpents, and beings with a single, enormous foot, and men with faces in their chests? As we discover more about the Lord's work, I am more than convinced that other wonders will be revealed to us – and that these wonders in time will be seen as commonplace.'

'Amen to that,' Claude exclaimed, fully onside.

'Harumph.' Outnumbered and outgunned, Mâitre Azimuth held his peace. He eyed me warily, but I felt that once he realised I really was just a fish that could speak, and not some existential threat to his small, well-ordered world, Cornelius would eventually warm to me.

As I hoped, the venerable *mâitre* soon became quite used to my presence at their little gatherings, and between them he, the good clergyman and the poet undertook to teach me the elements of their various areas of expertise. I learned stories from the Good Book, and that different peoples often had different ways of showing their devotion (wrong ways, according to Cornelius). I expanded my knowledge of Latin and absorbed some Greek as well, I listened to numerous examples of poetic forms (although of course Claude's poems were pure tripe), I learnt basic mathematics, some theoretical alchemy, that barbarians lived in the lands to the north, Moors to the South, Orientals to the east and the sea poured over the edge of the world to the west. 'Pure hearsay and unproven,' Father Flammarion protested. 'He questions the wisdom of his superiors?' Cornelius Azimuth glared back. 'So, all that water just pouring away into nothingness.' snorted Flammarion, 'How is it replaced?' Cornelius retorted his friend was stepping on dangerous ground. Scholars from the East maintain that the Earth is spherical, that the sea doesn't pour anywhere, grinned Flammarion. 'Blasphemy, infidels!' Cornelius spluttered. '*Du calme, du calme!*' the priest smiled, 'Nothing is proven.'

And so, my education continued. With the help of a small blackboard and chalk I also quickly learned to read, but with fins rather than hands I was never to master writing. Not only was I a carp who could speak, I was becoming an educated carp.

Seasons passed, but mostly Parisian life remained unchanged. News would filter down to the riverbank of the fluctuating war between the French and the English and their Burgundian allies. After striking out a couple of times, Jeanne d'Arc had finally won the trust of the dauphin and was put at the head of a force on the march to lift the English siege of Orleans. I thought it prudent to keep shtum about my very slight role in putting Jeanne in touch with her voices; although I tried to remain officially neutral in the affairs of humans, I couldn't really see any way in which this was going to end well.

No one was more surprised than me when she pulled it off. No need for me to go over very familiar ground: Jeanne was instrumental in the crowning of the dauphin as Charles VII of France at Rheims, and turning the tide of war against the Brits. I was deeply saddened by her capture, show trial and burning by the English in 1431, but considered that perhaps a brief, stellar existence was preferable to a lifetime of washing rags and staring into space. I hoped so.

It was another five years before the English grip on Paris was finally loosened, by which time the second bridge from the Ile de la Cité to the Rive Gauche was still only three-quarters complete. A vast wooden framework housed the construction of the structure's spans, while scaffolding still surrounded the work on its two remaining part-built stone piers. The city elders had intended that the bridge be finished for Charles VII's triumphal entry to Paris, but the work had evidently proceeded at a snail's pace due to the years of uncertainty over the city's eventual masters.

Two topics preoccupied our little waterside group: King Charles's procession through the city streets of Paris to the palace on the Ile de la Cité due to take place the next day, and, far more importantly, Claude's latest infatuation.

'It's the real thing this time, *mes amis*.' Claude clasped his hands dramatically to his chest.

'You've said that the past seventeen times,' smiled Father Flammarion.

'The widow Pommard has a beauty beyond compare.' Claude was undaunted.

'She has her own teeth, or most of them,' said Cornelius.

'Her hair is as lustrous as a cascade of morning dew.'

'You've never seen her hair,' said Father Flammarion, 'she always keeps it well covered. You don't know if she has any hair.'

'Her hair is wonderful, I just wish she'd let me see it.'

'I expect you're going to say her voice is as a tinkling fountain,' said Cornelius.

'Have you been peeking at the ode I'm going to serenade her with?' said Claude.

'You're serenading her?' I asked.

'That's why I came by rowing boat,' said Claude. 'I found out she lives above the apothecary on the *pont de la cité*, so I'm about to row my boat directly below her window and woo her with my latest composition.'

'*Bonne chance*,' said Father Flammarion.

'*Bon courage*,' said Cornelius.

'I'm sure it'll all go swimmingly,' I exclaimed after him as he rowed splashily away from the bank and up the river. 'You can always hope she's profoundly deaf,' I added softly.

With Claude trying his luck with the widow Pommard, our conversation reverted to Charles VII's grand entrance to the city. The two venerable men discussed the city elders' fear that the English would stage some kind of attack to demonstrate for once and for all that they were going nowhere.

'I thought they were retreating from all their strongholds,' I said. Of course my stance was strictly neutral, but that didn't mean I was uninterested in current affairs.

'They've had numerous setbacks,' said Father Flammarion, 'but take King Charles out of the equation and all the momentum would vanish from the French advances.'

'The English and Burgundians would hold sway once more,' said Cornelius. 'The martyrdom of Jeanne d'Orléans would count for naught.'

'Not that she sacrificed herself willingly,' said Father Flammarion under his breath.

'But precautions have been taken,' said Cornelius. 'Nothing will rob the French of their birthright and nothing will prevent Charles's grand arrival.'

'Can precautions ever be one hundred per cent?' said Father Flamarion.

'You'll see,' said Cornelius with certainty. 'All the city gates are triple guarded, the streets are constantly patrolled. Plus, great chains have been laid across the river downstream of the metropolis, to prevent English boats from sailing up from La Manche.[4] All will go without a hitch, mark my words.'

'I pray you're right,' said the good Father.

'What could possibly go wrong?' I wondered to myself. In my near 400 years on Earth, I'd learned that plenty can go wrong.

Our musing was disturbed by a bad smell carried down the river by the gentle breeze. Bad smells from the river were commonplace; this one was worse than most. Then a splattering and spluttering heralded the return of our intrepid troubadour, who turned out to be the source of the revolting odour.

No sooner had he started to woo the fair widow than she'd emptied an entire pan of excrement over his head.

'Let me guess,' said Father Flamarion, 'she didn't like your poem.'

'It was my voice,' said Claude glumly, 'she said I sounded like alley cats fornicating.'

'So I guess your romance with *la veuve* Pommard is over,' I said.

'Far from it,' Claude answered. 'She never even got a chance to listen to my love poem. Tomorrow evening I return, but you'll come with me and recite the ode in my place. Lower your voice one octave and you'll have a fine troubadour's timbre.'

'You're serious?'

'*Absolument.*'

'What could possibly go wrong?' I wondered once more.

The next day, the city almost burst at the seams with exuberant celebrations as Charles VII made his glorious entrance. A long procession of dignitaries, nobles, knights and clergy followed His Majesty in a grand procession as he entered the gates to the Left Bank, traversed its narrow streets, then crossed the Seine to the Ile de la Cité, and made his way into the Palais du Roy. The people were wild with joy, in fact a number of the city elders remarked that the celebrations at least equalled those when Henry V of England had entered the city a generation earlier.

Parisians ate and danced and sang and drank and made merry late into the evening; there was cavorting in the streets, puking in the gutters and knee-trembling in the alleyways, as the city laid down the foundations for the mother of all hangovers the next day. Those in charge of the king's protection were both relieved and triumphant; of the hated English there had been not a sign.

I hesitantly followed Claude as he rowed upstream towards the Pont de la Cité. By now the delirious furore had died right down, bar the occasional burst of drunken singing and the sound of vomit splattering on cobblestones.

'You're absolutely sure about this?' I asked.

'Of course,' said Claude. 'This night *la belle Pommard* will melt into my arms.'

'Supposing she actually *likes* your poetry, there's still the matter of your rusty-gate voice. I can't speak your lines permanently.'

'Ha – once she hears the lyrical beauty of my verses, she'll cease caring about the slight imperfection of my speech.'

'And she'll forgive you for using a fish as a voice actor?'

'Without a doubt, you wait and see.'

'If you say so.'

'Oh, ye of little faith! Just remember your lines and leave the rest to my genius. Look! Her window's open! Quickly, Gisella, do your thing!'

While Claude held the boat steady in the flow beneath the bridge arch, and the gaping second storey window above it, I nervously cleared my throat and began my recital—

'Oh maiden fair, with whom no damsel can compare,
Your lustrous beauty draws me hence, my soul laid bare,
Your nose so straight, your breast so plump, your satin skin luminescent,
You leave me gasping, short of breath, and monstrously tumescent....'

'Jesus bloody Christ!' bellowed a very Parisian basso-contralto voice from above, 'won't these *sales cochons* ever leave me alone!'

'B-b-but...,' Claude tried to protest.

'All right, lover boy, just let me fetch you a token of my appreciation.'

While this affectionate badinage was taking place, I'd become aware of a swishing sound approaching rapidly from upstream. A large-sized barge, carrying no lights, was rowing swiftly under the bridge arch, straight towards us. From it I heard hushed voices, English voices.

'Keep the noise down, 'Arry...!'
'Old 'er steady!'
'Quit pokin' me with yer sword!'
'Then stick yer arse in, mate!'

There was no time to warn the distracted Claude. I shoulder-barged his boat and knocked him into the water, a split second before the speeding barge splintered it to matchwood. Simultaneously *la veuve* Pommard emptied a large pail of putrid slops from her window (and make no mistake, she'd been partying very hard), which landed right on top of the craft's helmsman.

This smelly mishap had the effect of temporarily blinding the fellow and causing him to lose hold of the giant, paddle-like oar that served as the barge's rudder. That, coupled with the damage caused by the collision with Claude's rowing boat to the vessel's prow, led to a catastrophic loss of control. It careened on downstream, until it smashed into the scaffolding surrounding one of the part-built new bridge's piers, causing an avalanche of wooden cladding and stonework from the upper part of the structure onto the stricken barge below. Those soldiers not obliterated by falling beams and masonry were dragged under by their chainmail.

'Whoopsie,' I muttered as I nudged the groggy Claude, who clung to an oar, towards the shore. The quicker we disappeared the better.

'What's going on?' Claude gasped, spitting out water. 'What was all that noise? Who's shouting?'

'I think there's been a bit of an accident. Nothing to do with us. Just hang on and keep shtum.'

The next morning revealed the full extent of the disaster. Not much of the bridge remained, apart from three of the piers. My normally tranquil haunt near the end of the Ile de la Cité was bustling with troops, tents, wagons, officials, river folk, scavengers, hawkers and a smattering of bleary-eyed women of the night, hopeful of a bit of extra trade. All manner of boats bobbed on the water, scuttling to and fro, as every possible item of salvage was pulled from the water. It was a wonder there were no further serious collisions and fatalities. Timber and nails, a canvas sail, oars and rowlocks, swords, crossbows and daggers, it was all fair plunder. And on the grass, in two neat rows, lay upwards of three score of very dead men-at-arms in chainmail. The word was that somehow an attack on His Majesty's person by the feared English SAS (Special Assassination Squad) had gone catastrophically wrong – praise the Lord – with the result that the fourth Seine bridge, so near to completion, was no more. The dastardly Rosbifs had bypassed the great chains across the river by covertly travelling overland to a point upstream of the city, had stolen a barge, and sailed downriver completely undetected. A fiendishly clever assassination plot that was only foiled through the will of God. According to the official version, that was.

Claude had little idea of what had gone on, and I reflected it was probably best that matters stayed that way. His heartbreak over *la veuve* Pommard plunged him into the most dismal slough of despond for the best part of three days, but shortly afterwards the silly grin on his whiskery face announced a new amour. Big Lisette, who ran a fish stall at the smaller market on the Rive Droite, had given him a small perch with his weekly pike – an unmistakable gesture of true passion.

I was none too keen on anyone who traded in dead fish, but Father Flammarion and Cornelius were for once cautiously optimistic about their friend's chances. Big Lisette was well known to them, and Cornelius remarked that this time he certainly wasn't punching above his weight. Flammarion grinned he wasn't so sure, better not let her get on top.

'That was unworthy of a churchman,' snorted Cornelius, unable to suppress a grin.

'Philistine barbarians,' snorted Claude as he stomped off. It was agreed that an indignant strop was infinitely preferable to yet another bout of lovestruck bleating.

Life settled into its familiar pattern of convivial meetings at the riverside and my continuing education. Father Flammarion was excited by every new development in the arts and sciences – and it was a time when new ideas were aired on an almost weekly basis – while Cornelius, the man of science, maintained there was nothing worth knowing that couldn't be found in the Good Book.

Flammarion was particularly thrilled by news that a kind of revolution was taking place in painting way to the south, in the Italian states of Venice and Florence and Milan, and also the Papal States. Not really knowing what a painting was, I was intrigued.

The kindly priest appeared the next day with a small wooden panel, on which there was a colourful depiction of Mary and the infant Jesus. It was beautiful! Flammarion explained that it was painted with egg tempera, egg yolk mixed with pigments, but you could also paint with pigments directly onto plaster, which was called fresco painting. I became really enthused when he added there was a completely new medium called watercolour, and asked how I could get hold of some watercolour paint.

'Whoa there,' said Father Flammarion. 'It means the paint is water soluble, not that you can paint with it underwater.'

'Oh.'

'It would all dissolve and float away.'

'Oh.'

'And if you tried to paint on paper it would go to mush.'

'Ah.'

'And you need to use paintbrushes to paint pictures. How would you hold the bushes?'

'To be honest I hadn't thought that far ahead.'

'There's a reason no one has ever heard of any fish painters.'

'Or women painters,' said Cornelius, pitching in for the first time.

'Of course women can paint,' said Flammarion. 'Plenty of women paint, they just don't make a big song and dance about it.'

'It's unnatural,' grumbled Cornelius. 'Nowhere in the Bible does it say that women can paint.'

'I don't think it says they can't either,' said Flammarion. 'Women have a perfect right to paint.' He glanced towards me. 'And so do fish, even if they, er, can't.'

As the discussion meandered onwards my attention wandered. It appeared things were happening down in the hodgepodge of states in the Italian peninsula. Not just advances in painting. A rebirth of art and learning, of the sciences and philosophy – of civilisation itself. By learning from the ancients, scholars, scientists and artists were forging an exciting way forward for the future, and I wanted a part of it.

Any form of travel was far from straightforward in those days, especially foreign travel, and most particularly if you were a fish. With my friends' help I was able to pore over maps and discuss my options for making the long journey to Italy, but no simple solution presented itself. The shorter route would be to swim up the Seine, down the Saône, enter the Mediterranean and maybe fin it up the Arno to Florence. Simple. Except that between the headwaters of the Seine and the Saône there lay at least twenty leagues of rough terrain, and finding someone to pack me in a big box of wet pondweed to make the transit was never going to be easy. The alternative was to make my way down the Seine, round Normandy and Brittany, traverse the Bay of Biscay, make my way around the Iberian Peninsula and enter the Mediterranean that way. I guessed that would be a longer trip than my trip across from the Thames to the Rhine a decade or two back. Far, far longer, my friends assured me.

The trundled past, and while my dream of travelling to Italy remained a constant companion, the means still escaped me. My three good friends lived out their brief lives (actually all three of them made it past seventy, which was pretty damn good in the fifteenth century), and I found a handful of new confidants amongst their acolytes. But their combined brainpower still failed to suggest how I was going to achieve my southern odyssey without setting off on the mother of all swims. Until, that is, His Majesty Charles VIII set his heart on a new campaign to claim the Kingdom of Naples.

Thanks to advances in artillery and musketry, the French army was now the most feared in Europe. Through the early 1490s, iron foundries around Paris and Saint Étienne worked at full pelt, producing deadly ordnance in preparation for the invasion. Some whispered that King Charles had designs on all of Italy, while others maintained he just enjoyed seeing fortified cities blasted to smithereens, and troops reduced to *andouille* by pairs of chained-together cannon balls. Regardless of which opinion one adhered to, an invasion was imminent. While the initial incursion involved the army crossing the Alps to take Milan, reinforcements of armaments and ammunition were to set sail from Marseilles to Livorno, in order to replenish the French troops on their southwards march.

This hefty consignment was to be taken by boat up the Seine, transported by wagon train over to the Saône, and shipped downriver down to the Med and thence to the fleet at Marseilles. My friends clubbed together for my transport – a large chest stuffed with sodden pondweed – and bribed a foot soldier to keep me topped up with water for the duration. Charles could invade Naples all he wanted; I was on my way to Florence. As that worn old saying goes, what could possibly go wrong?

The trip up the Seine? A doddle. Then apparently we branched off into the Yonne for as far as it was navigable. *Pas de problème*. Overland via a train of wagons to the upper reaches of the navigable Saône. Bumpy but supportable. It was then that things started to go a little bit awry. The friendly soldier who'd been tending my needs during the trip should've released me straight into the Saône, but instead my box was hoisted through the air and onto something that I had a horrible suspicion was another boat. This wasn't in the script; where was my friendly soldier?

When the boatmen cast off, the barge I'd been shoved onto – obviously seriously overloaded with lethal ordnance – sailed downstream for a few metres, and then simply stuck fast on the bottom. I listened with mounting panic as the crew discussed the situation. The barge was too far from the shore to be unloaded again, so the only options appeared to be to dump the cargo into the drink, which could well involve the crew losing a head or two, or wait it out until the river level rose again, which could also involve a loss of heads. The men had a dilemma, and I had a very serious problem.

It was only late spring, but the weather was unseasonably hot. Without its topping-up of fresh water, the weed in my chest had lost any oxygen it might have been carrying, and I began both to asphyxiate and bake in equal measure. What had happened to my tame foot soldier? The selfish bastard had only gone and died of dysentery, leaving me in the lurch.

Calling out was to no avail, my throat was too dry and I could only emit a pathetic croak. I was convinced that this was curtains for poor old Gisella, baked in a box on a run-aground barge. It was then that salvation came in the unlikeliest form: the first and only time I've ever been indebted to a cat.

Horace, the barge cat, had become increasingly obsessed with the smell coming from my chest, which wasn't surprising considering I was ripening horribly. A couple of boatmen eventually agreed that there was something decidedly off about my chest, and crowbarred off its lid. Taut as a clock spring Horace pounced, but I was too quick. Even in my dilapidated state I used the last of my strength to flip out of my prison, bounce off the barge's deck, and plunge into the life-giving, cooling water of the Saône. It was elixir, bliss. Horace's plaintive miaowing faded into the distance as I glided downstream.

Unseasonably warm weather, blue skies, a gentle meander through valleys of beautiful rolling countryside, I greatly enjoyed my sedate cruise down the Saône. My ever-sensitive lateral line warned me of great atmospheric turbulence to the east, and from time to time I picked up the rumble of distant thunder. Remembering the maps I'd studied, I surmised there were violent storms breaking out over the Alps, but they weren't going to affect me, were they?

When I reached the confluence of the rivers Saône and Doubs my complacency was shattered. The Doubs was in a rotten mood. Rising up in the Alps, it was carrying a large volume of floodwater from all the storms, plus all sorts of debris and drowned livestock. This was not pleasant, but on I ploughed.

I'd meant to stop and have a look at the famous city of Lyon, but under the strained circumstances I just went with the flow and sped right past it. Then an ominous rumbling threw my poor old lateral line right out; I was rapidly approaching the confluence of the Saône and the Rhône. If the Doubs had been grumpy, the Rhône was bloody furious. The water was a seething brown froth of sludge, uprooted trees, a few dead cows and even, unmistakably, an almost complete cowshed that had been carried away. Not that I had much time for taking in the sights. I was buffeted from all sides by all manner of flotsam and jetsam, and the sheer force of the turbulent current put me through hell. A fish's first instinct in a flood is to try and find slack water. Ha – fat chance! I was carried helplessly downstream for league after league, through an appallingly beastly night and into another grim and punishing day.

At length the mighty Rhône (the Saône was the Rhône now) lost the worst of its violence. The water was still high and very coloured, and still carried all manner of flood-borne detritus, but at least I could actually control where I was swimming. Visibility was still down to less than a metre, so I decided to peek above the surface to see if I could get my bearings. Ahead of me was a sizeable town, more like a city really, with a magnificent palace and a fine, imposing stone bridge. I reckoned it could only be Avignon. There would surely be a port in the town where I could rest up for a day or two and recover from my buffeting.

As I cruised towards the bridge I noticed I was swimming beside the grandaddy of all oak trees, yet another victim of the violent spring flood. I distanced myself from the tree and swam gracefully beneath one of the bridge's many arches. The tree didn't. It smashed right into one of its sturdy supporting columns, demonstrating that it wasn't so sturdy after all, and brought three spans of the structure crashing down into the river. I only narrowly avoided being mashed into *soupe de poisson.* Not again, I groaned. I hoped no one was going to blame me for this latest disaster.[5]

Of course, no one noticed a large carp in the murky water, and I was able to steer myself into the city's port, where several boats of varying sorts and sizes were moored alongside a long wooden wharf. Naturally there was a buzz of excitement and consternation among the river folk, from which I deduced that (a), nobody was blaming me for the bridge's collapse, and (b), the bridge had a habit of collapsing every decade or two, because Avignon's builders weren't very good. At least no one appeared to have been on the bridge at that point. Satisfied that all was well – apart from the city lacking a bridge once more – I sank to the riverbed and slipped into delightful oblivion for the next couple of days.

Notes

[1]*Daube de venaison.* Venison stew.
[2]*Pain perdu.* Bread and butter pudding.
[3]*Palais du roi.* King's Palace.
[4]*La Manche.* The English Channel.

[5]The bridge at Avignon had a proud history of falling down. The venerable folk song, 'Sur le pont d'Avignon', actually recounts people dancing on it. They did so at their peril.

Chapter Seven

The Holy City. How Gisella makes friends with the greatest savant of the Age, becomes pally with the Borgias at the Vatican, and brings the first manned flight to a premature end

A very refreshed carp continued her journey down the Rhône, which by then was a more placid, happier place to be, passing the sun-bleached city of Arles and entering the brackish waters of the Bouches-du-Rhône. There I spent another day acclimatising to the salty water before leaving the Camargue[1] and entering the Mediterranean. My study of maps and my sophisticated sense of direction told me which way to go: I had to turn left.

Some of my fellow fish I recognised, such as grey mullet and bass, while others, red mullet, bonito and the spiky *rascasse* were new to me. In its charmingly inarticulate way, a grey mullet warned me to steer clear of the colourful rascasses – they may be small but their spines are poisonous. If one got too close, apparently saying the word *bouillabaisse*[2] would send it scuttling for cover. 'What does it mean?' I asked.

'You don't want to know,' said the mullet.

I swam steadily eastwards, knowing that sooner or later I would leave French waters and enter Italian. Naturally I hadn't been able to bring a map with me, so I relied on eavesdropping fishermen to get my bearings. Sure enough, after about ten days the fisherfolk were speaking a different language as they cast their nets. I listened hard, and soon started to pick it up. *Parliamo italiano.* Simple.

Gradually I found myself following the coast in a south-easterly direction, and then generally southerly. I remembered my maps. This was the Italian peninsula. All I had to do was keep swimming and keep a sharp lateral line for any mention of the River Arno.

My seaborne diet was mostly shellfish and shrimps – not too shabby at all – in fact pretty delicious. (We carp are suckers for *fruits de mer*. The array of carp baits based on prawn, squid, fishmeal and tuna is mind boggling, and we carp just love 'em.) Being in a new environment, I was also mindful not to become part of some other creature's diet. Deep in rocky crevasses there were sinister moray eels, which looked easily big enough to take several chunks out of me, while further out at sea large shadowy forms glided by – sharks of some kind I was sure. Very few freshwater fish could trouble me, but this was a different ball game. I did my best to remain on full alert.

About a month into my trip I entered a river estuary, which the pilot escorting a small cargo vessel had helpfully mentioned was the Arno. Next stop Florence and the Renaissance, I joyously told myself, but of course I had to spend another boring twenty-four hours reacclimatising myself to fresh water.

I was wrong about Florence, for after only a day's swim I found myself passing a fortified town with a very distinctive landmark: a decidedly wonky tower. I'd forgotten about Pisa. While I was deliberating whether to hang around or stay, I became aware of a clanking sound approaching. It was some kind of boat, constructed a bit like a barrel, driven by what I soon learned was a propeller, with a funnel sticking out of its top. The astonishing thing about it was that it was sailing underwater, with only the very top of its funnel breaking the surface. So astonished was I that I failed to get out of its way and hovered there like a comatose haddock as it rammed into me.

'Qu'est que tu foutes, putain!' I bellowed. Which can loosely be translated as please be careful.

'*Pardonnez-moi,*' answered the chap in the barrel in French, but with a heavy Italian accent. 'I really should try to invent some sort of window for this thing.'

The odd craft surfaced, its barrel lid – or hatch if one wants to get technical – popped open, and a bearded gentleman of middling years popped his head out. He appeared completely unfazed by exchanging words with a large carp.

'*Ciao*,' he smiled. 'Are we speaking French, or do you have any Italian?'

'It would only be polite to attempt Italian I suppose. *Buongiorno, mi chiamo Gisella…*'

'Splendid, though maybe you need work on your accent; you sound a bit like a Parisian tavern wench after a heavy night. And your lopsided manner of swimming might persuade the more cynical among us that you've had one over the eight. But no matter, I am known as Leonardo da Vinci – painter, inventor, sculptor, botanist, architect, cartographer, physicist….'

'*Ben alors*, I came looking for the Renaissance and I found it in one person!'

'Not entirely, but I am a little bit of a polymath I suppose. Where is it you're heading, looking for the Renaissance?'

'I'd thought Florence was as good a place as any. Lots of good stuff going on there I heard.'

'It's true, it has a fine reputation as a hive of arts and science, but I wouldn't go there right now if I were you; the French army is occupying the city, and the hungry troops might just prove partial to some *cannelloni alla carpa*.'

'Oh. And would their presence there have anything to do with you sailing down the Arno in a sunken barrel?'

'You're an astute fish,' said Leonardo. 'I'd been hanging out in Milan, but when I got wind of King Charles and his men approaching I scarpered to Florence, where the good old Medici kindly stumped up the moolah for me to put my submersible boat together. But no sooner had I hammered in the final nail than word had it the Frenchies were on the march to Florence, so *io vado*, and here I am.'

'Is there anything you've done to upset the French?'

'It's more what I don't want to do that's the point. People always want me to invent weapons, which I'm actually quite good at. But King Charles already has weapons of mass destruction, capable of decimating armies and pulverising city walls. Do I really want to enable him even more?'

'I can see your point. Will you be safe here?'

'Who knows, maybe the French will come here too? Push comes to shove, I'll head back up the river and lie low in Empoli.'

'That thing can go upstream? I'm truly impressed.'

'A simple system of pedals, chains and cogs that drive a propeller, and it's steered by a rudder. There are still a few bugs to iron out, such as seeing where I'm going when I'm underwater, but so far so good. I'd love to build something as streamlined as a fish, though.'

'Well, I could name a few fish that look like a barrel, but I get what you mean. Are there any other ground-breaking projects you're working on?'

'Scores of them. An improved irrigation pump, a writing machine, a self-playing pipe organ, a flying machine.'

If I had eyelids I would've blinked. A flying machine sounded truly screwy, bonkers. But then again Leonardo had already conjured up a type of boat that could travel underwater – albeit a fairly crude one with no means of seeing where one was going – so who was I to judge? That was the sort of thing I'd travelled to Italy to experience, but now I was there it appeared I was at risk from thousands of hungry French soldiers, who probably fancied a fish supper. Surely there had to be some safe haven in such a big place.

'Is there anywhere the French aren't going to march into?' I asked.

'You could always try Rome,' said Leonardo. 'Naturally the Holy City is under the control of Pope Alexander, and he's made a treaty with King Charles to allow the French free passage en route to Naples, in exchange for not blasting the city to kingdom come – plus raping and murdering all the inhabitants of course.'

'Sounds like a canny fellow. And you haven't thought of decamping to Rome yourself?'

'I'd rather wait and make sure of my welcome. You never know which way things can turn with the Church. One of the reasons I'm well out of Florence is that there's a crazy friar there called Savonarola[3] who thinks everything I do is blasphemous, and he's very fond of setting people on fire. I doubt very much he'd take kindly to a vocal carp either. But Pope Alexander is a little more moderate, so maybe I'm being a tad over-cautious. I reckon you should be all right in Rome. Just keep your head down on Fridays.'

'Rome it is then.'

'Back down the river, keep south along the coast to a port called Ostia, turn left and you can't miss it. I hope our paths cross again, unique talking carp.'

'*Ciao, maestro*, hopefully see you in Rome some day.'

Barring the tedium of acclimatising myself back to salt water, and ten days later reversing the process again, the trip was pleasant enough. As ever the chatter of sailors and fishermen helped me find my way, and after only another day's swim up the Tiber I arrived in Rome very late on a moonlit night. All seemed quiet, but that was an illusion.

As I neared another of Rome's many bridges, I heard an urgent hiss of whispering, plus a man's anguished gasp. Three hooded figures, certainly females to judge by their stature and voices, were viciously assaulting a youngish man, and attempting to pitch him over the bridge's parapet. The fellow, foppishly dressed but quite muscular, was attempting to struggle, but he was quite obviously as drunk as a skunk, which made his attackers' work much easier.

What is it about fish and bridges, particularly me? Yes, they give us shelter, they're good ambush points if gobbling up smaller fish is your thing, they can keep the sun's glare out of your eyes, but they can also spell danger. I'd already sailed close to the wind with two bridge collapses, and a couple of centuries earlier Rodney de Yaxley had almost dropped onto my head from one. The young man struggling on the bridge above me went one better. He dropped like a stone, and, because I was gawping so intently, I failed to clear out of his way in time.

It was already dawn when I started to regain consciousness. Things appeared to be happening very quickly. I was floating on my side by some steps that led from an embankment down to the river. The victim of last night's assault was being hoicked out of the water by several hooded men, some kind of guards judging by their demeanour, whose capitano affirmed that the deceased – for the young man was very dead – was none other than Giovanni Borgia. A cursory sniff told of a night of drunken debauchery, but the pulped state of the back of his head also told of violent assault, though whether a casual street robbery or assassination it was too early to tell. Whoever perpetrated this outrage would be mercilessly hunted down, and His Holiness would have to be informed.

Groggy as I was, I clocked that I'd be wise to vamoose before I became embroiled in what was evidently some major intrigue – and no doubt very unhealthy for a fish. Oh, slow-witted carp. Before I could move a fin strong arms plucked me from the water and threw me roughly up the steps. Before I knew it I'd been manhandled up onto the embankment, where a couple of the hooded men eyed me greedily, and muttered something about *pesce brasato.*

'*Un momento, capitano!*' I exclaimed. All the men turned and gawped at me. 'You can't braise me, I saw everything. I'm an eye witness.'

'*Madre di Dio*,' gasped the captain. 'Are you some kind of demon?'

'No, I'm a carp. And if you refrain from knocking me on the head I'll tell you what happened to this unfortunate young man.'

The captain was clearly out of his depth and continued to look dumbstruck, but fortunately one of his subordinates had half a brain and suggested that they'd lose nothing by listening to what I had to say.

'Very well,' said the captain, gathering what few wits he had. 'But we'll take it to the Lady Vanozza, she'll know what to do. And don't forget, His Holiness must be informed as well. Fratelli, Maldini, off to the Vatican, now!'

As the captain and the remaining guards hurried me along a series of narrow backstreets, past the averted eyes of the emerging street traders and retiring ladies of the night, I found it increasingly difficult to breathe.

'Is it far to where we're going?' I gasped. 'I need water.'

'Not so far,' said the guard with half a brain. 'In fact,' we turned yet another corner, made our way through the narrow entrance of a nondescript stone building, and entered a large courtyard, 'we're here.'

The building's unassuming street aspect hid a sumptuous urban palace with a beautifully set-out courtyard. Exotic flowers and shrubs occupied much of the space, along with various pieces of classical statuary, while in its centre was a generously proportioned circular pool, whose central fountain took the form of a stone Neptune, alongside mermaids and a fanciful dolphin spewing water. Not that aesthetic appreciation was my foremost concern.

'Water,' I gasped. To my immense relief I was flung into the pool.

It took a good ten minutes for me to start feeling myself again, during which time I was aware of screaming and loud voices inside the palace. At length, a striking, richly dressed lady of middle age, her dark grey hair interwoven with strings of pearls, stormed out of one of the doors and strode towards me. Her face was streaked with tears, but even in her grief you saw a person who wasn't to be taken lightly. 'My son's killer will be found,' she told the captain, who scurried along behind her. She had a voice that dripped honey, but I was also aware of an indomitable disposition. 'And whatever agony Giovanni suffered when his life was snuffed out will be meted out one hundredfold to his assassin.' Then she stopped and looked me in the eye.

'So, this is the miraculous talking fish. I am the Lady Vanozza Cattanei, consort to His Holiness Pope Alexander and mother of his children. And you are?'

'Gisella. Carp. Pleased to meet you.'

'Ah, do I detect a hint of French? Tavern French, if I may be so bold? Please don't get me wrong, I saw a fair bit of the insides of taverns in my past life, but we don't speak about that anymore.'

Why do people always associate me with taverns, bawdy houses, nightclubs? So my voice has a few rough edges, so shoot me already. Anyway, I digress.

Vanozza turned to the guards, thanked them for doing their duty, and told them they were dismissed.

'Are you sure, my lady?' said the captain. 'This fish could be dangerous, you can't be too careful.'

'Seriously, capitano? What's she going to do, blow water in my face and drown me? No, I can assure you it's quite safe to leave us.'

'*Signora.*' The captain clicked his heels – a tad resentfully I thought – turned, and led his men out of the courtyard.

The Lady Vanozza turned back to me. 'So, you saw everything?'

'Yes. Or rather I witnessed the final denouement.'

Vanozza nodded encouragement.

'Last night, as I was swimming up the Tiber, I approached one of the city's bridges. On it three cloaked figures were attacking your son, who was clearly far too *bourré*, rat-arsed in other words, to defend himself. His arms were raised, but his attempts to ward off the blows were completely ineffective, and, as he collapsed, they managed to haul him up and push him over the bridge's parapet.'

'Anything else?'

'Yes. Judging by their stature and voices, his assailants were women. I'm pretty certain of it. Beyond that I haven't got a clue. Giovanni must've landed right on top of me, because the next thing I knew it was getting light and the guards were fishing him and me out of the drink.'

'Interesting,' Vanozza pondered. 'My first suspicion, naturally, was Cesare, but for all his faults he'd never get women to do his dirty work.'

'Cesare?'

'His older brother. Pardon. You evidently know nothing of the Borgia dynasty, but why would you? You're a fish.'

'Pardon my ignorance. I've figured out how kings and queens work, but this pope business is new to me.'

'Very well, potted history, I'll keep it nice and simple.'

'You don't have to, I'm not a mullet.' I thought that, I didn't say it.

'When my *special friend*, Rodrigo Borgia, assumed the papacy a few years back, he became Pope Alexander VI and I was promptly stuck away out of sight. He's a great dad though, and has always done his best to look out for our four children. That's why Cesare, the oldest, was appointed a cardinal, earmarked for a future papacy, and Giovanni, the second oldest, made *comandante* of the papal army.'

'Got you so far.'

'And that's the problem. Cesare hates being a priest and loves fighting, while Giovanni never sticks – stuck – at anything for long, except drinking, gambling and whoring. Cesare should've been a soldier, while Giovanni, well, he was a piss-poor general, but it doesn't make much difference now. However, Rodrigo would never see it. Giovanni is – was – the apple of his eye, the golden boy who could do no wrong, however much he screwed up, and he'll be completely distraught.'

'And you suspected that Cesare might've wanted to create a job vacancy in the papal army?'

'You're clearly smarter than the average carp. I have to admit the thought crossed my mind. Cesare has a furious temper, and I could see him doing for Giovanni in the heat of the moment, but getting a bunch of women to do his dirty work for him? No. He's far too macho for that. He's completely feckless and utterly fearless, but one thing he isn't is a coward.'

'So?'

'So I make my way to the Vatican and share my grief with the father of my children. It's at times like these that he forgets we're no longer supposed to be an item. And I'd better get to him before he does anything rash about Cesare. He's normally a very placid man – but you never know with those quiet ones.'

Left on my own, I explored my new home. The *palazzo* and courtyard were indeed splendid, built fairly recently around the remains of an ancient Roman villa. I was intrigued by a very faint gurgling sound from beneath me, which I subsequently learned was part of the original Roman drainage system that ran under that part of the city. One of the basement passages gave access to a smelly old drain, which was filled with only water after rainfall, and otherwise just contained a sticky morass of mud and ordure. Vanozza's minions found it very convenient for disposing of all kinds of detritus, which only added to its ripeness.

My pool was about a metre deep and a good ten metres across. The fountain kept the water aerated – not that we carp need our habitat to be mountain-fresh like oxygen-hungry trout and grayling – and the abundant water lilies kept the pool sweet and fragrant. Even if people neglected to feed me I'd do okay with all the bugs and water snails, but I rather hoped a few Roman delicacies would come my way too. I'd be fine in there, but if my stay was to be for any length of time it would start to feel like a prison. I was alone in the pool, with only a few frogs and newts for company – and they're no company at all. Food, yes, companionship, no. Then I reflected that

I'd just had yet another narrow escape, and a bit of stir craziness was certainly preferable to ending up braised.

It was a couple of days before I saw another human being, a girl in her late teens, dressed in the manner of a noblewoman, with long blonde ringlets and the kind of smile that turns young men's legs to minestrone. She headed straight for my pool and dropped to her knees.

'Mama told me about a talking carp, please don't let it be bollocks.'

'It's not bollocks at all, *signorina*, please excuse the accent.'

'It's *signora* unfortunately, but that's something we don't speak about.'

'*Signora* then. Does your mama talk bollocks? She struck me as a very serious lady, but then we didn't meet under normal circumstances.'

'I wouldn't ever call meeting a talking carp normal, but I get your point. All of Rome is weeping for poor Giovanni. Except perhaps the legions of gamblers, husbands, whores and innkeepers he owes money to, or has cheated, or insulted, or cuckolded. But enough of that. I couldn't stand papa's constant wailing for another instant, I had to get out of the papal palace before my head exploded.'

'I take it you're—'

'Lucrezia. Papal offspring number three, and by far the prettiest. Don't get me wrong, I loved my deceased brother but let's face it – he was a dickhead. I won't say he had it coming to him, but absolutely no one can be surprised. And while papa's usually a lamb he's really got it in for Cesare, although he knows Cesare had nothing to do with the killing. It's more that he knows the dice have fallen rather nicely for Cesare, and he can't forgive him for that. Mama's in there keeping the peace, waiting for the storm to blow itself out so to speak, and sooner or later he'll go back to his beloved grapevines, and she can get back to running the Catholic Church.'

'Come again?'

'Mama's the real power behind the Vatican, everybody knows that. They call her *Signora Papa*, but she's the one who really wears the white cassock. Papa's into viticulture in a big way, and he'd far rather spend his time tending his grapes than his flock; he puts in a shift at the Vatican from time to time to keep up appearances, but otherwise lets mama do all the thinking.'

'This is a lot to take in. Your mum running the show, the pope being an amateur winemaker.'

'He's a highly accomplished one, actually.'

'Not to mention having the Lady Vanozza as a mistress and fathering several children. I thought the priesthood was supposed to be celibate.'

'Celibate my arse, they're all at it. Even the *saintly cardinal*, Giuliano della Rovere, who has accused papa of sedition, simony, incest and a whole bunch of other venal sins, has whelped the odd bastard here and there. Papa's not perfect, in fact he's had a succession of mistresses, but thanks to mama his is a pretty good papacy.'

'And the Lady Vanozza's all right about the other ladies?'

'She's long since tired of papa's grunting and groaning, as she puts it. If she gets an itch there's always a willing stableboy to scratch it. The latest papal mistress is the fragrant Giulia Farnese, and mama is more than grateful to her for keeping his hands to herself.'

'Formidable lady, your mother. So she's the one who keeps the Vatican ticking over. But – here's the thing: I've just about got the idea of how kings operate, telling everyone what to do and all that, but what is it that popes do? I know the Pope is the church's head honcho, but what does the job actually entail?'

'A pope is God's senior representative on Earth. Even higher up the ladder than kings.'

'So he's a king of kings?'

'One down from that, actually. He administers faith, hope and charity. He gives everyone spiritual guidance, from kings and cardinals to peasants and beggars, he bestows blessings and leads prayers, oversees education, ensures good people have a roof over their heads and food in their bellies.'

'Gosh, that's wonderful! Food and shelter for the poor and downtrodden! It's revolutionary almost!'

'Food and shelter for the poor? That *would* be revolutionary – what an absurd notion! No no no, we make sure the *nice* people of elevated birth don't have to go without. The poor and downtrodden? They're used to that sort of thing, aren't they?'

I thought back to Father Flammarion's scripture lessons and was confused. 'Didn't Jesus champion the poor and the downtrodden? What was all that about rich men passing through the eye of a needle, and him washing his disciples' feet?'

'Yuk,' Lucrezia grimaced. 'You wouldn't catch me doing that. You've got to understand, the Church often talks in metaphors. No one's washing anyone else's feet, and rich men don't have to pass through the eye of a needle to get to heaven – they simply have to come up with a suitable donation to the Mother Church.'

So the papacy dishes out faith, but it certainly comes up short on hope and charity. Again, I thought that rather than said it. Not so different from kings then, except popes ruled in ecclesiastical matters while kings ruled in matters of power. But that was shortly to change.

A commotion of voices interrupted our conversation, and Lucrezia hushed me and told me to take cover under the lily pads. Cesare was coming. She loved her brother dearly, but he was unpredictable at the best of times and she didn't know how he'd react to a talking carp.

Cesare just looked wrong in a cardinal's robes, like a rugby player turning up at a soirée in a cocktail dress. Long hair tightly knotted behind his head, a substantial beard that couldn't hide his forceful chin, machismo that almost crackled, in other words rugged good looks that suited an action hero far rather than a candidate for the papacy. And his attendants, while dressed in priests' robes, were certainly militiamen rather than ecclesiastical.

'Come, sister,' he said. 'We've nabbed Giovanni's killers. You don't want to miss the burning, do you?'

'Who was it?'

'Three common strumpets. Their sister whores soon gave them up when we started brandishing a hot poker or two. It seems they wanted revenge on him for dosing them with something nasty – stealing their livelihoods.'

'I'm not sure I blame them,' said Lucrezia quietly.

'Tish, sister. You don't go around killing Borgias and not pay the price, even if our brother was a licentious, mendacious inebriate. We Borgias have to be untouchable, no matter what. We all have to put in an appearance. Mama's already there.'

By burning of course Cesare meant the three unfortunate young women were about to be burned at the stake, just like poor old Jeanne d'Arc. The world of nature is pretty brutal, dog eat dog, eat or be eaten, lots of ripping, rending and grinding, a hotbed of pain and premature death, both sudden and lingering, but the human race's sheer inventiveness in curtailing other humans' lives is unrivalled anywhere in the world of nature, especially when it comes to executions. Stoning, hanging, being chucked into pits of snakes, flaying, beheading, garrotting, poisoning, sawing in half, crucifixion, boiling alive, etc., etc., and of course burning at the stake. It appeared that burning at the stake was a favourite of the all-merciful Church.

Life in the pool at the Lady Vanozza's palace turned out to be quite pleasant. I missed the freedom of roaming in rivers, but on the plus side I was safe, I had an excellent diet of natural food plus whatever various people saved me from their dinners, and a ceaseless supply of gossip from Vanozza and Lucrezia. They gave me the lowdown on the latest scandals in the curia,[4] and came to rely on me for weather forecasts because I was 99.9 per cent accurate.

There was a constant flow of people to the palace, those from whom my existence was better kept hidden, and those who could be trusted to meet a linguistically gifted carp without having a meltdown. Niccolò Machiavelli was a frequent visitor, one of the few people the worldly wise Vanozza trusted for advice.

One day when the courtyard was otherwise empty, he confided in me that increasingly Cesare was leaning on him for guidance, which he found rather disturbing.

'They all come to me like I'm some sort of super agony uncle,' he said. 'Everyone's got the idea I'm wonderfully clever and really good at scheming. Wise as a parliament of owls and cunning as skulk of foxes. I reckon it's because my eyes are so close together.'

It was true. Niccolò was a beanpole of a man, whose clothing always looked too short and baggy for his frame. And his eyes were set very close together, giving him a somewhat sly, squinty look.

'I do have a genuine talent though,' he continued. 'I'm really good at telling people what they want to hear, in a way that sounds fiendishly cunning and insightful. It's all hot air though, and I'm scared that sooner or later people are going to see right through me.'

'And Cesare?' I prompted.

'He's volatile, and I suspect he's capable of great violence. Once he gets some real power God knows what might happen. He gives me the willies, and the last thing I dare do is to tell him any home truths.'

I thought of what Lucrezia had told me about Cesare's unpredictability, and reckoned that maybe Niccolò's fears were well founded.

'Maybe you can keep him from going too over the top, be a calming influence.'

'Easier said than done,' said Niccolò glumly.

As per the agreement brokered with Charles VIII, the French army and all its deadly ordnance bypassed Rome en route to its seizing of the kingdom of Naples, and the Holy City breathed a collective sigh of relief.

But change was in the air. Cesare now had his way and was appointed Gonfaloniero, or in other words chief of the papal armies, which he proceeded to enlarge and re-equip. His first acts with his new, improved fighting force were to occupy and annexe the Romagna and Marche. It was apparent to all that he didn't intend to stop there, and of course Niccolò Machiavelli could see that there would be consequences.

One afternoon I was in conversation with Lucrezia about herbs and balms – as it happened she was very keen on natural remedies and alternative therapies – when Vanozza hurried into the courtyard to tell us that Rodrigo was on his way. Papal visits to the *palazzo* were very rare by then, and always a sign that something was definitely not right.

'That lad's going to be the death of us all,' the pontiff panted as he shuffled up to us by the pool. He was short and rather round, his once jet-black hair now salt and pepper, his cheeks pink and his chins a little bit wobbly. He gave every appearance of being accustomed to a lot of sitting and eating and drinking. Wearing white definitely didn't suit him. 'Charles has got a bee in his bonnet about the papal army mobilising, and frankly I don't blame him. We promised not to engage in any military shenanigans, and look what Cesare has gone and done. Word has it the French army is marching north again – and this time I think they're going to pay us a little visit.'

'I thought they'd all caught something horrid,' said Lucrezia.

'Most of them have,' said Vanozza. 'But the fact that they've got nasty sores and dripping thingies just seems to make them even crosser.'

'Plus they've got their wretched cannons, which Cesare's men can't possibly match,' said Rodrigo.

(It's possible that this is when people started calling syphilis the 'French disease', or perhaps that was just a generic bit of Frog-bashing. Many believed the disease was imported via the recent voyages to the New World, but personally I think Native Americans have had enough to put up with without being accused of giving the rest of the world a dose on merely circumstantial evidence.)

'Calm down, sweets,' said Vanozza. 'There's got to be a way out of this.'

'That's why I've come to you, Nozza, you always know what to do.'

'Pass. Time was when I could put Cesare on my knee and give him a stern talking to, but I think that ship has sailed. Have you asked Niccolò's advice?'

'The famous Machiavelli is supposedly Cesare's official advisor now, but anyway, no one can find him; he might've done a bunk to Florence.'

'You've been strangely silent all this while,' Lucrezia said to me. 'Any thoughts?'

'Ah,' said Rodrigo. 'The miraculous carp I've heard whispers about.'

'At your service, Your Eminence.'

'Of course some may say that a talking fish is the Devil's work, but I say we're all God's creations, and you most certainly are one of them.'

'Amen to that.'

'And our little problem?' said Lucrezia. 'That thanks to my idiot brother we're all going to die?'

'You could all run away. Or in my case swim.'

'And leave the Holy See at the mercy of the French?' Rodrigo's chins trembled as he shook his head. 'I'd prefer a solution that doesn't leave Rome a smoking ruin.'

'Come on, Gisella,' said Vanozza. 'You're not usually short of an idea or two.'

These good people were really scraping the barrel asking a fish for advice, but in desperation I suppose people grasp at straws. I did my best to examine the problem logically. How does one stop a battle-hardened army bristling with cannons? You distract them. What are soldiers' favourite distractions? Fornication and getting bladdered. Well, they'd evidently done a fair bit of fornication, and much good it had done them. But surely that would only make them even thirstier for another bout of liquid distraction.

'Lucrezia,' I said. 'You're a whizz with herbs and potions, right?' She nodded cautiously. 'And Rome's cellars are reasonably well stocked with wine?' Rodrigo agreed they were. I turned back to Lucrezia. 'Is there anything you could knock up that would knock a soldier off his feet, yet be undetectable in a goblet of *vino rosso*?'

'Jesus Christ, one or two herbal infusions go slightly wrong and suddenly I'm a *femme fatale* poisoner! So a light-fingered chambermaid and a randy ostler who couldn't keep it in his codpiece died in unspeakable agony after one of my tisanes, so shoot me already. I'm sick of all the whispers and innuendoes. I'm a herbalist, in touch with Mother Nature – that's all!'

'Of course, quite understood. Natural remedies only. But do you know of any harmless 100 per cent organic tincture that would zap a full-grown man for a few hours?'

'Hmm, a low dose of any of the proprietary poisons would do the job, however, getting hold of the quantity we'd need is a pretty tall order, particularly given our timeframe. But perhaps there's something else we could use. We need to assemble a group of peasants who know the woodlands inside out, we've a mass of foraging to do, then *I'll* do the rest!'

'Capital,' grinned Vannoza. 'We'll have to get Cesare on board with this, but we must be careful to make him think it's all his idea.'

'That should be the easiest of our tasks,' said Lucrezia.

Ten days later, an advance guard of the approaching French army happened upon a dozen oxcarts hauling tuns of wine. At the sight of several very grumpy French soldiers, who appeared to be marching with a quite noticeable degree of soreness, the waggoners fled, leaving behind their cargo.

That evening the army set up camp a little more than a league from the Holy City. Within a short period of time all the soldiers, from highest to lowest, were rip-roaring drunk, and a little later their inebriation changed into another, far less familiar form of intoxication. Which is when Cesare Borgia led a modest force of his best men right into the heart of the camp. No one lifted a finger to stop them.

'*Oo la la, les belles couleurs*,' exclaimed a French soldier.

'Everything's gone all swirly!' gasped another.

'Newts and toads, newts and toads everywhere!'

'I never realised mud was so beautiful, it makes me want to weep!'

'I love everything, look, I'm making love to these brambles!'

The French were all at Woodstock and beyond. Lucrezia's distillation of nondescript little woodland mushrooms had done its work well.

Maréchal Leforge, who was barely in control of his limbs, lurched into the royal tent and reported to King Charles that a band of pixies appeared to be stealing all their cannons. His Highness, who was dancing with an enchanting group of nymphs and fauns, answered he couldn't care a fuck.

The next day some very sore-headed French scouts reported to green-looking King Charles that Rome was suddenly guarded by the most fearsome array of ordnance, backed up by the papal army. It had been reported a few days earlier that Cesare's men were on the verge of mutiny or mass desertion, but now they appeared to be in great spirits, and were belting out a medley of very unecclesiastical insults. '*Putain de merde*,' Charles spat. 'That's our ordnance they've got, you imbeciles. *On nous a enculé*.[5] There's nothing for it: we march north. This whole venture's been a bloody disaster, and I'm going to catch hell when I get home.'

'I think we caught it already,' sighed one of the scouts.

Disaster averted, our daily lives returned to normal. The French army fought a couple of engagements as it headed for home, but essentially Charles VIII's Italian adventure was over. Our lives may have settled back into a pleasant groove, but we were all too aware that Cesare, cock-a-hoop after his triumph over the invaders (according to him it was his triumph, anyway), was preparing his army for further conquests. He now had his eye on the northern states.

'Rodrigo I could always handle,' Vanozza complained to me. 'But Cesare is cut from different cloth altogether.'

'You mean…?'

'No, you impertinent carp, Rodrigo is Cesare's papa, one hundred per cent, but they couldn't be less alike. Rodrigo always does what I tell him, but Cesare is a complete loose cannon.'

'And now he's now got scores of them too,' I chipped in unnecessarily.

'Like an idiot with hundreds of loaded guns,' said Lucrezia.

'Enough already,' said Vanozza. 'He evidently fancies himself as some kind of latter-day Roman emperor, bent on a programme of military expansion and conquest throughout the northern states, and there's apparently nothing we can do to rein him in.'

Over the next two years Cesare made only the occasional fleeting visit to Rome – to deliver progress reports to his father on how his campaigns were faring, and tap up the curia for yet more funds to keep his men paid, fed and supplied. The ailing Rodrigo despaired of his bellicose son, pleading that the Catholic Church should be an empire of faith rather than military might and territorial acquisition, but his entreaties fell on deaf ears. All Europe would bow to Rome, and then.... But first things first. There was the rest of the peninsula to conquer.

Initially the seized French artillery gave the papal army an enormous advantage over the forces of the northern states, but, as in all arms races, the opposing factions soon procured deadly ordnance of their own and a bloody stalemate ensued. Cesare had his hands full either openly fighting or intriguing against his foes, or making and breaking alliances as the fortunes of war swung to and fro like a weathervane. A knife in the back was frequently as effective as decapitation by cannonball, but progress had virtually ground to a halt. What Cesare needed, what he craved, was a brand-new killing technology, one that couldn't be replicated by his enemies – the work of a genius, someone centuries ahead of their time.

One day the palace was abuzz with activity as the staff prepared for a special guest. I tried to ask who the VIP was, but unusually no one appeared to have any time to stop and natter with me. Then there was a creaking as the courtyard gates opened, and a cloaked, hooded stranger was ushered in – whereupon the gate was speedily slammed closed once more. Vanozza and Lucrezia bade the stranger welcome, and hurriedly sent for goblets of the new wonder drink of the age, introduced only that year from the New World, steaming hot chocolate, accompanied by almond *biscotti.*

The stranger swept back his hood and took a seat on the perimeter of the pool. From the back I could make out he was grey-haired, and certainly not in the first flush of youth. 'A very palatable beverage, my ladies. A fine antidote to several days of violent shaking in a prison wagon.'

'But we were assured you were Cesare's honoured guest,' said Vanozza, shocked.

'His invitation was somewhat compelling,' said the stranger. 'Somehow I didn't find a way of turning it down.'

Others might've guessed the stranger's identity by then; I didn't until he said his *biscotto* was too hard for his poor teeth, and Lucrezia told him the carp would certainly appreciate it. When he turned to give me the confection I recognised him immediately.

'*Maestro!*'

'Tish, Gisella, you know to call me Leonardo.'

'You know each other!' Lucrezia was delighted.

'We're old acquaintances,' I said.

'Old friends,' smiled Leonardo. 'We met only briefly, but this is an extraordinary fish and I'm honoured to count her as a friend.'

'We're honoured to welcome you as a guest,' said Vanozza. 'But it sounds as if you didn't have a lot of choice in the matter.'

'What's Cesare up to *now*?' said Lucrezia.

'It appears that I've become the Gonfaloniero's chief military inventor, although it's not an honour I asked for. Or wanted. But evidently Cesare can be mightily persuasive when he puts his mind to it.'

'Oh dear,' said Vanozza. 'Then we're your gaolers, albeit highly unwilling ones.'

Leonardo nodded.

'And I suppose slipping away in the dead of night isn't an option?'

'Eyes are upon me at all times,' said Leonardo. 'I wouldn't take three steps outside the palace before being grabbed. There's a project I'm developing, and I'm going absolutely nowhere until it's completed. At least I'll be working in comfort, that's one consolation.'

Every morning two of Cesare's goons called for Leonardo, and returned him to the palace at the end of the afternoon. Apparently his workshop was only two minutes away, and no expense was spared in providing him with all the assistance and materials he asked for – however bizarre.

The four of us – the maestro, Vanozza, Lucrezia and me – would get together every evening and mull over palace life, culinary pleasures, what an upstart the young Michelangelo was, the changing of the seasons, and all manner of other inconsequentialities. The genius of the age, two of Rome's foremost ladies and a unique talking carp, and our conversation was no more elevated than a tabloid gossip column. It was as if there was an unspoken rule that due to the involuntary nature of Leonardo's presence in Rome, it would've been bad taste to touch on politics or the invention he was unwillingly creating.

But I'm an inquisitive fish, and I became fed up with all the pussyfooting. One evening I asked the maestro plainly what he was there for.

'You remember when we first met I mentioned to you I'd had an idea about a flying machine? I thought you would. And you no doubt thought I was barking. Well, that's what I'm doing now.'

'And will it actually work?'

'Alas yes. The project's going better than I dared hope – unfortunately.'

I looked at Leonardo for an explanation.

'I should never have breathed a word about my idea to anybody, but it's too late to fret about that now. Cesare got wind of my idea and told me how helpful a flying machine would be for entirely peaceful purposes – town planning, mapmaking, speeding up communications. Well, I'm not naïve, I knew exactly what he had in mind and refused his overtures. Which is when he made me his unrefusable offer.'

'It still seems incredible. I mean, how does it work? Have you made something that's lighter than air?'

'As good as,' Leonardo enthused, producing a parchment from an inner pocket in his cloak. It was a blueprint, of the oddest contraption imaginable, at least that's how it appeared to me at the dawn of the sixteenth century. It comprised a sedan chair-like pilot's cabin, anchored below a large pair of bird-like wings, above which was attached a helicopter-like rotor. All the moving parts were connected by chains and pulleys.

'Very intriguing,' I said. 'What makes it go?'

'That's the clever bit,' Leonardo grinned, 'even if I say it myself. It's powered by my perpetual motion gadget, or rather it's as close as can possibly be to perpetual motion. I just pedal like hell to get it spinning, just like in my submersible, then the gadget drives the rotor by itself. The power comes from enclosing two very powerful magnets which repel each other, producing an enormous force that I use to drive the flying machine's moving parts.'

'If it really works, I can see why you don't want Cesare to get his hands on it.'

'It'll work. Imagine Cesare with not just one flying machine, but hundreds of them. Bigger ones. Big enough to carry explosives that can be dropped on your enemies, and flying high enough to avoid their musket fire. Frankly it gives me the heebie-jeebies, and I'm the one who's responsible.'

The prospect seemed absurdly farfetched, the sky dark with flying machines dropping tons of high explosives on innocent people, but I reckoned it would be prudent to avoid any chance of it if possible. 'You couldn't just make sure it doesn't work?'

'That was my first idea. Unfortunately, Cesare has offered me a bonus for producing a functioning flying machine: he'll graciously let me live.'

'Could you sabotage it?'

'Not a chance, Cesare has eyes everywhere. I can't lift a screwdriver without his goons eyeballing me. What's more, now the prototype's all but finished, Cesare is keeping a close, personal eye on everything. Questions, questions, what does this do, how does that work? The man may be uncouth, but he's a million leagues from being stupid.'

Cesare had arranged for a select viewing of the prototype's inaugural test flight, which, in honour of his dear mama, was to take place right in the *palazzo* courtyard. Of course the Borgia clan was to be present, along with the dukes of Milan, Padua, Mantua, Genoa and a representative of the Doge of Venice. No doubt his unsubtle subtext was, 'Look what I can do, better bow to my will before I obliterate you.'

On the eve of the demonstration Leonardo and I discussed what options remained. One obvious solution popped into my mind, which shocked me only insofar as we hadn't thought of it earlier. I told the maestro that if he could make the machine fly, surely when he took off the next day he could zoom off into the ether and get clean away. 'Bloody hell,' he said. 'Why didn't I think of that?'

Our conversation came to an abrupt halt when there was a sharp banging on the palace gates. Cesare had decided upon a surprise visit, and for some reason insisted on meeting Leonardo in the courtyard. He gave the maestro a curt greeting and then strode purposefully up to the edge of the pond. 'I can see you,' he said, peering at the water. 'Come out from under those lilies, I know you're there.'

Reluctantly I left my sanctuary.

'I've been waiting to meet the famous talking fish. You didn't think you were a secret, did you? My informants told me about you from the word go, but until now I had no reason to bother with you.'

I looked at him quizzically.

'They tell me you can foretell the weather, with great accuracy.'

'That's true,' I answered.

'Good.' He then turned to Leonardo. 'There's a change of plan tomorrow.'

Leonardo and I exchanged glances.

'A wicked thought occurred to me, and shame on me for having such a suspicious mind, but there would be nothing to stop you taking off in your contraption and just flying away.'

'But sire,' Leonardo protested. 'The idea never—'

'Shush! Just to remove any temptation I will carry out the test flight.'

'B-but the controls, surely you'd—'

'Pish and pish. I've studied everything you've done, and I'm perfectly certain I can handle it.'

Leonardo looked downcast. Evidently he believed Cesare was quite capable of flying his machine.

'You, *Signorina Carpa*, will give me an accurate weather forecast, to make sure the maiden flight goes smoothly, and you, *maestro*, will make sure the contraption runs without a hitch. Failure on any count and you'll both find yourselves bathing in my lamprey pool.'

At the word lamprey I went as white as a ghost carp, a reaction Cesare picked up on immediately. 'So, you have history with the foul beasts,' he grinned. 'A pond full of killer lampreys is the must-have accessory for every despot this year – I got mine from my old mate Ferdinand II of Naples, after he *accidentally* fell in and ceased to have any more use for it. And be assured they aren't any ordinary lampreys; those brutes can kill a man in minutes, so what they'd do to a large carp.... I shudder to think.'

After Cesare's departure the mood in the palace was sombre, to say the least. Leonardo confided to me that he'd been in secret communication with the new French king, who'd offered him asylum at the *Manoir Clos Lucé*, in Amboise, if he could only reach a certain Genoese ship moored at Ostia, whose captain was in the pay of the French. That seemed a pretty remote possibility under the circumstances. He added that he'd far rather see Cesare crash in flames and suffer the consequences, than be responsible for ushering in a new era of mechanised killing from the sky, but he reckoned he'd been completely outmanoeuvred by the young megalomaniac. Vanozza and Lucrezia sadly bade us goodnight, then I was left alone.

I had a dilemma on my fins. Everyone else appeared to have forgotten that I'd been charged with providing a weather forecast, after all the sky had been clear for a month, and it was easy to assume that's how it was set to continue. I knew what was going to happen, though. The question was, did I consider my life was worth more than millions of humans'? Tricky one.

The next day the sky was veiled by thin cloud, but it was very warm and there wasn't a breath of wind. Rodrigo joined Vanozza and Lucrezia by the pool, nodding grimly at each other. I felt for them. Admitting their closest and dearest was a certifiable, power-crazed psycho can't have been easy. Leonardo clucked like a mother hen as his flying machine was wheeled in through the gates from the street, both proud and protective of his brainchild, and in dread of it. The assembled dignitaries, nibbling at antipasti and sipping Chianti, were nonplussed by the contraption; what it lacked in size it made up for in bizarreness. It was certainly a novelty, but the rumours that it would carry a man up into the sky? Cesare was having *una risata*, certainly?

Cesare casually approached me and asked for the latest forecast – a few clouds were bubbling up that he didn't like the look of. I could sense that a mass of frigid air had descended from the Alps and was rushing south along the Apennines, while a plume of hot Sahara air was barrelling north, and they were going to collide directly over Rome in a matter of minutes.

'Nothing to worry about, sire,' I whispered back. 'Fine weather cloud, we're set fair. Carp's honour!'

Reassured, Cesare swaggered over to the flying machine, told the assembly they were about to witness the white heat of technology of the modern age, and clambered into the box-like cabin.

He appeared to be pumping the pedals, which, of course, were out of sight. His face was quickly reddening, however.

'Here, Leonardo,' he shouted. 'This thing's shite!'

'Keep pedalling,' the maestro answered.

Sure enough, the rotor started to revolve, very slowly at first, then more quickly, then a blur. Then, to a collective gasp, the flying machine inched up into the air. It rose, haphazardly, lurching from side to side and nearly clipping one of the palace's towers as it ascended – which would've saved an awful lot of trouble. But Cesare soon started to master the craft's controls, and his flight became more deliberate, controlled. All the while, what had been an innocent-looking build-up of fluffy clouds was turning into a brooding mass of inky thunderheads. The air, which minutes ago had been merely sticky and oppressive, now fairly crackled with evil intent. There was a vivid flash, then a crash of thunder that could've shattered granite. A few meaty raindrops amplified into a deluge in a matter of seconds – turning the whole courtyard into what looked like a lake almost instantly. The guests quit gawping at the flying machine and stampeded for the palace doors, while Leonardo and I remained rooted to the spot, gazing upwards. In the gloom and forest of pelting rain it was hard to see anything, but another crackle of lightning revealed a shredded flying machine plunging earthwards.

'Bloody hell,' Leonardo and I uttered in unison.

History records that Cesare's time was not yet up, and indeed he survived his fall from grace. But his plan to dominate the skies came to naught and his loss of face in front of his peers only exacerbated his curmudgeonly temperament.

In fact, minutes after we'd witnessed his descent from on high, the palace gates burst open again and in stormed a very battered and dishevelled Cesare, hellbent on vengeance, flanked by guards. As luck would have it, he'd landed right in the muck heap in the stable yard next door, which had given him a soft but very smelly landing. The fact that the pelting rain had washed him clean in a few instants had done nothing to lift his mood. Me? I'm afraid I was so terrified I was doing my finest traumatised turbot impression, but Leonardo still had his wits about him and grabbed me from the pond and flung me to the watery ground. He hissed at me to get a move on, so I slithered across the flooded ground as best I could, and followed him though the small doorway and down the stairway that led to the cellar. The buffeting I received flopping down the stone steps was extremely painful, but I was driven on by a mental image of giant, blood-sucking lampreys. The light soon faded, for the stairwell torches were unlit, but now we were guided by the sound of rushing water and the smell of ordure and worse. I'd heard about heading towards the light; we were heading towards the stink.

The underground drain was now carrying a torrent of stormwater, but either we risked taking the plunge or we'd fall into the hands of Cesare's guards, who were already in hot pursuit. In we leapt.

Now it was my turn to help Leonardo, who wasn't in the first flush of youth and was clearly struggling, so I shouted to him to put his arms around me and hang on. It appeared that we were alone in the drain; our pursuers had evidently thought better of continuing the chase, and I can't say I blame them.

Before long the water slowed dramatically, and at the same time the water level was rising quickly, so the headroom at the top of the tunnel was rapidly disappearing. This put the maestro in immediate peril of drowning, and I wasn't faring much better – the water was so choked with debris of all kinds I was finding it nigh on impossible to breathe. It occurred to me that we must be near the Tiber, and there was probably some sort of grille where the drain emptied into the river that had become choked up with grot. In which case there was a fat lot I could do about it, because I could no longer move. But then, just when hope seemed to be extinguished, there was a great gurgling sound and an enormous whoosh as the grille gave way and we, along with tons of rotting food waste, dead rats, old rags and innumerable turds spilled into the Tiber.

I helped Leonardo to the shore a hundred metres or so downstream, and we sheltered among the moored rowing boats at a tumbledown landing stage. Minutes dragged past, but the expected search parties failed to materialise. We allowed hours to elapse but no one was looking for us, at least not by the river. In fact, history records – absolutely nothing. Cesare was all too happy for the excruciating episode to be forgotten, and his honoured guests had far too well-developed survival instincts to prattle about it. Manned flight was to remain a pipedream for another few centuries, and a damn good job too.

Leonardo helped himself to a rowing boat and I accompanied him downstream to Ostia, where he was able to contact a friendly ship's captain and begin his journey to France. As for me, my hopes of finding a more enlightened society in Renaissance Italy hadn't exactly been fulfilled, but in all fairness I'd only really stopped in Rome, and seen little other than a palazzo courtyard – even if it was a very attractive courtyard, and for the most part I'd enjoyed good company.

Maybe I needed to give Italy another chance. But I was going to get as far away from Rome as I could without actually quitting the peninsula. That meant one destination: Venice.

Notes

[1]*La Camargue.* The swampy area around les Bouches du Rhône – the Rhône delta – which is famous for its white horses, known as Camarguais, its fearsome bulls, Taureaux de Camargue (the area has a tradition of bullfighting), and its mosquitoes, which are demonic.

[2]*Bouillabaisse.* The famous fish soup of Marseilles, made with rascasse, all sorts of other fish, shellfish, lots of olive oil, saffron, garlic, tarragon… served with croutons and aioli. Which we won't go in to now.

[3]Savonarola was an overzealous (okay, nutty) friar who had plenty of chutzpah and a knack for inciting folk to burn books, art and anybody he took a dislike to. He particularly disliked the Borgia Papacy, considering it corrupt and degenerate. He came to a sticky, or rather charred, end.

[4]*Curia.* The Catholic Church's ruling body/council.

[5]*Enculé.* Don't even ask.

Chapter Eight

Gisella meanders her way to the City of Canals, and helps an aspiring young painter of the High Renaissance period achieve an artistic breakthrough

After gaining my sea fins, which didn't seem so bad this time, I headed into the Tyrrhenian Sea and south along the coast. Having to swim to Venice meant I was definitely taking the scenic route, but the scenery was picturesque and I was in no great hurry. Whatever was waiting for me in Venice would just have to be patient.

I'd considered making a stop at Naples, but the constant rumblings of nearby Vesuvius were playing havoc with my lateral line, so I just kept going.

Not only was the landscape spectacular, the sea provided me with much to marvel at too. The waters of the Mediterranean were far clearer than those of the North Sea or the Bay of Biscay, and the array of aquatic fauna (I don't include myself here) continued to enthral me. Quicksilver sardines, morose morays, those gloriously garish red mullet, lurking octopuses, and the lightning-fast bonito tuna – oh my, how those fish could motor. A bulky lake-dweller like me isn't the most athletic of fish, but the bonito could leave even grayling and grey mullet for dead, and *they're* no slouches.

I took great care making my way around the Strait of Messina, for although the currents were swift and treacherous there was a great concentration of fishing boats. The strait was a busy thoroughfare for all kinds of fish, and the local fishermen evidently considered it worth risking their lives to reap the bounty. They even fished by night, for the lamps on their boats proved irresistible to silly sardines and the like. I swam below the level of the nets, and wasn't tempted by the baits that were dangled here and there. It might've proved amusing to see the look on a fisherman's face if he pulled out a big carp, but I didn't think it was worth getting a knock on my head for.

A fortnight into my journey I realised I was now following the coast in a northerly direction. I suppose I'd picked up a bit of navigational nous during my journeying, and I could remember all the maps Father Flammarion. I had entered the Adriatic Sea, and although Venice lay a gentle month's swim ahead of me, I so enjoyed the sights and flavours of the Adriatic ports, not to mention the equable climate, that I ended up taking far longer – a decade longer in fact.

The Adriatic coast was fascinating, and the ports of Bari, Pescara and Ancona were wonderful places for me to spend a few months in, listening to all the sailors' and fishermen's chit-chat. There's something to be said for travelling in the slow lane, and taking the time to smell the seaweed. However, after spending a winter in Rimini, I thought that maybe I'd dawdled for long enough and told myself that if I didn't get a move on to Venice the Renaissance could very well be over before I got there. No more distractions, Gisella!

Those unfamiliar with Venice probably have a mental image of the city as filled with gold-hued classical buildings, azure canals and gaily coloured gondolas, scenes of brilliant light, timeless elegance and beauty – much like a Canaletto[1] painting (such a cultured carp, I know). It isn't always like that, and certainly wasn't when I reached the fair city state.

For a start I smelt Venice long before I arrived there. What is the difference between a sixteenth-century canal and an open sewer? The answer is not a lot. I didn't have to acclimatise to fresh water because the Venetian canals are filled with seawater, but I did have to adjust my olfactory senses to the constant pong. Add to that the clammy, cold and drizzly weather, and my first impression of Venice was not a joyous one. Still, the water wasn't so polluted that it didn't support all sorts of fishes, including the almost ubiquitous grey mullet, whose dietary habits are sometimes far from sanitary. And apart from mullet scoffing the occasional unmentionable, enough food waste was dumped into the waterways to feed a thriving aquatic population.

As I explored the city's myriad canals I took care to pass under bridges with great caution: lesson learnt, hopefully. The other hazard was boat traffic, especially gondolas. These came in a variety of sizes, and varied from gilded luxury craft for the well-to-do, with cushioned seats and tasselled canopies to protect the nobs from the elements, to utilitarian transport for the hoi polloi, and shabby old cockleshells for transporting goods. Their one common denominator was the gondolier, who propelled the boat by means of a large, rear-mounted paddle, or *remo*. Those bloody things could slice the top off a carp's head if one weren't careful.

As evening approached, the mass of boats rapidly thinned out. I soon overheard the reason why: Venice was now at war with the Papal States and France! If a week is a long time in politics, a decade is an aeon. Pope Alexander had snuffed it, his old enemy Cardinal della Rovere was now Pope Julius II, Cesare Borgia had legged it to Spain, where he was embroiled in yet more internecine unpleasantness, and Julius had palled-up with the French to curb Venice's territorial ambitions – or seize the gateway to trade with the East[2] – depending on which way you looked at it. In other words, there was yet another bloody stupid war, and, because there was a great fear of spies or a sneak attack by night, a curfew was being enforced. Troop-manned gondolas patrolled the waterways, and anyone caught out after dark risked prison and a few choice tortures. That, of course, didn't apply to carp.

After three days of wandering to and fro, I reckoned to have found my bearings in the city. The thing about Venetian houses and palazzos was that most of their entrances and windows all looked out over water – heaven for a large scaly fish that had a penchant for snooping. It was also very useful to know where all the best bakeries and kitchens were situated, and when food waste was tipped out into the drink. I soon became a connoisseur of the scores of different pasta varieties in vogue, and also scraps of what has more recently become known as pizza. This was a rounded flatbread topped with tomato, cheese and whatever else the cook thought of on any given day. I certainly didn't object to the tartness of anchovies or olives, but drew the line at the maniacs who topped them with fruit. A crime against gastronomy!

My favourite bakery, Cannavale's, was situated right next to a large artist's atelier. Cannavale's back entrance opened to the river, and was used for both receiving supplies and dispatching deliveries, while the neighbouring studio had three large canal-side windows, presumably for the light.

I soon discovered the atelier belonged to a venerable and venerated painter named Giovanni Bellini, who had a couple of apprentices working under him. I'd come to Italy to get a flavour of the Renaissance, and apparently the art of painting was undergoing a revolution during these turbulent years, so could this be my chance to see what all the fuss was about? The trouble was, the paintings were obviously all in the atelier while I was outside in the water. I considered my best chance to cop an eyeful of art was to befriend the *Signor* or one of his underlings, so I took to hanging around outside the workshop in order to learn more about the exotic creators working within, and whom I could approach without undue risk of becoming an unusual pizza topping. I soon came to recognise the gentle, slightly breathless voice of the *maestro*, Giovanni Bellini, as well as his two apprentices, Tiziano and Paolo. While Signor Bellini was softly spoken there was something compelling about his speech, while his charges both demonstrated the brazen excitability of youth, with frequent raised and sometimes angry voices. But who would present himself as an ally?

Within a couple of days, the choice had been made for me. The weather had changed dramatically, from gloomy and damp to bright sunshine, and I had taken to basking near the surface to absorb some of the glorious warmth. Young Tiziano, meanwhile, finding the atelier stiflingly warm, sought out the canal in order to cool down. Wearing just a loincloth, he leapt from one of the windows and landed in the water a metre away from me. 'Oi!' I exclaimed. 'Didn't your mamma tell you to look before you leap?' It was out of my mouth before I had time to think.

'*Mamma mia!*' Stunned, Tiziano expelled a mouthful of water, but he regained his composure with impressive speed. 'A thousand pardons. I never expected a talking *carpa* to be swimming by. Especially in salt water!'

Tiziano – known to his mates as Titian – impressed me instantly. Mainly because he was unfazed by meeting a talking fish, but also because he showed no inclination to bop me on the head. This fine young man turned out to be more than happy to show me the wonders of Venetian art, which he did by holding up paintings at the atelier windows whenever there was a slack moment. To say I was

impressed was an understatement. Back in Paris Father Flammarion had shown me some fine egg tempera paintings, but the oil-painting revolution taking place in Venice was taking the art to a different level. Human figures were depicted so much more realistically, the compositions were so much more fluid, the sense of perspective more believable, the colours more luminescent (okay, okay, I'll stop being so frou-frou, but these guys could paint).

Over the next four weeks Titian became increasingly busy, but not so much that he didn't have time to share the odd lunchtime pizza with me at the bakery steps. He explained to me that although he was only sixteen he'd been given a fantastically important commission.

'I image that's quite a coup for someone as young as you,' I said.

'Well yes. But of course the *maestro* would be doing it if he weren't confined to his bed.'

'I thought I hadn't heard him for a while.'

'He thinks he's got the sweating sickness, but if he had we'd all have caught it. No, it's gout again, and the poor blighter's completely immobile.'

'And? The big commission? You're not going to keep me in the dark.'

'Well.' Titian looked from side to side to make sure we weren't being overheard. 'It's all hush hush, but there are secret talks between Venice and the French about a treaty, and attacking the Papal States. As a gesture of friendship, the doge[3] is to present a painting of the French ambassador's beloved daughter, Brigitte, to his excellency at an unofficial viewing in the atelier tomorrow. But because the *maestro* can't even hold a paintbrush at present—'

'*Sacré bleu*, he must trust you a lot! I bet Paolo's jealous.'

'That's not the half of it! He hates the fact that I'm a better painter than he is, and worse, I'm not a Venetian. His family has canal water in its veins – he has a million relations throughout the city – while I'm from a remote village in the foothills of the Alps. An upstart bumpkin.'

'And? There's got to be more to it than that.'

'No. I swear it. Or rather maybe. There may have been a little bit of a thing between me and his sister Sophia. Once. Or just a few times. And now of course he hates me even more.'

'You're not worried he'll try to sabotage you?'

'Actually, he's given me a very wide berth for the past few weeks. Sulking no doubt. In fact, with the *maestro* tucked up in bed, I've been allowed to work in perfect peace.'

'They've left you alone painting the ambassador's daughter? That's very broad-minded!'

'No way, Brigitte's *molto bella*, and very well chaperoned at all times. I work from sketches I made of her at the ambassador's *palazzo*. But now the work is finished, and by midday tomorrow I'll know if I have a glittering future as a painter or a career whitewashing walls.'

As the sun started to set behind the city skyline, Titian left to return to his nearby lodgings. I hung around near the atelier, feeling just a little uneasy on my friend's behalf. Maybe this good-natured carp was starting to become just a little bit cynical about how outraged, jealous humans sometimes react, but I didn't trust Paolo to allow Titian's moment of glory to take place without a hitch. And it wasn't long before a dim light appeared in the atelier window, and then a glimpse of a familiar silhouette: Paolo. Then there was a slight ripping sound from within, so I wasted no time in finning it over to Titian's digs to raise the alarm.

Fortunately he was finding it impossible to sleep, so when I called at his window he appeared almost immediately. Due to the curfew going by street to the atelier wasn't an option, so he dropped quietly into the water and swam after me as I retraced my route. I couldn't sense any gondolas nearby, so fortunately the coast was clear.

Back in front of the atelier our worst fears were confirmed: a soggy rectangle of canvas floated in the water, and we didn't have to guess what it was. Not without difficulty Titian clawed his way up to and in through the window, but when he struck a light there was no sign of Paolo. With so many friends and relatives among the guards and gondoliers, it was obvious that he could move around with impunity during the curfew, and had the run of the city.

Not only was Titian's beautiful portrait of the comely Brigitte ruined beyond repair, but in its frame, under a silken veil, there was now a canvas of unsurpassed hideousness. Barely able to believe his eyes, my friend held it up at the window for me to see. In the moonlight you could just about tell it depicted a woman, sort of, but it was all cubes and angles and badly painted blocks of colour. Everything was in the wrong place. The eyes were where the mouth should've been, the ears on top of the head, and hair and hands and feet all higgledy-piggledy. And to cap it all, there was an unambiguous pudendum right in the middle of her face.

'*Putain*,' I gasped. 'You said Paolo can't paint, but that's ridiculous!'

'Imagine if they'd unveiled it tomorrow morning.'

'That would be the end of any treaty between Venice and France. And I don't suppose you'd come out of it too well either.'

'I'd be hung, drawn and quartered for sure. That's all Paolo cares about. So what if Venice ends up burned and pillaged.'

Titian wasted no time in cutting the offending canvas to sheds, but there still remained the problem of not having a painting to show the next day.

'Maybe you can say you got artist's block?'

Titian shook his head.

'How about running away?'

'I'd never even get out of the city.'

'Then you'll have to paint another picture. A good one.'

'In a single night? That's insane!'

'Do you have any better ideas? You've still got all your sketches to work from. Maybe you won't be able to do all the fine detail, but surely you can catch Brigitte's essence. I don't know what else you can do.'

'Harrumph,'

'Very well, give up then. But I can already hear those knives being sharpened up.'

'All right already, I don't have much choice, do I? But if I'm still around to tell the tale tomorrow afternoon I'll be one shocked painter.'

To my immense relief Titian was around the next afternoon. After the throng of dignitaries had left the atelier, he appeared at the window, a wide grin pasted across his face. He recounted to me what had happened.

That morning the doge, the ambassador, Brigitte, and all their assorted flunkies and hangers-on, had assembled in the studio for the grand unveiling. Even the doddery Bellini had been helped from his sickbed to attend his protégé's moment of triumph, and of course Paolo was there, a very smug look plastered over his face. Standing next to his easel, on which stood his silk-shrouded artwork, Titian was a bundle of nerves. After a fanfare and a couple of pompous, meaningless speeches, which did nothing to improve the young painter's anxiety, the moment of truth arrived. Titian told the guests to step back, for the work was newly finished and the paint still tacky. He swept the picture's silk veil aside, and there was a collective gasp. Especially from Paolo.

'It's most, er, unusual,' said the doge.

'It doesn't look finished,' said the *maestro.* 'The background isn't so much painted as hinted at.'

'It's crap,' Paolo sneered. 'Look, you can see all the crude brushstrokes.'

'I like it,' said Brigitte. 'You can see fleeting sunshine. The light's so real. It captures a moment in time. And I look *très mignonne!*'

The ambassador clapped his hands together. '*C'est magnifique!* It gives such a real impression, a glimpse of a beautiful maiden on a spring morning. Mark my words, this painting is the shape of things to come!'

The doge and Maestro Bellini exchanged looks of great relief, but from Paolo came an outraged roar. 'That jammy bastard's lucked out again!' A knife flew through the air, nicking Titian's ear and removing the doge's domed hat, before embedding itself in the frame of an easel. Paolo tried to flee but was grabbed before he'd run three steps, and, accused of attempting to assassinate the doge, found himself facing the same fate he'd intended for his rival.

The painting, unconventional as it was, was declared a great success, and the dignitaries spoke of young Titian as definitely the painter to watch over the coming decades. The *maestro* was most thankful for the artwork's success, but quietly warned his apprentice that any repeat of his outrageous experiment and he'd find himself out on his ear.

Because delicious smells were wafting from Cannavaro's, I joined my young friend to enjoy some celebratory spiced pastries at the bakery steps.

I was sorry that I never managed to take a look at the ground-breaking portrait, but supposed that Titian would soon produce some more paintings in his new style. No way, he answered. While the French ambassador obviously had very advanced aesthetic tastes, he didn't think the art world was quite ready for *the art of impressions.* No, he was going to work on light and colour and form, but his artistic development was going to be more evolution than revolution.

I didn't want to puncture the feelgood mood by pursuing the point, so I changed the subject and remarked how delectable the spicy confections he'd purchased were. Especially the little brown ones, they were almost addictive. They were made with fenugreek, Titian said, another spice imported from the East. Apparently all sorts of spices were imported from Constantinople by Venetian merchants, but they were becoming rarer and more expensive because – surprise, surprise – another conflict had sprung up between Venice and the Ottomans – who ruled Constantinople, and naturally controlled all trade from the Orient.

Much as I'd enjoyed my stay in Venice and my friendship with the young painter, I felt another bout of itchy fins coming on. Part driven by curiosity, but admittedly also motivated by the haunting aroma of fenugreek and other intriguing spices, I decided Constantinople was to be my next destination.

Notes

[1]Peter Paul Rubens was famous for paining ample ladies, George Stubbs was famous for painting horses, and Canaletto was famous for painting Venice. Such a cultured carp.

[2]The city state of Venice was Europe's gateway for trading with the Ottoman Empire and points further to the east. It was therefore of great strategic and economic importance.

[3]The doge was the city-state of Venice's highest official. The word is derived from duke, though why they couldn't just have used the word duke is unclear. Though elected, the position was for life. That resulted in quite a few lives being mysteriously short.

Chapter Nine

The magnificent. Gisella befriends a magnificent conqueror and goes to live in a palace

Fifteen years later I finally turned into the Bosphorus and approached the magnificent city of Constantinople. I'd dawdled a bit along the way, learning a clutch of new languages, admiring the views, and frequently seeking sanctuary in order to avoid the continual seaborne battles the various powers insisted on waging. The feared corsair Barbarossa[1] was a scourge of Western shipping, as were the Barbary pirates, but ships from Italy and Spain weren't averse to attacking Ottoman traders either, when the opportunity arose. During a renewed bout of Venetian and Ottoman fleets knocking seven bells out of one another, I'd passed a few pleasant years in the city state of Dubrovnik, which had wisely remained neutral and closed off its harbour when too many cannonballs were flying, and Piraeus also proved a useful bolthole. Of course, the baked dainties their many bakers produced were an attraction, but not wanting to be blown out of the water was rather persuasive too.

On reaching Constantinople I quickly learnt two things. One, that Constantinople wasn't called Constantinople anymore, it was Istanbul. The second was that Turkish was rather different from English, French, Latin, Italian, Bulgarian and Greek, and it was going to take me a few days to learn it fluently.

I hung around the harbour area listening in on conversations and enjoying the aromas from the dockside spice warehouses. The port was crammed with more ships than I'd ever seen, from the sleek corsair vessels used for fighting and raiding, to galleys bristling with cannon, and the myriad traders, which, unlike the more warlike ships, relied solely on sail power rather than rows of oarsmen gathering blisters.

The skipper of a small merchantman, being loaded with the most aromatic sacks and barrels, was grumbling that if only he could get permission to trade with the port of Valencia he could double his profit, but even more than a generation after the last Moors had been booted out of the Iberian Peninsula, trade with the Spanish ports was still to be properly re-established. My Turkish must've been improving because I could understand most of what he was saying, but I knew that actually speaking the language would be another kettle of fish. The mate, who didn't appear to belong to the first rank of intellectuals, said that His Magnificence the Sultan Suleiman had just returned in triumph from the conquest of Belgrade, so it may well be worth asking him about trading with Valencia. That was cloud cuckoo land, the skipper snorted, an old seadog like him would have more chance of reconquering Spain single-handedly than getting an audience with the sultan.

I was so absorbed with snooping that I never realised I'd drifted over a drop net suspended from the side of the ship, and before I knew it I'd been hoicked up into the air. I'd escaped from a similar device just outside Paris a couple of centuries earlier, but this time I wasn't so lucky. I was rudely dumped onto the deck, where a couple of the crew members and the mate peered greedily down at me. As I flopped helplessly around, there was a word repeated amongst the sailors that I couldn't help understanding: supper. This was no time for me to be shy and retiring.

'You mustn't eat me, I can help you,' I hoped I'd said.

'Pardon?' said the intellectually challenged first mate. 'You say you want your shoes shined?'

'Skip,' one of the crew members turned to the captain. 'There's a fish here talking utter bollocks.'

I tried to compose myself – not easy under the circumstances. 'I – can – help – you.'

The captain looked down at me. 'What – the – fuck – do – you – mean?'

In halting Turkish I did my best to explain my idea to him. In short, if he were to present His Magnificence (it was a fair assumption that the sultan was the head honcho around there) with a truly exceptional gift, such as a talking carp, maybe his request to trade with Valencia would be looked upon favourably.

The first mate looked acutely disappointed. 'I say we eat the fish.'

'No,' said the skipper. 'That actually makes sense. We'll take him.'

'Her.'

'*Her* to the Topkapi Palace, and present her to the sultan.'

'It would make a lot of sense if I actually arrived there alive, so could you fetch me some water?'

A barrel of water was quickly produced, and, once immersed, I gratefully gulped in the scummy harbour water. Rather than being whisked straight to the sultan's palace, however, I had to endure a wait of several hours on the ship's deck while the skipper had disappeared to deal with the people who mattered. The first mate was vocal in his desire to have me kebabbed, but fortunately his colleagues managed to convince him that replacing a talking fish wouldn't be very easy, and if anything happened to me *he* would be the one who ended up on skewers.

Just when I was starting to think the captain had been given the bum's rush, he reappeared with a large group of exotically dressed palace flunkies. My very indecorous barrel was bundled off the ship and onto a most decorous palanquin, and I was whisked away through the streets of Istanbul.

The Topkapi Palace is reckoned to be one of the world's most beautiful structures, but from inside of a barrel I didn't get the chance to enjoy an overwhelming first impression. After much manoeuvring and jolting, my barrel was emptied into a large stone pool, or bath rather, in a vast interior chamber. It was filled with fresh water, a little too warm for comfort, but it was sweetly scented with rose petals and cardamom, so I thought it would be churlish to complain. The walls of the chamber were made of the most exquisite, multicoloured and multipatterned faience, punctuated by towering, pointed arches. Okay, I'll stop with the Niklaus Pevsner, but it was fabulous, and it turned out that it was just one of the palace's hundreds of rooms.

Next I became aware that the room was filled with very richly dressed people, most of whom wore the most exotic, turban-like headgear, and all of whom were staring expectantly at me.

Amongst them was the humble sea captain, who looked frightened out of his wits. The man with the fanciest headgear – it really resembled a giant, bejewelled onion – pointed at me and demanded that I speak. It flashed through my head that perhaps human rank was denoted by the size and opulence of what they placed on their heads. For instance, my writer friend Geoffrey Chaucer had worn a modest floppy hat, while the pope had worn a much bigger and more dashing titfer, but by virtue of his outrageous crowning glory alone, I surmised the chap speaking to me had to be the sultan, and on that evidence he was very, very important indeed. The temptation to address him as Onion Head was nearly overwhelming, but fortunately the vision of skewered chunks of fish sizzling over a charcoal fire drew me back from the brink.

'Your Magnificence,' I would've bowed if I could. 'At your service.'

I thought I'd said at his service, but in fact it had come out as *at his circus*. No matter. The sultan was delighted. He granted the skipper's request for permission to trade with Valencia, saying it was high time they started profiting from new markets, and then clapped his hands, indicating that the gathering was to disperse. He then told me I was his honoured guest, and we would converse by and by. In the meanwhile, I was to work on my Turkish, and to that end, and to look after all my needs, I was assigned two concubines from his harem. These young ladies pampered me with *rahat lokum*[2] and dainties flavoured with cinnamon and cardamom and fenugreek, and tittered so much I thought my swim bladder would burst with irritation. Within days, though, my Turkish was near perfect, but the girls were still amused by the wonky carp with the raspy foreign accent.

True to his word, Sultan Suleiman paid me regular visits and we talked of many things. He was enraptured by my life story and especially by my longevity, for which he was certain I would agree that Allah should be thanked. He thought the Normans sounded barbaric and the English little better, although I attempted to persuade him that his vision of them as a race of dung-hut dwellers who lived on a diet of wurzel mash was a tad outdated. The French, he conceded, were reasonably cultured, as were the Italians, but they'd all taken part in numerous crusades, and they were all infidels – for which he insisted they'd pay a heavy price.

Although the sultan grudgingly conceded that the Christian countries produced a number of thinkers, poets and artists, he maintained nothing could compare with his expanding Ottoman Empire for culture and learning. Every art one could think of was encouraged under his reign, all forms of learning, for he wished posterity to remember him for ushering in a golden age of Islamic culture, for making Istanbul the centre of the world for poetry, architecture, music, mathematics, astronomy, painting, ceramics, philosophy, humanities and of course the worship of Allah.

'And if one wasn't a Muslim?' I'd ventured. The sultan told me that being an infidel was a grave error and naturally the best thing for non-Muslims to do was convert, but his was an enlightened regime and religious minorities were tolerated – after all, Istanbul sustained Catholic, Orthodox and Jewish communities. All that was required was that they live within their own strictly delineated enclaves. Naturally infidels couldn't expect court or government positions, and if they were called upon to fight they were always in the first rank of cannon fodder, but they made useful tradespeople and servants, and actually no power on Earth could prevent the blighters from trading.

Not exactly a fair deal, I thought to myself, but then I reflected that religious tolerance was probably still in its infancy. After all, in Chaucer's England Lollards and Wycliffites had been an endangered species, and in Rome Muslims and Jews had been tolerated only when there was profit to be made from it. I knew that Jews had been massacred in Spain, and before I'd left Venice there had been talk of booting out the Semites from there as well. When I looked back I reckoned the most broadminded people I'd known had been Geoffrey Chaucer, the famous plagiarist, and the kindly old Jesuit priest, Father Flammarion. And Leonardo probably. Not that long a list.

Suleiman was often accompanied by his grand vizier, Emre Pasha, a tubby, splendidly moustachioed, affable-looking fellow, who radiated bonhomie. He contributed little to our conversations, but would constantly nod affirmatively and chuckle his approval at his master's wisdom. He too often brought me little treats, and declared the talking fish was indeed a marvel. Emre Pasha appeared to be everybody's friend, and was considered a most able and trustworthy deputy to His Magnificence.

During the sultan's frequent long absences, Defne and Irma continued to be my chief source of company – always under the watchful eye of a towering eunuch called Safat, which was apparently mandatory for any concubine leaving the confines of the harem.

The limited swimming space in my pool plus the over-rich diet of sweets and cakes were taking their toll on my normally svelte waistline. In fact, I was becoming decidedly tubby. Anyone familiar with angling will have seen those trophy shots of gigantic, bulging carp caught from French commercial lakes – affectionately known as gut buckets – well, I was getting to be like one of them, and no amount of swimming round and round and round my pool was taking off any of the excess pounds.

During the sultan's longest absence to date, I finally lost patience with the girls. I suppose I was frustrated with my indolence and gluttony, and tired of my companions' incessant tittering. I simply snapped at them to stop simpering so bloody much; no way did I believe they were as empty-headed as they made out, so could they please talk to me like a normal fish.

'We only do it for his benefit,' said Defne in a hushed voice, glancing over her shoulder at Safat, who as ever stood impassively under one of the arches.

'He looks to me as if he's fallen asleep,' I said.

'Not a chance, but I think he's finally twigged that we're not meeting with any men,' said Irma, 'so I suppose we're safe to speak now.'

'Wow,' I said. 'It sounds as if being a concubine is a real bundle of fun.'

'It has its compensations,' said Defne. 'Many of us come from minor aristocratic or even ordinary backgrounds, so having a daughter in the sultan's harem confers kudos and privileges on our families. Even wartime captives have much to be thankful for – being a concubine is preferable to being raped and butchered. The harem is rather like a village, there are the favoured girls and the drudges, the in-crowd and the Nesry no-friends. We have to make the best of it, because for us life doesn't offer any alternatives.'

'Scores of ladies and one man,' I said. 'How on earth does that work?'

'The sultan's magnificent potency is more than enough for us all,' said Irma with a wry grin. 'Or so he'd like to think. Actually, getting a night with him is a less than yearly event for most of us, and a night is something of an exaggeration – in reality it's about six minutes.

Most nights he spends with his favourite wife, Roxelana, and the best of Ottoman luck to her.'

'You don't sound too bothered.'

'We lesser ladies tend to make our own amusements, if you get what I mean,' said Defne. 'Some even take the risk of secret liaisons with palace guards and the like, but most of us are too chicken. The consequences of getting a baklava in the oven when you haven't consorted with His Magnificence for over a year are pretty unthinkable. No – self-sufficiency is very much the order of the day in our community.'

'Don't you miss contact with the outside world? I know I do, and I'm still one of the newcomers here.'

'We can form a pretty good picture of what's going on beyond these walls,' said Irma. 'For a start you'd be amazed at what we learn from the sultan's pillow talk. He tells his bedmates all his plans and achievements and concerns, because he can't even start to imagine that any female will understand a word he's saying. There's a veritable grapevine of information within the harem. Plus news manages to filter through from all sorts of other sources – for instance, we know from a courtier's wife exactly how our master's campaign in the West is progressing.'

'*Ben alors!* Spill! I've heard nothing for the past few years.'

'Well, it seems that the Ottoman army occupied Buda and placed a puppet on the Hungarian throne. Suleiman's forces are now besieging Vienna, but are encountering stiff resistance,' said Defne.

'The human race's appetite for war seems to be without limit!'

'We're told Vienna is the gateway to the Holy Roman Empire and the rest of Europe, and Suleiman has been known to mutter about world domination in his sleep,' said Irma.

'Plus it's now personal,' said Defne. 'Not only did negotiations with King Ferdinand of Austria break down, he was overhead muttering that it was hard to take someone with a giant onion on his head seriously.'

'Now Suleiman has sworn to butcher every man, woman and child in the city, which probably accounts for the stiff resistance they're putting up,' said Irma. 'Our armies have ground to a halt and are running short of supplies.'

'It'll be to no avail, though,' said Defne. 'A great fleet of ships from the Turkish navy has set sail to relieve the Ottoman forces. It's travelled via the Black Sea and into the River Danube, and will probably pass Buda within a month. Once it reaches Vienna it won't be able to attack the city itself, because scores of Austrian cannons overlook the river's approaches, but reprovisioned by fresh supplies, armaments, ammunition and men, the Ottoman army is certain to break the deadlock.'

'Poor Vienna,' I sighed.

'Suleiman's very sensitive about his headwear,' said Defne.

'But massacring tens of thousands of innocent people does seem a tad extreme,' said Irma sadly.

Not only was Vienna facing an existential threat, I soon found my own future in immediate peril. That night a tittering and guffawing penetrated the usual hush of the palace, and into my chamber staggered Emre Pasha, clearly pissed as a newt, supported by two giggling and dishevelled concubines, whose state of inebriation was only a notch or two below the vizier's.

This wasn't great news for yours truly because: (a) the pasha was completely rat-arsed, which was definitely not kosher in the Ottoman Empire (even if it was far from unheard of), and (b) he was clearly on better-than-first-name terms with the two young ladies. I fervently hoped he'd remain oblivious to my presence, because if the penny dropped that his indiscretion had been witnessed, his affability might turn out to be skin-deep.

No such luck. He lurched over to my pool and immediately I hovered stock still, barely moving a fin, and mimicked a gentle snoring. Those who know fish will be aware that we do not sleep as such, and we certainly can't close our eyes because we have no eyelids, so I was banking on Emre's befuddled condition to get away with my slumbering charade. He stared intently into my blank (I hoped) eyes for several seconds, blinked, as if his ability to focus was letting him down, and then abruptly turned and re-joined his companions. I bubbled a gentle sigh of relief as they teetered out of the chamber, but only time would tell if my sham snoozing had saved my neck.

Very early the next morning my worst fears appeared to be unfolding. A large sack over his shoulder, Safat the eunuch made his way into the chamber – with remarkable stealth for such a large man – followed by two shadowy, cloaked figures. '*Merde*,' I sighed to myself.

'Shh,' Safat urged as he set the sack down. 'Emre Pasha has ordered me to poison you, so we're going to have to be quick.'

I then realised the cloaked figures were Defne and Irma. 'Emre's obviously got some kind of grudge against you, so he wants to eliminate you and then tell the sultan he discovered you were a spy,' said Defne.

'Denouncing folk as spies is the pasha's go-to method of elimination,' said Irma. 'And Suleiman is so paranoid he falls for it every time.'

'No hope of denouncing him and saving my hide?' I said hopefully.

'The word of a fish, two concubines and a eunuch against a grand vizier's?' said Defne. 'Not on your Nelly.'

'Don't worry,' said Safat. 'We're going to do a swap. I bought a big old carp at the Jewish night market, and that's what we're going to show Emre Pasha as proof that his order was carried out.'

'And?'

'And you will be a free fish once more,' said Irma.

'This, good friend, is where we part ways,' said Defne.

'We'll miss you,' said Irma.

'And don't worry about the treacherous pasha,' Defne added. 'You obviously saw him doing something he didn't ought to, and it's not hard to figure out what. His boozing and leching are bound to be exposed before long, so we can guarantee his days are numbered.... then he'll be erased from history.'

I looked up at Safat. 'I thought you were the sultan's man, yet you're helping me.'

'I am indeed the sultan's man – and not the pasha's! Now – you'd best look away.'

Safat emptied a very dead carp from the sack into the pool, and I couldn't help taking a morbid peek at it.

'I know it doesn't look much like you,' said Safat, 'but the pasha's eyesight isn't very good, and he won't see the difference – believe me. Now we must hurry, the palace is waking.'

Praying the giant eunuch wouldn't betray me, I allowed myself to be bundled into the sack, and then submitted to being swung across his shoulder and bumpily carried away.

No more than four anxious minutes later I was dropped from the sack into chilly, briny water. No time to acclimatise myself, I was obviously in the Bosphorus. I thanked my gallant rescuer, and then concentrated on drawing the salty water through my gills and trying to clear my head. A free fish again after so long in a glorified goldfish bowl, I needed a plan. Normally I tended towards heading directly away from any area of human conflict. As was once said in a popular human entertainment, I stuck my neck out for nobody. Not that I had a neck. But the idea of thousands perishing because of a throwaway remark about onion-shaped headwear stuck in my throat. And if I tipped the good people of Vienna off about the new peril they faced I wouldn't really be taking sides, it would be up to them if they did the sane thing and fled for the hills. Besides, I needed a really vigorous swim in order to shed the results of a destructive Middle Eastern confectionery habit.

Notes

[1]*Barbarossa*, aka Red-Beard. He was a notorious pirate from the Barbary Coast of North Africa who specialised in attacking European shipping. He later was made an admiral in the Ottoman navy, and tasked with attacking European shipping.
[2]*Rahat lokum*, Turkish delight. In the Levant it's not just eaten at Christmas.

Chapter Ten

The Blue Danube. In which Gisella ascends Europe's mightiest river, has a contretemps with a large fleet of ships, saves a great city from a gruesome fate, and discovers Viennese pastries.

Yet again I was indebted to my old Parisian friends for my geography lessons, for I navigated my way through the Bosphorus, up the Bulgarian coast of the Black Sea and into the Danube delta without undue difficulty. My saltwater companions were gradually replaced by freshwater fishes, and for the first time in my life I found myself among a high population of carp – common carp, such as myself.

My joy at finding myself among my own kind was very short-lived. Anglers will tell you the carp is the most intelligent of fish. Wily, discerning, hard to bamboozle and quick to learn from any mistakes. Well, let me tell you, *I* am the most intelligent of fish; my fellow carp are at best very dull conversationalists, uninterested in anything bar eating and avoiding being eaten, and in all probability would lose a game of chess against a barnyard chicken. But of course my fellow carp don't have the benefit of being able to converse with humans, and to be fair they make a pretty good job of being fish.

Besides carp there were scores of other fish species, some familiar, some not. The ones that caused me a bit of concern were the sturgeon, because they could be so vast, and catfish, which were not only enormous but voracious predators into the bargain. I hadn't felt at risk from any pike for centuries, but the biggest of those moggies could certainly do me some real damage. They were easily capable of eating swans or dogs or any comparable animal. Fortunately, there was an abundance of bream, ide,[1] and Danubian barbel to preoccupy them, so as long as I kept my wits about me I reckoned I could keep out of harm's way.

Under normal circumstances I would've taken my time over the trip and done some sightseeing, but I passed through the Balkans with barely a pause. The splendour of Belgrade came and went, and I swam straight past Mohács, which had been razed in the course of a couple of recent battles anyway.

All the while the excess pounds were melting away from me, turning me from a sluggish pond-dweller into a torpedo-shaped, Olympian river carp. As any angler will confirm, river carp are one of the hardest fighting fish, while their endomorphic lake-bound cousins often behave like sedate old dowagers, disturbed during afternoon tea. Hup-two-three-four, on I ploughed.

I'd hoped to overtake the Ottoman fleet by the time I reached Buda, but as I approached the city the only boats I saw were normal run-of-the-mill river craft such as ferries and barges. On the left bank, Buda looked to be a lively, thriving city, with scores of grand houses and an imposing hilltop castle, while on the opposite bank, the township of Pest was obviously the poor relative. I swam up to a busy wharf on the Buda side to listen in for some information, but nothing had prepared me for the frustratingly opaque Hungarian language. Even with my grounding of French, English, Italian, Latin, Turkish, etc., etc., I barely understand a single word.

I turned to a Danubian barbel that was holding station in the gentle current. Barbel aren't exactly members of the aquatic brains trust, but it did manage to convey to me that there had been ships. Ships big. Ships many. Ships gone. To be honest the barbel had exceeded my expectations.

Promising myself that one day I'd return to learn that most baffling of languages, I continued my upstream journey, but even when I reached Bratislava, or Pozsony or Pressburg according to one's origin, there was no sign of the fleet. Although on the wharf-side a number of different languages were being babbled I didn't linger – I simply had to get ahead of the fleet.

When I finally caught up with it dusk was falling, and it had halted for the night. The ships were moored along both riverbanks, or anchored further out in the main flow, scores and scores of sleek galleys, seemingly extending as far as the eye could see. I realised it wasn't so much a fleet as an armada. I caught various snatches of conversation from the decks as I threaded my way between the vessels, as well as the clinking and clanking of ships' chains and the creaking of the rigging.

'Pretty tough, those Viennese.'

'Arquebusiers.'

'Carnage.'

'Had their chips now.'

'Won't know what hit them.'

'Tomorrow.'

'Ka-boom Christians.'

'Women.'

'Plenty loot.'

From these fragments it didn't take a genius to figure out that the Ottoman reinforcements were full of confidence and looking forward to some rather splendid rape, pillage and carnage. The fleet wasn't simply carrying fresh manpower and provisions, many of the ships were laden with high-grade ammunition, the finest arquebuses, which would be able to pin down the deadly Viennese marksmen, and large-bore cannon, that could actually penetrate the city's monolithic walls.

No more than a couple of miles after leaving the fleet behind me, I reached the fringes of the besieging army's encampment, which spread for miles over the razed approaches to the beleaguered city. It was now a cold night, with a mix of clear spells and the odd spot or two of sleet – not the sort of weather for fish to be very active, but all the same I had the feeling something wasn't quite right. Then it hit me: there were virtually no other fish around, apart from a few undersized roach, barbel and ide.[1] I knew the invaders had pretty much run out of ammunition and food, so I guessed the hungry soldiers had gone in for a spot of fishing to supplement their scant rations. A one-masted riverboat, illuminated by a brazier of glowing coal on its deck, bobbed on the water, its sail lowered. It was manned by two men, one hauling a net and the other propelling the craft via its large, gondola-like rear paddle. I remembered the Italian fishing boats in the Mediterranean used lamplight to attract fish; evidently a couple of the Turkish troops were trying the same approach in the Danube – or perhaps just keeping warm on a chilly late autumn night.

As for the encampment itself, along the riverbank the darkness was pierced by the flickering light of innumerable campfires, and from the water I could make out a forest of tent tops and plumes of smoke. The groups of soldiers visible to me looked dishevelled and beaten as they huddled around meagre bonfires or glowing braziers, while the wisps of conversation carried on the breeze were mostly drowned out by the groans of the sick and the cries of the wounded. Being a carp I had no experience of warfare and battlegrounds, but this didn't strike me as an all-conquering army, vast as it was. Little wonder they were in desperate need of reinforcements.

As I contemplated man's mania for self-destruction, I made the fundamental blunder of swimming straight into the riverboat's waiting fishing net, whereupon I was quickly and violently hauled up onto the deck and into the arms of one of the men. More than shocked and hurt, I was angry.

'*Putain de bordel de merde!*' I bellowed as the fellow tried his best to hold onto me. 'Leggo of me, you bastard! Piss off!'

Of course he was no match for thirty pounds of solid piscine muscle, even enveloped in netting, and my frantic thrashing about sent him reeling backwards into the glowing brazier in the middle of the deck, sending it flying and scattering burning coals everywhere.

Shrieking that I was a demon, spawned from the bumhole of the devil himself, the netsman scrambled to grab an iron bar to brain me with, but his companion, alert to the fact that a talking fish was probably the least of their worries at that juncture, grabbed him by the waist and sent the pair of them tumbling into the water.

Most sailors run a tidy ship, but these guys were soldiers and the boat's deck was anything but tidy – in fact on it lay a jumble of unfurled sails, large jars of lamp oil, bundles of kindling, additional dry nets, a couple of bags of coal and a case of illicit hooch, all of which very quickly contributed to a crackling blaze. I rapidly untangled myself from the net and executed a neat backflip into the water, then I looked on as the unmanned boat was carried downstream and away from the camp. Several soldiers on the riverbank stood and stared as the illuminated craft got smaller and smaller. They all agreed that that did not bode well.

The night watch of the Ottoman fleet's leading ship watched in fascination as the small light he'd spotted upstream grew bigger and bigger. By the time he clocked that something wasn't as it should be, the burning riverboat was already bearing down on him.

'Fireboat!' he yelled. 'Sound the alarm! We're being attacked!'

Trumpets were blasted and the message was relayed down along the fleet, the threat growing ever more exaggerated from boat to boat, thus the word spread like wildfire. By the time the warning arrived at the hindmost vessels, they were apparently under attack from an armada of fiery galleons, backed by an army of hundreds of thousands – apparently elephants were mentioned too.

Some of the ships desperately tried to raise anchor, the others to slip their moorings, all pretty much at once, and all very haphazardly. The result, naturally, was a crazy mass of collisions and gridlock, followed by the mother of conflagrations and a series of massive explosions – the fleet was carrying an *awful* lot of gunpowder. The night sky lit up like day.

The two official versions of that night's events differ surprisingly little. The Viennese, whose scouts had let them down appallingly, had no idea about the approaching armada and mistook the river-borne catastrophe for a spectacular thunderstorm. And rather than admit that the pride of Ottoman sea power had been allowed to go up in smoke in a matter of minutes, the official Turkish report on the siege of Vienna made absolutely no mention of the relief fleet whatsoever, and simply noted that there had been one helluva a storm that night. Nothing to see there. And of the two fellows whose spot of night fishing had contributed to the debacle, history is silent. They probably did the clever thing and deserted, like many hundreds of others.

The next morning, I saw that the besieging army was already starting to strike camp. The walls of Vienna remained un-breached, and Suleiman had regretfully reached the conclusion that a combination of dogged resistance, hunger, poor supply lines, draining morale, the bloody flux, and a score of other deadly ailments had rendered any further attrition pointless. Swearing he'd be back, he had ordered the retreat.

What struck me as I approached Vienna was the scale of its fortifications – great zigzagging battlements skirting the city, punctuated by roundels bristling with cannons. The enceinte was bordered on one side by the Danube, and elsewhere protected by a canal drawn from the river that acted as an encircling moat. On closer inspection the defensive walls were heavily pockmarked by cannon fire, and in some places it looked as if they wouldn't take much more punishment before collapsing. The air reverberated to the pealing of a hundred church bells as the burghers rejoiced. The quaysides thronged with people, and flags and banners fluttered from virtually every window of all the grandiose city buildings.

By rights I should've been welcomed as the Austrians' hero, but of course they had no idea of the imminent danger they'd been in, let alone that a talking carp had played a part in their deliverance. And, to be frank, I had rather mixed feelings about having inadvertently blown an unknown number of humans to kingdom come, even if by doing so I'd certainly saved the lives of many times more. Anyway, I didn't speak their language, so I was going to have to spend the next day or three swotting up the German tongue.

The next day, a great fanfare heralded the arrival of such a grand boat it could only be a royal barge. I couldn't yet follow what was going on, but several times I heard the name Archduke Ferdinand mentioned. With much pageantry the vessel docked opposite one of the city's grand gates, and was greeted by a deputation of dignitaries. Stepping down the gangplank, His Archdukeness was unmistakable: this tall young man had a crag-like nose and imposing lower lip, and was decked out in an ermine cape and crimson velvet jerkin and pantaloons – plus everyone else was behaving in a most obsequious manner towards him. The most senior of the city officials, the Bürgermeister, bowed low.

'*Willkommen zurück in Wien, Eure Majestät*,'[2] he grovelled.

Archduke Ferdinand turned to his chief flunky. '*¿Qué dice, González?*'[3]

'*Wir hoffen, dass Sie einen angenehmen Aufenthalt in Böhmen hatten, während die Kämpfe stattfanden*,'[4] said the burgermeister.

'*¿Qué?*' said the archduke.

'*Realmente no quieres saber, Su Majestad*,'[5] said the flunky.

That was great. Now I had another two new languages to learn. However, being a carp of moderate brain at least, I had little trouble gleaning one or two things from this exchange. Although he ruled Austria Ferdinand was evidently Spanish and spoke no German, and the good people of Vienna were less than delighted that their exalted ruler had bravely skipped off to Bohemia when the going got tough. Personally, I'm all for turning and running away to live another day, but I could see how the archduke might've been seen as dubious leadership material.

Over the following years I was proved wrong about Archduke Ferdinand. He added Holy Roman Emperor to his titles, acquired a far better hat into the bargain, and when Suleiman the Magnificent returned to complete his unfinished business a few years later, the Ottoman army was again repelled – this time without my assistance.

I stuck around Vienna for the next few decades, although my task of learning German along with some useful Spanish phrases had been accomplished in a matter of days. The winters in Vienna took some getting used to: being coldblooded my metabolism would slow right down, but I still kept myself safe and as long as I fed every few days I survived pretty well.

The city proved hard to leave because I was able to ascend various drainage channels into the centre and get my fix of human gossip, not to mention discarded odds and ends of pastries from the many fabulous bakeries as well. People would have us believe that a Viennese artillery officer named August Zang invented the croissant and its many delectable variations in the nineteenth century. I can confirm that is an absolute *connerie* – he found an old cookbook dating from 1517 and cribbed a bunch of recipes from it. Sixteenth-century Vienna was awash with delicious pâtisseries, as my expanding waistline once more bore witness.

I desperately needed a change of lifestyle, and that would have to involve another bout of travelling. I just needed a little bit of extra impetus to force me away from the pastries. That eventually came with the news – third- or fourth-hand admittedly – that a queen now sat upon the throne of England. Up until then the only rulers I'd come across had been men, and even though I'd become quite chummy with ex-King Harold for a while, they hadn't collectively impressed me very much. Would a woman make a better fist of it? Anyway, a few hundred years earlier I'd set out to visit London only to make a wrong turn and go to mainland Europe instead. Now it was time to put that right.

Notes

[1]The ide looks like a cross between a roach and a chub, and in large rivers can grow bigger than either. You'd eat one if you were hungry. Very hungry.

[2]'*Willkommen zurück in Wien, Eure Majestät*,' Welcome back your majesty.

[3] '*¿Qué dice? González?*' What's that he's saying, González?

[4]'*Wir hoffen, dass Sie einen angenehmen Aufenthalt in Böhmen hatten, während die Kämpfe stattfanden*,' We hope you had a very enjoyable stay in Bohemia while all the fighting was taking place here.

[5] '*¿Qué?*' '*Realmente no quieres saber, Su Majestad*,' What? You really don't want to know, your majesty.

Chapter Eleven

Perchance to fish. How Gisella returns to England, becomes friends with a modest genius, and helps create a literary legend for the ages

What can I say? Yet again I mooched along, meandered and dawdled, being a fish prone to procrastination. I'd say I was a fishy *flâneur*,[1] except I always had my destination in mind.

One fine summer's day I swam into a harbour that turned out to be in the port city of Cadiz. I'd taken my time journeying from Austria, several years in fact, and was becoming impatient to reach England and see how humans fared under a woman's rule. I wanted to catch up with the current affairs of the world before continuing my trip, and ships and harbours were always good places for overhearing idle chitchat.

The port was rather the worse for wear. The walls of the fortress overlooking its approaches were pitted with cannon shot, as were all the nearby buildings, and several burnt-out, half-sunken men-of-war blocked a good portion of the harbour. Most of the vessels I spotted were small coastal merchantmen or fishing boats, but as luck would have it supplies were being hoisted onto the one large galleon present. I sidled alongside to glean the gossip.

My patchy Spanish was a little rusty, but being fluent in French and Italian anyway, I had no problem following what was being said.

'Rather them than me,' said one of the dockers on the quayside, glancing up at the ship.

'There was me thinking you'd bend over backwards to join the fiesta,' said one of his colleagues. 'Where's your spirit of adventure, *amigo*?'

More dockers joined the discussion.

'After that friendly little visit we had from the Brits last year?'

'Ah, but they'll be joining an enormous fleet at Lisbon.'

'Making a reciprocal visit, *en el espíritu de la verdadera amistad*.'[2]

'Render unto Sir Francis Drake the gifts he brought to us.'

'Say what you like though, those English are fine seamen.'

'Explosive company you could say.'

'Absolutely! I reckon our *compatriotas* can count on a very warm welcome from our English cousins.'

'But our lads'll show them how to party. Warm English ale is small beer compared to hot-blooded Spanish sack!'

From what I could make out the Spanish were about to sail en masse to England on a spectacular fraternal visit. After witnessing so much skulduggery and warfare over the past few centuries, I was overjoyed that nations were willing to pour so much effort into what amounted to a massive gesture of goodwill; not only did I want to be a part of it, all I had to do was follow the great fleet of ships and I'd be led straight to my destination. Oh happy day.

As planned, the galleon from Cadiz joined a great armada of great ships that had assembled at Lisbon. There were both warships, with twin rows of cannon ports, and stout merchantmen, probably upwards of 120 vessels. When they arrived in England there was going to be one hell of a party!

All I had to do was follow the fleet, and by doing so I crossed the Bay of Biscay directly towards the British Isles, instead crawling all the way up the French coast until I reached the narrowest spot to cross the English Channel.

It was only as the armada approached the Lizard peninsula of Cornwall that I began to realise I might've just misread the situation a little. A cannonball pitched into the water just a few feet to my side. Bells rang, bugles trumpeted and lookouts shouted: the English astern, the English astern!

Of course swimming just under the water's surface I was the very last to see what was going on, but I soon pieced it together. First of all, the English weren't rolling out a red carpet. A much smaller fleet of English warships had set out of Plymouth, skilfully tacked against the hearty south-westerly breeze that had sped the armada towards the Channel, and had manoeuvred itself behind the Spaniards.

The English men-of-war, while smaller than their Spanish counterparts, were speedier, more nimble, and carried superior ordnance. It turned out that the Spanish were masters of close-quarters naval engagements, boarding and hand-to-hand fighting, while the English were content to stay out of their range and rake them with cannon fire. I was content to get the hell out of there.

While the sea battle – which in reality was more a succession of skirmishes – headed eastwards up the English Channel, I decided to head west. I still had a hankering to visit England after all that time, but reckoned I'd be better off avoiding the argy-bargy taking place to the east.

After rounding Land's End, I followed the coast of the southwest peninsula and headed into the silty Bristol Channel. I'd intended to make a stop at Bristol, but became rather distracted by the vast clouds of migrating elvers, which I found absolutely delicious. Before long I found myself being carried along by a fierce riptide and, as the surge of water was funnelled into the River Severn, a series of speeding waves formed. At first it was frightening, but after a few minutes I felt nothing but exhilaration as I was borne upstream at dizzying speed. Whee![3]

By the time the waves dissipated, I found myself approaching a city and racked my brain for its name, but as soon as I arrived at a long, busy wharf, my curiosity was satisfied. Ornately painted on the bow of a river barge was: *Candice-Marie – Gloucester.* Of course, I should've remembered my geography lessons, but maybe at 500 years old I was starting to go a bit gaga. I shook my head. *Putain!* I still felt fit as a fiddle.

Several small merchant ships and barges were unloading barrels and loading large bales, but many people were also clamouring to board smaller boats to journey upstream. The reason for this frenetic activity became apparent when a town crier mounted a crate on the dockside and announced the latest developments from the south of the country: an invasion force from Spain, a veritable armada, buoyed by an additional army encamped in Flanders, was expected to invade the mother country from one day to the next – and anyone who didn't fancy a forcible conversion to popery was strongly advised to leg it – or boat it – to the hills.

Everywhere I went seemed to be beset by conflict. Cold-blooded or not, it made my blood boil. You try to see the best in humans and then they go and— I fanned water through my gills and did my best to calm down. I'd come across quite a number of good, or at least okay, people in my time, it was just a shame that en masse they couldn't co-exist for more than a couple of years without resorting to barbarism.

Although it took place 500 years earlier I still had vivid memories of the Battle of Hastings, so I decided to follow the example of the Gloucester folk and head for quieter climes further up the River Severn. Leaving the city behind, I heard the doleful, reverberating chime of a single bell from Gloucester Cathedral – a sombre message to all that things were not well with the world. I pressed on.

As I neared another riverside town, my lateral line alerted me to the fact that the atmospheric pressure was dropping alarmingly. Right on cue rain started pitter-pattering down – the overture to a forthcoming deluge. Naturally a downpour wasn't going to send a fish scuttling for cover, but there are downpours and downpours. Although the worst of the weather was still centred on Wales, it meant one thing for the Severn – and that was a serious flood. I'd been caught up with one of those in the River Rhône and had no wish to repeat the experience, so I kept a sharp eye open for a calm tributary from the east to escape into.

At Tewkesbury there was such a river,[4] so I swung a right and found myself swimming past water meadows and fields of wheat and barley. Picturesque villages punctuated the river's meandering course, but soon the green and pleasant land was blanketed by diagonal sheets of rain. Gradually the water level started to rise, but I had faith that this river wasn't going to get anywhere near as angry as the Severn.

My steady progress came to an abrupt halt when I reached the pool of an impressive weir. *Zut.* There was plenty of natural food in the weir pool, indeed the numerous bream rooting about in the silty riverbed looked plump, hale and hearty, but getting stuck in the lower reaches of an unknown river with just dull-witted bream for company hadn't been part of my agenda. I wanted to avoid any chance of getting caught up in another war, but I also knew that if I spent any time there I'd end up so bored I'd beg the first fisherman who came along to catch me.

Then I became aware of a few other large fish in the weir pool. They were sleek and silver and flecked with tiny black spots and enviably athletic. They were salmon, and with the rise in the river level they weren't hanging around. One after another they zoomed towards the thundering weir and leaped up and over it. I was seriously impressed.

In my Topkapi and Viennese incarnations I wouldn't have considered trying to emulate those show-off *silver tourists*, but the last few years of negotiating powerful sea and river currents had left me in tiptop condition. I took several large gills-full of water.

Two sodden farmhands on their way home had stopped by the weir to gawp at the ascending salmon despite steady rain. 'Did'st see that?' said the first.'Did oi see what?' said the second.

'A carp. A bloody great carp just tried to leap the weir.'

'You're touched, Burt.'

'It were a carp, I swear it. Didn't make it though. Fell straight back down.'

'Your eyesight's going.'

'There it is again! Bloody hell, it's game!'

'Did you see any pixies too? The rain must've got into your brain.'

'Look! It's having another go! You must've seen it – it made it that time! Third time lucky!'

'Lay off the cider. They says it makes you see things.'

'Says Mr Hollow-legs, who gets home on his hands and knees every night! I'd say that's why you couldn't see it.'

And so they carried on bickering as they resumed their squelchy walk.

The rain eventually cleared, although it remained distinctly chilly for the time of year. I continued my ascent of the river through a pleasant landscape of cornfields and coppices, sleepy villages and enclosures of both sheep and cattle. A few more weirs blocked my path, but none that I couldn't scale. What I wanted to find was a nice little town, beyond any possible war zone, where I could eavesdrop some juicy gossip and filch some tasty human tidbits. Was that so much to ask?

At length I arrived at just such a town. A substantial bridge spanned the river ahead of me, while to the left-hand side of it was a higgledy-

piggledy mass of densely packed, half-timbered houses, and a large church that overlooked them from the vantage of a slight rise. To my right was a water meadow, filled with spiky sedge grass, kingcups and several cascading willow trees.[5] I thought that this would make a very pleasant place to stop, providing of course there would be no pitched battles, cannon fire or sieges to shatter the peace. Then it occurred to me that something was missing from this idyllic picture.

At first I thought that there wasn't a single human being in sight, but then I spotted a lone angler, slumbering in the shade of a willow on the meadow side of the river. He was a slight fellow, in his early twenties perhaps, with a silly goatee beard that probably compensated for the fact that his hairline was already in serious retreat. He didn't cut a very impressive figure, nor was he a very impressive angler. His rod was badly warped, and his threadbare braided horsehair line looked as if it would part if he hooked anything more lively than an arthritic gudgeon. Not that that was likely; on his hook was the most unappetising morsel of mouldy bread crust. Still, he looked a picture of perfect peace, and at least he didn't seem to be posing much of a hazard to my fellow fish.

'I thought as much!' bellowed a strident female voice.

The hapless angler awoke with such a start he slithered down the bank and into the water. At the same time a well-built woman, in her early thirties perhaps, strode juggernaut-like across the grass towards the water's edge. 'You can't hide from me, I knew you'd sneaked off again.'

It occurred to the angry woman and me at pretty much the same time that the angler wasn't trying to hide so much as drowning. Just feet from the riverbank the water was deep and the current perilous thanks to all the extra water, and without help the poor chap didn't stand a chance.

'Jesus bloody Christ!' exclaimed the woman, alarm now matching her anger. She made no move to leap in to the rescue, however, which I considered a mark of common sense. Swaddled in skirts, bodices and aprons she would've sunk like a stone – a pointless sacrifice.

Naturally I shot downstream of the fellow and then did my best to support him and keep his head out of the water. Rather than try to hang on to me, though, he flailed around like an electrocuted eel, and nearly took one of my eyes out. 'Just hang on, you idiot!' I shouted. He continued to flail but somehow, in spite of his efforts to batter me to death and drown himself in the process, I managed to guide him back to the shore, a good 200 yards downstream from where he fell in, where a strong pair of hands grabbed him under the arms and heaved him up onto dry land.

I was exhausted. '*Nom de dieu*,' I gasped. 'Some people just don't want to be helped.'

People display a wide variety of reactions when they hear me speak for the first time. This formidable matron was taken aback for a brief moment, but then answered me in a very matter-of-fact tone. 'That's a fact – this feckless wastrel will do absolutely nothing to help himself. I don't know why I bother with him, I really don't.'

The young man sat up and coughed out some more river water. Then he shot me a surprised look, but thought better of saying anything.

'He needs taking home and warming up,' I said. 'I hope your – son? – will be all right.'

'He's my husband actually, but don't worry – it's an easy mistake to make.'

'I'm perishing,' said the shivering young man, stating the blooming obvious.

'Get yourself home and get out of those wet things,' said the woman. 'I'll follow anon.'

Still dripping, the fellow sloshed off across the meadow towards the bridge, shooting me repeated uncomprehending looks as he went.

'It's not every day one meets a talking fish,' said the woman. 'A fish that talks with a foreign feminine lilt to boot. What brings you to our fair—' A sudden and almost calamitous pealing of church bells stopped her in mid-sentence. 'Something's afoot,' she exclaimed. 'Pray it's not the Spanish. I must away, but promise me you won't go anywhere. I'll be back when I can. The chance for discourse with a large, bronzed, lopsided fish is irresistible.'

Before long I saw excited, joyful people streaming from the town's streets and onto the river embankment. Bells continued to ring, flags were waved and hats tossed into the air. Whatever was afoot, I guessed the Spanish weren't about to come marching in after all.

A good couple of hours later the lady returned to the meadow and updated me on events. Not only were the Spanish not invading the realm, their armada had been roundly defeated and put to flight. The English navy had attacked the invasion fleet with fire ships and broken their formation, but what had really done the damage was the great storm that had broken after the English had withdrawn to re-provision, whereupon the would-be invaders had been scattered and driven out into the North Sea. Many had sunk, and many more were no longer in any condition for combat. The threat was over.

After hearing the wonderful news from the town crier, Anne had returned home, swaddled her husband in blankets and given him warm milk laced with mead and honey. Then she'd hurried to renew our acquaintance.

She was eager to know all about me, so I gave her the concise version: that I'd been touring Europe for half a millennium in search of...some kind of enlightenment maybe? Upon hearing a woman was on the throne in England. I had returned to these shores after a gap of nearly 200 years, to see if the feminine touch was any better than all those male rulers.

'Actually, good Queen Bess is our third in a row,' said Anne. We were on first-name terms by then. 'The first one only lasted a few weeks, the second was a tyrant, and Elizabeth is passably good – at least in comparison.'

'I heard her dad was a real stinker.'

'And not just to his wives. He really wasn't a good advertisement for the institution of monarchy, but one isn't supposed to say that, even now. How can I put it? The current regime is still tyrannical, but in a much more pleasant way.'

'Don't worry, not a word of this shall pass my lips. So, stating an opinion out loud isn't a recipe for a long and healthy life?'

'Oh you can – just as long as you're smart about it. Put it in a play or a poem, preferably one that no one understands, then you're not in danger. If no one reads it, you're doubly safe.'

'There speaks the voice of experience, I guess.'

'You could say that.... I write a bit, but being a woman of course I have no audience. Nobody reads anything by a mere woman.'

'So much for *Matriarch Regina* – I expected better with a woman ruling the country. Being a writer without an audience must be frustrating.'

'I'm bursting with ideas, but what with having to take up the slack because Willy's such a useless lump, I don't get the time I'd like to put pen to paper.'

'You and him. I don't mean to be rude, but I just don't get it.'

'An arquebus wedding, I'm afraid. All the result of too much mead during a Midsummer's Eve revels. I really don't know what got into me.'

'Hmm, I've got an inkling.'

'Smutty fish.'

'Don't pretend that you're shocked. What does he do, anyway?'

'Precious little. He flits from job to job, but he's such a slacker he invariably gets the heave-ho after a few days. I knew he'd got the boot from the tannery when he didn't come home stinking yesterday, and finding him out fishing wasn't the most brilliant bit of detective work. He loves his fishing, even if he seldom comes home with anything. The only thing he has any talent for is mimicry, but that doesn't make money and I'll wager it'll get him into real trouble one day. He's got the common sense of a toasted crumpet. In the meanwhile, I have to try to make ends meet. I cook pies, sew garments, craft ditherwhimsies and the like for wealthy visitors – anything for a few pence. And that's all on top of being a mother of three young children.'

'And you write as well.'

'When I can find the time. But over the years, I suppose I've built up quite a collection of work.'

'Could you read me some? I'd really like to hear what you do.'

'Now I'm shy. It's not very good, really.'

'*Bon courage*, what've you got to lose?'

'You'll laugh at me. Besides, I'm hopeless in front of an audience.'

'Really? I took you for a modern, self-confident woman, someone who doesn't suffer fools gladly.'

'Exactly.'

'All right, all right, if you don't want to you don't want to. But why bother writing then?'

'Very well. You're right I suppose. I'll bring some samples tomorrow. But don't be too hard on me, I'm only an amateur.'

'Don't worry, I'm only a fish. I'll be nice, I promise.'

I had to wait until midday the next day, but then Anne appeared at the riverbank with an armful of parchments. 'You're sure about this?'

'Of course I am. Living in a river one can get a little starved of culture.'

'Very well, I'll begin with a sonnet.' Looking very uncomfortable, she cleared her throat. I tried to look encouraging, but when you're a carp it isn't that easy.

'Shall I compare thee to a drizzly day?
Thou art plainer and more desolate.
Rough winds do shake the wither'd buds of May,
And dank, wet summers really grate…'

Anne paused to gauge my reaction. 'It's meant as an ode to a young man.'

'I'd guessed that.'

'It's terrible, go on, you can tell me.'

'You could end up with a black eye, but it's not terrible. Could do with a tweak here and there, but you're definitely onto something. Go on, I want to hear it all.'

Anne completed the sonnet, and then read me an excerpt from one of her historical plays, Henry VIII Part I.

'I think you're good,' I said. 'Some rough edges…could use a bit of tidying up…a few word changes here and there…and maybe penning a hatchet job on Henry VIII is a tad unwise after everything you told me.[6] Maybe go back a few Henrys? You should be safe enough with, say, the Fifth? But – and this is speaking strictly as a cold-blooded freshwater fish with no literary background whatsoever – I think you have a real talent to work with.'

Anne nodded eagerly.

'Right. We're going to go over everything – everything you've written. We're going to make sure your artistry dazzles even the most severe of critics, then we'll think about getting your name out there in lights. Your work will inspire generations, you'll show the world a woman can write as well or if not better than any man. The capital will fall at your feet.'

Anne suddenly crumpled. 'If only. But I don't think fame and fortune is going to work for me. I'm plain Anne Shakespeare (although everyone still calls me Annie H hereabouts), mother of three, provincial housewife. To be frank, the idea of having to adopt a whole lot of la-di-dah airs and graces with a lot of windbaggy bigwigs in London fills me with horror, although I wouldn't say no to living a little more comfortably.'

'What about posterity?' I gasped. 'What about the empowerment of women?'

'Oh I want my work to be known – I want people to read my poems and attend my plays – it's just that I don't need to be the one taking the credit.'

Anne could see I was dejected.

'I'll carry on writing, but we should let the world believe Willy's the author.'

'Seriously?'

'Don't you see? I'm a homebird and Willy will love all the hobnobbery down in London. He might make a halfway decent actor to boot – he can schmooze with the nobs and I'll churn out the scripts. That's as long as you'll still help me cross the t's and dot the i's.'

If I had arms to cross I would've crossed them.

'Please. If we make a success of this Willy will send me money – he's a plonker but he won't dare cross me – and I'll be able to live comfortably doing what I love. We know women can do anything men can, but we'll have to wait a little longer for the world to wake up to it.'

I gave in. What else could I do? We spent most afternoons during the following months tidying up Anne's work, and, to be honest, the basis was already there for some truly memorable creations. Naturally Willy was brought into the scheme, and did his best to pull his not very considerable weight. He cooked and cleaned and looked after the children quite a bit of the time, and didn't seem to mind the ridicule directed at him by friends and neighbours, who thought him an effeminate pantywaist. In fact he wasn't a complete numskull; he simply had the attention span of a stickleback, and no aptitude whatsoever for creative or innovative thinking.

The following spring Willy was despatched to London with a satchel full of manuscripts. I was despatched to Lechlade in a large wooden crate, crammed with sopping pondweed, with instructions to the courier to revive me with a tot of whisky prior to dumping me in the River Thames. The plan was I'd keep an eye on him, and prevent him from selling Anne's work for the price of a tankard of porter.

Talking of reviving liquids, I have to confess a decent single malt makes a very fine alternative to all the French variations of firewater, but perhaps a decent *hors d'age* Armagnac remains my favourite. That said, the Scotch did a sterling job of setting me to rights and I started my swim down the river towards the capital in fine spirits. It had been agreed that Willy and I would meet up at the foot of London Bridge in a month or so's time – he was to look out for me every morning.

It almost broke my heart having to bypass Oxford without stopping and chinwagging with many of the learned souls from the university. I imagined all the fascinating conversations that must've been taking place on the grassy riverbank, before a backdrop of dreaming spires, as I allowed the current to carry me on my journey. I earmarked the city for a future visit.

The river meandered pleasantly through the Thames valley and past the towns of Reading, Slough (which was more of a village really, and not one I had any compulsion to stop at) and Windsor, before speeding up at a place called Teddington, where I sensed the unmistakable turbulence of rapids ahead of me. Worryingly powerful ones. Although there was much slacker water to either side of them, I'd left it too late to get out of the main flow, so I braced myself, and, trying to keep my nose pointing downstream, was swept into the very worst of them. Through a maelstrom of white water I shot, narrowly avoiding several large, submerged rocks, and then scraping my belly along a rough, gravelly riverbed. I'd made it with no more than the odd bruise. Naturally my chief worry was lost scales, but I was pretty sure they were still intact.

There was now an unmistakable tang of salt in the water, brackishness, which told me that I was now in the tidal reaches of the river. My fellow fish downstream of the weir were the usual suspects, roach, bream, pike, perch, etc., but with the addition of a few flounders – those little flat fellows who look as if an anvil has been dropped on top of them, who swim up from the sea. I knew the big city was now only few hours ahead of me.

Mindful of my dubious track record with bridges, I was extremely circumspect when I passed under London Bridge. Although perhaps not the largest bridge I'd ever seen, it was certainly the most impressive, supporting something like 200 buildings, up to seven storeys high. Some were shops, others residential, even palatial-looking, and its central roadway was permanently thronging with people. More than just a bridge, it was like an entire township on stilts. If I brought that one down there really would be hell to pay.

Naturally, with so much waste ending up in the drink from it, from privies in particular, the water downstream of the bridge wasn't a particularly nice area to hang about in. Most fish gave it a wide berth, except for a shoal of grey mullet, who, let's face it, sometimes have pretty disgusting eating habits. Those silver tourists, migrating salmon and sea trout, hurried through as quickly as their fins could propel them. Myself, I put up with the putridness for the sake of great art. You could accuse me of putting on la-di-dah airs and graces, but a promise was a promise.

It was on my tenth morning of hanging about below the bridge that Willy finally deigned to turn up. Naturally I greeted him very curtly, but the insensitive clod remained oblivious to my grumpiness. I asked him how his hobnobbing had progressed, whether the literary and theatrical worlds had embraced the Shakespearian genius yet.

'Good progress, good progress,' said Willy. 'I've already got a theatrical agent.'

'That's a start,' I said cautiously. 'So are any of the plays being performed yet?'

'Not yet, actually. Sig said I needed to make a few changes.'

My lateral line tingled an acute warning. 'Such as?'

'Well, there are far too many words in the plays, audiences will just get bored. And we need song and dance routines, lots of singing. Music. Fiddles, trumpets, sackbuts. That kind of thing.'

'Really. You don't think Anne and I may have something to say about that?'

'I reckoned you might. That's why I asked Sig to come along.' Willy put two fingers to his mouth, gave a sharp whistle, and a bouncy little chap in an overstated velvet outfit and oversized ruff came bounding down the riverbank. He too had lost much of his hair, but compensated for that with such a growth of facial hair it was next to impossible to guess his age.

'Sig Poliakoff, theatrical impresario at your service,' he beamed. 'So this is the famous talking fish I've heard about, such a pleasure to meet you. I've been telling this schmendrick he needs more pizzazz in his work. Words, words, words, the punters get tired of words really fast. You lose them in the first few minutes and you never get them back.' If he was surprised at meeting a talking fish, he gave no outward sign of it.

'Harrumph,' I snorted. 'So you're suggesting we tear up months and years of hard work in order to add some trilling and clodhopping.'

'Precisely, my scaly, French-sounding friend. No entrepreneur ever got poor by aiming for a really low common denominator. Give folk a good belly laugh and set the feet tapping – that's how you clean up.'

'And supposing, just supposing, Willy makes a change or two, have you found a theatre for his material?'

'Early days, early days. Trust in Siggy, I have fingers in all sorts of pies.'

'So that's a no, then. And do you have a contract with Willy yet? Anything on paper?'

Sig proudly flourished a tatty piece of parchment. 'Right here. All shipshape and in order, signatures on the dotted line.'

'Can you hold it closer? I can't see the small print properly.'

Sig obligingly held the shabby little document right in front of me at the water's edge. 'It says something here about ten per cent,' I said. 'So there's some kind of fee involved?'

'Finder's fee, paper fee, transport costs, catering, ink fee, my valuable time. It all adds up.'

'So, in the end, if I'm not in need of spectacles, Willy gets ten per cent and you get ninety?'

'No need for specs,' the beaming Sig nodded. 'An amicable arrangement and a win-win situation. Our boy is destined for great things!'

Willy, bless him, looked as if he was counting sheep. Like I said, the attention span of a stickleback. I realised Anne would ignite like a barrel of black powder if she got wind of this arrangement, so I took action. With lightning speed for such a large fish, I leapt from the water.

'Aie, aie!' Sig bellowed to Willy. 'Your fish just ate our contract!'

The parchment was horrible and I knew it would play hell with my digestion, but it was a price worth paying to preserve the Shakespeares' prospective legacy.

Sig recovered his composure with admirable speed. You don't keep Sigs down for long. 'Ah well, easy come, easy go. Wait!' He clasped his head in his hands. 'The act to end all acts, and it's right in front of my nose!'

Willy and I peered at Sig sceptically. At least the scales had been removed from Willy's eyes regarding Mr Poliakoff.

'I can see it now,' Sig clapped his hands together delightedly. 'Siggy and his amazing talking fish! Yes! You could sing too. And wear a little costume! Audiences will love it. I – we – will be a sensation. The theatrical phenomenon of the decade, even the Queen will come and see us! Here, quickly, let me draw up a contract!'

Sig needed deflating and he needed deflating fast. 'We could be a sensation or we could get done for witchcraft.' I'd stopped Sig in his tracks. 'Not everyone's as, er, broad-minded as you, Sig. Folk are superstitious. We could easily end up hung, drawn and barbecued for our efforts, I'm pretty sure that would draw a crowd too.'

'Perhaps you're right,' Sig sighed. 'It's not as if the Sigs of this world don't have to tread carefully at the best of times anyway. What a duo we might've made though, huh?'

Willy and I nodded sympathetically.

'And singing-and-dancing Shakespeare plays are out too I suppose?'

Again we nodded.

'I guess it's back to cheap card tricks and flogging impotence potions again. But fear not for Siggy, for something always turns up.'

'By this time Willy and I were feeling quite sympathetic to old Siggy.

'Before I go, one thing. I don't know why I'm telling you this because it can't possibly profit me, but they frequently perform boring stuff like yours at James Burbage's[7] theatre, at Shoreditch. It's actually called *The Theatre*. It may be worth taking your stuff to him. Can't do you any harm, anyway.'

The rest, as they say, is history. Anne had hit after hit in The Theatre, fronted of course by Willy, who became quite an accomplished actor thanks to his talent for mimicry. Learning lines wasn't his forte, but with much prompting he gradually trained his mind to master several parts.

After a few years at The Theatre the company moved to the Globe, by the river, and gained an ever more enthusiastic audience, including Queen Bess – although to my chagrin she remained one of the monarchs I never got to meet.

I'd usually run the rule over the manuscripts Anne sent from Stratford, but she no longer needed any input from me. Perhaps I'd helped to boost her confidence in those early days, but as writers go she really wasn't too shabby at all. She also produced a prolific quantity of sonnets, nearly all of which were published and immortalised. Who hasn't got their favourite? One that wasn't published, for very obvious reasons, would still make me blush if carp could blush. My memory is hazy, but I recollect that the first few lines went like this—

'My fish's scales are nothing like the sun,
Coral is far less pale than her eyes' pale;
If snow be white, why then her belly's dun;
If weeds be wires, long wires dangle from her tail….'

It still brings a tear to my eye.

Notes

[1] *Flâneur*. One who wanders in a pleasant, aimless way. Usually in Paris, but not always.
[2] *'En el espíritu de la verdadera amistad,'* In the spirit of true friendship. The previous year a small English group of ships under the command of Sir Francis Drake had launched a sneaky attack on Cadiz, destroying a large portion of the Spanish fleet. Rather fancifully this episode is known as Singeing the King of Spain's Beard.

[3]It seems that Gisella had surfed the Severn Bore, a sport that wasn't to gain popularity until centuries after.
[4]From Tewkesbury Gisella entered the Warwickshire Avon. Actually, there are three River Avons in England, the Hampshire Avon, the Bristol Avon and the Warwickshire Avon, so when people talk about the river Avon they should be specific, because one can't be a mind-reader.
[5]Stratford-upon-Avon, as it happens.
[6]Ann very wisely took Gisella's advice and scrapped her Henry VIII plays.
[7]James Burbage was one of the first great actor/impresarios. He created the second purpose-built theatre in the land, 'The Theatre', and one of the first repertory companies of actors, 'The Lord Chamberlain's Men'.

Chapter Twelve

No smoke without fire. How Gisella hits the road, enters the not so glamorous show-business industry, encounters a compleat angler, and becomes involved in a conflagration that changes the face of the capital

I became accustomed to hanging around the big landing stage where people alighted from riverboats to visit the Globe Theatre. I deeply regret that I never found a way to attend any of the performances, but I was able to gauge that Anne Hathaway's plays were enormously successful. Through courtesy I was still encouraged to run my eye over all new work, but of course I had nothing to add to such works of genius.

All manner of people attended the theatre – royalty, traders, nobles, soldiers and streetwalkers. And food stalls selling chops and sweetmeats and ribs and puddings and pies sprang up all around the venue – who says fast food is anything new? Fortunately for me, Elizabethan folk weren't all that litter conscious, and all sorts of half-eaten tidbits ended up in the water. Even the dumbest flounder or bream got to know when punters streamed out of the Globe and set about guzzling discarded greasy treats, but there were plenty of tasty pickings for all.

Of course I met with Willy quite frequently, and was most impressed by how he'd grown into the role of playwright / poet / actor. In fact, he was quite unrecognisable from the hapless bumpkin who skived off menial jobs in order to dangle a line in the Avon. He never got too big for his boots, however, because he was always aware that the goose that laid the golden manuscripts could always switch off his supply.

Willy was also kept in line by the threat of wifely visits to the theatre. On one occasion in the autumn of 1602 Willy, who was playing Ophelia, happened to spot her in the audience, and when they met up for a chat after the performance she left him in no doubt that she could reappear at any time. In other words, if he indulged in any showing-off or facetious ad-libbing she'd know about it. He nodded; message received loud and clear.

Anne made sure to seek me out and we had a very convivial catch-up, but her distaste for the capital remained, and I believe that was the only occasion on which she actually made the trip.

Anyway, sadly, that was the last time I got to meet her. I fully intended to return to Stratford, but the complexity of the journey always put me off, I'm ashamed to say. I'd swum to Vienna after all, so a short trip to Warwickshire shouldn't have been that daunting, but during that time I'm afraid inertia got the better of me. Time took its toll on Willy, and apparently there was some mirth at his leaving Anne his second-best bed in his will. Actually, that was one of his little jokes, for over the years the income from her writing had allowed her to live in great comfort – she was just never flashy about it.

The Globe continued as the capital's must-visit theatrical venue until it burnt down following a production of *The Tempest*. It was rumoured that the fire was started by a doddery retired admiral who wasn't too careful where he tapped his pipe. After all, no-smoking rules were still centuries off, but that was just a rumour.

For a few years I was at a loose end. I meandered up and down the London reaches of the Thames, but didn't make contact with anyone who might've shown me the bright lights of the big city. There were crowds, noise, great buildings on both sides of the river, frivolity, gaiety and drama, but I remained an onlooker who couldn't actually see very much.

It was when I was making a nostalgic visit to the landing stage near the spot where the Globe Theatre had stood that a vaguely familiar voice hailed me.

'Oi, fish, over here!' It was a beaming, bearded, bouncy gent, over-dressed in clothes that might have been fashionable several decades previously. With him was a much younger facsimile, albeit with more hair on his head and less on his face.

'*Ça alors*,' I laughed. 'If it isn't Sig Poliakoff. Well bless my fins!'

Sig introduced me to his son, Sol (I'd never have guessed!), and confessed that our meeting wasn't exactly an accident. He'd been looking out for me for quite a long time in fact, because he'd had an idea. He was going to make me an offer I couldn't possibly—

'The answer's no,' I said.

'Oi, such an attitude! At least hear me out. It's true, I've never quite been able to forget the idea of us forming a double act. We'd be great, no one would ever have seen anything like it!'

'And when we're eviscerated for demonic practices we'll draw quite a crowd too.'

'No, no, no, bear with me. I've thought of a way around it. We do our double act, a few tricks and jokes and witty repartee, but we pretend it's a ventriloquist act. We pretend it's really me speaking. Come on, a carp that performs tricks will be a sensation in itself, and no one will be able to accuse us of witchcraft. It's a trained animal act. You get acrobatic dogs, prancing ponies, dancing bears. Why not a fish?'

'Pop's right,' said Sol. 'It can work.'

'And just how am I supposed to appear on stage?' I said. 'In case you missed it, I breathe water.'

'No problem,' beamed Sol. *Nom de dieu*, he was a chip off the old block. 'I can build a big tank for you, three sides caulked planks and one side good quality glass. We mount it on a drop-side wagon, and that'll serve as a stage.'

'You can really make a tank like that?' I asked.

'I'm good with my hands,' said Sol.

'There's already a travelling fair that's interested in taking us on, we could really make a go of this.' said Sig.

'Sounds to me like you're already counting your chickens,' I said. 'Isn't that a bit presumptuous?'

'Such cynicism from a fish. If you prick me, do I not—'

'So you've seen that play too.'

'Indeed, and I've a bone to pick with Mr Shakespeare. all that stereotyping, such a *kolboynick*...[1] But no matter. Yes, I tested the water, and I'm sure we'd get the punters rolling in.'

'Keep talking.'

'Think of it. The carefree life of a travelling performer.'

'I have a carefree life as a carp.'

'You'd get to travel the length and breadth of the country, visit places you could never reach just stuck in rivers, take in all the sights.

Come to think of it, how much do you see, swimming about under the water?'

Sig's relentless hard sell was wearing me down and I confess that his point about my restricted sightseeing struck a nerve.

(A fishy digression here, please bear with me. You'd think that swimming in a river we'd have a very restricted view of what happens on the riverbank, but that's not quite the case. Because of the refractive index of the water's surface, light always travelling in straight lines except for when it doesn't, etc., our field of vision is rather greater than you'd imagine. That's why when an angler is keeping low, trying to stalk a trout for instance, he still gets spotted and the fish vamooses. Even dumbos like trout. Lecture over.)

Okay, so I get to see a certain amount above the water, but never as much as I want to. High riverbanks, embankments etc., forget it. I had to admit it, Sig was chipping away at my resistance.

'Imagine, Gisella, we'll visit the most wonderful places, see the most beautiful sights, castles, cathedrals, mansions, mountains, forests – or you can continue marking time in the Thames with roach for company, waiting for someone to chuck in a rotting apple core.'

'*Assez!*' I exclaimed. 'I submit. You talked me into it. Just don't try to con me with any dodgy contracts – you remember what happened last time.'

'My face is red. No contract. This is a three-way thing, you, me and Sol, all equals, hand on heart.'

My tank and our wagon were ready within a month, and we journeyed to join Surprendo's Travelling Fair on a common near the village of Hampstead, a few miles to the north of London. Oh, brave new world! For centuries my only overland travel had been in boxes packed with pondweed, and I didn't miss it. (I quite missed my tots of Cognac and the like, but actually Sig soon spotted my weakness and would provide a modest hit of vodka at the end of a hard day. Vodka was never my favourite tipple, but Sig retained a taste for it because it was what his forebears used to drink back in Białystok.) I feasted my eyes on all the overground sights, and we reached the fair's encampment far too soon for my liking.

The larger-than-life Signor Surprendo might have been Spanish or Italian or Romanian or anything to the south of Dover, he was a towering figure in the most flamboyant clothing, which was an enormous contrast to the more toned-down fashions of the day. He twirled his magnificent moustache and asked us to show him what we could do.

We were abysmal. I don't even remember our repartee, but it was certainly banal beyond belief, and my *tricks* amounted to my leaping a couple of feet into the air and landing back in the tank. Bravo.

To our amazement, that's exactly what Signor Surprendo cried out. He applauded wildly and told us that the ventriloquism was absolutely first rate – or *bellissimo* – and a carp doing tricks on command was astonishing. It was time to meet the rest of the troupe.

I suppose the fair would be called a circus in the modern age, but back then circuses hadn't been invented (unless you were an ancient Roman), and rather than assemble in a big top all the acts took place in separate booths, tents and wagons. The fair comprised of food stalls, selling sweet and savoury snacks, Madame Belnitziskaya the fortune teller, Zoltán the fiddler, Cedric the strongman and prize fighter, Franz and his prancing Pomeranians, Ejigu the Abyssinian juggler, Igor and his melancholic dancing bear, Yi-Bei the acrobat, Ferenc and Kati from the Hungarian Puszta with their balletic horses, plus various spouses and children, who all played a role in the running of the operation – and now Siggi and Gisella, the amazing "talking" carp, the newest members of the troupe. They were very precise about the inverted commas.

Sig and I were well aware that we had to up our game regarding our performance, so we set about widening our repertoire with a degree of urgency. Sig had an able wit, however, and I had a knack for picking things up, so we soon cobbled together some sort of routine. I mastered some intricate backflips in my tank, and perfected my aim in squirting mouthfuls of water at patsies in the audience.

The Rights of Man and Fish

When we put on our first public performance we were all nerves. For all his chutzpah, Sig was breaking new ground, and I don't think many carp had performed on stage before me. After Ejigu had done his juggling turn, Signor Surprendo ushered the public towards our wagon and lavishly introduced our act; my tank's curtain was pulled back and I found myself facing perhaps seventeen surly-looking, very rustic punters. Eek!

Dressed in his finest, swinging a walking stick, Sig swallowed hard and then launched forth. 'I say, I say, I say, my wife's gone to Northern Italy.'

'Genoa?' I stammered.

'I should say so, we've been married for twenty years.'

The was a deadly pause, punctuated by a few gasps.

'I say, *mon brave*,' said I, 'what did the bald man say when he was given a comb?'

'I don't know, what did the bald man say when you gave him a comb?'

'He said *I'll never part with it!* Boom boom!'

The audience was mesmerised.

'That lopsided fish, it's actually speaking!'

'You can see its mouth moving, it's real!'

'Incredible!'

'It can't be!'

'It's the old fellow, I saw his beard twitch.'

'That's a weird accent he's putting on.'

'Girly. And foreign.'

'They ain't half good though.'

Sig ploughed on. 'I know a man with one leg called Frank.'

'*Pas vrai!* What's his other leg called?'

'Rubbish!' cried a member of the audience, who just happened to be Cedric the strong man, loosely disguised in a long coat and floppy hat. I leapt three feet into the air and blew a mouthful of water several paces, right into his face.

How did our meagre crowd take to this sophisticated fare? They loved it. I strongly suspect that even our rather lame banter had gone over most of their heads, but that wasn't important. They roared with laughter and applauded until their hands were sore. The other acts continued and folk danced to Zoltán's frenetic fiddling – he reckoned his playing was very much in the *cigány*[2] tradition, but that was being very kind – we'd cleared our first hurdle, and were still feeling pretty high when the fair wound down for the night and Sig, Sol and I said our goodnights over a nightcap of vodka.

Our next performance was at the village of Kilburn, where we played to an audience of thirty. Again, their reaction could hardly have been more enthusiastic. On we went, Barnet, Stanmore, Rickmansworth, Uxbridge, and then the thrill of playing in Watford. Everywhere, folk came out to see us and marvel at the incredible talking carp. Of course, they were reassured that it was the little old fellow who was really doing all the talking, but it was such a novel act that the rubes just loved it.

Naturally my tank needed cleaning out every few days, and refilling with fresh water. Sol, who acted as a kind of jack-of-all-trades and understudy to his dad, carried out this job without complaint, and every time we passed close to a river or pond I was released into the water to zip around like a demented dace for an hour or two. The tank was grand and I was seeing the world from a completely fresh vantage point, but it also made me feel a little stir crazy at times.

Nights in front of a campfire were intimate and fun. Our wagon would be pitched a little way from the others in order to prevent the secret of my unique gift being revealed, but fortunately no one appeared to take umbrage at that. We'd feast on leftovers from the food stalls, enjoy our tots of vodka, and talk of our personal histories and whence we came. I kept my 600-year history mercifully brief and vague, but it turned out that the Poliakoffs were just as well-travelled as I was.

Following a performance during which an uncouth lout had shouted at Sig to go back where he came from (he'd answered Shoreditch, actually), Sig and Sol explained how their family had its roots in Białystok, in Poland / Lithuania, but a succession of pogroms against the Jews there had forced them to leave. The family had gone on to Bohemia, then Hungary, then the Ottoman Empire, then Italy, then Spain and then France – and in every one of them the treatment of them and their kind had forced them to move on. The Poliakoffs had finally washed up in England, where Henry VIII, that kindly old monster, had recognised that having a few Jews around made sense for the kingdom's economy, and was prepared to tolerate them. Sig's father had been a shoemaker, but he himself had never shown an aptitude for it. Nor for banking nor for trade, which some would have you believe all Jews have a talent for. After the death of his wife Deborah from the typhus, he'd tried his hand at a host of things without finding his calling, which is why he and Sol had ended up on the fringes of what would now be called the entertainment industry. So some oaf telling him to go back where he came from was therefore like water off a duck's back. Of course, there were still people who believed that Jews were in league with the Devil and ate Christian babies, but Protestants and Catholics were mostly too busy hating one another to waste much energy on a handful of Semites. He and Sol still quietly observed the odd Jewish festival such as Hanukkah, but they didn't make a song and dance about it. You keep your head down and you make a living, what are you gonna do?

I noticed over time that Signor Surprendo was giving me the odd sidelong, questioning glance. Naturally I wondered if he'd cottoned on to our little secret and resolved to be on my guard. Then, one evening, following a particularly well-received show, he wandered up to my tank and told me I'd excelled myself.

'Why, *merci, monsieur,*' I blurted out. *Merde!* I'd gone and put my fin in it now.

'Well, well,' he chuckled. 'We all suspected there's more to your act than meets the eye for some time now. Good old Siggy's become just a bit too blasé; if you're going to play at being a ventriloquist it's best not to be stuffing your face with lardy cake at the same time. But don't worry, your secret's completely safe with us – after all, we're all outsiders from all over Europe and beyond, so what difference does it make that you're a carp? We're troupers and we stick together.'

I bubbled out my relief. It had been awkward keeping quiet among this lively and friendly group, but now we'd be able to take part fully in the social life of the fair.

We melded into the most tightknit of bands, a true ensemble in every sense of the word. The next few decades were at the same time terribly hard work and extremely happy. I'd met all manner of humans up until then, but I could honesty say I'd never found such honest, faithful and worthwhile people in all of my 600 years.

Father Time took his toll, and Sig, after a short period of decrepitude and deeply distressing senility, passed peacefully one night in his sleep. Signor Surprendo was the next to go, never really recovering from being bitten by a wild boar that had been scavenging some food waste. Mortality can be so tragic and banal at the same time. Sol replaced Sig and our act continued, while one of Signor Surprendo's nephews took up the master-of-ceremonies mantel. Performers left and performers joined, the fair endured.

Having performed at a village not far from Stratford-upon-Avon, we were about to hit the road when distant cannon fire has heard. A fleeing family of farm labourers told us that Parliamentary and Royalist forces were going at it hammer and tongs at Edgehill,[3] and if we had any sense we'd make ourselves scarce too. We didn't need telling twice.

Being outsiders, we never had a very in-depth knowledge of the issues at stake during the Civil War, save that the Parliamentarians believed that parliament should be the supreme power in the land, and King Charles, being a king and a firm believer in the divine right of kings, believed it should be him. The sheer barbarity of the fighting, town turning on town and neighbour betraying neighbour, ensured that any sympathy we may have had for either side was completely lost.

We went about our business. People still needed entertaining, perhaps even more now that the rest of life appeared so grim and tenuous. It didn't matter if a community had parliamentarian or royalist leanings, folk flocked to the fair and spent a few hours enjoying some good old unsophisticated fun.

Even those supporting Cromwell's side were shocked when King Charles was beheaded, and the country braced itself for living under the New Order. Puritanism held sway. The frivolity, vulgarity and sheer lewdness of the *ancien régime* was anathema – if that wasn't too much of a papist word.

Was that the death knell for Surprendo's fair? Of course not. Unless you were born a killjoy you still wanted to let your hair down from time to time – laugh at some tomfoolery, dance to some raucous fiddle-playing, marvel at a fish that appeared to be speaking – those things were hard to suppress.

We still trod warily, mindful that there were always going to be some zealots who equated entertainment with Devil-worship, but we survived the Commonwealth[4] intact and rejoiced at the Restoration – which meant that although the nation was again ruled by someone whose position owed everything to his family connections, we were no longer fearful that some jumped-up martinet was going to have us closed down and imprisoned – or worse.

One early summer's day, after we'd put on a show at Walthamstow, just to the north of London, I was enjoying a few hours' R and R in a sluggish stretch of the River Lea. Close by I spotted a middle-aged gentleman, soberly dressed, who was fishing with a very clear air of expertise. Cautiously, and staying deep enough to avoid being seen, I took a peek at his terminal tackle. A finely braided horsehair main line, swan-quill float weighted just-so by a few split lead shot, catgut trace and a sharp hook baited with a large pinch of honey-dipped bread. I was right, this chap was no dilettante.

My attention was then taken by a largish pike that hovered nearby, clearly intent on ambushing some roach. I told it in no uncertain terms to push off, and after it had grumpily shuffled away all hell broke loose as a large tench made a silly mistake with the angler's bait and was hooked.

I watched, fascinated, as battle commenced. The angler's rod hooped over as the tench shot out towards the middle of the river, but the line held firm. Steady pressure told on the fish, so it kited to one side, aiming for the sanctuary of some willow branches that drooped down into the water. Sudden side strain turned its head, making it change directions and plough back into open water, where the struggle turned into a war of attrition: any line gained by the angler the tench recovered, to and fro, back and forth. It no longer had the strength for another rush, but it wasn't ready to give up the ghost quite yet either. All of a sudden it turned and belted towards the bank, where it wrapped the line around a sunken root and left the angler resigned to an inevitable snap-off. Off the tench swam; I knew it would work the hook loose within a couple of days and be none the worse for its narrow escape.

If the tench's triumph wasn't altogether unexpected, the angler's response certainly was. Instead of cursing, he put his rod down and applauded wholeheartedly. 'Oh bravo, sir, well fought!'

He examined his severed line and found it coated in fish slime, a tell-tale sign of the species that had escaped him. 'Of course, a *Tinca tinca*, one should never underestimate a tench.'

I couldn't resist it, I had to have a word with this most refined of fishermen. Popping my head above the water I said, 'You're quite right of course, those *Tincas* are the most resourceful of fish. Except for us carp, of course.'

The angler landed on the seat of his trousers, but quickly recovered his composure. 'Goodness, who would've thought it: a talking *Cyprinus carpio*, of quite enormous proportions, and from *la belle France* if I'm not very much mistaken.'

'*Exactement*. Gisella, at your service.'

'Izaak Walton, angler and gentleman.'

'I couldn't help noticing your, er, unusual reaction to losing a big fish.'

'But was it not magnificent? At no point did I think it would get the better of me, yet I'm now convinced it was playing me rather than the contrary. I doff my hat to it.'

'I've always understood that you humans catch fish in order to eat – in that respect you're little different from other carnivores, whether mammals, birds or fish – but for you yourself, it's about the pursuit rather than the result, isn't it?'

'I hadn't quite considered it that way but you're right. It's the sport of it, the art. You see I find fish endlessly fascinating, in fact I love them.'

'You have a funny way of showing it.'

'Yet it's true. For me, and many others I'm certain, fish are the most mysterious and wonderful of God's creations. Would that I could spend my entire life studying them, and catching them too of course.'

'So you worship us and bait hooks for us.'

'I suppose that's hard to explain to a fish. In fact it's hard to explain to anyone who isn't an angler. But I fish for the joy of observing, understanding and handling such beautiful creatures, and keeping them to eat is of little importance to me. I just as often return them to the water, for making the capture is the crux of the matter rather than the aftermath – although I confess a plump trout pan fried with butter and almonds can be a temptation.'

Mr Walton made a good case, and truthfully I didn't feel we carp had a metaphorical leg to stand on. We're not above eating small fish from time to time, even if we're not quite killing machines like those uncouth pike.

'You say it's hard to explain angling to non-anglers. Have you tried?'

'I confess not, and it's definitely a failing. Fishing has given me decades of the most refined pleasure, and I should probably attempt to share that with the world.'

'A book perhaps?'

'I'll call it *The Competent Angler*. Or maybe *The Contemplative Angler*.'[5]

Loath as I was to leave this fascinating conversation, I realised it was high time for me to go and rendezvous with Sol. I knew he'd start to fret if I was very late.

'I'd keep an open mind on that title if I were you, but good luck with the project and take care not to cast at any carp. If that tench gave you a going over, just think what a big carp would do.'

By the 1660s Sol had left his youth far behind, and he and his wife Miriam had a strapping son called David, who of course was learning the family trade. While theatre, song and dance, and of course travelling fairs, were once more a boom industry life should've been rosy, but another less savoury industry was also enjoying a revival: witch-finding. Some said it was a way of finding someone to blame for the plague pandemic that had broken out in many cities – something the circus had avoided by keeping to rural locations – but in my opinion, it was a plain old mix of superstition, sadism and misogyny.

Everyone had heard of the feared Matthew Hopkins, the country's unofficial Witchfinder General, but he had an acolyte called Peter Glyssop, who was if anything even more fanatical and ruthless than his mentor. It was said that he had a particular hatred for people's grans, in other words he was a grotesque misogynist, but in fact he saw sorcery in anyone he took exception to, and had all sorts of ways of 'proving' it.

As luck would have it, when we were preparing for a show in Hungerford, word reached us that Glyssop was in town and planned to attend. That was enough for the Poliakoffs and me, our wagon was hurriedly packed for travelling, and with the setting sun we made to leave the camp. Alas, we were too late.

If one has any preconceived ideas about what a zealous witch-finder should look like, Peter Glyssop didn't match them. Mine had been of a gaunt, puritanical figure with long ratty hair, hollow cheeks and the thinnest of lips, but here was a jovial-looking chap, decked out in the latest flamboyant fashion, sporting a wig that must've cost a clerk's monthly wage. Unlike his band of sombre, horrid-looking followers, he was grinning from ear to ear.

Sol, David and Miriam were seized, and the rest of our comrades told to stay back or suffer very serious consequences. The witch-finder turned to me and told me he'd been looking forward to this rendezvous for a very long time. That the show's ventriloquism act was a sham was by then a very badly kept secret, and he intended that the talking fish should suffer a prolonged and grotesque punishment for witchcraft and being in league with the Devil.

'You've got it all wrong,' Sol protested. 'I'm simply brilliant at throwing my voice.'

'So you say this scaly creature is just an ordinary fish, that does tricks?'

'Exactly.'

'What do you say, fish?'

Naturally I kept shtum.

Glyssop drew his sword. 'And if I run you through and eat you for my supper, what do you say then?'

'*Putain de merde!* Okay, I can speak, but I'm no witch. I'm just an ordinary, er, talking fish.'

'That's more like it,' Glyssop grinned.

'I'm willing to undergo trial by water. You know, if I float I'm a witch but if I sink I'm innocent.'

'You must think I was born yesterday. There's no need for a trial; a talking fish is by nature an abomination in league with dark forces, and even worse, you're a foreigner.'

There were boos, hisses and catcalls from his followers.

'Now, stand back and let justice—' The sudden, unmistakable cocking of flintlocks stopped him in his tracks. He and his men – they were all men – stepped back as a new group took centre stage. They looked truly sinister. They wore long, dark cloaks, masks that obscured their faces, large medallions that depicted a wild boar's skull within a pentagram, and, perhaps most importantly, they all carried rather lethal-looking firearms.

Most of us had no idea who these newcomers were, but Pete Glyssop clearly did. 'Opus Azazel!' he croaked.

(Another little digression: since Tudor times secret societies had flourished in England. Some were Protestant, some Catholic, some even atheist, and some just plain barking. Some were quite well known, such as the Freemasons and the Knights Templar, but most of them you probably haven't heard of. That's hardly surprising because they were secret societies.)

These guys were well organised. They clearly knew all about me and had prepared for this intervention very meticulously. I was manhandled out of my tank and placed in a crate filled with wet pondweed, so evidently my captors weren't planning to bump me off immediately. For some reason, that didn't fill me with optimism. I presumed my companions were unable to do anything to help me, and neither were Peter Glyssop and his goons for that matter. Very soon I felt the bumpety-bump of being transported in some sort of carriage, and little by little I slipped into that beastly semi-comatose state I hadn't been subjected to for centuries.

At length I came to. Although I was still in my crate, fresh water was being poured over me and someone gave me a tot of whisky – very superior whisky as a matter of fact. I managed to focus my eyes and saw that I was in what could only be a very large kitchen. Racks and racks of bottles lined an entire wall, while all manner of cooking implements hung on another. I could make out there was a great fire burning in the recess of another wall, with a spit for roasting suspended over it, and a big cauldron to one side. Had I been invited for dinner or was *I* the dinner, that was the question?

One of my captors, sans mask now, leaned over me. Beneath his cloak he wore fine, crimson velvet, his jet-black hair – his own, not a wig – was bunched up behind his neck and he sported the most magnificent, pointed moustache and beard. I could say he looked positively diabolic.

'As you've probably gathered, you are now the honoured guest of the Opus Azazel Society, Lucius Grimwood at your service.'

'Guest or captive?'

'Both, *Madame*, or is it *Mademoiselle*?'

'Let's cut the *conneries*, I have a feeling that's going to be immaterial before long.'

'They told me you were intelligent. That's why we went to such pains to get hold of you. That and the fact you have a magic gift of speech, and have mastered several languages.'

'You want me to teach you German? Italian? I can teach Turkish too if you want.'

'Very droll, my dear fish. In a way we want to make use of your gift, but it's more your magic that we're interested in.'

'Ah.'

'You see we're an occult society, with a keen interest in demonology. We're also *bon viveurs* and devote much of our time to fine dining, heavy imbibing – hence the unique collection of the finest malt whiskies – and the most degrading debauchery. We're quite sure Old Nick himself approves of what we get up to.'

'I'm no expert on religion, but aren't you a bit worried about the burning torments of Hell once you drop off your perches?'

'Not in the least. That's where all those churchy types get it completely wrong, you see. The Devil approves of sinning, and by Beelzebub we all break the Ten Commandments on a regular basis. We're rotten to the core. So do you seriously think that when we pop our clogs the Devil's going to punish us? Quite the opposite, there's a special corner of Hell reserved for us where we'll live in utmost luxury for eternity. We'll be his VIP guests.'

'I see. And where do I fit into this hare-brained scheme if yours?'

'We want your polyglot magic so we can travel across Europe doing foul deeds, and to do that we're going to eat you.'

Merde. I suppose that being a large fish I'd always run the risk of ending up on a serving platter, but I still felt this was a pretty pathetic end to my 600-year story.

'I have some pre-prandial lechery to attend to,' Lucius continued. 'But wee Jock here will see to everything.' Wee Jock was a hairy six-foot-seven giant in a kilt and a pinnie. 'What are you going to prepare for us, Jock?'

'Carpy-leeky,' he grinned. 'A delectable ragout of freshwater fish with leeks, pearl barley and neeps. It'll be a triumph.'

'I have no doubt,' Lucius smiled as he turned to leave. 'I'd say *au revoir*, Gisella, but I'm afraid it's plain old goodbye.'

Once we were alone, I told Jock he didn't have to do this.

'Och but I do, they'll have my guts for garters if I let you go. But, here's an idea. Maybe a wee tot of the hard stuff afore ye go?' He took a dusty bottle from one of the racks and uncorked it.

'I wouldn't say no. And it would be impolite of you not to join me.'

He poured a generous measure of whisky into my mouth and then necked his own glass.

'Nice,' I said. 'But it didn't quite hit the spot. Another little one maybe?'

'Aw, there now. I'd promised Kate I was off it. But you don't often get to cook a talking carp, and this really is a quite delectable wee drop. So what the hell.'

Many, many Scotches later Jock could barely stand and I was pissed as a newt. He made the decision he'd better cook me before he passed out and attempted to lift me out of my crate. I'd love to say that I made a heroic bolt for freedom, knocked the giant Scottish cook flying and made good my escape, but of course that would've been completely absurd.

What actually happened was that I was too slippery for the sozzled Jock to hang onto so he dropped me, and I went skidding over the floor and into all the racks of whisky, which came crashing down and smashed all over the flagstones. I was dazed rather than hurt, while Jock just blinked uncomprehendingly. A pool of neat single malt radiated across the kitchen floor until it met the crackling fire, and a few little blue licks of flame started to rise from it, just like flamed brandy on a Christmas pudding. But that was just the phony war. With a great whoomph the kitchen was suddenly filled with flames and smoke, and Jock immediately sobered up and took to his heels. Not having legs I was at a disadvantage, and kind of remember having thought that at least those mad bastards never got to eat me before I blacked out.

I came to outside in a city street, being carried by David, who, as it turned out, had covertly followed my carp-nappers and waited for an opportunity to rescue me. Several buildings behind us – most of them were wholly or part wooden – were already ablaze, and panicking Londoners were fleeing. I looked up at a street sign and saw that we were just about to leave Pudding Lane.

I think I was just about on my last gasp when David rushed me down a set of steps and dropped me gently into the Thames. Naturally I couldn't see what was happening on dry land, but I didn't have a very good feeling about it.

'It's bad, isn't it?'

'It's bad.'

'Very bad?'

'You can see it spreading before your eyes. It's going to engulf the whole city by the look of it.'

'People are getting out?'

'It's a stream of humanity. Folk are salvaging what they can, but mostly it's just a case of grabbing an armful and running. It's an inferno.'

'Maybe this is what the city needed to get rid of all the plague breeding grounds. A reset. A cleansing, even.'

David shot me a withering look. Of course he didn't buy it.[6]

Fortunately it was low tide, and David was able to make his way to safety by following the riverbank downstream. I accompanied him but our mood was sombre.

We reluctantly agreed the time had come to move on. There was no going back to our carefree fairground life, and anyway, David admitted he'd always enjoyed his hobby of working with leather, and was thinking of taking up the old family tradition of shoemaking.

As for me, I felt the call of the continent. I didn't know if wee Jock had got out of the building in time – I rather hoped he had, although I suspected that his employers were even then discovering whether or not their theory about receiving a convivial welcome in the underworld was quite correct – but if he had survived then perhaps the world would know that the culprit for the conflagration was an inebriated carp. It's also quite possible people would smell his breath and conclude he was both drunk and doolally, but that wasn't a risk I was prepared to take.

Having said a fond goodbye to David I set off towards the North Sea. Waters and pastures new.

Notes

[1]*Kolboynick*. Schmendrick. A stupid person, a jerk, an unfortunate.
[2]*Cigány*. Hungarian Romany. A form of virtuoso violin playing, but evidently not in all cases.
[3]The Battle of Edgehill, 23rd and 24th October 1642. The first major engagement of the English Civil War. The result was a stalemate, allowing both sides respite to regroup for more subsequent butchery.
[4]The Commonwealth describes the period between the execution of Charles I and the restoration of the Monarchy when England, Scotland and Ireland were governed by Parliament as a republic.
[5]Sir Izaak Walton wrote 'The Compleat Angler', the most famous fishing book of all time.
[6] The Great Fire of London, 1666. It did in fact generate a massive bout of urban renewal. Thank Gisella for that.

Chapter Thirteen

A year in the life of Gisella Carpova. How Gisella discovers how harsh a northern winter can really be, witnesses the founding of a great city, and inadvertently helps quell an uprising

Retracing the route I'd taken 300 years earlier, albeit in much kinder weather this time, I eventually found myself scenting the muddy aroma of what I now knew was the River Rhine. Left, right or straight on? Eeny, meeny, tiny scale, catch a minnow by the tail. It appeared I was turning left.

After a couple of days, the cliffs and beaches to my right-fin side gave way to what looked like an enormous, manmade seawall, that carried on for mile after mile. I soon reached a great sluice gate in it where a vast amount of fresh water was being pumped into the sea, which intrigued me greatly, but waiting for high tide to see if I could swim through it struck me as foolhardy. The chances were I'd end up chewed to pieces by the mechanism – which surely was designed to expel an excess of fresh water from within, while keeping out seawater and stray fish. I carried on along the sea wall.

Another couple of days saw me rounding a large, low-lying headland, and entering a wide estuary that split into several branches. Here there was plenty of shipping, a veritable rush-hour of ocean-going vessels, coasters and sturdy barges, so I simply followed the traffic and found myself entering a great harbour, protected by a very low jetty that extended for at least a mile. Behind the jetty was another expanse of water, this time dotted with barges and much smaller craft, which were sailing to and fro between the larger ships and the entrances to four wide canals, that led into a most handsome-looking city.

I swam into one of the canals and saw that to either side of it were tall, almost stately brick-built houses, several storeys high. There was a constant exchange of goods between the boats and the buildings, busy-ness everywhere, and a collision of smells that was almost overwhelming.

There were three main canals in the city, but these were interconnected with several lesser ones. Different areas dealt with different trades, I soon found out, some of them not at all nice to be near, but when I picked up the heady aroma of fenugreek I knew I was heading into the spice district, and I'd found my home for the foreseeable future. Fenugreek, cinnamon, cloves, pepper, star anise, nutmeg. My kind of place.

Hanging around the barges I soon picked up the lingo. It wasn't hard, a bit like someone with a heavy cold speaking German. I learnt I was in Amsterdam, and ships from Amsterdam traded pretty well all over the world – thus the imports of exotic spices from East Asia. I also learnt that Amsterdammers like pastries, and odds and ends of rather nice treats were always ending up in the water. All I needed to make my stay perfect was a little intelligent company and conversation, but no opportunities presented themselves, so I prudently kept my own company for a few years. Winters were colder than I'd been used to and the canals would ice up for weeks at a time, in spite the locals' best efforts to keep them clear for trade. What I found most strange and disturbing was the sound of people skating on ice above me – it played hell with my lateral line.

Gradually I felt my wanderlust creeping back. Maybe it was the knowledge that ships leaving the port were travelling to destinations all over the world, but old Amsterdam was getting awfully familiar. I was also intelligent enough to know that while I was reasonably comfortable pootling around the coasts of Europe, any ocean voyage was bound to be fraught with peril. I wasn't about to allow my natural curiosity to lead me into the belly of a whale, thank you very much, so travels to far-flung exotic shores were a non-starter for this stick-in-the-mud carp.

It was then that fate stepped in. One balmy summer's night, when all respectable burghers had gone to bed, my repose was shattered by the sound of inebriated singing on the quayside. Followed by a big splash.

Naturally I swam to see if I could give the tipsy reveller any assistance, and discovered him foundering badly under the weight of his sodden clothing, and grasping for something to cling onto. He grabbed onto me with a degree of desperation that was really painful, so I told him not to be such a bloody *klootzak* and let me guide him to the nearest steps. That shut him up and thereafter he was as docile as a lamb.

Once he was sitting on the top of the canal-side steps to get his breath back, the fellow looked almost sober again. A shock's good for that.

'Did I really hear you speak, or was it that sneaky *aquavit*?'

'It was me all right. You could've saved me a tot of that hooch, you know.'

'Urgh. Never again. I'm not used to knocking back that much.'

'Then what did you do it for?'

'We were celebrating. A group of us are setting off to help build a new city way up north tomorrow, so we decided to let our hair down a little.'

'Really? And where is this brand-new city?'

'On the fringes of Russia – or what were the fringes of Sweden until very recently. The Russian Emperor, Peter, wanted a port on the Baltic Sea to open up trade with the rest of Europe, so he captured a remote Swedish fort on the mouth of the Neva River, and he's having a new metropolis constructed there on virgin marshland. We're engineers, and being Dutch we're experts at land drainage, canals and the like. My own speciality is building pontoon bridges – I just love 'em.'

'A complete new city on a swamp. *Incroyable!* That's one hell of an undertaking.'

'Vast. Enormous. The emperor drafts in tens of thousands of serfs and soldiers every year to carry out the work, but we have his personal assurance that they're fairly paid for their labour and well-treated. Otherwise we'd certainly have thought twice about signing up.'

'So that's why you were sozzled.'

'We heard the Russians like their vodka. We thought we'd better get in training.'

'Don't get too well-trained, or you may never build that city.'

The engineer got gingerly to his feet. 'Better catch an hour or two. Don't want to miss the coach.'

'You're going overland, not by ship?'

'Take a boat and we could be attacked by the Swedes, travel by coach and it could be brigands. We're going to take our chances with brigands.'

'Best of luck.'

'My name is Piet van Klarrt, if our paths should cross again. Thank you for saving me. Tomorrow I probably won't believe this ever happened.'

I reckoned there was a reasonable chance that our paths would cross again, for the lure of more travel and seeing a brand-new city rising from swampland was more than I could resist. I'm a carp who likes to have a plan.

My journey northwards was most pleasant. After rounding the Danish peninsula I found myself in a very different sea, with minimal tides and very low salinity. It was most refreshing. Apart from the fish one would expect to meet at sea – flounders, cod, herring – I now started to encounter pike and perch and zander and bream – all very much freshwater fishes. What a strange place.

Gdańsk, Riga, Tallinn, all places I would've loved to stop and get to know, but my curiosity about the new city rising from the swamp kept me swimming. Late summer in the Baltic, the sky was blue and the sun twinkled, but increasingly I began to notice it was lacking real warmth. So it wasn't the Mediterranean, *ben alors*, but I wasn't complaining. I was covering new water, with more discoveries to be made.

I passed many vessels sailing in both directions, but there was no sign of any aggression from any quarter, so I thought back to Piet van Klarrt, and hoped that he and his colleagues hadn't made a mistake in choosing to travel to St Petersburg by road.

It was another fine autumnal day when I finally approached what could only have been the nascent city. It looked as if two river estuaries entered the sea about 200 yards apart, and on the land sandwiched between them stood a redoubtable fort.

A little exploration showed that the fortress was actually on the largest of three islands that stood in the delta of the Neva River estuary, and the twin estuaries I'd first seen were actually just the two largest branches of the watercourse. While I couldn't see a great deal of what was taking place on dry land, it was obvious that the most massive construction project was taking place.

The riverbed reverberated to the thud-thud of wooden piles being driven deep into marshland to form the foundations for future buildings. Elsewhere, on two of the islands, some buildings were already in various stages of erection. The grandest of them were being built in brick and stone, but most were wooden. Also, on the north bank a much larger, stone-constructed edifice was going up. This had to be the head honcho's crib, the Czar Peter's place.[1]

In at least two spots it looked as if canals were being excavated, and a large port area was being built. So far, all the visiting cargo ships were having to drop anchor in the sound, and unload their cargoes onto smaller boats for bringing ashore, so the sooner some proper wharves went up the better. While in some places oozy mud was being scooped up from the riverbed, in others boatloads of rocks were being dumped into the water to provide a more stable riverbed. Everywhere there were boats, big boats and little boats, scuttling like water boatmen. I could understand why Piet and his companions had been hired. In the long term proper bridges would no doubt be constructed, but in the meantime a temporary solution had to be provided, and a pontoon bridge or two would save many thousands of precarious boat trips.

All this labour required labourers, and at any time hundreds upon hundreds of workers were engaged in various menial, backbreaking and frequently hazardous tasks. To a human they may have resembled ants, but to me they were more like water fleas. Zip, zip, zip, hither and thither. And all these unfortunates were overseen by armed guards who didn't hold back in cracking the whip. I had a feeling that when my soused engineer learnt that the workforce was well looked after, he'd been sold a big pack of *conneries*.

I was able to swim fairly close to many of the worksites without being seen, as the water was constantly churned up and muddy, which is how I quickly picked up the basics of Russian. Although the language was quite unlike any of the others I spoke, the conversations I was listening in on ('Put your backs into it, scum!' and 'Aargh, what happened to my leg?' and so on) weren't exactly complicated. I soon felt that if necessary I'd be able to communicate with the locals.

Although most of the ground being developed was indeed very marshy, as I'd been told, some areas were obstinately rocky, and where shovels and pickaxes and blood, sweat and tears failed, gunpowder was used. I wished someone had warned me. As I swam past a granite outcrop there was a vast bang, my swim bladder nearly burst, and I came within inches of being sushied by falling rocky debris. In a blind panic I shot away, instinctively heading towards the quietest water I could find.

It took me a fortnight to recover. I'd ended up in a very calm, shallow and reedy backwater, far from the building work and mayhem of the emerging metropolis. Although there were water beetles, worms and crayfish to eat, food appeared to be getting scarcer day by day. That, it dawned on me, was because it was getting colder. Much colder. The sky had gone slate grey, and a few fat flakes of snow were wafting down. I thought it would probably be wise to get my bearings before I ended up iced-in.

The snow quickly intensified, and I could see it was settling thickly on the frigid ground beside the watercourse. Along the shoreline I eventually came across a vast shantytown of the roughest hovels, most of which were made from discarded building scraps and torn old tents. The whole area was fenced in, but its gate hung wide open; I thought it looked like some sort of prison, but with neither inmates nor guards. It looked like hell on Earth, except in this case hell had frozen over.

Then I saw the camp was in fact inhabited – after a fashion. A few lost-looking souls wandered aimlessly in the snow, their clothing – worn and torn animal pelts and assortments of rags – by then almost perfectly camouflaged in the white-out.

One of them, clearly skeletal even under his bulky garb, shuffled his way down to the riverbank to fill his canister with water. Even under his heavy beard – all the inmates were similarly hirsute – I saw his eyes were listless and jaundiced and his cheeks deeply sunken. He looked about ninety.

I was appalled and, caution be damned, I felt I had to speak to him. 'Who did this to you? What is this place? Is it a prison?'

The inmate looked up, his senses so dulled that not even a talking fish got a reaction out of him. 'It's the Melenski labour camp. One of many.'

'You mean you're working on the construction?'

'We were. Until it shut down for the winter. It appears the snows have come early this year.'

'But there are so few of you. What's happened? You look as if you've been in a war.'

'At least they kill you quickly in a war. We've been left behind to die because we're too weak to travel. Everyone else has been sent home.'

'That's appalling! Isn't there no one from your home who can help?'

'Ha! Even if there were, it would take them all winter to reach me. I come from a small village called Gornopravdinsk, on the River Irtysh. It's near the Ural Mountains – and about as far away as one can go.'

Tears started to well up in the poor man's eyes. I didn't interrupt him. 'I was the schoolteacher there – or so I liked to think. Of course there isn't a school as such there, but I did my best to teach the rudiments of reading and writing to anyone who was interested, which amounted to a mere handful. But, as the bastard son of a count who must remain nameless, I had leisure on my hands and a love of books that I was keen to share. Anyway, when they came for men they weren't too fussy about who they grabbed. That mad Aleksandr Denisovitch, whose nose is always in a book, who can't see a barn door without his spectacles…' (I suspected his spectacles were long gone.) '…taken by the Tsar's soldiers to break rocks and dig ditches – God sometimes has a very strange sense of humour. I sometimes wonder if I've been missed; I think I was quite well-liked, for even although many of the villagers had no time for reading and writing, and regarded me as slightly cracked, they all loved a good story. And I told a very good story. And I won't be going back there.'

I said nothing. There was nothing I could say.

'Enough of that,' Alexandr said. 'It was all a lifetime ago, even if it was only months. Now we eat. I presume you're hungry, *Mademoiselle Poisson.*'

'Yes. I mean, have you enough? Did they leave you food?'

'Have no worries on that score.' Alexandr turned and trudged away into the whiteness.

I wondered whether he'd gone to fetch his fellow inmates. I wondered whether they had a mind to include fresh carp in a diet that can't have been gourmet fare. Unworthy fish. He soon returned with a large bowl of some sort of grainy mush.

'It's millet. That's been our mainstay all the time we've been here. It's not even good millet, it's riddled with creepy crawlies, and because of the wet it started fermenting ages ago, but at least it's plentiful. Our supply will outlast us, that much is certain.'

He placed several handfuls of the stodge in the margin, and I gobbled it up. I had to admit the fermentation and all the bugs enhanced it greatly as far as I was concerned, but I appreciated it probably wasn't to most humans' tastes.

Even as I finished eating I was aware of the cold intensifying. Alexandr saw the peril I was in at the same time that I was making up my mind to move on. No need for me to perish too, he told me, the backwater would be frozen solid within a couple of days, and I needed to find deeper water. I should continue eastwards, and I'd soon find myself in Lake Ladoga, where I'd be able to over-winter in safety. I said my inadequate farewells to this gentle, kindly man, but how to you say goodbye to someone whose days, and maybe just hours, are very strictly numbered?

Lake Ladoga was nothing short of an inland sea. When I entered it, its surface was mostly ice-free, but that changed within a couple of days, and I found myself in an eerie, silent and mostly dark aquatic wilderness. This was a bit of a culture shock for a carp who enjoys a certain amount of hustle and bustle and good company.

I soon discovered that away from the shore the lake was immensely deep, and I had no intention of exploring any watery abysses and meeting whatever terrifying beasties that might've been lurking down there. I soon found where I was most comfortable, in areas about ten metres deep, over silty lake beds.

(Pause for a very short scientific explanation about icy lake water. The layer of water just under the ice is beastly cold and no sane fish would hang about in it. Then there's a transitional layer called the thermocline, where warmer and colder water mixes, below which all the lake water remains at a constant four degrees centigrade, however cold it gets above the ice.)

Naturally I chose the four-degrees water, at a depth that didn't squash my swim bladder too badly. It can be so uncomfortable. Although my metabolism had slowed down considerably, I was still able to scratch about in the silty lakebed for the odd aquatic worm or bug when I needed nourishment, and thus I adapted to life under the ice.

Why didn't I try to leave the lake? Well, for a start everywhere was iced over, and that certainly included the River Neva as it passed the new city. And actually, I didn't feel like it. In the chilly Ladoga water, I simply felt lethargic and demotivated – a carp suffering from existential gloom. Do I want to eat a worm or not this morning? Pah, *je m'en fous.*

Of course I wasn't alone. A variety of fish lived and ate and were swallowed under the ice, and for the most part they seemed far less affected by the chill than I was. I guess they were used to it; I felt very effete and southern. There were several unfamiliar species, including something like a northern vendace[2] that was disgustingly lively in the cold, plus sedate sturgeon, cold-eyed zander, packs of marauding perch and psychotic pike. Thankfully none were quite large enough to view me as prey.

There was occasional activity above the ice as well. Passing horses and sleighs, and anglers who bored holes in the ice and bamboozled gormless carnivores that somehow mistook shiny bits of metal or feathers for small fish. More fool them. But mainly it was a quiet existence and, as winter advanced, a very gloomy one. I could really understand why so many humans liked to overwinter by the Mediterranean.

Days and weeks and months passed, and little by little my mood improved as the mornings and afternoons became lighter. The onset of spring at last. I've heard about how northern people, Scandinavians and Russians, go a bit bonkers when the sap begins to rise, and, after having spent a winter in Lake Ladoga, I can well understand them.

One bright afternoon my lateral line was assaulted by crashing, grinding and booming sounds that made me think the lake was under an artillery bombardment. Of course, it was the ice melting and breaking up, which appeared to be a trigger for the pike and perch to get very frisky, and me to have a good old forage for some delicious, crunchy crayfish. Things were looking up, my appetite was returning.

While I was keen to see what was going on down the Neva at St Petersburg, I also found it very hard to drag myself away from the glut of new life that abounded in the lake's margins. Reeds and water lilies were growing almost before my eyes, and pondweed seemed to reappear pretty much overnight. For the delectation of a large carp, crayfish and freshwater shrimps and succulent water snails abounded, while insect larvae, big juicy insect larvae, were emerging everywhere. If I were inclined to be pretentious I could've called this Brasserie Ladoga, but heaven forbid.

After a month of grazing and gorging, I finally decided the time had come to swim west. It wasn't hard to find where a slight movement of water turned into a current, and by following the current I eventually left the lake and found myself in a wide river – which could only be the Neva.

My river cruise was most pleasant, with unexpectedly warm sunshine drawing me to the surface, from where I could see the distant verdant, tree and scrub-lined riverbanks slipping by. Because the river was so deep there was little weed in it, and it was still early in the year for much weed growth anyway, but the sun's rays on water that was heating pretty rapidly had the effect of producing a sudden and extensive algal bloom which, if left unchecked, would soon start to cause problems. Islands of clogging algae were floating downstream.

Was I worried? I was too preoccupied with sunbathing to care. After four days I reached the point where the river started to split into different branches – the river delta – which meant that I was approaching St Petersburg. Whether I'd intended to or not, my course remained bang in the middle of the main channel. I was now caught up in an iceberg-like clump of cloying, unctuous algae, my back exposed to the air, sun and breeze. *Merde*, my slothfulness had left me appallingly vulnerable.

I soon heard voices, and saw that ahead of me a major algae clearing operation was taking place. Men on oversized skiffs were frantically hauling up great wodges of algae with boathooks, rakes, shovels and anything else that came to hand, and dumping the slimy, oozing mass on the riverbanks. I then saw why. Downstream from them the current sped up, before reaching a most impressive impromptu bridge that spanned the river in the distance, linking the main island, on which stood the fortress, with the north bank, where a mass of impressive, classical buildings already dominated the skyline. The pontoon bridge, which was composed of scores of barges moored side by side, and spanned by a wooden roadway, carried a bustling mass of men, horses and carts. My old acquaintance Piet had evidently been very busy. The clean-up crew was obviously trying to prevent the mass of algae from reaching the bridge, because while the structure looked reasonably sturdy, it was already carrying a considerable weight of traffic. A very risky weight of traffic, by the look of it.

It occurred to me that there was an abnormal commotion taking place on the bridge, and given the choice I'd rather get away from my yucky green raft than get swept right down in it. Obligingly a couple of strong pairs of hands hoicked me up into the air and into an algae-filled boat.

'What a whopper!' cried one of the boatmen.

'It'll feed the lot of us,' said another.

'Quickly,' said the third. 'Bop it on the head!'

'*Lâchez moi, bande de salauds*,' I screamed and started thrashing about for all I was worth. 'Bog off, leave me alone!'

To my utter dismay my outburst only made my persecutors more determined to hold me fast, and all three of them did their utmost to smother me and pin me down in the sopping mass of algae in the middle of the skiff. Which, from their point of view, was a mistake.

With no one at the tiller, their skiff picked up speed in the current, and whacked straight into another algae-laden boat, which had been on its way to the shore. The shock of the collision pitched everybody into the drink, including one very relieved carp, whereupon two entangled, heavyweight, out-of-control boats careened on downstream towards the bridge.

It was only then that I realised what was really taking place. The pop and crack of musket fire told me that all was far from well on the structure. To my horror, I could see that a great crowd of labourers, armed with cudgels, shovels and pickaxes, was surging across it towards the north bank, while a much smaller number of smartly attired soldiers were doing their best to hold them back. In spite of their being armed with muskets and bayonets, which they weren't coy about using, their cause already looked lost. Which is when two unmanned, out-of-control, algae-crammed boats changed the course of events irrevocably.

Me and bridges, eh? Another one to chalk up – but I have to say that a *pontoon* bridge was a first for me. Dozens and men and horses were tossed into the river but, more importantly to the big picture, the entire central portion of the pontoon bridge had been taken out, and the attack on the north bank had effectively been halted.

From a safe distance I watched the aftermath of the brief but bloody conflict. Unable to press home their attack on the north bank, the massed ranks of workmen had nowhere to go, and then had to face another large force of soldiers that had assembled to their rear. Apparently when the uprising had begun the main garrison of troops had been trapped in the fortress, but a short time after the bridge's unfortunate breach they'd managed to break out, and now order was being restored.

Having seen the labourers' wretched living conditions last year, I had no doubt where my sympathies lay. And while I didn't blame myself entirely, I had to admit to myself that perhaps I inadvertently had just a little bit to do with the workers' uprising failing.

All through the day gunshots and cries could be heard. Groups of labourers were rounded up and marched off, while some individuals were simply forced to their knees and summarily executed. I don't know how many unfortunates lost their lives that day, but I surmised from overheard snatches of orders and pronouncements that the vast majority of the protesters would be pardoned once the ringleaders had met their just desserts. Well, they had to leave someone to build their ruddy new city, didn't they?

Several boats were now criss-crossing the river, as it would obviously take several days to repair the damage to the bridge. Closely guarded labourers began clearing up the debris from the conflict and making good the damaged sections of the pontoon's wooden roadway, while patrols still strutted back and forth, poking bayonets hither and thither, trying to root out hiding revolutionaries. Apparently, the leaders of the attempted uprising were still at large.

The person who found them was me. As I swam under the bridge's wreckage – that cyprinid curiosity again – I came across seven ragged figures taking refuge in a large air pocket in a capsized barge. Feeling a twinge of responsibility, I took a chance and addressed them.

'Please don't be alarmed, gentlemen, you'll give yourselves away, but I think I can help get you out of here.'

The men were clearly alarmed that a talking carp had rumbled them, but they had the presence of mind not to cry out.

'First of all you need to get away from this boat, because it's bound to be moved before long. Can everyone swim underwater?'

The men all nodded.

'*Formidable*, then what we need to do is try to reach the north shore. Of course we'll have to do it in stages so you can come up for air, but I'll choose spots where you hopefully won't be spotted. Are there any questions?'

'Plenty,' said the slightest of the fugitives, a slim young man with a straggly beard. 'But they'll wait. I agree we need to get out of here.'

'*Alors*, on the count of three—'

Fortunately all the men were reasonably strong swimmers, and just about managed to negotiate the considerable river current. Our first stop for air was in amongst some woody debris that clung to one of the pontoon's intact barges, the next amongst some clumps of weed in the lee of another barge, and then in the shelter of a waterlogged tree that had floated downstream. Thus, stage by stage, we reached a large reedbed on the north shore, just a short distance from the start of the bridge. I knew that regarding this as a safe haven would be a big mistake, so we headed upstream in similar fashion until the men were simply too exhausted to carry on. We stopped for the night at a wide inlet, where an overhanging willow formed a partial curtain around a large patch of water lilies. This was an absolutely ideal spot for a carp to hole up, but maybe less so for a group of humans on the lam, but any port in a storm as they say.

'This is all rather unreal,' said the young man, sitting up against the willow trunk. 'Not just being rescued, but by a talking carp.'

'It'll be real enough if we get caught,' said one of his companions.

'I take it you're what the soldiers would describe as rebels,' I said.

'Too right,' said another of the men. 'We couldn't take it anymore.'

'We've had it up to here.'

'We've had it with fourteen-hour days.'

'We've had it with sleeping on flea-infested straw.'

'We've had it with whips.'

'We've had it with beatings.'

'We've had it with bloody millet all the time.'

I didn't mention I liked millet. Especially fermented, and with lashings of juicy creepy-crawlies.

'It's not reasonable,' said the wispy young man. 'Especially since none of us actually volunteered to be here in the first place. We weren't looking to overthrow the tsar, we just wanted him to agree to treat us all a lot better. I'm sure he doesn't know half of what goes on, so we wanted to grab his attention.'

'So you weren't actually staging a revolution, attempting to overthrow the monarchy?' I said.

'Not at all,' said the young man. 'Call it a form of collective bargaining.'

'And if he wouldn't agree to our demands we were going to kill him,' grinned a comrade. 'But we rather hoped that it wouldn't come to that.'

Beyond avoiding a bayonet in the gut or gunshot in the back of the head, I wondered if any of the fugitives had any thoughts about what to do next. Sure, we could keep on running, but it might be useful to be running somewhere in particular.

It was Leon, the ectomorph, who answered. He said it was a long way off, but the city of Novgorod[3] would probably be a good place to disappear. Folk there were none too keen on all the tsar's modernisation and new-fangled ideas – especially considering a new city would take trade away from them. New city, same bossy regime. They'd be safe in Novgorod until the heat died down, then they'd all be able to return to their various homes.

Leon doubly proved his worth by knowing, in theory at least, how to get to Novgorod; he'd studied maps, and was able to tell us that we had to make our way up into Lake Ladoga, and then find our way to the Volkhov River, which enters it from the south. Novgorod lay about 150 miles upriver.

As soon as it started to get light we prepared to set off again, but the approach of voices sent the fugitives scuttling for cover. A large boat, crewed by a score of well-armed guards, rowed close by, and it was thanks only to the cascade of leafy willow branches that they failed to pick us out. Chastened, we decided to wait until nightfall to make a move again, but we'd still have to be extremely cautious. I said that to reach Novgorod they'd need two things: a boat and me. I'd be able to guide them by night and be their eyes and ears, for we carp are habitual night feeders and have no problem finding our way about in the dark.

Naturally the escapees were fascinated at being befriended by a talking carp, and Leon asked me during a quiet moment why it was I'd decided to help them. I certainly wasn't about to admit that my chief motive was guilt, so I waffled on a bit about my encounter with Aleksandr Denisovitch the previous year, and how I sympathised with the plight of the forced labourers, and natural justice, et cetera, et cetera – all of which was true by the way – and fortunately Leon didn't pursue the matter any further.

One of the men was able to steal a fishing boat from a nearly riverside village late that evening, so we were soon able to begin our journey to Novgorod in earnest. It would make for a better story if

I reported that we encountered numerous thrills, spills and further narrow escapes, but actually our journey was pretty uneventful.

When it was safe to do so we crossed to the south side of the river, and, upon reaching the lake, made our way cautiously alongside its south bank until we entered the Volkhov River, and headed upstream. We journeyed by night and laid low by day, the men foraging for food wherever we stopped. With the balmy summer arriving nature was bountiful, both for the fugitives and for me.

In spite of all the noise back in St Petersburg, I believe the manhunt for my friends had been called off fairly quickly. Gradually we were able to relax a little, and not restrict ourselves to solely travelling during the brief northern nights. After a while we were even able enjoy the quite magnificent landscape we passed through.

One bright day we reached a stretch of river that passed a venerable walled city. While the emergent St Petersburg was all bright and new, in the ultra-modern Classical style, Novgorod was ancient and exotic, filled with tall, colourful buildings with spectacular onion-like domes. I would've loved to stay and get better acquainted with the place, but there appeared to be no waterways actually leading into the city, and anyway I was becoming very aware of the passage of time. I'd made it through one Russian winter and had no desire whatsoever to stick around and repeat the experience. I said a fond farewell to the comrades and, with an exuberant swish of my tail, set off back downstream.

The building work at St Petersburg had advanced considerably since my hurried departure, and even from a safe distance out in the Neva I noticed that a number of things had changed. The labourers I could see all looked better fed and better dressed; the guards were no longer whipping them or shouting at them as if they were the scum of the earth. Maybe the era of collective bargaining had not yet arrived, but I thought that Tsar Peter had probably had an almighty shock when the mob tried to storm his palace, and had ushered in some much needed changes. Maybe he'd been a kindly humanitarian at heart and hadn't realised what had been taking place on the building sites and in the camps. And maybe pigs had wings. I swam under the rebuilt and strengthened pontoon bridge and headed for the Baltic. Russia: stunning country; beastly climate.

Notes

[1] He would become known as Peter the Great, also known as Peter the Mariner, because he loved ships and helped Russia become a naval power. The great city he created was called St Petersburg. Then Leningrad. Then St Petersburg again.

[2]The vendace is one of the Whitefish group of fishes, which all tend to live in cold northern lakes and are becoming increasingly rare. Apparently they're very distant relatives of the salmon and herring families, and also rather good to eat. Gisella pleads ignorance about that.

[3]Just to confuse matters there are two Novorods, Veliky Novgorod and Nizhniy Novgorod. Fortunately, Gisella and her companions were heading for Veliky Novgorod; Nizhniy Novgorod is considerably farther away and would've been an absolute nightmare to swim to.

Chapter Fourteen

Mein Befreier, der Karpfen. Gisella discovers music in a big way, thwarts a lunatic, and aids a maestro

After leaving Denmark in my wake, I reached a wide river estuary which looked well worth exploring. By ascending the river I'd be heading in pretty much a southerly direction, which led me to believe that I'd be reaching warmer climes. That was the theory, anyway.

I soon reached a large port, which of course was a wonderful place for soaking up information. Here's what I learnt: the port was part of the great city of Hamburg, Hamburg was one of the centres of the Hanseatic League, that I hadn't got the foggiest notion of what the Hanseatic League[1] was, the city had several canals, but not as many as Amsterdam, and that I was swimming in the River Elbe, which was evidently navigable for quite a long way inland, because it carried a considerable volume of riverboat traffic.

I spent a couple of days exploring the swimmable parts of the city, and found a couple of really first-rate bakers. Being a port, lots of spices were available, and some of the cinnamon and cardamom bun crusts that people discarded were really superb. Okay, I have a sweet tooth, but I told myself I was building myself up for the winter, just in case it turned out chillier than I'd anticipated. Some of the buildings, which were mostly in the Gothic style, looked as if they were true architectural treasures, but naturally from the canals I could only really get glimpses of the tops of them. The nearer the port area one swam the rougher the city became, despite its veneer of gentility and prosperity; ladies of the night and inebriated roughnecks ensured that only the well-armed or foolish ventured there at night.

Fascinating as Hamburg was, I stuck to my plan and headed south. The weather was still temperate and there was a good supply of natural food, as well as whatever edible refuse people chucked into the drink at the various towns and villages along the way. By refuse I mean the knobbly ends of loaves and stale cakes, by the way. I'll eat some fairly yucky stuff if necessary, but for heaven's sake I'm not a grey mullet.

Following the Elbe south and east I'd hoped to be heading into a warmer climate, but over the course of a few days the mild autumnal weather took a turn for the colder. My lateral line was telling me a thing or two I didn't want to know. I hoped I hadn't made a terrible mistake, but I was basing my calculations on lessons taught to me by the kindly Father Flammarion in Paris some 300 years previously, and maybe I'd been oversimplifying things somewhat. What was it about extremes of climate in large landmasses he'd spouted on about? *Merde*, silly carp.

One more slightly clement day, I was swimming past a very pleasant, medieval-looking city when I picked up the strains of a most heavenly sound. At the end of a manor house garden that stretched right down to the riverbank, a small group of women, warmly dressed in long coats and bonnets, were singing to the accompaniment of two violins. I'd never been in a position to take much notice of music before – mostly I'd heard drunken caterwauling or the scratchy fiddle-playing at Surperendo's travelling fair – but this glorious harmony was of a completely different order. I was transfixed, enchanted, ecstatic even. Where had music been all my life?

As the musicians finished their recital and made to return to the house, I couldn't help blurting out a heartfelt *Bravo!* Sometimes I wear my emotions on my pectoral fin. One of the ladies must've heard me, because she turned and made her way down to the water's edge and gazed directly at me. I'd thought that by sinking to a couple of feet deep the colour in the river would mask me, but her eyesight was better than I gave her credit for.

'That was you, wasn't it.' She wasn't asking a question. I looked back up at her. She must've been in her thirties, her coat and bonnet were made of quality fabric, and she radiated bourgeois self-confidence. In fact, despite encountering a speaking fish, she appeared quite calm and unfazed, and exuded no sign of malice whatsoever. I rose to the surface again.

'I've never heard anything like that. What you sang, that sound, it was simply beautiful. Did you compose it? *Ma parole*, I've been missing out on something very special for an awfully long time.'

'It's Bach.'

'Pardon?'

'The music, Bach. Johann Sebastian Bach's *Komm, du süße Todesstunde*,[2] a cantata.'

'Well, whatever a cantata is, that Johann Sebastian Bach is a flaming genius, and your singing was magic, pure magic!'

'*Vielen Dank*.'

'There's just one thing, though. Why were you performing outside on an autumn afternoon? Wouldn't you be more comfortable indoors? Preferably in front of a vast audience that would certainly love your singing?'

The lady let out a sad sigh. Would that life were that simple. She explained that women were not allowed to perform in public, and most certainly never to sing sacred music, and as for their ever singing in a church or cathedral, that was absolutely and completely *verboten*. I protested that I'd never heard anything so absurd. Why shouldn't women sing? What a complete lot of *ordures*.[3] She answered with a sad nod.

My new friend explained that most songs and choral music had parts that suited women's voices, especially Bach's, yet only males were allowed to sing. For alto, contralto and soprano parts young boys were used, and sometimes even adult men who'd undergone a grotesque form of mutilation in order to prevent their voices from ever deepening. That was why if women wished to perform music of any kind, they had to do it in private; if their families were supportive they could sometimes practise and recite at home, but just as often they were forced into covert get-togethers wherever they could find a secluded space, such as their gathering that afternoon.

Franke and her musical friends had formed the Magdeburg Ladies Bach Appreciation Society, but for all their musical accomplishment, they never got to perform in public. This afternoon had been her turn to host a session, but as her husband, a tone-deaf banker, forbade any such nonsense under his roof, they'd had to avail themselves of the garden.

Whatever the risk, I made up my mind that I'd have to meet this Johann Sebastian Bach. I seldom forgot that with each new human contact there was the danger that I'd be seen as a creation of the Devil, the result of witchcraft or a hot dinner, but I'd been fairly lucky so far, and I thought I'd probably be in reasonably safe waters with the master composer. My reasoning was that surely someone capable of creating work of such stunning beauty wouldn't react negatively to me. Sometimes I wonder how I ever reached twenty, let alone nearly a thousand years old.

Franke told me that the last she knew, Johann Sebastian had been working in Weimar, under the patronage of Duke Wilhelm Ernst, better known as Duke Willi, but no one had heard anything of him for the past few months, so she couldn't be certain I'd find him there. I thought Weimar would probably be the best place to start looking, and asked for directions. It was forty leagues to Weimar as the bird flies, but as the fish swims it was considerably farther. I had to continue up the River Elbe until I reached the third tributary on the right, the River Saale, and then hang another right into the River Ilm, then carry straight on until I reached Weimar. Simple.

The journey was simple, but only up to a point. I had no problem continuing to ascend the River Elbe, nor did the Saale present me with any problems, but the Ilm was a different matter. It wasn't exactly a big carp river, in fact calling it a river was overstating the case. The Ilm was a pretty trout stream, punctuated by numerous low weirs and shallow rapids, that ran through pleasant rolling countryside. It happened to be the trout spawning season, and anyone stopping to admire trout leaping over various obstacles would've been shocked to see a big old carp following suit. All the trout shaking that thing over the gravelly spawning beds cast me brief puzzled glances as I passed them by, and the numerous roach, chub, dace and minnows that also inhabited the stream respectfully moved out of my way. I hoped Herr Bach would appreciate the trouble I was going to in order to make his acquaintance.

I wasn't far from giving my journey up as a bad job when I approached a sizeable town, and what looked like a splendid palace on its outskirts. That, I thought, looked like a suitable place for a duke to reside. From the river I could only see one of its aspects, but apart from tall buildings it had a tower, a partial surrounding wall and – a moat. A small bridge spanned the moat's outlet into the stream, which at that point was thankfully a little deeper and more sedate than further downstream, so naturally I swam into it to see what I could discover.

The oval-shaped moat gave added protection to the palace's main building and tower, while another, larger bridge gave access to its ornate gatehouse. Both the buildings and the wall were stuccoed, and built in the German Baroque style. There was also a garden, comprising scattered fruit trees and a number of vegetable beds, and below them a grassy leisure area with seating, that led down to the water's edge. Continuing around the watercourse, I came to the moat's inlet from the river, which poured onto a waterwheel, that was for some reason festooned with copper wires. I didn't spend any time pondering this oddity, however, because the sweet tones of a violin began to sound some distance behind me.

I hurried back to the garden area of the moat, where I saw a full-figured man, in his early thirties perhaps, engrossed in playing his violin by the water's edge. In spite of the sublime music he was making, his face seemed burdened by the woes of the world. Eager to hear every note to its fullest, I swam up so close the top of my head and my back emerged from the water. Taken back, the man lowered his instrument.

'Don't stop on my account,' I said. 'That was absolutely beautiful.'

The man gasped and almost dropped his violin into the moat. 'Are you some demonic apparition sent to increase my torment?'

Oh dear. He was one of those. 'I'm just a carp, good sir. A carp that happens to like fine music. Not that I know anything about it, I just know what I like.'

'Pardon, *Fräulein Karpfen*, perhaps I'm doing you an injustice.' He removed his wig to scratch his closely shaved head, an involuntary action. 'I don't know what's what since I was, um, detained at Duke Willi's pleasure. Frankly I'm rather rattled.'

'*Quoi?* You mean you're being kept prisoner?'

The man gestured towards a fellow who can only have been a guard, sitting against the trunk of a distant apple tree, nonchalantly smoking his pipe. Whatever we were doing was evidently of no interest to him at all, but I had no doubt that if the prisoner made any sort of move to escape he'd be on his feet in an instant.

'Alas, since I tendered my resignation as the count's *Konzertmeister* I've been held captive here – he's not a man you want to cross, as I've found out. I really don't know what he expects of me, I'm so out of sorts I can barely compose any more, and as for *Konzerts*, I only ever have an audience of one now.'

'No prizes for guessing you're Herr Bach,' I said. 'I've journeyed a long way to pay my respects to you, but to find you in this situation? It's shocking! I really don't know what to say. I heard some of your music played at Magdeburg and I was enchanted, blown away by it. And here you are, living like a convict, it's appalling. But you're still playing.'

J. S. Bach played a couple of notes on his violin. They sounded like a lament. 'Until I was locked up I was working on a number of keyboard pieces. Plus a handful of violin partitas. The one I was just playing, the Partita in D Minor for solo violin, is what I've been tinkering with most recently, but my heart's no longer in it. You can get a caged canary to sing, but the notes may sound a little sour.'

'Not to my lateral line, maestro. But surely you could escape? The moat isn't that wide. Even if you can't swim, I could help you get across it.'

'And then what? Where would I go, how would I hide? The guards would come after me and the townsfolk are too frightened of Count Willi to take me in. No, I'm afraid I'm stuck here, at least until the count has a change of heart, whenever that will be.'

His pipeful finished, the guard got to his feet. I took it that the maestro's fresh-air sojourn was coming to an end and melted away into the deeper water. But I soon discovered that Johann Sebastian had a daily half-hour break which he took in the garden when the weather was fair, and we'd spend that time chatting and enjoying a few of his solo pieces on the violin.

The trouble with fine music and good conversation is that they can be so engrossing that you let your guard down. One damp morning we met as usual, and although I was enjoying a conversation with Johann Sebastian I was aware of a rapid drop in the atmospheric pressure. Not a good sign, and a bloody pain in the swim bladder. The misfortunes a fish must bear, eh? No matter… The maestro was so wrapped up in telling me about the influence of great Italian composers – such as Antonio Vivaldi and Arcangelo Corelli – on his music, that we failed to notice someone had been listening in on our conversation. He was a lanky, sallow-looking fellow in old-looking clothes and a scraggy wig. Although he must've been a similar age to Johann Sebastian, his outdated clothing and curmudgeonly demeanour made him look rather older.

'Those Latins have great talent,' he said, 'but they cannot hold a candle to you, maestro.'

There was no need for any introduction, this was obviously Count Willi, but he introduced himself to me nonetheless.

'*Mademoiselle, ravi de faire votre connaissance.* May I congratulate you on your German. You have retained your charming Gallic accent, but your command of our grammar is impeccable.'

'Thanks,' I said guardedly.

'Not many people are bilingual, but for a fish – why, you're a phenomenon. Tell me, do you speak any other languages?'

Oh, boastful carp, you should've kept your big gob shut. 'Well, English. And Italian. And Spanish, Turkish, Dutch, Russian, a smattering of Hungarian, and of course Latin and passable ancient Greek. You could say collecting languages is a bit of a hobby of mine.'

'Capital!' The count clapped his hands together. 'You'll be just the fish to help me with a little experiment I'm running.'

Oh no I won't, I thought. I zipped off as fast as my fins would propel me, but to my dismay I found the exit channel from the moat had been cut off by a wire grille. Worse, some net-wielding guards were paddling after me in a shallow-bottomed boat. Off I shot once more, but to cut a lengthy chase short, there was no way I could prevent the inevitable – I was as a goldfish in a goldfish bowl.

It turned out that Count Willi had been aware of my presence for some little time, and had already made preparations for my participation in *the furtherance of science*, as he put it. One of the palace's cellar rooms had been transformed into a laboratory, filled with a variety of apparatus that I couldn't begin to comprehend. It was all utterly alien to me, but there were lots of tubes, coils, cylinders, dials, wires, straps, switches, levers, and the devil knows what else. For me there was a large glass aquarium, brim-full of water, which was complicatedly wired up to a flat, bed-like contraption by its side. My alarm was only ratcheted up further when Count Willi tried to reassure me that he wasn't mad.

'This little set-up is a *mind facsimile* device,' he explained. 'It can transfer all mental faculties from one brain to another. It was actually invented by an Englishman called Neville Braithwaite, but I used it to crib all his knowledge and unfortunately he ended a gibbering brassica. It's one of the system's kinks that has yet to be ironed out: knowledge can be transferred, but not duplicated.

'Old Neville was a real wonk. He'd swotted up all the electrical experiments by luminaries such as Hauksbee, Gilbert and von Guericke, and made this giant leap forward all on his own – until of course I appropriated all his hard work. This whole contraption runs on electricity, which is produced by the turning of the waterwheel at the moat's inlet. The only drawback is that there needs to be a reasonable flow of water to power the system. The greater the flow, the more juice. It's simple.'

'And where do I come into all this?' I asked.

'Hmm. Let me explain.' How I hate explainers sometimes. 'In recent years I've become something of a misanthrope. To put it mildly. People – all their petty concerns, their squabbles, their ambitions, their vanity, their smells – I've come to hate them. All of them. Yet I love beauty, especially the beauty of art, and of music, and of J. S. Bach. Therefore I want to absorb all his genius, so I can have his music in my head. For ever.'

Jesus wept.

'The trouble is, there are still one or two bugs in the system that need ironing out. Turning my donors into *Blumenkohl*, cauliflowers, is of no consequence, they're no longer any use to me, but some of the abilities that are transferred aren't always perfect.'

Even as I lamented my forthcoming demise, my lateral line was tingling like crazy, warning me that outside the dramatic pressure drop was unleashing a rather severe meteorological event, or, okay, a bloody great storm. Judging by the sound of lashing rain from outside, it was even more powerful than the downpour in Rome that spiked Cesare Borgia's guns. Something told me it would work to my advantage to let the dotty count rabbit on a while.

'For instance,' he continued, 'I zapped our cook, old Frau Bauer, in the hope that I'd become a master chef, but while my *Sauerkraut* is perfection, my *soufflés* are still a complete flop. Hopeless. I can't risk that with J. S. Bach; what if my fugues were to flop too?'

I felt a fresh surge of power from outside, then there was a crack of thunder, but Willi was too engrossed in tinkering with his apparatus to take any notice.

'You still haven't explained why I'm next in line for the treatment.'

'Simple, my dear polyglot carp. Who wouldn't want to master as many languages as you, and if the process isn't quite perfect yet, who's going to complain if I get a Turkish subjunctive a little awry? Not me, anyway. Plus, in your case, I get to have a delicious dinner afterwards, so it's a win-win situation.'

'Not for me it isn't.' What was it with crazies wanting to crib my linguistic skills? Lazy so and so's, it could take me literally days to learn a new language!

'Alas no,' said the count as he lay on the flat bed and placed a wire-festooned, helmet-like contraption on his head.[4] 'You don't come out of it so well – but I'm not going to lose any sleep about that.'

The rain continued to hammer down outside, and I could only think that Count Willi thought it of no consequence, or was somewhat hard of hearing. One thing was certain: the little river would already be carrying a great deal of extra water.

'Auf wiedersehen, Fräulein Gisella,' said the count as he pushed a lever by his side. Several things happened simultaneously: the room was illuminated by blue light and filled with a sharp metallic odour; bolts of lightning flashed through the apparatus, into my tank and across to the recumbent count, who went into violent convulsions as his wig fizzled and smoked; while I, instinct kicking in at the last millisecond, leapt from the water and landed painfully on the stone floor.

Great, I thought, I'd avoided being boiled alive only to asphyxiate slowly on the cellar's frigid flagstones. Minutes ticked by and I could feel my life force ebbing. The count, meanwhile, who I'd assumed to be dead, gradually came to, groaned, and lurched to his feet. Then he caught sight of me, and exclaiming 'Oh, you poor fish!' scooped me up in his arms and slid me as best he could back into the aquarium. The water was uncomfortably warm, but at least I could breathe again.

It wasn't just that Count Willi looked as if he'd been raked from the embers of a fire, his entire countenance had changed. Somehow he looked – pleasant. Kindly. If extremely singed.

'I hope that's better, my dear *Karpfen.* Is there anything I can do for you? Anything to make you more comfortable?'

'*Schnapps*,' I croaked. 'Gimme Schnapps!'

A generous slug of the fiery liquid and I felt much more like my old self. The count, however, couldn't have acted less like his old self. He apologised for treating me so cruelly, and called for the maestro Bach so he could apologise to him as well. We quickly pieced together how the day's strange turn of events had taken place.

In short, the river's flash flood drove the waterwheel-powered turbine so fast, the mind facsimile device was catastrophically overloaded and blew up, causing major, and hopefully permanent, changes to the count's very singular grey matter. He confirmed that all the talents he'd absorbed through the machine had been wiped: he could no longer remember what gravity was, so all his scientific nous was gone, and he was sure that if he attempted to boil an egg it would probably explode. And, even more dramatically, from behaving like the world's sourest misanthrope, he was now acting like a latter-day Francis of Assisi. From Rasputin to Mary Poppins in a flash, so to speak.

The reformed Count Willi couldn't have been more contrite about holding Johann Sebastian prisoner, and urged him to take up the new post he'd been offered as *Kapellmeister* to Prince Leopold of *Anhalt-Kothen*, which would undoubtedly further his already illustrious career. A very relieved and thankful Bach made his preparations to depart.

As for me, I could feel another change in the weather approaching, and this time it was for the colder. We decided it would probably be better for me to over-winter in the palace's moat, which was deep enough for me to survive in relative comfort even if it did ice over. Count Willi pledged that his men would always keep a small area free of ice, and fresh *torte* would be available whenever I wished. I was no fan of winter ice, but under the circumstances I could've done a great deal worse. Throughout the colder months I had frequent conversations with Willi, whose sea-change appeared to be permanent. In fact, his goodness was so cloying I ended up wishing he'd curse a bit or go and kick a dog – but then I remembered what a bastard he'd been and was thankful.

Notes

[1]The Hanseatic League was a trading confederation of cities around the Baltic, a kind of precursor of the European Union. By the

Eighteenth Century it was a completely spent force, but mentioning it sounds smart.

[2]*Komm, du süße Todesstunde.* Come, sweet hour of death. Gruesome title, beautiful music.

[3]*Ordures*, conneries, load of old rubbish.

[4]Mary Shelley Schmelley… There's a reason Frankenstein is described as a Gothic novel.

Chapter Fifteen

Enlightenment. Gisella spends some more time in the Netherlands, learns about the evils of the slave trade, and then gets to hobnob with the great thinkers of the age

The last of the winter snow was still melting when I took my leave of Count Willi, who, being a very reformed despot, was quite tearful at my parting. I'd enjoyed his company a great deal but swimming round and round that old moat had become extremely tedious and the *Wanderlust* was upon me. I wasn't that keen on swimming in snow-melt – the fledgling Ilm was running high, cold and a sicky milky colour – but my urge for a change of scenery was overwhelming.

The Saale was an improvement and by the time I reached the Elbe my progress was far more comfortable. As the current calmed and the water deepened I slowed down – what was the hurry? Spring was unfolding, the days were lengthening and warming. In the more secluded stretches – although I always kept an eye out for fishermen – I'd drift just under the surface, luxuriating in warm sunshine. On the riverbanks the reedmace was shooting up, catkins festooned the draping willows and newly hatched duns and sedges were gingerly taking to the air, while under the water the streamer weed and water cabbages were almost growing before my eyes, water beetles zigzagged crazily and the roach, dace and bream clearly had more on their tiny minds than just finding food. The magic of spring; everything fresh. I was on a mission: a mission to enjoy life and meander where my fancy took me.

Hamburg I'd visited the previous year, so I drifted my way onwards into the North Sea, and then turned left and retraced my earlier route along the Netherlands' coast. Amsterdam I'd lived in for a few years before my Russian interlude so I continued my aimless journey until I reached another fine city built on the coast. I followed a shipping channel into its harbour where I rapidly got my bearings. Apparently I'd arrived at the Hague.

The Hague wasn't as big as Amsterdam and had far fewer canals, but it was equally posh and if anything some of its buildings were even finer. The canals I could follow led me past wharves, warehouses, factories, shops, town houses, mansions and, most importantly of all, bakeries. Carrying on, I reached open country that was dotted with whitewashed cottages, windmills and tulip fields. Well, I knew the tulips were there because I overheard conversations about them, but I never got to see them because I was down in the water and the pancake-flat countryside was forever out of view. I thought back to the happy years I spent travelling through England with Surprendo's Circus, taking in all the panoramas from my wonderful travelling aquarium, and wished some benevolent soul would build me another. Silly carp. I had to keep my wits about me because every so often I had to avoid large drop nets and various other types of fish traps, but although they were more than sufficient to bamboozle a bream or an eel, they weren't about to snare a well-travelled carp. Not this one, anyway.

Town and country. It was most pleasant. Although I'd set out to travel when I left Weimar I found that the Hague and its environs catered for nearly all my needs, so I found myself spending the summer there. Of course, that could've been something to do with the discovery of De Styl's, the finest pâtisserie in the land, built on higher ground and dominating the surrounding countryside. The bakers habitually threw all sorts of scraps and misshapes into the drink, where I was more than happy to hoover them up.

This indolent and gluttonous life inevitably led to an expanding midriff; I was getting like those big carp in commercial fisheries that do nothing but guzzle boilies. I set off into the country for some hard swimming and a strict regime of silkweed and water snails.

I followed the canal system several miles inland. I knew the land had been claimed from the sea, protected by great dykes, drained, cultivated, and cross-hatched with smaller canals and ditches, and I marvelled at mankind's ingenuity – they can be quite clever when they're not blowing one another to pieces. At length I reached an area that had every appearance of being uncultivated, or otherwise neglected, so nature was reclaiming it. It was overgrown with reeds and rushes, with the odd stunted willows dotted here and there, while the channel I was following narrowed until it was hemmed in by a jungle of reeds, banks of pondweed, and pockets of horrid-smelling ooze.

I would've turned back except, after having eaten revoltingly healthily for several days, I was getting cravings for something more satisfying than boring silkweed. My ultra-sensitive sense of smell detected something far more appetising than *plantes aquatiques biologiques*,[1] and that something was evidently located deep within the jungle. *Bon courage*, I plunged into the least inhospitable gap in the forest of reeds and headed on. As it happened, I found myself following some sort of watery tunnel, a well frequented thoroughfare used by all manner of fish, particularly eels. They have the reputation of being slimy, but apart from their tendency to keep themselves to themselves I've never had any problem with them.

At length I emerged into what seemed to be a large, oasis-like pond, deep within the reedy forest. The appetising aroma I'd picked up was cooked beans, *flageolets* to be exact, scattered on the pond bed – not unlike an angler's groundbait. Ahead of me was dry land, and on it a very hairy man, who was frantically pulling in a large net, that happened to contain, me! The scattered beans *were* groundbait, and they'd lured me into a cunning trap. Naturally I struggled like a mad fish and ripped the net, which had obviously seen better days, to shreds.

'*Bordel de merde!*'[2] cried a loud voice. That was just what I was going to say; to my surprise someone was speaking fluent and very colloquial French. I took a closer look at my would-be captor. At first sight I thought that he looked like a hairy old hermit, dressed in rags, but then I realised he was actually a hairy young hermit. And he wasn't happy. 'Oh me, oh my, that was the last of my good nets. It'll take days to fix it.'

'Sorry about your net,' I said. 'But I'd really rather not be caught if it's all the same to you.'

The young man ended up on the seat of his tattered breeches. 'What madness is this? Am I hallucinating now? I should've known those odd little fungi were dodgy.'

'I'm real enough, *mon ami*. People often have a bit of a funny turn when they meet me, but they get used to me pretty quickly, and I'm sure you will too.'

'François-Marie Arouet at your service,' the young man affected a respectful bow. 'A privilege to meet you, and how joyful to speak to someone again after all these years.'

'Even if it's a fish.'

'I've been stuck out here for five years so I'm not about to get picky about chatting to a talking carp, particularly one that speaks with a charmingly vulgar barroom lilt. In fact I feel honoured, mademoiselle. And I'm really sorry I tried to catch you.'

Looking around, I saw that François-Marie was standing on what looked like a large island in the middle of the reed jungle pond. He had a hut, built from old ships' timbers and rush bales, patched up with daubs of mud. Nearly all the dry land was cultivated, with beanpoles, cabbages and no doubt many other vegetables that remained out of my line of sight. I was sure he had quite a story to tell, and pressed him to tell it to me.

'Where to begin? At home I guess, where else? My father, who's a lawyer, and a complete uptight prick, expected me to go into the family business. I found the law deeply boring and refused. Don't get me wrong, I was a prick too back then, but probably the polar opposite of uptight. I lived for drinking and carousing and trying my luck at the tables, which didn't exactly endear me to Papa.

'Exasperated with me, he shipped me off to the Hague, where I was given the position of clerk to His Excellency the French Ambassador, I suppose in the hope that with a bit of responsibility I'd start to grow up. Fat chance. Nearly all my pay went on wine, women and games of chance, and the rest, as they say, I frittered away.

'In spite of my utterly hedonistic lifestyle I did actually come to form a more solid attachment. I started seeing a young lady named Catherine Dunoyer, otherwise known as Pimpette. God she was gorgeous, a pert bottom you could die for. And there, my scaly friend, I choose my words carefully.

'To put it crudely, I was rogering a Prod, slipping it to a Huguenot. And for a supposedly devout young Catholic in the service of the semi-senile but malevolent Roi Soleil,[3] that was definitely not kosher. I didn't know it, but my superiors quickly formed the idea that this dissolute clerk, this dandified wastrel, had suddenly gained value, by shtupping a detested Protestant.

'Late one night I was hauled from my bed by two cloaked thugs, whacked on the head, bundled into a sack, and spirited away. When I came to again I could feel I was being rowed along in a boat. I was both scared and outraged. I demanded to be set free, asked if my captors had any idea who they were dealing with, and told them the king would be informed of their treachery.

'Highly amused, they answered they *were* the king's men. At a time when the French monarchy wanted to stir up trouble with the Huguenots, I'd played right into their hands. They'd be rid of an idle waste of air, my disappearance would be blamed on barbaric Calvinists, and help incite further anti-Protestant hatred. A win-win situation, but alas not for me. Another blow to the head, but this time a clumsy, glancing one, knocked me senseless again.

'My assassins found a quiet spot that was to their liking and started to shove me overboard. Adieu, François-Marie. It was a very awkward manoeuvre, however, and as I was heaved over the gunwale a corner of my sack snagged on a rowlock, nearly capsizing the boat, before it ripped free and I plummeted several feet to the canal bed. The shock of cold water quickly brought me round again, but because my sack was weighted with rocks there was no hope of my making it to shallower water. It was then that fortune decided to shine on me. As I struggled I found the rip in the sacking and frantically tore at it until I was free, then, almost passing out once more, I kicked upwards and surfaced near what looked like a dense reedbed. I hadn't made my escape quite yet, however, because as they rowed away one of my tormentors must've heard me splashily swimming towards the shore and raised the alarm. *Merde!* I dived into the thickest area of rushes, and crawled and floundered my way away for dear life. A couple of gunshots rang out, but I just carried on slithering ever deeper into the rushes and reeds, on and on, until I was utterly lost and completely disorientated. Whichever way I turned, the vegetation just became thicker. Until after an age I emerged into this clearing.

'As you can see, they never found me. And as you can see I've never found my way out of here either, and it's not for want of trying. I found this island little different from what you see now. A hut, equipped with all the basics for a self-contained if restricted subsistence, such as nets, fish traps, tools, boxes of seeds, etc., and a large, cultivated area, which then had been neglected for some twelve months or so.

'My predecessor? His remains lay in a hammock suspended between two willow trunks. I guess he'd been dead for about a year when I found him, but at least it looked as if he'd departed peacefully enough. One of the first things I did was to give him as decent a burial as I could, under the circumstances. Who was he? Certainly some sort of hermit, his existence looked very well-ordered if solitary. Had he been a land-drainage worker who'd decided to put down roots? An escaped convict? A simple misanthrope? I'll never know – but what's certain is that I owe him my survival thus far.

'Apart from working hard just to exist, I've had a lot of time to think. I have little regard for my old self. My God what a plonker I've been. A young jackanapes whose only thought was the next bit of skirt or bottle of grog. But looking at the society I left behind, I've come to realise that so much of it is pomp and vanity and hubris. The megalomania of the monarchy, the pomposity of the priesthood, the absurdity of the aristocracy – don't get me wrong, I miss my fellow mankind, but seeing the folly of so many of my fellow humans from such a distance certainly changes one's perspective. You must forgive me for wittering on so. You don't know what it's like not to speak to another person for years and years.'

I certainly did, but I had no wish to interrupt my new friend's flow.

'I've learnt valuable lessons. There's no meaningful life without a certain amount of work and pain, and the highborn and pampered should realise that. Sometimes I've been convinced I was going gently potty here: the gorgeous summers, when I've felt that this must surely be the best possible of all worlds; and the miserable winters, when I've had to conclude that sadly that has to be the case. The deafening echo of my own thoughts. The almost endless round of chores. Today I'm going to set my eel traps and mend my nets, then I'll fix the roof, and then I must go and work in the garden.

'But now, after all this time, I have company. I can't tell you what that means to me. However, I fear I won't last more than another year, if that even. My nets are all decaying, my eel traps rotting, and the soil in my vegetable patch no longer produces as it used to. My self-sufficiency no longer appears to be sufficient. Maybe I'm destined to end up like my mysterious predecessor, unless you happen to know a way out of here, that is?'

'I was going to come to that,' I said. 'How far can you swim underwater?'

'Sixty, maybe seventy feet? I swim a fair bit during the summer.'

'It'll be touch and go, your choice. But if I lead you out the way I got in, there's a fair chance you'll make it.'

'What've I got to lose? Lead on, fair fish.'

We slipped an old, torn strip of fishing net over my head, and with François-Marie holding onto the other end of it and swimming after me, we submerged into the murky, watery tunnel under the reeds and kicked on. I'm quite accustomed to finding my way about in total darkness, but for my companion the experience must've been terrifying. Maybe I'd underestimated the length of the swim because it seemed to take forever, but just when I was sure I'd helped drown the young man we burst out into open water.

How François-Marie choked and gasped for breath; he was conscious but it had been a fearfully close-run thing. I wished I had some hard liquor to help revive him – I could've done with a good slug too – but of course there was none to be had in the middle of a Dutch canal. Once he was breathing more normally again, François-Marie had a sudden moment of doubt. What if Louis XIV's men were still after him? Was he still in danger? It was Louis XV now, I reassured him, I was sure he'd been long forgotten, but maybe he'd do well to adopt a new identity and make a completely fresh start anyway.

'A spanking new nom de plume,' François-Marie grinned. '*Formidable!* I have plays to write, pamphlets to pen, feathers to ruffle! I shall champion a fresh look at life and be fearless in my critiques!' Evidently, he'd forgotten his brief collywobbles a few seconds earlier.

I, on the other hand, was fearful. I hoped my young friend wouldn't be too fearless because that way he could end up in a sack again, or on a scaffold. There was no guarantee the new Louis would be any less devious than the old one, but I supposed staying in the swamp wasn't an option. We said our farewells, and I looked on as the young rebel splashily tried to flag down a passing barge. Was this the best of possible worlds? I wondered. *Ben alors*, it was the one we were stuck with. *Qu'est-ce qu'on peut faire?*

I over-wintered at Le Havre,[4] which, as the name implies, gave ample protection against the worst of the seasonal foul weather. Then it was onwards once more, drifting lazily around the Cotentin Peninsula, and then around the rugged Brittany coastline. Eventually I reached another major river estuary where, on a whim, I headed upstream.

The river was the Loire, and with night falling I soon reached the great port city of Nantes. Lights twinkled prettily in the town as well as on the scores of ships that were moored along the quays and anchored out in mid-river. I carried on, eager for a spot of sightseeing in rural France. I'd heard about the fabulous Chateaux de la Loire and now I was going to see them.

Many of course lay out of sight from the river, but others, built on higher ground and dominating the surrounding countryside, had grand views of the Loire – which meant I had grand views of them. Saumur, Villandry, Amboise, Blois, and on various Loire tributaries lay Chinon, Loches, Chenonceau… The splendour of these architectural marvels, plus the idyllic bucolic scenes of jolly peasants toiling in the fields, all combined to give me a bellyache. Maybe visitors to the region in subsequent centuries have ended up *chateau'd out* too. And as for the jolly toiling peasants, it dawned on me that perhaps they looked jolly only from a distance. I recalled the peasants in the village of Yaxley, in Kent, a few centuries earlier. Their lives hadn't exactly been jolly, and it didn't look as if things had changed

much for these sons and daughters of the Loire Valley. The antidote for me was to visit a town. A big one.

I returned to Nantes in daylight and found that the river was split into two branches, the larger of which was bordered on both sides by more than a mile of wooden wharves. Almost countless ships were moored along them, or so it seemed to me.

Inquisitive as ever, I swam along beneath the hulls of ship after ship, hoping to glean nuggets of knowledge, or just some plain old gossip. It was under one such vessel that I literally collided with a fellow, wearing just his breeches, who'd dived deep below the waterline and was scraping barnacles and crud from the ship's bottom with some sort of trowel.

'Have a care, *Monsieur*!' I cried.

'Sweet Jesus!' the man answered, recoiling and knocking his head against the ship's hull. I thought I'd better help him back to the surface.

'Sorry about that,' I said. 'I didn't mean to shock you.'

'Indeed, *Mademoiselle*. You probably don't meet talking fish every day, but what do I know? This is a very odd country.'

'So you're not from around here?'

'Take a look at me and have a guess.'

'*Alors?* Is that a trick question?'

'The fact that I'm black might be a bit of a giveaway. And it also explains why I'm the one who's got the shit job of scraping all the gubbins off the bottom of the ship.'

'So? We carp come in all sorts of shapes, sizes and colours. From ghostly white to nut brown to autumnal crimson, or almost. The thing is, we're all carp.'

'Humans aren't always so egalitarian, and it certainly isn't by my choice that I ended up here.'

Joseph – who explained that for some reason Africans were often renamed after characters in the Bible – had been a fisherman in a remote coastal village in West Africa. One day slavers arrived and set all the houses on fire. The younger, fitter villagers were taken into captivity, while the elderly, the infirm and the infants were all put to the sword.

Along with scores of other Africans, Joseph was chained in the hold of a ship, and endured day after day of pitching and rolling, foul food, non-existent sanitation, plus abuse and out and out brutality from many members of the European crew. All of which was before an added disaster befell: disease, which rampaged through the ship without regard to status or race. The mortality rate was somewhere above eighty per cent, and Capitaine Remy feared that without more hands on board *l'Esperance* would founder as soon as the next squall hit.

As one of the few males still able to stand, Joseph, or Ikenna as he was still called, was released from his shackles and made to help aloft in the rigging. Having spent all his life sailing around the coast Ikenna was good with boats – very good. A natural, even on a ship that was completely alien to him. And when a storm did hit, and it was one bastard of a storm, it was Ikenna who took charge of the wheel and kept *l'Esperance* facing the mountainous swell, and somehow prevented her from keeping a rendezvous with Davey Jones.

It was an almost skeletal version of *l'Esperance* that limped into Guadeloupe, but the miracle was that she had made it at all. The skipper might have been an inherently weak and evil man, but there must've been some glimmer of fairness buried deep inside him; he recognised that all the survivors on his ship, few as they were, owed their lives to Ikenna, and agreed to recommend him to another skipper – of a reputable merchantmen this time – as an ordinary crew member and a free man. As for *l'Esperance* itself, Capitaine Remy was going to have to wait several months to hear from the ship's owners as to whether they wished for her to be repaired, or to cut their losses and break her up for scrap.

Thus Ikenna embarked upon a life on the Seven Seas, and in the process became known as Joseph. As indignities go, *boff*, there are worse ones. He'd learnt French and become a true *matelot*. Had he considered going back to his village? Well, there wasn't a village anymore, was there? And really and truly, the West Coast of Africa was no longer a safe place for black people anyway.

I learnt that the issue of slavery was a complicated one. The trade was almost as old as so-called civilisation, and in Africa certain tribes were responsible for the practice as well as Arab and European slave traders. But what the Europeans were doing, which they were apparently so very efficient at, was mechanising and corporatizing the process. Conducting it on a scale hitherto unseen. Most of the ships moored up at Nantes were involved in the slave trade, massive fortunes were there to be made from it, and it wasn't just the French. English hands were every bit as bloody, and as for the European countries that didn't have a finger in the slave-trade pie, it wasn't as if they didn't wish to.

I was profoundly saddened by all this information, but not really that shocked. I knew that humans routinely did the most appalling and unbelievably cruel things to each other – but using your fellow man (and women in their millions too) for commercial gain, based largely on them living in the wrong place and the wrong time – and their pigmentation – was about as obscene as you could get.

Joseph told me that on his travels he'd met many fellow black people who hadn't been caught up in slavery. In all the French ports he'd called at, plus many English ones too, especially London, he'd come across black people in a variety of walks of life, but you still had to be a bit cautious with native whites. Many were okay; some, though, were liable to turn on you for no good reason. But he'd heard whispers, rumours, that men of reason were talking of change. That the old order needed to be moved aside, that a more equitable future was on the horizon. Or maybe not. He'd heard an awful lot of absolute bullshit in his time.

I was left thoroughly dispirited by my brief conversation with Joseph. This unassuming and gentle man had been through so much and still displayed no visible rancour. It was only thanks to the encounters I've had with so many decent, kind individuals over the years, personal friendships, that I didn't renounce all contact with human beings on the spot. People en masse can be so incredibly shitty.

I thought back to my trips all over Europe and realised that there was probably no safe haven from people's rottenness anywhere. But being honest, as much as I despaired of humanity's flaws, I was also hooked on their sociability; on friendships, learning, art, gossip, laughter, and cakes, certainly cakes, so there was no way I was genuinely ready to turn my back on them. However, Nantes, beautiful city as it appeared to be, had turned sour for me. I found I was missing England, warts and all. I was pretty sure that no one really blamed me for the Great Fire of London, and even if some had, what were the chances that they'd still be alive? Maybe I'd even encounter some of the new breed of enlightened humans Joseph had talked about. But first I needed to source some brioche. Being so near La Vendée, France's breadbasket, I couldn't possibly leave without tucking into some brioche.

How London had changed in the few decades I'd been away. Gone were most of the cramped half-timbered houses that leant in on one another, plunging the narrow streets into perpetual gloom and putting passers-by in peril of emptied chamber pots or plummeting roof tiles, and in their place were wide, well-ordered thoroughfares, lined by sturdily built stone or brick houses, in the classical and Baroque styles. Well, that's what had happened to the areas that had been flambéed when the Opus Azazel nutcases had attempted to cook me, otherwise there were still areas that looked in dire need of urban renewal, and none more so than the London docks. Miles of wharves, moored ships, water taxis, dark satanic warehouses, abject hovels, fetid heaps of rubbish, seedy taverns, bordellos, dry docks, silted-up creeks, mud-bound wrecks, dark menacing lanes and alleyways, and crumbling boarding houses.

It was a fascinating area, and although I'm tempted to say that all human life was there, there were precious few posh people, or rather those that ventured there took great care to ensure they wouldn't stand out in the crowd.

The *raison d'être* for the area was obviously shipping, and that meant it teemed with a great many seamen and dock workers – along with those who live amongst and off them. Looking up from the murky water I'd see traders, footpads, conmen, fishwives, whores and pimps, dandies slumming it and risking their necks, tinkers, buskers, slops men, hawkers, and a host of others who couldn't be identified at a glance. The rough edges of humanity.

Remembering my conversation with Joseph at Nantes I kept an eye out for anyone who looked like him, and realised that humans came in a variety of shades. Hitherto I'd only really noticed that they were usually a sort of pinkish colour, but down at the docks there was a variety, especially amongst ships' crews. If one travelled upstream to the posher areas of the city, however, the faces were overwhelmingly pink – apart from the very odd servant maybe. This all tallied with what Joseph had told me, not that I'd had any reason to doubt him in the first place.

While the docks were wonderful for human-watching, the people there were usually quite careful about the food waste they chucked into the drink, or, to be more precise, they didn't actually waste that much. Most of them couldn't afford to. And most of what did end up in the water wasn't all that palatable, unless you were a mullet. However, further upriver it was a different story; the well-to-do thought nothing of discarding really appetising dishes, and my sweet tooth never seemed to suffer from cravings for very long.

One feature of city life for the upper crust was aquatic pageantry – great flotillas of river craft carrying exalted passengers and staging shipborne feasts and even concerts. Ever since the 'Water Music' was first performed for King George several years earlier, Lord Mayors' shows and similar galas generally featured fine music and dining. That, for a carp who appreciated the very best pâtisseries and Baroque music (and I don't think it's disloyal to say I found Handel to be very nearly Bach's equal as a composer), was utter bliss.

Several years slipped past pleasantly enough, except for a couple of the winters that were uncomfortably chilly – but they were nothing like my experience in Lake Ladoga so I shouldn't complain. I missed having people to talk with, but knew better than to force any contact with humans. It would happen when it happened.

And then it did. I heard a voice I recognised instantly, even if that voice was speaking a different language from the one used during our first encounter. Stepping off a water barge and onto a landing stage at Wandsworth was none other than the chap who'd been living in the swamp near the Hague – older, greyer and way, way more smartly attired, but the very same unwilling hermit. 'François-Marie!' I exclaimed, as soon as the boatman cast off from the shore again.

Monsieur Arouet turned around confused, then he looked down and recognition spread across his face. 'Gisella, *par example!* What a wonderful surprise to find you here amongst the Rosbifs. What brings you here?'

'Simple wanderlust in my case, but I would ask you the same thing, François-Marie.'

'Ah, my name is now Voltaire, Monsieur de Voltaire. As you advised years ago, I changed my name and haven't really looked back. And to answer your question, I'm here in London because I got into a bit of a tiff with a silly aristocrat with no sense of humour, and was given the choice between a long stint in La Bastille and spending a few years here.'

'I think you made a wise choice.'

'Indeed. In spite of all my misgivings London turns out to be quite *agréable*, in fact I've made many like-minded friends here.'

'Then you've done better than me. I've been missing a good natter these past few years.'

'This we must rectify! *Écoute*. There's a group of us that meet up on Tuesday afternoons at Mrs Poskitt's coffee salon in Wandsworth. It has a garden that leads down to the river, so I'll suggest we all get together outside next week; they'll be elated to meet an intelligent carp, I guarantee you.'

'It sounds excellent – but are you sure no one'll throw a wobbly at meeting a talking fish? People can be very funny.'

'*Mais non*. They're all very enlightened, I assure you.'

The sun was shining brightly when I swam up to the lawn behind Mrs Poskitt's Coffee Salon. Monsieur de Voltaire was already present, along with eight others – all apparently intrigued at the prospect of meeting a talking carp. Voltaire eagerly introduced me to the group, who comprised Alexander Pope, Jonathan Swift, Joseph Butler, Lady Mary Wortley Montagu, George Berkeley, Sarah Duchess of Marlborough, Samuel Johnson and John Gay.[5] Before we could engage in any conversation, however, the kindly but robust Mrs Poskitt, followed by a young girl, bustled out of the salon's rear door carrying trays of coffees.

'I don't know what's wrong with you people,' she tutted. 'Hot coffee on a day like this. I told you I managed to get hold of some ice so you could've had iced coffee, but oh no, you had to have them steaming hot.'

'Madam,' said John Gay. 'That's the way coffeehouse society works. We meet, we agree that reason and logic must prevail, that none of mankind's problems can ever be solved by violence, and we drink *piping hot coffee* – it is thus and cannot be otherwise.'

'You're all touched,' said Mrs Poskitt. Then she turned to me. 'How about you, dear, will it be piping hot coffee too?'

'I'm not much of a coffee drinker actually. I don't suppose you'd have a tot of anything stronger, would you?'

'A girl after my own heart. I've got some cooking brandy in the kitchen that I keep for emergencies – although I seem to have emergencies every day. Would that suit?'

'Absolutely. Please.'

I didn't normally require Dutch courage to help ease me into conversation with new people, but looking at this gathering of well-dressed and well-spoken folk, whom Voltaire had spoken so highly of, I thought it couldn't possibly do any harm.

'A fish with a taste for the grape,' smiled Jonathan Swift.

'An occasional snifter,' I said, 'and largely medicinal.'

'Are you suggesting that Gisella here is a *Cyprinidus bibulous*, Mr Swift?' said Dr Johnson.

'Surely not,' said Joseph Butler. 'I think we should marvel that God in his infinite wisdom has given this fish the gift of speech – and the fact that she enjoys the odd wee tot is neither here nor there.'

'However your gift came about, you're something of a talented linguist, are you not?' said Voltaire. 'How many languages do you speak?'

'Getting on for twenty I guess,' I said. 'French, English, Dutch, German, Italian, Spanish, Russian, Latin, Greek, a little Magyar, Turkish….'

'I speak Turkish too,' beamed Lady Mary Wortley Montagu. 'I was Ambassador in Istanbul for a while.'

'Formidable,' said Sarah, Duchess of Marlborough. 'And they say women don't have an aptitude for languages.'

At this point Mrs Poskitt returned with my brandy. A very large tumbler of brandy, which she poured down my throat in one large hit. 'Cheers, sweetie,' she winked, 'in this company I guess you can use it.' Whoosh, wow! Fire spread to every part of my body, and I felt any inhibitions I might've had tumble away.

'Of course we girls can speak languages as well as any man,' I said. The brandy had gone straight to my head. I was used to wee nips, not ruddy great tumblers full. 'And God didn't teach me, I'm self-taught.'

'Oh my,' said George Berkeley. 'No one is suggesting you're not immensely gifted, we're saying it was surely the Heavenly Father who gave you that gift.'

'Ah, but it was Gisella herself who learnt all those languages,' said Alexander Pope. 'It was through her own free will and talent that she became such an amazing linguist.'

'And you're saying this polyglot pisces mastered most of the tongues of Europe sans divine intervention?' said Dr Johnson.

'Oh hark, Mr Wordsmith,' said John Gay. 'Never use one word when you can cram in twenty.'

'Maybe that's why your silly plays are so threadbare, Mr Gay, maybe a richer lexicon would give your oeuvres a little extra oomph,' said Dr Johnson, reddening. 'But to put it simply, so that even you will understand, sir, it was most certainly through the intervention of the

Good Lord that this denizen of the deep ended up far cleverer than you.'

'So it was the Heavenly Father's intervention was it? Not the Heavenly Mother's?' said Lady Mary.

'Maybe attributing a woman's gifts to some paternalistic deity is just a little bit insulting,' said the Duchess of Marlborough, using her fan to mask her irritated blush.

'Blasphemy,' spluttered Joseph Butler.

'You've got to admit it,' said Alexander Pope. 'This image of God as a whiskery old geezer, sitting up there on a cloud, is only one way of regarding the divinity.'

'Maybe God is a woman,' said Lady Mary.

'*Qui veut dire que Dieu n'est pas un poisson?*' The Devil made me say it, I was sloshed.

'Steady on,' said Swift.

'Saying God's a fish? This is an outrage!' cried Berkeley.

'Perhaps we should just agree the divinity is gender and species neutral,' said Pope.

'Absolutely!' exclaimed Lady Mary.

'Look at you, fluttering your eyelashes at Alex again,' said the Duchess of Marlborough. 'You know he can't resist a comely smile and shapely ankle.'

'Pah,' said Jonathan Swift. 'It's not as if you didn't become a duchess through your feminine wiles in the first place.'

'Take that back!' The duchess fanned herself furiously.

'Never!' cried Swift.

The outraged duchess snapped shut her fan and hit Jonathan Swift over the head with it. He retaliated by removing his wig and shoving it down over her head so her face was completely covered by it. 'There,' he cried. 'A vast improvement!'

'Why, you egregious bogtrotter!' exclaimed Dr Johnson, leaping to the duchess's defence and planting a punch in the middle of Jonathan Swift's face.

'By dose,' yelped Swift, staggering back. 'You've bloody broken by dose!'

'See what you've started with your heavenly paternalism?' Alexander Pope turned on puce-coloured George Berkeley, who proceeded to tip the remains of his cup of coffee over Pope's head.

Infuriated by the assault on the esteemed satirist, Lady Sarah kicked Berkeley in his nether regions in a very unladylike way, while the saintly but seething Joseph Butler landed a smart kick up the duchess's backside, and John Gay, still stung by his earlier slight, took to walloping Dr Johnson over the head with a rolled-up treatise on violence never being the way.

Thus the meeting of the most enlightened minds in the country, a group dedicated to reason and the peaceful resolution of any kind of conflict, had descended into a mass brawl. Voltaire stood back and observed the fracas with me. I have to admit I was starting to get a headache and suggested that we should retire. What did we learn? Chiefly that Jonathan Swift needed to keep his guard up better, and the Duchess of Marlborough had a piledriver of a right hook.

Notes

[1] *Plantes aquatiques biologiques.* Organic pondweed. It sounds better in French.

[2]*Bordel de merde.* Bother.

[3]*Le Roi Soleil.* The Sun-King, Louis XIV

[4]*Le Havre.* The Haven, or The Port.

[5]The group at Mrs Poskitt's coffee salon were all stalwarts of the Enlightenment. Gisella's is the only account in which they're all gathered together at the same time. Quite understandable, under the circumstances.

Chapter Sixteen

A tale of two hairdos. How Gisella meets a bunch of revolutionaries, becomes a royal companion, and then helps form a blueprint for the future of man- and fishkind

Monsieur de Voltaire thought he could better pursue his quest for enlightenment back in France, where he was sure people would've forgotten about any past *faux pas* and he could resume being very quietly subversive. He admired England's parliamentary system, its relative freedom of religion and its constitutional monarchy, but if the quest for enlightenment resulted in a punch on the nose he reckoned he might as well be back on home soil. Besides, he missed Diderot and Rousseau and all the old crowd. Yup, it was off to Dover and back across the old Manche for him.

As for me, I had to admit the idea of swapping lardy cake for croissants rather appealed. How long was it since I'd previously spent time in Paris? It had to be something like 400 years and seriously, no one could blame me for historical bridge-damage anymore. I too would head south, but unlike my erudite friend I was in no particular hurry.

How Paris had changed. For a start, there were now seven bridges spanning the Seine, and the city had expanded way beyond its original walls. As far as I could see from the river the old parts of it weren't so different from a few centuries before, although some fine stone buildings had been added, but the outward spread from the old boundaries was astonishing. In some areas the housing looked quite respectable, but others made the London dockland look – almost posh. As for the old riverbanks, most in the city were now stone-built embankments: good for overhearing pedestrians' chitter-chatter, but bloody hopeless for seeing what was going on. Fortunately there was plenty of boat traffic, numerous landing stages and of course the seven bridges, so I was able to keep up with the preoccupations of the day. It appeared that people had two main topics of conversation: the excessive shenanigans of the great and the not so good, and how much food was in the shops on any given day. This was not the Paris of Father Flammarion, Cornelius Azimuth and Claude de Gaillac.

I spent several years meandering up and down the metropolitan reaches of the Seine, and naturally I was familiar with all the best spots to find appetising foodstuffs – and where to forage the boring, healthy stuff when necessary.

It was another period in which I didn't do too well for human company. While I knew the Sorbonne was tantalisingly close by, I never managed to contact any of its luminaries; the grassy riverbanks of the Île de la Cité, where I'd spent such enjoyable and informative times with Father Flammarion and Cornelius, had been replaced by stone walls, so while any number of fascinating people were certainly passing me by, I was never able to meet any of them.

When I did finally make contact with people again it was under rather odd circumstances. One day I'd drifted aimlessly downstream from

the city and entered a backwater in order to soak up a little sun. Somehow I'd ended up a little closer to the bank than I'd intended, close to where a middle-aged woman appeared to be using a big stick to wallop an enormous pile of rank and malodorous, hairy animal skins that lay festering in the shallows. All of a sudden I found it impossible to breathe. Something appeared to be poisoning my gills. I attempted to swim back out into deeper water, but my fins failed me and I couldn't move. Okay, time to press the panic button.

'*À moi! À l'aide*!' I bellowed. 'Please, I'm choking here!'

Mist was descending over my eyes. *Putain*, what a miserable way to go.

'What the blazes do we have here,' said a deep but feminine voice. Strong hands grasped and pulled me a little way upstream from the vile heap of pelts, which had obviously been leaching toxins into the river water. Fresh water entered my gills. My saviour was the middle-aged woman, but as yet I couldn't see her very clearly.

'Was it my imagination or did you actually speak?'

'Cognac,' I gasped. 'For pity's sake gimme cognac!'

'Do I look as if I'm made of money?' said the woman. 'I can offer you a hit of *eau-de-vie*, but that's about it.'

I nodded feebly and she turned, ascended the riverbank and disappeared into a doorway. While I waited for her to return I glimpsed my surroundings for the first time. The woman's house was wood-built and pretty rough and ready, but its windows all had glass and it was obviously well cared for. It was a little larger than the few neighbouring dwellings, which evidently made up a small riverside village. What she was doing pounding a pile of animal pelts soaked in deadly poison remained a mystery to me.

She soon reappeared with a plain bottle and a glass, with a man in her wake. 'I haven't been on the sauce, Patrice,' she said to the chap. 'You just see.'

She poured a decent measure of clear liquid into the glass and tipped it into my open mouth. Yipe! Fire! God it was rough, it scorched my throat as it went down. These people must've been on the breadline if they couldn't afford better hooch than that. 'Hit me again,' I gasped.

Although I couldn't speak for the state of my stomach, the second drink helped restore my senses and I was able to focus slightly better on the two humans. They were both of a similar age, she dressed in a long, coarse smock and bonnet, and he in canvas breeches, a rough shirt and a leather apron. The woman was evidently quite well disposed towards me, but I still didn't know how Patrice would react. 'Thanks,' I said. 'A most welcome drop, I feel much better.'

'Well, I'll be damned,' said Patrice. 'You were right, Madeline, it does talk.'

'I think I almost killed it with our washing lye, but it looks fine now.'

'It's still sort of lopsided though, are you sure it's quite okay?'

'Hello, I'm swimming right here. And I'm a lady carp, not an it,' I said, sounding more irritated than I'd intended, 'and I'm afraid the lopsidedness is permanent – the result of an encounter with an uncouth *brochet* a very long time ago.'

'*Pardon*,' said Madeline. 'No offence intended.'

'None taken. And sorry if I sounded a little snappy. I'm really thankful you rescued me, Madame, and also for the *eau-de-vie*. I needed a little fire in my belly after that experience.'

'You're welcome to another glass,' said Madeline.

'Thank you, no. Two's cool, three for a fool.'

'Are you sure?' said Patrice. 'It's not every day you meet a talking carp. I think I need one, and I'd be surprised if Madeline doesn't too.'

'You know me too well, *cochonnet*,' said Madeline.

'Ah well,' I demurred. 'In that case it would be impolite not to join you.'

Thus lubricated, we fell into an easy conversation. It turned out that Patrice was a periwig maker, hence all the animal hair that of course needed thorough washing and soaking in lye – that ghastly mix of pig fat, saltpetre and urine that had nearly poisoned me – before it could be fashioned into hairpieces. I'd become accustomed to seeing men wearing wigs for the past century or so, but I hadn't realised how much class and status was bound up in the whole business. For the aristocracy and upper crust only a powdered wig made from human hair would do, and that would be bought from a master craftsman from the esteemed Guilde des Perruquiers[1] no less. The lower orders often went wigless, but if you were an aspiring trader, or clerk, or some kind of lackey such as a coachman, a wig was an aid to stepping up the ladder. If you want to get ahead get a wig. But the cheaper sorts of wig, generally made from goat- or horsehair, were made by unaffiliated craftsmen such as Patrice, and cost a fraction of the deluxe variety. Patrice and Madeline scratched a living from this, but Madeline also took in washing and did mending in order to help make ends meet.

Regardless of their restricted means they were a generous-spirited couple, and they invited me to share their lunch of bread, *saucisson sec* and rather ripe cheese. It was actually very good. They told me to stop by any time I was in their part of the river, they'd always be glad to see me. And so I did, and always found a welcoming chat, *casse-croûte* and glass of firewater.

Over the next few months I learnt that while Patrice and Madeline sold their wares to the aspirational and social-climbing, their sympathies lay very firmly with the *Sans Perruques* – the Wigless – a political group who championed the interests of those who couldn't even afford a goat-hair hairpiece. Bread prices were high and labour, when work could be found, was cheap. Patrice may have worn a wig to show off his wares, but in spirit he was no wig-wearer. Which turned out to be just as well.

One evening I was drifting contentedly downstream from the city when I caught sight of four men in a boat, one in his thirties and the other three perhaps a decade younger, paddling downriver for all they were worth. I soon saw the reason why. On a bridge immediately in their wake several armed soldiers had assembled, and proceeded to fire their rifles at them. The biggest of the fugitives, a hulking great fellow, had the ingenious idea of capsizing the boat to afford them some cover from the whizzing lead balls, which proved very effective. They propelled themselves by kicking their legs doggy-paddle style and thus continued downriver, the only drawback being that they couldn't see where they were going.

I saw they were heading straight towards a sunken barge in a shallow backwater, so reluctantly I intervened. I had no idea who these fellows were, but the odds against their surviving the next few minutes weren't looking too good, so I sped up to them and told them to follow me. I soon led them back into open water and on down the river, but it occurred to me that I hadn't really thought that far ahead either: the fugitives were unable to generate much speed in their upturned rowing boat, and the troops were bound to find boats themselves and give chase. I had to find a safe haven for the escapees or the game was up.

I soon smelt the familiar, disgusting stench of pig fat, urine and saltpetre, in other words lye, and knew we were close to my wig-making friends' atelier. And to my relief a great pile of sopping animal hair, manky old pelts and discarded scraps of fabric lay on the riverbank.

Having scrambled onto dry land, the four men looked a sorry sight. They wore well-cut clothing, but it was soaked and festooned with strands of weed, as was their long, dripping hair. The shock of being rescued by a talking carp, plus the unnerving experience of being shot at, appeared to have robbed them of the gift of speech and they simply stared at me imploringly. It was their choice, I told the four men, either they held their noses and got on with it, or they could carry on wallowing their way downstream until the armed men caught up with them – which would most likely be much sooner than later. No debate was necessary. We quickly sank the boat, which had been in danger of going down anyway, then, retching and gagging, they burrowed their way under the revolting mound.

The soldiers were quickly on the scene. A couple of boats sailed up and down the river, scanning the water, while several armed goons made a house-to-house search. Dressed in their nightgowns, Patrice and Madeline stood silently back as the soldiers poked around everywhere – everywhere except the stinking pile, which, inexplicably, none of them were willing to approach.

The very least Patrice and Madeline were owed was an explanation. The troops had left, and although occasional patrols could be heard marching up and down the road that ran through the village, the river was now soldier-free. Having gingerly emerged from the stink pile, the four bedraggled and reeking men looked very abashed.

'I'm sorry,' I said, kicking proceedings off. 'I didn't know what else to do with them.'

'Who are you?' Madeline asked the men.

'Jean-Paul Marat,' said the eldest of the fugitives. 'And may I present citizens Georges-Jacques Danton, Maximilien de Robespierre and Camille Desmoulins.'[2] All three gave a respectful bow.

'And perhaps you can explain why the king's men are after you?' said Patrice.

'We were at a meeting when the soldiers arrived and broke things up,' said Robespierre.

'What kind of meeting?' said Madeline.

'You don't want to know,' said Desmoulins.

'Yes we do,' said Madeline. 'You're putting us in danger and we deserve to know why.'

'It was a meeting of the Sans Perruques,' said Danton – the chap built like a brick outhouse. 'We discuss ideas such as an elected parliament and the rights of man.'

'We've heard of you,' said Patrice. 'It's just as well we're on your side.'

'Normally our secret meetings go without a hitch, but this time we must've been betrayed,' said Danton. 'The troops burst in on us and started making arrests.'

'Tell them the rest,' said Marat.

'There may have been an incident between my boot and a soldier's jaw,' said Danton.

'And another soldier's manhood,' said Desmoulins.

'Which without doubt put both men in hospital or worse,' said Marat.

'Meaning that if we're caught we face the hangman's noose, or deportation at the very least,' said Robespierre.

Marat, meanwhile, had started furiously scratching his arms, legs and face.

'Sorry,' said Madeline. 'The hair heap's riddled with nasties.'

'It's not that,' said Marat. 'I have a skin condition. The river water appeared to soothe it, but now I'm drying off again it's driving me nuts.'

'Staying here isn't an option,' said Patrice. 'You're bound to be discovered when we open the shop again. But what to do with you? You can't just walk out of here.'

'Unless anyone has another boat I think we're going to have to,' said Marat, still picking at his neck. 'We must reach a place of greater safety, and the sooner we're gone the better as far as you're concerned too.'

'It's madness,' said Patrice. 'The soldiers will be looking for four smartly dressed young men, without – wigs.' He, Madeline and I exchanged knowing looks. We'd all three tumbled on a solution at exactly the same time. The first thing was for the Sans Perruques to lose their flowing locks.

Within a matter of a couple of hours the fugitives had been transformed. Marat had been transformed into a schoolteacher, Desmoulins a clerk, Robespierre a coachman and Danton a farrier (in clothing that Madeline had worked very hard to let out) – all wearing Patrice's off-the-peg periwigs. Calling me Citoyenne Carpe, they thanked me profusely for saving their bacon in the first place, and then turned to the kindly couple who were risking their necks for them, and swore their undying gratitude.

The foursome slipped away at half-hour intervals, then all was silence. As far as we could tell they'd all made good their escape. Relieved but embarrassed that I'd put them in such danger, I apologised profusely to Patrice and Madeline, but they told me not to be so foolish. They were glad I felt they could be relied upon, and were proud to have helped the Sans Perruques. All they needed to do now was explain to their customers that the clothes they'd brought in for mending had been replaced by some rather natty, posh people's threads.

Normality quickly returned to the little wig workshop, and as ever I visited whenever I swam that far downriver. Being gentlemen of upstanding morals, Marat, Danton, Robespierre and Desmoulins had sent word of their safe escape, and made sure their wigs and outfits were generously paid for. The thought occurred to me that Patrice and Madeline were possibly putting their own livelihoods in danger by supporting the Sans Perruques, because of course a society that turned its back on wigs wouldn't have much need for wigmakers either, but then they were people of upstanding morals too.

Late one afternoon Madeline and I were having a good old moan about how much sawdust was being added to the *saucisson sec*, when we realised an exceptionally finely dressed lady, swathed in silks, velvet and brocade, with an impossibly bouffant hairdo, was standing behind us, jaw wide open, listening avidly.

'Who the fuck are you?' Madeline demanded, before clapping her hand to her mouth.

The lady was so shocked by my presence she completely ignored what was certainly a treasonable remark. The newcomer turned out to be none other than La Reine, Marie-Antoinette, whose carriage had lost a wheel just outside the workshop. It just happened that the main Paris-to-Versailles road was impassable due to subsidence, and in taking a detour the royal coach had come to grief in Madeline and Patrice's village. Marie-Antoinette, being only human after all, needed to attend an urgent call of nature (very likely due to a tired array of *fruits de mer* on a visit to *le Comte de Bernicourt*, whose chef deserved to be flayed), and had hurried through the atelier in search of some kind of privy. Finding none she had burst out of the back door, only to stumble across a roughly dressed *artisanne* and a large talking fish. She commanded me not to go anywhere and disappeared behind a bush.

Madeline and Patrice kept a respectful distance behind us as the Queen engaged me in conversation, as did a lady companion and another flunkey.

'It's true,' I said. 'As you've heard, I can speak, and I have a reasonable level of education.'

'Really you should be addressing me as Your Majesty,' said Marie-Antoinette, 'but as you're a fish I think we can dispense with all that. Just call me Marie-Antoinette.' The lady companion and the flunky let out audible gasps.

'Have you had the gift of speech for long?' asked Marie-Antoinette.

'Longer than I care to think about. I guess I was born like this, and I picked up French simply by listening. But isn't that how everybody learns language, by listening?'

'If only. Surely you've picked up my accent – pure Viennese. And the books I've had to swot up to get even the basics of French grammar.'

'Well books aren't much use to me underwater, although I have no problem reading. No, I just listen. I've learnt quite a few languages like that, although I still haven't really got the hang of Hungarian properly. It's a bit of a quagmire, that one.'

'So you can speak German?'

'Fluently.'

'Then you're coming with me. I won't hear any argument.'

Madeline and Patrice looked as alarmed as I was.

'Have no fear,' said Marie-Antoinette. 'I will make sure you travel safely, and there's a wonderful lake for you to live in at my pleasure gardens, at Le Hameau,[3] close to my personal palace at Versailles, Le Petit Trianon. I so miss conversations in my native tongue – we'll have such fun times together, I guarantee.'

I made it very clear that my presence at Versailles should be a secret, because I had no intention of being gawped at by all the twits and sycophants at court, nor did I fancy being the subject of scientific experiments by any of the royal physicians. Marie-Antoinette gladly agreed; she said she valued her rare moments away from all the palace hubbub greatly, and my presence at Le Hameau was to be a closely guarded secret.

Madeline and Patrice were crestfallen at my departure. To thank them for bringing me to her attention, Marie-Antoinette appointed them official wigmakers to the lesser members of the royal entourage, but they didn't look particularly delighted. Perhaps they had the gift of second sight. I distinctly heard Madeline mutter something about lickspittles, flunkies and toadies, but fortunately no one else picked up on it. That fact was, when Her Majesty wanted something, she got it.

In all fairness, my transport arrangements were flawless. I was packed into a teak trunk, swaddled in the most luxurious, sopping wet streamer weed, and suffered no discomfort at all on the short trip to Versailles. Upon my arrival at the lake at Le Hameau I was carefully unpacked, given a very generous tot of the finest marc cognac I've ever tasted, and released into the water. Thus I began a new chapter as the Queen's piscatorial confidante.

The lake at Le Hameau was roomy and sufficiently deep to be comfortable in all seasons. It was surrounded by pleasant landscaped mock-countryside and, continuing with the bucolic theme, bordered by some brand-new buildings, of dubious architectural provenance, that were intended to look like a farm. Tame livestock roamed freely, along with a few flunkies dressed up as peasants: it was Marie-Antoinette's pastoral theme park.

My companions in the lake were mainly other carp, along with a handful of tench (good old stalwarts and of course not to be underestimated), plus hordes of tiny rudd, which could be very irritating when they tried to mob any food that was thrown in. A swish of my tail and they gave me plenty of room, however. The sheltered, pampered existence enjoyed by the royal household was evidently shared by the resident fish.

I ended up feeling quite sorry for Marie-Antoinette. Most historical accounts describe her as over-entitled, vain, scatterbrain, capricious and capable of great unthinking callousness. Okay, she *was* over-entitled, vain, scatterbrain, capricious and capable of great unthinking callousness, but what could you expect of the not terribly gifted product of a milieu that did everything to encourage such traits? She was kind to her intimates, enjoyed the animals at Le Hameau's little farm – although she got her companions to pet the baby lambs for her – and she was very nice to fish. Her infamous remark 'Let them eat cake'[4] is probably apocryphal (however plausible), but as far as we fish were concerned she made sure we all had ample quantities of brioche to consume.

All manner of court and social gossip came my way via Marie-Antoinette and the select few from her entourage permitted to know about me, but I heard precious little about what was happening out in the wider world. I gleaned little snippets about unrest in Paris and some of the provinces, about unease in Prussia and what pigs the English were, but mostly I was subjected to tittle-tattle about such and such a duchess who'd lost a fortune at the tables, and this and that count who'd copped a dose from a chambermaid.

Parties and balls occupied much of the Queen's attention, and for some reason she insisted on sounding off to me about what should be served, which dances should feature, the music that should be played, and most of all, what she would be wearing. In fact, in fair weather she insisted on trying out various outfits by the lakeside in order to gauge my opinion. In vain I told her I was a fish and *haute couture* wasn't one of my areas of expertise. Her full skirts, tight bodices, her *robes volantes*, her flounces, her *négligées*, her *chenilles* and corsets and *paniers* were all pretty much lost on me, but I made the right noises and was positive about the dresses she especially liked. During those brief years, I believe I gained invaluable insight into the psyche of the pampered elite.

If she was a keen fashionista, she was absolutely potty about hairdos, and by hairdos I mean the most outrageous architectural constructions that aristocratic women wore upon their heads. These weren't just bouffant perms, they were Baroque and Rococo works of art, kitsch at its most ostentatious. The starting point was hair, and hair was sometimes used in these creations, but they also frequently included feathers, ribbons, flowers, dolls, jewels, and any other objects that were deemed to make a statement. They were small scale but intricate tableaux, miniature *installations*, and the more important you were the more outrageous your headpiece had to be.

With her birthday approaching, Marie-Antoinette naturally wished for a new hairpiece to surpass all others. Hundreds of noblewomen would be among the guests attending the celebrations at Versailles and if any of them were to outdazzle her in the head-decoration department she'd be mortified – it would be a fatal blow. Naturally Monsieur Peazi-Teazi was sent for.

I'd met Ramon on several occasions before, he was a favoured guest at le Petit Trianon and Le Hameau. In fact, I remember our first encounter very clearly. Marie-Antoinette had brought a slightly built fellow, with a brilliantly white, tightly curled wig, dainty little moustache and oh so fine lime-green velvet clothing to the lakeside, and introduced him as the royal hairpiece-maker.

'Designer, please,' he said in an effeminate voice. 'Other people simply make hairpieces – I *design* them.'

'A thousand pardons,' smiled the Queen. 'This is Ramon Peazi-Teazi, and he designs the most to-die-for hairpieces.'

'A pleasure to meet you,' I said.

'*Au contraire*.' Ramon bowed low, displaying immaculate *sangfroid* at meeting a talking carp. 'The pleasure is all mine.'

Her attention required by a lady-in-waiting who was in floods of tears for some reason, Marie-Antoinette left Ramon and me to converse. 'You wouldn't believe what she wants me to do this time,' said Ramon, his voice instantly an octave lower. 'She only wants to put a scale model of a ship in my next effort, just because the French navy gained a heroic victory over an English fishing boat near Saint Helier.'

'So, every hairpiece you make – er, design – has to have some sort of—'

'Gimmick?'

'I was being polite.'

'No need. These things are fads, and the faster my clientele moves on to the next fleeting sensation the better it is for me. Last month it was all birds. Would you believe Her Majesty had a headpiece with a live canary in a tiny little cage? She loved it until it crapped on her head.'

'Just as well it wasn't an ostrich.'

'They take some making, some of these thingummies. They want this, that and the other in their hairpieces, and then they moan they're too heavy. But you'd be surprised what some ladies will put up with for the sake of fashion. I wouldn't want to parade about with several pounds of cloth, twigs, jewellery, birds' nests and God knows what else on my bonce, I can tell you. I'm surprised more of them don't develop neck muscles like prize fighters.'

'Well Her Majesty still has a slim and swan-like neck. Sort of.'

'I take extra care to keep hers as light as possible. Valued customer and all that.' He looked round at the sobbing lady-in-waiting, still being comforted by the Queen in the pathway some distance away. 'I do hope that's not on my account.'

I waited for an explanation.

'We might have had a little thing going on some time back,' he said hesitantly. 'All this *frou-frou* act I put on is pure theatre. I actually love the ladies – a little too much I'm afraid, as my recent visits to the town apothecary for tincture of mercury following a brief encounter with one of the chambermaids will attest – and my over-the-top camp act is purely to convince the husbands of my lady clients that I pose no threat.'

'Very cunning,' I remarked.

'What are you two ladies gossiping about?' said Marie-Antoinette as she returned from the sniffling young lady, who still dabbed her eyes with a kerchief.

'*Oo la la*,' Ramon tittered. '*Mais cette jolie carpe est trop charmante!*' He gave a low, elegant bow and took a couple of steps back.

'Very good, Ramon, run along now,' said Marie-Antoinette. Ramon gave another exaggerated bow, and turned and swept away in an oh-so-fluid movement. 'That fellow's more of a queen than I am, but no one can beat him for glorifying the royal noodle.'

For her birthday Marie-Antoinette had, of course, told Ramon she wanted something that put all his previous work in the shade. Something to blow all the competition out of the water. For once at a loss, he wandered down to the lake with his sketchpad and pencils and complained to me that he was drawing a blank. What was there that he hadn't created before, short of putting an elephant or the Parthenon on the Queen's head?

While we were racking our brains a small carp leapt clean out of the water, trying to snatch a sedge-fly. 'Marie-Antoinette quite likes fish,' I said.

'Indeed, but more specifically she likes you. You've been her favourite companion since way back in fact.'

'Don't you dare even think of it!'

'Of course not, *poisson idiot.* Can you see her carrying thirty odd pounds of fish flesh about on her noggin? No, I should make a very lightweight clockwork model of a carp, and place it in a hairdo that looks like a pond. It would have a swimming movement, and if I could find a way of making it blow bubbles—' He hurriedly sketched out his idea and it looked ingenious. Unique.

'That's fantastic.'

'Thank you, Mademoiselle Carpe. You're my muse, my inspiration!'

He hurried away, bubbling with enthusiasm, but alas, his *chef-d'oeuvre* would never gain its desired audience.

Odd bits and pieces of news spread as far as the lake at Le Hameau, and even the woolliest heads amongst the royal household couldn't escape the feeling that great change was in the air. Marie-Antoinette often confided her disquiet and frustrations to me, but I never had the impression she felt any personal sense of foreboding. It was all rather generalised, remote even.

When Ramon came to present her with the finished hairpiece for her birthday bash she was enraptured. It was a most wonderful creation, complete with a little bronze-coloured, mechanical fish that blew bubbles, and she declared that no one would ever possess anything to match it. She'd treasure it forever. After she and Ramon had shown it to me at the lake she hurried back to Le Petit Trianon to stash it in a safe place, leaving its creator and me to catch up. He told me he doubted that he'd be available to join the forthcoming festivities – he had a few commissions over the Manche in England, and added that anyone with any sense would follow a similar course. Paris was just getting too rough, and that went for the rest of the country as well.

Even when the Bastille was stormed, Marie-Antoinette only remarked that Louis had dithered instead of putting his foot down with a firm hand, and the mob was being allowed to get away with murder. Apart from maintaining that her husband gave too much ground dealing with reformers and clinging to the ideal of an absolute monarchy, she had little interest in politics – it was as if the turmoil gripping the land had nothing to do with the occupants of Versailles.

Thus, when a crowd of revolutionaries finally turned up at the palace and took all royals and their entourage into custody, they were not only affronted, they were actually surprised too. As for me, I very quickly realised I was going to have to keep my head down. Le Grand Palais, Le Petit Trianon and the farmhouse at Le Hameau were all occupied by revolutionary guards and functionaries, and, in common with nearly all the common people, they were hungry. As ever there was not enough bread – and not enough cheese or sausages or puddings or anything else for that matter – but there were fish in all the royal lakes, so out came a plethora of fishing rods.

It was carnage. The lake's occupants, accustomed to being hand-fed by flunkies, actually fought one another to get at the fishermen's baits. It was like shooting rats in a barrel. Myself, I found it dead easy to avoid the anglers' crude hooks, but as a result I soon started to experience real hunger. It had been all fine and dandy when HRH and her minions were heaving brioches and *crêpes Suzettes* into the lake every day, but now there was precious little to forage, and any hatching insects were quickly picked off by the obnoxious little rudd. I have to confess here that in a few moments of weakness I scarfed down a rudd or two. Well, we carp aren't vegans, are we? All sorts of creepy-crawlies make up our diet in the wild, along with immature fish when we're hungry, and what are most modern carp baits based on? Fishmeal or animal protein. Plus fenugreek and maple syrup in the *crème de la crème* of boilies of course.

As the fishermen whittled down the lake's fish population, a greater share of the water's natural foodstuff was available for me. It was back to a diet of water beetles, snails, hatching flies, worms and anything else that kept body and soul together. Okay, it was really very healthy, but constantly having to be on the lookout for predatory humans definitely wasn't. From being the *numero uno*, most favoured fish, I had now gone onto the critically endangered list. If there had been a way out of there I would've taken it, but there wasn't.

It was late one evening, a good year later, that a cloaked figure ghosted up to the lakeside and very gently whispered my name. Marie-Antoinette and Louis had managed to escape from custody in Paris, but instead of making a dash for sanctuary in Hapsburg Austria, she'd insisted on returning to Versailles to say adieu to me – and, as an afterthought, pick up her treasured carp hairpiece. Of course it was a doomed endeavour: Le Petit Trianon was crawling with revolutionary guards and her hairpiece was doubtless long gone, but she did manage to reach the lake under cover of darkness and bid me an emotional, tearful farewell. Her detour proved fatal. The lost hours meant that the pursuing guards caught up with her and Louis at Varennes, and set in motion the inexorable chain of events that led eventually to their rendezvous with the hereafter.

In the meantime I wasn't experiencing the best of times. Soon enough the new residents of Le Hameau gave up fishing in my lake because, as far as they were concerned, there were no fish left to catch. That was something of a relief, but I still had to be constantly vigilant and keep well out of sight, because had anyone got an inkling there was a thirty-pound-plus carp swimming around, my life wouldn't have been worth a bean. I didn't find it easy. My thirst for gossip meant I was always tempted to swim close to the bank in order to keep up with current affairs.

What I did manage to glean made dismal listening. The old order, comprising the royals, the aristocrats, the clergy, the judiciary, the rich merchants etc., were being swept away, but more to the point they were being carted to the new-fangled Madame Guillotine. Having listened to the likes of Voltaire, Pope, Johnson, Marat, Danton and company I'd come to appreciate there was a need for change, but in my humble opinion lopping off thousands of heads seemed to miss the point of the Enlightenment somehow. Especially when I learnt that quite often those falling victim to the Terror were simply the victims of property grabs, old scores being settled, sexual jealousies and the like.

It was during a very hot summer's day that my cover was blown. The weather had been unusually warm and exceptionally dry for months, and consequently my lake's water level had dropped alarmingly. And of course one evening I was spotted, in fact I was surprised it had taken so long, because for a few days I'd been swimming around with my back out of the water.

Several men leapt into the muddy water, and hard as I tried to dodge them, it was only a matter of time before several pairs of hands grabbed hold of me and dragged me to the shore. Did I bow to the inevitable? Did I resolve to meet my maker with quiet dignity? Was I as composed as so many of the great and the not very good when they knelt before the guillotine's keen blade? Was I hell. I flipped and struggled and if I'd had any teeth I would've bitten like crazy too.

'Leggo of me,' I yelled. 'You can't do this to me, I'm too young to die.' Well, no one had any idea how old I actually was.

'Ooh, *la vache*,' gasped one of my captors. 'What have we here?'

'A talking fish from a royal lake,' said another.

'Must be an aristocrat fish,' said a third. 'I say off to *la guillotine* with her.'

'No way,' I protested. 'I'm a common carp. Common as muck in fact.'

'She *sounds* like one of us,' said another revolutionary.

'Anyone can fake an accent,' said the first captor. 'Off with her. Someone fetch a washtub and a tumbril.'

Before I knew it I'd been dropped into a washing tub filled with water, which was still unpleasantly soapy, and heaved onto the back of a tumbril. The situation was getting truly desperate. It was time to drop a name or two.

'I know Georges-Jacques Danton, and Camille Desmoulins, and Maximilien Robespierre.' My captors hesitated. 'Jean-Paul Marat, *c'est un bon copain*. A mate.'

'She's bullshitting,' said a captor.

'What if she isn't? What if she's really chums with Marat, and he gets to hear that we took her for the chop?'

'Citizens,' I said. 'There's a simple way to resolve this dilemma. You'll have to ask citizen Marat if he knows a talking carp called Gisella, and when he says yes you'll have the satisfaction of knowing that your heads will remain attached to your bodies.'

Within a couple of hours I was sharing a bathtub with the great man in his lodgings on the Rive Gauche. I say bathtub, but this contraption was big enough for two, and had by its side a table on which stood a bottle and a glass. Like the hated aristos, he evidently appreciated the good things in life. His skin complaint had worsened over the years, so he spent a considerable portion of every day immersed in tepid water, from where he attended to the affairs of the day and conducted numerous meetings. For his modesty, and to my relief, he always wore a loincloth, and I noticed that his wineglass was never far from his hand. I mentioned, but that didn't matter – they were good stories of *rouge*.

He was delighted to see me again, and told me with no false modesty that without my intervention, back when I helped save him and his fledgling radicals from the king's soldiers, there's no doubt that the glorious revolution could never have taken place. He wasn't a stupid man; he saw I wasn't exactly bowled over by his statement.

'I know the killing's got just a bit over the top,' he said. 'The people are angry, they've put up with a lot. They have to vent.'

'You don't think the venting's gone totally crazy? It's as if no one's safe now, no one at all.'

'Alas, you're right, gentle carp, these are uncertain times. Georges, Camille and Max have voiced concerns for their own safety, and even I don't know what the fates may have in store for me. Some say the country needs a strong man to take it in hand, perhaps a military man such as that young upstart Colonel Bonaparte, but he's a tedious little oik who'll never amount to much. No, the fervour will burn itself out in due course, and La France will see a glorious, egalitarian new age.' He took another sip of his wine. 'Ah, this Gaudichots Domaine is truly excellent. A shining example of the viticulturist's art.'

'So once the head-culling dies down you're going to have an egalitarian society?'

'*Exactement*.' He held up a manuscript. 'I've been working on some amendments to our revolutionary *Rights of Man* declaration, trying to see how we can give everyone an even fairer deal in the future.'

'Such as the right to carry on living and not being guillotined?'

'That's a work in progress.'

'Okay. How about everyone having the right to vote on who's in charge? That seems fair.'

'Whoa there, Gisella. One step at a time. We want responsible people voting, and that means land-owning types. How can you make an informed choice if you don't have skin in the game? Maybe when we've improved people's education we can widen enfranchisement a bit, but that's got to be an evolution rather than a revolution'

'And there was me thinking this was a revolution.'

'It is – but one step at a time, huh?'

'Where do you stand on the slave trade? It's absolutely barbaric, you've got to have banned that.'

'Well actually that's a work in progress too. Of course we think it stinks, and long term it's got to go. But we'll need the support of the slave owners to push our reforms through, so we're stepping very gently for now.'

'How very egalitarian. *Mon dieu.* Passing quickly on, your document is called the *Rights of Man.* I take it that means woman too? Surely one's gender should have no bearing on one's rights as a citizen.'

'Harumph. Of course in *theory* women should have equal rights, no question at all. But it'll take time. Much has to change first. After all, it's the man who earns bread, the woman who tends the home. But be assured, in decades to come the role of women will have our closest attention. However, for the time being, sexual equality must just be a principle; an aspiration rather than a fact.'

'So it really is the *Rights of Man* – masculine gender, full stop. What about us fish? Have you even thought of the rights of fish?' I'm afraid I was off on one. 'You humans eat us fish in our millions. Where's the justice in that? We, the fish, demand equal rights with Man!'

Marat scratched his chin thoughtfully. 'It's true, we do eat lots of fish. But don't you too? Doesn't the pike eat the bream and the zander the roach? Fish are trampling on fishes' rights all the time. Can you put your fin on your heart and tell me you've never partaken of fish?'

'Is there a clause in that document about having the right to remain silent?' Of course, there had been those rudd back at Versailles – and they were by no means the only small fish that had passed my lips. I'm an omnivore, so shoot me.

'I thought as much. How about we insert a section about fish having a *theoretical* right not to be eaten? That fish have the inalienable right not to be eaten, only, er, they must state it verbally or the clause is null and void?'

'Well, I guess so.'

'And we'll rename the document *The Declaration of the Rights of Man and Fish.*'

Our discourse was disturbed when a young lady was announced, a certain citizen Charlotte Corday. 'Ah, Corday,' Marat pondered. 'I know that name. The de Corday d'Armonts, minor aristos from

Normandy – Caen I believe – I'd kind of assumed they'd all lost their heads.'

'A distant branch of the family,' said Charlotte Corday. She was in her twenties, plainly dressed but with straw-coloured hair and a pleasant, fresh complexion. She hardly batted an eyelid at seeing a large carp in the tub with the great man. With hindsight, that should've put me on my guard. 'I believe they actually escaped,' she continued. 'Last I heard, they were in rented accommodation in East Grinstead. As for me, I happen to be from Bordeaux.'

'Ah,' said Jean-Paul, turning to me. 'That means citizen Corday is no doubt a Girondin. For the uninitiated, they're a moderate faction that supports gradual reform and the institution of a British-style constitutional monarchy, but they can generally be reasoned with.'

Citizen Corday told Marat she wasn't there to discuss the status quo or the monarchy or any such piffling issues, she had come to see him to talk about wine. 'Papa is a wine merchant. He acts for several of the big *domaines* of the Gironde region, and they're all hurting.'

'Some excellent wines,' said Marat, 'but continue.'

'It's your beastly naval blockade to stop us selling our wine to the Rosbifs. The Brits love their claret, and they make up the largest part of our market by far.'

'And they're our enemies. Not getting their claret fix is hurting them.'

'Not nearly as much as it's hurting us. And if we can sell them wine again they'll all end up sozzled, and wouldn't you prefer a sozzled enemy to a grouchy, sober one?'

'They always have their warm ale, which I wouldn't wish on anybody, but I take your point. We don't want our wine producers to go hungry, and lifting the blockade would be a friendly gesture to our friends the Girondins. I don't see why we shouldn't lift it.'

'Thank you,' the relieved young lady curtsied, but then her nose wrinkled and her sunny smile vanished. She picked up Jean-Paul's three-quarters empty glass, sniffed at it, and grimaced. 'This is from a south-facing slope, six leagues north of Baune, one valley across from the Saône. There's no mistaking it, it's a Gaudichots Domaines '74….'

'Why, yes, and jolly nice it is too!'

'It's a fucking *Bourgogne*! You traitor! You insult me, a native of Bordeaux, home of the world's greatest vignobles, and a Girondin to boot, by drinking vile Burgundy filth in my presence!' Almost quicker than the eye could follow, she produced a long stiletto and plunged it repeatedly into Marat's chest. 'That for your idiotic Montagnards, and that for your moronic revolution, and *that, that and that* for your bloody filthy Burgundian swill!'

I recoiled in shock, but still managed to cry out in alarm. Two attendants were on the scene in a matter of seconds and dragged the furious, writhing Charlotte Corday away from the inert Marat, but the damage was done: the hero of the revolution was dead. Me – I needed a shot of cognac desperately. *Eau-de-vie* would do.

They say booze kills, but I never realised it could do it as quickly as that; I knew that what really killed Marat was his penchant for fine wines, but I was canny enough to realise that a faithful account of events wouldn't tally with the mythology that had already built up around him. When questioned by a couple of revolutionary prosecutors, I simply stated that citizen Corday had assassinated Marat for political reasons, and they agreed it was an open-and-shut case. No time would be lost in taking the perpetrator to her appointment with Madame Guillotine.

By then I felt my sojourn in revolutionary Paris had run its course and requested to be released into the Seine. I was – but the two brain-dead oafs who carried me to the river in the smelly old washtub jolted me around horribly, and then simply threw me off one of the bridges. I landed with the most excruciating bellyflop, and floated helplessly downriver for a good half hour before I regained control of my fins. *Bon dieu*, I felt rough. A short time ago I was debating the rights of fish with a hero of the Revolution, but now my focus was solely on the survival of Gisella.

Although I still felt like death, I decided to make a brief stop to see whether my old friends Madeline and Patrice, the wigmakers, had weathered the storm. I found them older and greyer but still very much alive; they'd got out of the hairpiece trade, though, and now tailored a natty line of utilitarian revolutionary clothing from scrap fabric. We were able to share a frugal lunch of *saucisson* and crusty bread before I resumed my journey.

After my experiences in the capital, I felt every one of my 700 odd years. Every fin and every scale felt arthritic, and as for my poor belly, it felt sore as hell. It was time for this old fish to retire and I thought back to Ugolin, the cook at Count Roland's manor back when I first encountered the human race prior to the Norman invasion, and his tales of his native Provence, where the sun always shone, the weather was balmy, the air scented with lavender and rosemary, et cetera, ad infinitum— That would be ideal for this old carp. Down to Le Havre and turn left then.

Notes

[1] *Guilde des Perruquiers.* Snobby wig-makers for snobby people, a closed-shop union.

[2]Marat, Desmoulins, Robespierre and Danton. At this point they were but fledgling dissidents. For the very, very long version about them read Hilary Mantel; for the concise alternative persevere with this book.

[3]*Le Hameau.* The Hamlet. A rural idyll.

[4]'Let them eat cake.' It was supposedly brioche actually, but let's not split hairs.

Chapter Seventeen

Manon du Moulin. Gisella is saved by a family of Provençales, spends considerably more than a year in Provence, and helps invent a highly dangerous substance

If I'd hoped a long sea voyage would be restorative I was sadly mistaken. Progress was slow, and storms in the Bay of Biscay didn't help. Rather than plough on towards the northern Spanish coast, I headed into the Gironde Estuary in order to call in at Bordeaux and see if I could get my chops around some decent calorific human food. *Moules* and *crevettes* and lugworms are all very well, but this sore and weary carp felt in need of some comfort food, and that meant pâtisserie.

From what I was able to see, Bordeaux was a very fine city, with a large, teeming port, crammed with seagoing ships. Of course, since I'd started my long journey south the wine blockade had been lifted, and tuns of claret were being loaded onto merchantmen almost round the clock.

What really captured my interest, however, was a group of travellers tottering over a gangplank onto a much smaller, single-masted craft, that had a team of eight rowers. Initially I busied myself surreptitiously slurping down a half-eaten pastry that a little girl had thrown in (which the Girondins apparently called *chocolatines,* but I knew as *pains au chocolat*), but then I gleaned that the vessel was about to leave for Sète. Well, Sète didn't mean very much to me, but then I learnt that from there it was but a short hop from there to Les Bouches-du-Rhône, and then on to Avignon. My lateral line immediately prickled. If this was some sort of cunning

shortcut to the Mediterranean, then I'd be able to reach Provence without the endless and wretched business of rounding the Iberian Peninsula.

Initially I tried following the riverboat up the Garonne, but the water was thick with mud and I soon lost sight of it. No matter – following such a major river upstream didn't exactly overtax my navigation skills, and the going would've been easy had I not been feeling so lousy.

Little by little the water clarity improved, and I saw that I wasn't the only fish migrating upstream. The Garonne was doing a lively piscine tourist trade with several salmon, sturgeon and allis shad (a sleek migratory fish that looks a bit like a cross between a sea trout and a herring) also making their way against the current. Also present – surprise, surprise – were literally tens of thousands of grey mullet, which were completely at home in fresh water and quite happy to ascend several rapids. Unfortunately, the river wasn't quite so docile now.

In the middle reaches of the river we frequently had to ascend uncomfortably fast water and heavy flows – which I found hard work, as did the rowers on the numerous riverboats I encountered. Sail was fine under normal conditions and in the sluggish stretches, but where the river sped up the boatmen definitely worked up a sweat. And these were normal, low-water river conditions; looking at the riverbanks, it was clear that the Garonne sometimes suffered almost biblical floods, which meant there was always an element of risk attached to the voyage, and travelling in winter would be extremely hazardous.

Although I still felt gruesome, I couldn't resist the temptation to explore such intriguing tributaries as la Baïse, le Gers and le Tarn, and towns such as Agen, Condom and Montauban, which ended up slowing my journey by four years. I'd hoped my poor, painful stomach would eventually show signs of recovering, but actually my condition just seemed to deteriorate. I needed to press on, otherwise I felt I'd never reach my balmy, fragrant destination.

At length I reached Toulouse, the famous Ville Rose, and had I not spotted a riverboat entering a lock to the side of a backwater I might easily have missed my turning. I followed it in, then waited uneasily as the lock gates were closed behind me and the enclosure started to flood with water from a couple of unseen, powerful sluices. Such turbulence! As if I wasn't uncomfortable enough to begin with. But then the gates at the other end of the lock were swung open and as the riverboat was towed out of it I followed. It had been traumatic. I'd hated the experience and prayed I wouldn't have to go through it again. Ever.

Little did I know. Actually, I soon got used to passing through canal locks, and had I not been in so much pain – and of course mullet-headed – I might've admitted to myself that the experience was quite invigorating. But this grumpy old carp wasn't going to confess any such thing.

Unfortunately I missed out on the Toulouse experience. I caught glimpses of its magnificent buildings, with their distinctive pink brickwork, its markets, its southern *joie de vivre*, but by then I didn't care. I ploughed onwards. I learnt I was in the Canal du Midi, one of the engineering wonders of the modern world, but all I wanted to do to get to the end of it as quickly as possible.[1]

After a couple of days I realised I'd reached the canal's highest point, and the subsequent locks were taking me on a downward gradient. Whoop-de-doo. Castelnaudary, Carcassonne, Narbonne. *Bof!* I swam grimly on. The canal seemed to go on forever. Into l'Étang de Thau, where I saw and took no notice of thousands of exotic pink wading birds, standing on one leg in the shallows. On I swam.

I should've rejoiced at passing Sète, and my arrival in les Bouches-du-Rhône should've filled me with glee, but I felt too ill to be bothered. The fires of hell seemed to be burning in my stomach. All I really wanted was to find a quiet, warm backwater somewhere and live out my last days in peace.

Funny I should've thought of peace, because it was brought sharply home to me that La France was at war. Sitting low in the water, close to the mouth of le Petit-Rhône, a French man-of-war was being towed by a couple of longboats. Only one of its masts remained, large portions of its hull and decks had been reduced to matchwood, and it was plainly unable to steer: the ship looked in as sorry a state as I felt. In spite of myself, I approached the stricken vessel to catch the boatmen's chatter about what had happened.

As I understood it there had been a major engagement between the French and the English fleets just off the Egyptian coast.[2] The

French ships had remained at anchor, lined up a short distance from the shore, confident they could withstand any attack. That had been a mistake.

The English fleet had divided into two, one half attacking the seaward side of the French line at a diagonal angle, allowing its ships to train their cannon directly at the French while avoiding most of the enemy's return fire. The other portion of the English fleet manoeuvred into the narrow channel between the French ships and the shore, and opened fire on their landward side. The French hadn't even prepared the shore-facing sides of their ships for battle, assuming all the action would take place to port, i.e. out at sea. Their starboard gun ports were closed and anyway, none of the cannon were in place. For the Rosbifs it was a turkey shoot; for the French carnage. It was agreed that Admiral Brueys deserved to be hanged for gross incompetence in his handling of the battle, except that he'd already perished on his flagship, *l'Orient*, which had been blown to smithereens when its magazine took several hits.

The direct result of the battle was the destruction of three quarters of the French Mediterranean fleet while, the English suffered little more than a couple of cases of seasickness and a midshipman with a splinter in his finger, but among the longboat crews there was also an overwhelming fear that while the French army was a force to be reckoned with on land, their lack of sea power left them very vulnerable.

Sobered by this latest demonstration of humankind's destructive tendencies, I was more determined than ever to find some final resting place – somewhere far from all the madness. I headed up the Rhône, then, for no particular reason, I took a right turn before reaching Avignon and found myself in a river called the la Durance (a fact that couldn't have interested me less at the time), and continued upstream. By this time I was barely conscious, my lopsidedness had become so pronounced I think I was swimming on my side, and my eyesight was going. In short, I was dying.

Little by little I came to again. As my sight crept back into focus I realised I was immersed in water, in some shallow kind of wooden trunk, indoors. A pretty young girl of about fourteen, with long straw-coloured hair, wearing the simplest of country dresses, was rubbing some sort of ointment into my poor belly. '*Enfin! Bienvenu, Mademoiselle Carpe!*' She then called out to someone in some language I couldn't understand. She was quickly joined by a middle-aged couple, a woman and a man, who like her wore the simplest peasant clothing.

'*Pardon*,' said the woman. 'We normally speak Provençal, our French isn't so good.'

'But we're trying,' said the man. 'Provence is part of Greater France, and we must all speak French now.'

Delicate as I felt, it didn't escape me that the two ladies glared at him.

Over the next few days my kindly hosts filled me in on what had happened during the ten days I'd hovered at death's door. It appears I'd somehow made my way up a tributary of the Durance called le Vairon, past a tiny village called Vairon-la-Romaine, right the way up to the mill pool of le Moulin de la Herse, a mill situated about half a league upstream from the village. (For those interested in that sort of thing the English for *vairon* is minnow. And the eponymous stream and village weren't very big. At the time I couldn't have given a fig about any of that.) They'd found me floating semi-conscious in the pool, and initially their intention had been to prepare a hearty *carpe à la provençale*, but they soon thought better of the idea. Firstly, my stomach had an ugly wound which was surrounded by some kind of horrid fungus, and secondly, I was deliriously babbling all kind of *conneries*. Demented nonsense about Marie-Antoinette's absurd hairdos and setting London on fire and helping King Harold escape from the Battle of Hastings, as well as assorted babble in a variety of strange foreign languages. In other words, a load of incomprehensible twaddle.

Esteve, Beatris and Manon had debated what to do with me. Esteve was nervous about having anything to do with a talking carp that made not one iota of sense, but he was outvoted by Beatris and

Manon, who pointed out that you don't encounter talking carp every day. They were going to look after me and see if I was capable of making any sense once my wound was healed.

It turned out that this charitable family ran le Moulin de la Herse, and Madame, Beatris, was something of a healer. At that time many country women continued to dabble in mysterious medicinal arts, although they still ran the risk of being accused of witchcraft, even on the cusp of the nineteenth century. Beatris treated my wound with poultices made from mouldy bread (brioche would've been preferable, but all that cream, sugar and eggs makes it a faff to make, not to mention expensive), and gradually I improved. Then, one day, still not feeling quite myself, I ate some of the mouldy bread dressing Beatris was trying to apply to me, and was sharply told off. It was then, however, that my recovery really accelerated. Beatris wasn't sure she'd be able to persuade many of her other patients to eat her mouldy bread cure, but it was clearing up my infection like a treat. The stuff tasted pretty awful, though, so I insisted on washing it down with a slug of pastis. (It's said that pastis is an acquired taste; I acquired it in a matter of seconds. But we carp are suckers for aniseed flavour – it's been used in baits for centuries.)

I was seldom without company during my convalescence. Beatris was practised, deeply knowledgeable, and extremely gentle in her treatment of me, and chatted about the wonders of nature, the herbs she gathered and the wild foods she foraged. She was a true daughter of Provence, and appeared to centre her entire existence on the Vairon valley. Her knowledge might've been gained in a geographically tiny area, but it was truly encyclopaedic.

Esteve aspired to be the opposite; he aspired to be French to the core, even if when he spoke the language he had a Provençal accent as thick as tapenade. While he was a hard-working miller and well-respected in the area, he was also an avid supporter of Napoleon. He saw Provence and *les Provençales* as part of a greater France, and was adamant that they should all speak French. Always eager to get another language under my belt, I requested a bit of conversation in Provençal, but it was immediately obvious that he expected me to help him brush up his French rather than he tutor me in his native tongue. Beatris and Manon would be the ones to teach me Provençal, which I learnt was the same as Occitan. Two birds with one stone, eh?

Esteve's big fear was the English. He was terrified that following the naval debacle at Aboukir *les Rosbifs* might invade at any moment. Doubtless Napoleon would build up France's naval strength once more, but in the meanwhile *La Patrie* was in grave danger, and it was up to all citizens to keep the wolf from the door. (Where in God's name was he getting this guff from, I wondered?) Still, he continued, he was developing a secret weapon for the defence of his family and property, and when I was well enough to return to the river he'd be happy to show me what he was doing.

Manon proved a competent nurse and a good companion. Like her mother she'd never left the locality, and the nearby town of Cavaillon was the farthest she'd ever travelled, but unlike her mum she had ambitions to see the wider world. On market days at Cavaillon there were stalls with all manner of goods, there were boys, whose eyes followed her wherever she went, and there was even a school, where people learnt to do numbers and read and write. But what she really wanted was to travel farther and wider. Maybe some day she'd get as far as Aix-en-Provence, or Arles, or even Avignon – some day.

She listened wide-eyed when I told her of my travels and the characters I'd met over the years. I don't know if she believed any of it, or in fact whether she'd heard of any places or people I mentioned, but that didn't matter – they were good stories, and they gave her a glimpse of a different world.

The time came when I was well enough to be released into the mill pool, just below the water wheel. The mill was powered by a sluice-controlled channel that led from the Vairon and poured, via the wheel, into the mill pool that lay below the mill itself, and to the side of the family's house. There was also a little boathouse attached to the wall of the dwelling that housed the family's rowing boat, which Manon quietly told me was used for fishing. The pool then narrowed once more into a modest, canalised channel, before re-entering the Vairon some seventy to eighty yards downstream.

It was good to get back into open water, and Manon accompanied me in the family boat as I enjoyed stretching my fins once more. My belly felt fine again, and I allowed myself a chuckle at how being chucked from a bridge had nearly been my downfall, when I'd been the downfall – directly or indirectly – of so many bridges over the years. A few circuits of the pool were enough. I had all the time in the world to build up my strength again.

Esteve, meanwhile, carried on developing his secret weapon. 'You may not know this,' he told me, 'but the stuff I sweep up from the mill floor can make an explosive mixture.'

'Really,' I said, not wanting to show off. I remembered very well how a combustible pile of chaff, dust and quern grit had barbecued a number of very unpleasant characters in a certain fourteenth-century Kentish mill, but I didn't want to appear a know-it-all.

'I mix chaff, dust and quern grit and pack it into old hollowed-out gourds,' he beamed. 'When they're ignited they flare up and explode. The trouble is, I haven't hit on a formula that's terribly destructive yet. Sometimes they bang, sometimes they fizzle, but they don't really cause that much destruction. I want something that'll blow up an entire platoon of *sales anglais*, but as yet I'd probably only singe a few whiskers.'

From the mill pool I was able to watch as he tried out his next prototype bomb at his test site – a dried-out old well that lay about eighty yards away. He lit the fuse, tossed the device into the well, ran for cover, and threw himself on the ground. Then there was a dull phut sound and a tiny puff of smoke rose from the well. 'Ah well,' he sighed. 'Back to the old drawing board.'

'I think I know what's missing,' I told him. 'Your mixture contains most of the ingredients of gunpowder, but it's missing something sulphurous.' How did I know this? I've picked up a few things over the years.

Esteve shot me a look that said *nobody likes a wise arse*, but he simply said, 'And where the hell am I going to get any sulphur?'

The next few years drifted by most pleasantly. As always Esteve milled the grain brought to him by local farmers and villagers, chatted about the war and their continuing fear of an English invasion, and carried on trying to make his exploding gourds more potent than Guy Fawkes Night sparklers. Beatris made him use an old stone hut some distance beyond the end of their vegetable garden for his experiments, not that there appeared to be any danger attached to his concocting.

By contrast Beatris's concocting was considered highly effective and won her much respect locally. When not helping her husband in the mill she disappeared into the countryside for hours on end, gathering plants and herbs, and then used them to prepare remedies far more effective than any on sale at the apothecary's in Vairon-la-Romaine, and she also used her herbal expertise in cooking up the most delicious meals.

Manon, meanwhile, grew up into a beautiful young woman. She had inherited her mother's independent spirit, so naturally they clashed. Beatris repeatedly told her it was high time she found a husband – after all, her four older sisters had all been married off at a far younger age – and it wasn't as if there was a shortage of eager suitors in Vairon, but Manon would just roll her eyes. She wanted to learn things, to see a bit of the world, to spread her wings, and talking with me had no doubt helped fan the flames. To her credit, if Beatris held me responsible for turning her daughter's head she didn't show it, but I think that deep down she knew Manon was going to make her own decisions in life, come what may.

I loved the region and saw no reason to move on. Because in places the sides of the Vairon valley dropped steeply down to the waterside, I was able to get good views of the surrounding countryside, which was simply magnificent. Lower in the valley were fields and fields of lavender, along with olive groves, almond and peach trees, while higher in the hills the cultivated land gave way to rough scrubland, *le Maquis*, heather, abounding with wild thyme, rosemary, dwarf pines and juniper. Even from the river I could smell the various scents of Provence, which were almost intoxicating.

I frequently swam down to the village, which I discovered was called Vairon-la-Romaine because an ancient Roman villa had been located there. All that now remained of it was a couple of broken stone columns, because over the centuries the locals had helped themselves to all the villa's stones, but the name had remained. I'd hang around near the village's bridge and watch the world go by, listen in to conversations drifting from the nearby *auberge*, and slurp scraps of bread thrown in by the baker's young son, who knew me simply as *le gros poisson*. The grown-ups never believed the tales about such a big fish in such a modest river, but I was a popular visitor with young Franck and his chums.

Our idyllic life was about to career right off the rails. One morning there was a cry of anguish from Esteve's ramshackle laboratory: some tiles had blown off the roof and numerous pigeons had got in and crapped all over his precious pile of combustible detritus. My by then fluent Provençal was enriched by several new words; when distressed, Esteve always reverted to his native tongue.

I called out to him that he shouldn't be downhearted. Not spotting that Beatris and Manon were desperately trying to shush me, I told him that could be just the breakthrough he'd been looking for. Bird poo contains all sorts of nasty chemicals, including sulphur, so maybe that was the vital missing ingredient. Under their breath the two ladies contributed still more to my vernacular Provençal.

A scant half hour later Beatris, Manon and I looked on, breath bated, as Esteve marched over to the old well, ignited his latest gourd bomb's fuse with a taper, dropped it into the void, and ran back for cover. Before he could even start his dive there was a truly massive explosion that left an enormous crater in the space the well had occupied, and sent tons of rocks and debris high into the air. How he wasn't maimed or killed outright by it when it returned to earth is a mystery, but he escaped with a few cuts and bruises. Water, meanwhile, was pouring through the breached riverbank into the hole gouged by the explosion, creating a brand-new pond.

When we all started to recover our hearing Esteve was exultant. Just let *les Rosbifs* set foot in their valley now! Just think of it. With his wonderful discovery he could help France win the war against the perfidious *anglais*. Facing his super-powerful bombs any army would be quickly wiped out, while the powder would at least double the range of the French navy's cannons. Hurrah, *vive la France!*

Beatris and Manon were furious with him for being a bloody idiot, and I wasn't in their good books either. Talk about giving an idiot a loaded gun. I decided that under the circumstances it would be better to make myself scarce for a few hours, and flitted downstream to the village.

From the near bridge I could see the edge of the village square, and in it several French soldiers had assembled a large group of the local lads and men. What I couldn't see I was able to hear clearly enough.

The soldiers were *recruiting* civilians for active service in the French army. The process wasn't so much asking for volunteers as press-ganging, and pretty well any male between fourteen and fifty who could stand up straight and walk ten paces was selected.[3] There were a few muted complaints, especially from distraught womenfolk, but the troops' major bellowed at them to shut the hell up. It was evident that he held the locals in very low regard; calling them all Provençal pigs was a bit of a giveaway.

'But who'll be left to keep things running?' complained M. Lefevre, the mayor. 'You're taking all our labourers and tradesmen. The village will die.'

'The women can do the work,' said the major. 'Anyway, there's bound to be a few cowards who've gone into hiding, there always are. Mind, if we find any of them, we bayonet them.'

It was then I found the baker's tearful son cowering in a bush down by the water. There was no colour in his face and he couldn't stop shaking. 'What happened?' I asked.

'The soldiers,' he sobbed quietly. 'They took *maman* away, and when they'd finished with her she was weeping and covered in bruises and could barely walk. And *papa*, they'd held him tightly, but when he cried out they stuck a big knife in him. I couldn't see if he was all right, I just ran.'

'You must stay hidden,' I told him. 'Stay hidden until the soldiers have gone.' I could do nothing to comfort him – I felt helpless and useless. Making my way downstream I came across Maurice, an amiable old village drunkard, lying half in the water, blood seeping from a wound in his neck. Apparently he'd been deemed unfit for active service. Hearing more voices, I made doubly sure no one could see me from the bank. Nearby, several soldiers were planning their next move.

'We've just about cleared up here.'

'In more ways than one.'

'Speak for yourself, I never got any.'

'Boo hoo for you, pal.'

'There's still a mill a short march up the river. Might be worth a look.'

'Oh yeah? Where that bloody great thunderstorm must've been. I half thought it was the bloody English invading.'

'Who cares? According to the mayor there's no suitable men up there, just some miller who's too old—'

'You haven't listened, have you, *mon pote*? There's no suitable men, but word has it there's a very tasty daughter.'

'Ah.'

'What are we waiting for?'

'And if we're caught wandering *off-piste*?'

'We're after deserters. Requisitioning rations. Anyway, it's only those primitive Provençale peasants, so who gives a rat's arse what we do? It's not like it's real French people.'

I'd heard enough. I was off back upstream at a rate of knots.

Esteve was simply incredulous. French soldiers would never act like that – they wouldn't besmirch the honour of *La Patrie*. He crossed his arms and refused to listen. Beatris and Manon had no such faith in the military, however, and with the sound of boots on gravel approaching we decided that I'd help Manon find a hiding place the soldiers would never find – in the Vairon.

She hurriedly made her way to a spot in the river upstream from the mill's feeder stream, and when I joined her I found a hollow beneath a rushing weir which concealed her perfectly. I was very fearful for Beatris and Esteve, however, so I cautiously made my way back along the circuitous route to the mill pool, where I was able to overhear some of what was going on in the house. It made harrowing listening. The soldiers knew they'd never find the girl in the fading daylight, but they'd discovered her clothing upstairs and insisted she couldn't be far away. They wanted to know where the old couple had hidden her, but not only would they not tell them, they could not. The men were very unsparing in their efforts to extract the information, however, and I knew they'd never survive the night if they weren't rescued. I returned to Manon. I'd thought what to do about the soldiers, but I'd need her help.

A little later the soldiers heard a voice from outside. It sounded as if it was coming from near the mill pool.

'*Maman*, *papa*, have they gone yet?'

'It's got to be her,' whispered one of the soldiers.

'Blimey, she sounds a right old scrubber,' said another.

'So what if she's been around the block a few times? I've gone without long enough and I'm not fussy,' said a third. 'Come on.'

Outside, the soldiers couldn't see me but they could still hear me. 'Oh hell,' I cried in an exaggerated voice, 'now I'm for it!'

The bit between their teeth, the soldiers chased my voice along the riverbank as I sped downstream. 'Help!' I cried, trying to sound as girly as possible. I redoubled my speed.

Further on downstream, the soldiers caught sight of a silhouetted figure in the mill's rowing boat. 'There she is. Me first, boys!'

When I reached the main river I carried on swimming at top speed, leaving the men well behind me. And when the soldiers reached the rowing boat they were a little surprised to find it contained a scarecrow holding a gourd with a little fizzing fuse in it, rather than a terrified young woman. The next instant they were wiped from the face of the earth.

Esteve and Beatris were much the worse for wear. They were covered in bruises and what may possibly have been small burns, plus poor Esteve's jaw looked out of kilter and he could speak only in a low mumble. We reckoned we had about a day's grace before the soldiers' comrades came looking for them – and they'd find parts of them were scattered over a wide area – which meant we needed to take urgent action.

The Dufresnes, who owned a nearby farm, were happy to supply their old neighbours with an ox and cart, and their sons, who'd emerged miraculously from *le Maquis*, helped the millers load their most useful belongings onto it. Before setting off, my dear friends came down to the mill pool to say goodbye to me.

They were off to Avignon, where they were sure relatives of Esteve would take them in. Manon was excited at the prospect of at last getting some learning, even if she had to beg, borrow or steal to acquire it, while Esteve, in a painful mumble, swore he'd not lift a little finger to help the French now, and promptly dumped his remaining explosive powder in the stream. Beatris was distraught at leaving the valley where she'd lived all her life, but she knew they'd never feel safe there again. The military had ruined that. As for me, I could've stayed put. I could've stuck around in beautiful Provence, but recent events had rather soured the mood and I too felt it would be prudent to make another move. Go to England, Esteve muttered. He was rooting for the Rosbifs from then on; as far as he was concerned, Napoleon and his followers could go and boil their heads.

I waited behind for a couple of hours while the toxic powder in the water dissolved and dispersed downstream from me. I looked around at the lavender fields and olive groves and expanse of fragrant *Maquis*. It was still only a degree or two removed from paradise. In the words of someone or other, I swore I'd return.

Notes

[1]Constructed during the reign of Louis XIV, The Canal du Midi (or Canal des Deux Mers; actually it has a lot of aliases) links the Bay of Biscay with the Mediterranean. It's considered one of the engineering marvels of the 17th Century. Eat your hearts out, Rosbifs.

[2]The naval engagement was the Battle of Aboukir Bay.

[3]By this time during the Napoleonic War the French army wasn't being too choosy about its intake of canon-fodder. Nor its recruitment policy.

Chapter Eighteen

Une partie de campagne. Gisella returns to England and meets a painter, a cartoonist and an eccentric royal, and has a rather odd literary encounter

I was determined to follow Esteve's advice. Not because I'd decided to take sides in the war – a plague on both their houses was my attitude, or at least a heavy cold – but rather it appeared very hard to think of anywhere that humans weren't knocking seven bells out of one another, and also I had an inexplicable hankering after some suet pudding. Being in the country of *crème brûlée*, *brioche* and *crêpes Suzettes* that probably sounds bizarre, but I found myself missing the kind of good, plain grub that someone's grandma used to make.

Retracing my swim up the Canal du Midi and down the Garonne wasn't nearly as arduous as my outward journey had been, and although I encountered the usual crummy weather in the Bay of Biscay I had no major setbacks, and at length made my way up old Father Thames and into London. The city had grown, naturally, but at first I could see little change. The docklands area was still poor, and the farther west I swam the more affluent it became.

Various items of food were still chucked from London Bridge, but the houses on it had vanished and the thoroughfare had been widened to accommodate a constant throng of people, horses, carts and carriages. I was also aware of another change: the water quality in the Thames had deteriorated still further. All the pie crusts, bacon rinds and morsels of jellied eel that landed in the drink now tasted rather odd – it took quite some getting used to. As for the people hurrying by, chatting and gossiping, most of them were displaying symptoms of advanced paranoia about an impending French invasion.

Not so different from France and the fear of an English invasion then, nor, for that matter, the panic that had surrounded the approach of the Spanish Armada in 1588. Even I knew that following the overwhelming defeat of the joint French and Spanish fleet at Trafalgar there was zero possibility of La Grande Armée crossing the Channel, but who was going to listen to a lopsided carp who no longer knew anyone in the country?

I spent the next few years cruising the Thames, rediscovering it all from Greenwich up to Lechlade. I knew you could expect a better class of scraps if you hung around Westminster or Windsor, or headed up the Cherwell into Oxford, but it was all pretty nice. Not the South of France perhaps, but its quintessential Englishness still had plenty of charm. These were good years, despite my not having made any friends.

This changed when I stopped to look at scruffily dressed chap of about forty who was fishing in the Twickenham stretch of the river. He had just caught and was releasing a sizeable chub, which in itself wasn't remarkable. Chub certainly aren't gourmet fare. What arrested me was the fellow's tackle: a thinner, more rigid rod than I'd ever seen before, coupled with a large-capacity, shiny new reel. This angler obviously spent more on his gear than his clothes. He gawped at me gawping at him.

'Bloody hell, what I'd give to catch you!'

'That, my friend, isn't going to happen.'

The man sat down with a thump, but soon recovered his composure. A good sign.

'That's some pretty snazzy kit you have there,' I said.

'Isn't it.' The angler showed no ill effects from being spoken to by a lopsided carp with a husky French accent. 'The rod's Tonkin bamboo, which is really stiff yet supple, and the reel's a brand-new multiplier. I had to send away to the United States for it.'

'Must've cost you a pretty penny.'

'Don't even go there. But I look at you and I don't think I'd stand a chance if I hooked anything your size.'

'Please! You're speaking to a lady.'

'Pardon, no offence. Foot in mouth strikes again, I'm afraid manners have never been my forte.'

'Think nothing of it. If I'm honest I think it's pretty good manners when people don't try to eat me. And I notice you put that chub back, so you're not really fishing for food, are you?'

'No, not at all. I just love fishing. It takes my mind off work, and talking of work I've just been feeling rather jaded about it all of late. Same old thing, I'm in a rut.'

'So what do you do?'

'I'm a painter. A paintings painter, not a house painter. And I've got a lot of work to do, and I just feel bogged down.'

'What kind of painting do you do?'

'Landscapes, mainly. Are you an art lover?'

'I don't get much chance to look at art, as you can imagine, but I did know a painter in Venice once. Long time ago, though.'

'Hmm, Venice. Maybe I should think of going on a Grand Tour again now this wretched war has finished. Meanwhile, I'm stuck with a commission to paint castles. Windsor bloody Castle next, and it's going to look just like all the others. Clean lines, clear colours, faultless brushwork, immaculate perspective, easy-peasy, blah blah. I'm in a rut.'

'I know Windsor. There's actually a rather good view of the castle from the river, a lovely little spot by an island. I could show you.'

'Why not? It's got to be done I suppose. I can make some pen, ink and watercolour sketches to work from. Tell you what, I'll hire a punt and bring a picnic, we can make an occasion of it. Does next Wednesday suit?'

'Any day. The name's Gisella by the way.'

'William. Joseph Mallord William Turner. Pleased to make your acquaintance, Gisella.'

Carp aren't very good at telling the time, which explains why I turned up at the Windsor reach of the river rather early. The sunshine was already pleasantly warm, however, swallows were dipping, and emerging damsel flies were clawing their way up reed stems. It was idyllic, a perfect English summer's day. I'd picked a spot near an island, with a grand view of the castle and its grounds close by, so I relaxed in the balmy river margin to wait for William to arrive on his punt.

'How now, fair fish, is this not the most *frabjous* of summer's days?' An elderly gentlemen was speaking to me, and he clearly expected an answer. He had long white, unkempt hair and a straggly beard, wore a

long, tattered gown of threadbare dark red velvet and went barefoot. The way his skin and clothing hung loose suggested that while he was now as skinny as a rake, he had probably been quite portly earlier in life. His appearance may have been rather odd – who am I to judge? – but he looked harmless enough.

'It's gorgeous,' I said. 'Absolutely perfect for taking in the sights.'

'Ah! Do I detect a delectable Gallic twang? Are you a visitor to our fair shores? Is this not a most pleasing aspect?'

'It's lovely, but I wouldn't exactly describe myself as a tourist. I've spent a fair amount of time here over the years.'

'An old hand then, although should I not say, fin? Excuse me – I've often been taken to task for my poor jokes. But that would explain your perfect English. I count myself as a fairly gifted linguist myself. German, Dutch, French, Spanish. In my former line of work it was expected, but it's all rather rusty now. However, enough about me – how boorish to speak about myself in the presence of such an unusual and talented visitor. If you're not a tourist would it be impolite to enquire as to what has brought you to Windsor today?'

'I'm meeting a chum for a picnic.'

'Formidable, I do so love a picnic. But I have no desire to intrude, so when your friend arrives I shall melt away like a dawn mist in sunshine.'

'Don't be a twerp, I'm sure there'll be no need of that.'

'*Si, ma chère carpe*, you've no doubt heard the saying, two's company but three's a crowd.'

While my new friend was rabbiting on I felt the unmistakable vibrations of an approaching boat, and looked round to see a punt being clumsily poled up the river towards us. On it, poling most clumsily, was William Turner, plus A. N. Other. The Other was a jolly-looking fellow at least twenty years older than William, who by his expression evidently thought his companion's boatmanship wasn't of the highest order.

'William,' I called. 'Over here!'

'I am melting away,' said my new friend. 'Melt, melt, melt.' Actually, he still looked very present.

William drew the punt to the shore and doffed his cap. 'Morning, Gisella, I've brought a mate if that's okay.'

'The more the merrier,' I said. 'I appear to have a plus-one as well.'

'The name's George,' said the unkempt man with a graceful bow. 'Delighted to make your acquaintance.'

'I'm William Turner,' William told George, 'and this here's Thomas Rowlandson.'

'How do,' said Thomas, who then scratched his chin thoughtfully. 'There's something ever so familiar about you.'

George just smiled.

'Blimey,' said Thomas. 'You're only the ma— Er, King George.'

'Mad King George,' George smiled. 'That's what they call me.'

'*Mais ce n'est pas juste*,' I said. 'He may be a tad eccentric, but I certainly wouldn't say mad.'

'It's all a charade,' said George. 'Techniques I gleaned from my good friend of yesteryear David Garrick, the *akk-tor*. It's all just to give me a modicum of P and Q. But if you try to tell anyone I'm not bonkers I'll start jabbering to the nearest rhododendron.'

'This is a turn up for the books,' said William. 'I suppose we'd better address you as Your Majesty or similar.'

'Don't you dare,' said George. 'You can save all that malarkey for my idiot son the Prince Regent. He wanted power, pomp and circumstance and he's entirely welcome to it. *Bon courage*, I say, *Viel Glück*.'

'That's a relief,' said Thomas.

'I know who you are now,' said George. 'You're the cartoonist chappie. You lampooned me mercilessly. That drawing of me being rogered by George Washington.'

'Not guilty,' said Thomas quickly. 'That was Gillray.'

'It was brilliant,' laughed George. 'All those cartoons are, and I'm well aware you have brought forth more than your fair share of them too. Worry not, my friend, you and your confederates perform a great service, and I'm most grateful for it. And as for all those pornographic prints you do—'

'Erotic,' Thomas complained meekly, 'and humorous. I don't think they'd get anyone that excited.'

'They're absolute magic. My dear chap – you cannot know how much I appreciate the way you chaps take down the great and the good and the pompous.'

George told us that over the years he'd become increasingly fed up with not just being a monarch, but the whole institution of the monarchy. The idea that a few generations back some ancestor of yours turned out to be better than anyone else at bashing people over the head, or getting others to bash people over the head, and on that basis you got to rule over everybody. Absurd! And all these meaningless rituals built up over the years to reinforce a ruler's status:

Black Knob performing a Buggaloo to confer the Order of Bishbashbosh upon yet another obnoxious sycophantic hanger-on. Pinning pretty ribbons and attractive brooches on ridiculously garish outfits, making everyone look like idiot popinjays. The grotesque accoutrements of power and the ridiculous symbols of obscene privilege. Fawning and arse-licking and backstabbing.

The longer he'd reigned the more he'd become disillusioned with the whole revolting pantomime. By the time the American colonies declared independence he was secretly on their side, and when Louis XVI and his missus were deposed he was heartily in favour of *la Révolution.* Naturally when he tried to speak out about his feelings he was gagged by Parliament and all his horrified advisors, and whenever he persisted in his heresy he was called unhinged and locked away. So, reluctantly, he mostly kept on script and performed his part and was a good, well-behaved king again. With a few minor relapses, of course.

It was lamentable about poor old Louis and Marie-Antoinette, but they really weren't the sharpest knives in the drawer – and what on earth possessed them to dither about in Versailles when they could've shown the revolutionary guards a clean pair of heels? (I thought it would've been disrespectful to point out that the royal couple came to grief only because the Queen Consort had insisted on a detour to say farewell to a certain carp.)

When the true scale of the butchery carried out during the French Revolution became known, George felt an increasing sense of doom. The hopes he'd harboured for a new, egalitarian society were melting away like summer snow. The fledgeling republic across the Atlantic was already riven by factional bickering, and it hadn't even got as far as abolishing slavery; and as for Revolutionary France, it was *liberté, égalité et* massacres.

Then, of course, came Napoleon Bonaparte. George had still kindled a slight hope that after a period of adjustment France would perhaps get its act together, but then *le petit Caporal* crowned himself Emperor and something inside him went *kaput.* He'd had enough. Everyone thought he was barmy anyway, so now he was going to prove them right. Georgy-Porgie was made Regent and got his greedy mitts on the reins of power at long last, and he was able to retire in peace as Windsor's resident looby-loo.

To begin with every move he made as the castle lunatic was closely monitored, but gradually, as he proved he was quite harmless and had no desire to wander off anywhere, he was left to his own devices. He had a minder who was supposed to keep an eye on him, but the fellow preferred to spend his days more pleasurably with a young widow up in the town.

'Don't get me wrong,' said Thomas, 'I'm no great supporter of the monarchy. But what would you replace it with?'

'You're asking the resident lunatic?' said George. 'Flubble.'

'You're just being a tease,' said William. 'You must've had some ideas on it.'

'I'm an old man, long since mothballed, and you want me to sort out the future?'

'Yes please,' I said. 'I'm sure you've had plenty of time to think this stuff through.'

'Maybe we can continue this over there?' said William. 'That island looks a wonderful spot for some watercolour studies, and I really should put brush to paper.'

George jointed William and Thomas on the punt and, with three men plus a picnic basket, several bottles and an assortment of art equipment on board, the craft looked somewhat overloaded. William successfully if precariously manoeuvred it across the river and moored it alongside the island.

'Your blueprint for a better Britain?' Thomas reminded George.

'Well, it's more a list of ingredients, but how about abolition of slavery, equal rights for women, no more hereditary titles, a widespread programme of decentralisation, the individual regions run by assemblies of representatives drawn from all walks of life, universal suffrage in the election of the aforementioned assemblies, no taxation without representation, nationally determined rates of pay for all jobs, fair land distribution, all businesses run as cooperatives, free universal education and health-care—'

'No wonder you were declared a basket case,' said Thomas. 'That's *far* too much sanity for the great and the good of the land to stomach.'[1]

'Amen to that,' said William, who'd pinned a dampened sheet of paper to his drawing board and was mixing some paint in his paint tin. 'Though if you get rid of all the aristos then most of my clients disappear in a puff of smoke.'

'Ah, but the common man – or women – will be better able to afford the finer things in life,' said George.

'Not at his prices,' said Thomas.

'You sell your prints by the hundreds,' said George, 'so why not William?'

'Because I sell original artworks,' said William. 'If you could get better reproduction from the printing process maybe that'd work, but at present the medium's better suited to Thomas and company.'

'Maybe printing will improve in the future,' I chipped in. 'Maybe someone'll invent a process that makes flawless facsimiles of fine paintings.'

'The horror,' said William, frowning as he applied brush to paper. 'Just imagine it. The great masterworks could end up plastered anywhere. The *Mona Lisa* on biscuit tins, *The Anatomy Lesson of Dr Tulp* on tablemats, *The Martyrdom of St Sebastian* on bedsheets.'

'Just imagine if they find a way of doing that with music,' I said. I was off on one, and no one had even opened a bottle yet. 'What if someone made a machine that could reproduce great music as well. A music-playing machine.'

'Eek,' said George. 'Queen Mary's funeral march by Purcell in physicians' waiting rooms.'

'Bach's double violin concerto in mail coaches,' said William.

'Mozart's *Requiem* in tavern taprooms,' said Thomas.

'Everyone help themselves to food,' said William. 'There's cucumber or tongue or pilchard paste between slices of bread, lardy cake and rock buns, and a choice of claret, porter, sack or brandy for those with a thirst. Maybe a snort or two of the grape will put a cork in that fish's flights of fancy.'

'Don't mind if I do,' I said unwisely.

The day passed by most pleasantly. There were a few fluffy, insignificant clouds in the sky, but nothing to ruin the sunshine. Bees buzzed, great crimson dragonflies zigzagged by, water boatmen scuttled. After eating their fill Thomas and George dozed while William carried on painting, but he painted with a frown on his face.

'Too stiff,' he muttered to himself. 'It's all so – correct. Just like everything else I bloody do. And it's boring. Pah!' He put his watercolour aside to dry in the sun and pinned another sheet of paper to his drawing board. I asked him for another brandy. It was my third, and I think he had a very liberal hand.

We weren't the only ones enjoying the river that day. All kinds of craft passed us by, from riverboats to tiny skiffs. Ever since the final defeat of Napoleon at Waterloo there had been a feel-good factor, and the recent fine weather contributed still further to a general mood of well-being. People were happy, good natured and exuberance prevailed. Then we heard the approach of an oversized rowing boat whose passengers, six women of varying ages, were far more than averagely exuberant. The two oarsmen, by contrast, looked as if they'd rather be anywhere than on the river.

'Yoo hoo, boys,' a middle-aged lady cried out to us. 'Look lively, I've seen more life in a barrel of kippers.'

George and Thomas awoke with a start. 'That's Maria Edgeworth, the writer,' gasped Thomas.

'Oi, you,' cried a young woman. 'Rowlandson. Are you going to put me in one of your smutty drawings?

'And young Mary Godwin,' William chuckled. 'She's a fine one to talk, the way she carries on with Percy Shelley.'

'Get 'em off!' roared a prim-looking, elderly lady.

'And that, if I'm not mistaken, is Jane Austen,' said George with a smile.

'Get 'em off yourself,' I roared back. I wasn't one hundred per cent sober. '*Espèce de veille morue!*'

'Some Frog floozy just called you an old codfish!' another middle-aged lady said to Jane Austen.

'Show your face, *sale pute!*' shouted Jane Austen.

'I'd keep mine hidden if it was anything like yours,' I slurred. 'Anyway, it takes one to know one!'

As the boat swished past several empty bottles were launched from it, along with a stream of jolly invective, some of which I believe was Germanic in origin. One of the missiles glanced off King George's head and another landed right in front of my nose, but the rest flew harmlessly wide.

'Ladies. Please!' said one of the oarsmen.

'Shut up and row, cute stuff,' said another lady of a certain age.

'Who *were* those people?' I said as the ladies faded into the distance.

'Fanny Burney, Jane Austen, Susanna Rowson, Mary Godwin and Ann Radcliffe,' said William.

'The finest lady writers of the age – otherwise known as the Green-stockings' Literary Circle,' said Thomas. 'It must be their annual beano, they're known for letting off steam.'

The heat of the day started to become oppressive – if you were a human. Being immersed in the Thames I was of course fine, except for a spinning head for some reason. Thomas and George complained they were baking, and William griped that he'd now reeled off a half-dozen quick watercolours and they were all crap.

'You're all hot and bothered,' said Thomas. 'Here.' He scooped up a wineglassful of water from the river and flicked a few droplets of it into William's face.

'Ah,' said William. 'More!'

'I can give you more,' I laughed. I leapt from the water and blew a mouthful of water over him.

'What th—' he cried.

I took his shout for approval and repeated the process, but it turned out he wasn't so cock-a-hoop about being sprayed after all. 'Aaargh, I'm soaked, and you've got river water all over my paintings!' He stood sharply up, knocking into George's back, and before we knew it the punt had rolled over and everyone and everything was in the drink. I made a mental note to limit myself to no more than two brandies at all such future events.

All the soaked paintings, art equipment and picnic items were heaved back into the righted punt, and we paddled our way back to the shore. My head was still spinning uncomfortably.

'Where's the punt pole?' William demanded.

'It's just there on the bank,' said Thomas.

'Good,' said William. 'Because when I get my hands on that fish I'm going to insert it where the sun never shines.'

'Your paintings,' exclaimed George. 'Look at your paintings!'

'I know,' William barked. 'Gisella's bloody ruined them. It's an effing disaster.'

'No,' said Thomas. 'Look at them. I mean *really* look at them.'

George was laying the soaked watercolours on some bankside bushes so we could all see them, me included. It was true that the paints and ink had run, and colours had bled into colours, but actually the effect was wonderfully harmonious. No more harsh lines – everything was correct, but it was all correct in a totally natural sort of way – organic rather than deliberately constructed. Spontaneous yet timeless.

'Well fuck me sideways,' said William.

'By George I think he's got it,' said Thomas.

'They're wonderful,' said George. 'These aren't paintings that engage the intellect, they engage the emotions and the senses.'

'Do you think you could do that back in your studio,' said Thomas, 'in oils?'

'Oh yes,' beamed William. 'A thousand times yes. Now I know what I'm looking for, I see a whole new phase taking shape! No matter what the critics may say, and I expect all the old fossils at the Royal Academy will be simply beastly, Joseph Mallord William Turner is henceforth an artist reborn.'[2]

'A new artistic genre has come to be,' said George.

'The three great Romantics of the age: Keats, Beethoven and Turner,' said Thomas.

'Aren't you going to thank me?' I said, trying to fight back my encroaching hangover.

'Thin ice, Gisella, thin ice.' But of course William wasn't angry, he was too exultant.

Before we took our leave of one another, Thomas gave me one final nip of brandy and a large wodge of lardy cake, which he assured me would settle my stomach. George said his minder would shortly have finished with his paramour and be on his case again, and William and Thomas wanted to head back towards Twickenham before the day was done. I must've been starting to feel a little better because I was getting that familiar itchy-fin feeling again – in other words, *wanderlust.*

Notes

[1]New ideas were slow to take root in George III's time. Whereas in this day and age, all progressive and humanitarian political ideas are warmly embraced. Oh yes.
[2]As we know from Gisella's chronicles, Titian had produced one impressionistic work several centuries earlier, but it was lost to the mists of time. The whole world knows that J M W Turner produced work that was a good fifty years ahead of its time.

Chapter Nineteen

The Gosditch saga. Gisella catches up with the Industrial Revolution, learns about the East India Company, takes a dip with royalty, and makes herself scarce again

On a whim I swam upstream, and as I approached Oxford I remembered promising myself a visit to the university some 200 odd years ago. Thanks to the chatter I heard from passing boats I had no trouble finding my destination, and located the perfect spot for insinuating myself into the company of the university's savants by the grassy banks of the River Cherwell, a tributary of the Thames, close to a majestic college building in the Gothic Perpendicular style.

I didn't have long to wait. Four whiskery gentlemen tottered down to the riverbank and laid out a picnic of fine-looking victuals – pork pies, chicken legs, more meats between slices of bread (which the gentlemen described as *sandwiches*), various pastries, rock cakes and a couple of dusty bottles. I looked longingly at the bottles, and then shook my head. The men were dressed in long, black gowns, wore odd, flattened caps with tassels dangling from them, and between them probably had an accumulated age of over 300 years. Nothing compared to a certain venerable carp, but quite respectable for humans.

I listened avidly to their conversation, but to my great disappointment found it did little to elevate my levels of learning.

'Overcooked, this chicken.'

'Not mine. It's a little bit chewy – I don't think it's cooked enough actually.'

'Nice pork pie though. Lots of scrumptious jelly.'

'Pork pies should be heated though.'

'Rubbish. You don't know what you're talking about.'

'Gentlemen! Each unto their own.'

'Very passable drop of port, this.'

'Not bad. But the 1779 is better.'

'Well, only a nincompoop would dispute that. But when did you last lay hands on a '79?'

'Ugh. Why do they leave the crusts on these sandwiches?'

'Chuck them. That's what I do.'

Unlike the erudite picnickers I had no qualms about noisily slurping down the crusts that landed nearby, which of course gave away my presence.

'My word,' said Oxford don number one, 'what a big fish you are.'

'I'm a carp actually. And there's nothing wrong with these *sandwich* crusts at all.'

'A carp that speaks with a rather common French accent,' said don number two. 'Phenomenal!'

'Well, I'm a common carp. *Cyprinus carpio*.'

'A learned common carp,' said don number three. 'Fancy that. I imagine there's much you can teach us.'

'Actually, I was rather hoping to learn from you,' I said. 'This is a university, isn't it?'

'Indeed. *Maudlin College* to be precise,' said don number four. 'Though it's spelt M-a-g-d-a-l-e-n, for the uninitiated. It has a very fine kitchen, but the sandwiches are a let-down.'

'Fascinating,' I said. 'Although I hoped we could get into some rather more erudite discourse, such as whether the French Revolution was a direct result of the Enlightenment for example?'

'As I see it,' don number one scratched his whiskers thoughtfully, 'the Enlightenment helped usher in a more prosaic approach to French cooking: *Liberté, égalité et potage pour tout le monde* etc.'

'Conversely the revolution also provided a boost for *haute cuisine*,' said don number three. 'All those cooks who served the thousands of aristocrats who went the way of *la guillotine* were forced to go independent and opened up their own restaurants. Good food became available to the hoi polloi. The democratisation of gastronomy.'

'Plus many masterless chefs fled over the Channel and opened up eating houses here,' said don number two. 'There's one in the town, *Les Quat' Saisons*, I can recommend it highly.'

'It does a wonderful *filet de veau à l'estragon*,' said don number four. 'And a memorable *carpe à la sauce m-o-u-t-a*—'

'Harumph. Moving quickly on,' I coughed. 'Maybe we should discuss literature. Shakespeare: the greatest English writer, or are there any other contenders?' (I wasn't about to get into the real provenance of Shakespeare's works, however aggrieved I felt about poor old Anne Hathaway.)

'Look no further,' said don number one. 'Shakespeare. Not one iota of doubt.'

'Take Falstaff,' beamed don number two. 'Both a gourmand and a gourmet. No one could polish off a roast swan like John Falstaff.'

'Ah, but who can forget Sir Toby Belch in *Twelfth Night*?' said don number four. '*Dost thou think, because thou art virtuous, there shall be no more cakes and ale?*'

'You're all forgetting *Antony and Cleopatra*,' said don number three. '*Eight wild boars roasted whole at breakfast – and but twelve persons there*'— Surely they're the greatest of Shakespeare's gluttons.'

'Is there any subject you're happy to talk about other than food?' I asked.

'Not really,' said don number one. 'At our time of life it's the only thing that really interests us.'

'There is something that you could tell us, though,' said don number two. 'Being French and all that.'

'A question that has plagued us over the decades,' said don number three.

'Which offal makes the best andouillettes,' said don number four, 'cow or pig?'

Feeling that my quest for personal enlightenment had hit the buffers, I sadly bade the four epicurean dons farewell and headed back to the Thames. Dreaming spires (well, the tops. You couldn't see that much from the river) and bread crusts are my abiding memory of Oxford University, which is a bit of a shame.

A little way beyond the city I caught sight of a very narrow but rather long boat being towed by a couple of sturdy fellows into a lock, on the north bank of the river. I'd seen larger barges on the Rhine, Elbe and Danube, but this was a smaller craft, more suited to narrow waterways. Intrigued, I followed it into the chamber and went through the familiar whooshing, churning sensation as water gushed into it, raising the water level to that of the channel beyond in a matter of a few minutes.

Once freed from the lock the barge was hitched up to a pair of carthorses (pairs appeared to be most common, although smaller vessels with lighter loads were often pulled by single horses), which proceeded to plod their way along the path that followed the canal bank, towing it behind them. This, I very quickly gathered, was the Oxford Canal, and the barge was en route to the north Warwickshire mining area to pick up a cargo of coal.

What had I been missing? While my eye had been off the ball a vast canal network had been created covering most of England. I'd made good use of the Canal du Midi in France, but now the Brits had embraced canal transport in a big way and given me a way of exploring most of the country. After several hundred years I was about to venture north of Watford. Oh, brave new world!

Locks slowed my progress slightly, but I had to admit I preferred using them to leaping over weirs in rivers. Putting up with a little bit of effervescence and waiting for the next barge (and how often you'd wait for an hour before two or three turned up in a row) was a small price to pay.

I passed through a green and pleasant land, of sheep and cattle farming, wheat and barley fields, and numerous orchards. The small towns and villages that lay en route were sleepy and picturesque, suggesting a way of life that hadn't changed in hundreds of years. It was a bucolic wonderland. On the barges there was much chatter about the town of Birmingham, which was now only a few miles distant. I imagined it would be another gem of antiquity, like Oxford or Stratford or Gloucester.

Of course it wasn't. I approached Birmingham at night, and nothing on earth could've prepared me for what I encountered. I was familiar with the concept of Hell, and Birmingham by night perfectly matched what had been conjured up in my mind's eye. Night was supposed to be dark but here it was ablaze, illuminated by countless fiery, spark-spewing furnaces in scores of vast, satanic iron-smelting plants, belching out clouds of choking smoke. It was noisy: crucibles clashing, carts clanking, molten iron hissing, men shouting, whistles shrilling. It was smelly: acrid ash and coal dust penetrated everywhere, rendering the canal water as thick as soup and stinging the eyes and clogging the gills. Swim deep and you risked maiming yourself on the debris that lined the canal bed, swim shallow and you were in immediate danger of collision with barges. I couldn't see how humans could possibly survive such in an alien environment, and as for fish.... I pressed on, praying to whoever or whatever watches over carp who've lost their way to deliver me to sweeter water, and in spite of a number of near disasters with sunken coal carts, trolleys and looming barges, I gradually left the toxic zone behind me. Little by little I became aware of light penetrating the murky water, then, wonder of wonders, I caught sight of the sun. It was setting; I'd been in that nightmarish poisonous gloom for the best part of twenty-four hours. Canal travel was great, but somehow I'd have to find routes that avoided the worst of those appalling *manufactories*, as I believed they were called.

It was a long, long process, incorporating numerous detours and not a few U-turns, but on my grand tour of England I successfully avoided Stafford, Stoke-on-Trent, Crewe, Manchester, Liverpool, Runcorn, Huddersfield, Sheffield, Doncaster, Leeds, York and Chesterfield. Which was a shame, because some of those places might've been rather nice – but after my Brummie experience I wasn't going to take the risk.

What I did learn, because barge folk chatter just like everyone else, was that the nation was in the throes of mass industrialisation. All manner of goods were being produced in the new manufactories, and the manufactories gobbled up vast quantities of coal and iron and wool and cotton, and what fed these raw materials to the manufactories was the canal network. It was an industrial revolution, no less. The bargees were kept constantly busy, but they reckoned they had it far better than the poor souls on the manufactories' production lines. It was often repeated that while the French Revolution took place to liberate people and failed, the Industrial Revolution was created to enslave them and succeeded. And poison them, I thought to myself.

I'd overheard a lot of talk about a brand-new canal, a third Pennine crossing no less, which was due to be opened in the very near future. Running from Kendal to Ripon, the Gosditch Canal – named after one Josiah Gosditch, the canal's benefactor – was one of the highest canals in the country, and incorporated a magnificent iron- and stone-built aqueduct that spanned the Ure Valley. The given reason for its construction was the transportation of raw materials between the manufactories on either side of the Pennines, but some wags also suggested that it was a vanity project by J. Gosditch Esq., he of pots of New Money, to help him climb the social ladder.[1] The canal also passed close to his newly constructed country pile at Marsborough, Gosditch Manor. Naturally I found the idea of navigating a brand-new canal most appealing. If there was any heavy industry along it I could always turn back.

Its westerly section connected with the Lancaster Canal at Kendal, and there I had the good fortune to tag along behind a small barge carrying a team of navvies up to where I understood some work was still being carried out. The first thing I noticed on entering it was how acidic the water was. It had a real tang, although it wasn't actually that unpleasant once you got used to it. I now know that the high acidity was due to its water being drawn from the peat bogs in the moorland hills. It was heady stuff. With hindsight I'd add it could've done with a splash of soda.

Apparently the canal itself had been completed, but Mr Gosditch had another project in hand, and I had a vessel to chaperone me through all the canal's locks. It wasn't long before we were climbing, and yes, there were plenty of locks. En route I learnt that that the men's employer was a right bastard: with him you worked twice as hard and twice as quickly for half the rate, so no wonder a great deal of shoddy work slipped through the net, but what choice did a working fellow have? It wasn't as if jobs grew on trees.

We stopped for the night at Sedbergh, where the men made camp and I fed on the scraps that they tossed into the water, then, late in the afternoon the next day we navigated the spectacular aqueduct that crossed the Ure Valley. I say it was spectacular but that was because the boat's passengers were all deeply impressed by it; I myself could only notice that the waterway narrowed somewhat for the crossing, and that it was encased in sturdy cast-iron plates that were riveted together.

Shortly after we ascended one more lock, then the men moored their vessel and made camp again. They were visited by a stocky, bewhiskered man in a suit of finest tweed. He dressed like a sixty-year-old, but couldn't have been a day over twenty-five, with a face that looked as if a smile would cause him excruciating pain. The workers all respectfully addressed him as Mr Gosditch Sir, so I surmised I must've heard his name wrong before. Work was to begin the next morning, at seven sharp, and he expected the job to be completed within a day. A fair day's pay for a fair day's work, that was his motto – at which the men all exchanged covert sour looks. I decided to stick around and see what the *fair day's work* involved. Curiosity killed the carp, as the saying goes.

The next day saw the navvies hacking away at the canal bank with picks and shovels for all they were worth. I stuck around like a gawking idiot because every so often a discarded bit of ham rind or pasty crust came my way, and I still wanted to see what they were up to. Then, approaching midday, the men all leapt clear as suddenly water started to surge through the breach they'd excavated in the canal bank, and naturally I was sucked into it too.

Buffeted and battered, I was carried downhill with the torrent of canal water for nearly two hundred precipitous yards until it finally slowed and then calmed altogether. I was barely conscious and unable to get my bearings, but after feebly swimming in a few circles I ran aground close to a muddy bank, and, resting in a few inches of water, I could move no more. '*Au revoir*, cruel world,' I gasped. 'To end my long, eventful life in a muddy ditch, such a terrible anti-climax.'

'Ay up,' said a loud voice. 'Who's a bloody melodramatic fish then.'

I looked up and saw Mr Gosditch Sir staring down at me. He clearly didn't know whether to be shocked or amused by me, but amusement appeared to be winning. 'You're not in *any* ditch,' he continued, 'you're in *my* new estate lake, thank you very much, and I certainly didn't expect it to have any fish in it yet, let alone ones that speak with a Frog accent. In fact, what kind of fish are you?'

The news that I was in a lake was reassuring. Maybe I wasn't on the verge of an inglorious demise after all. I wriggled into slightly deeper water and righted myself back into my usual lopsided posture. 'I'm a carp Mr Sir,' I said. 'A common carp.'

'Well, I won't hold that against you, but where does this Mr Sir codswallop come from? The name's Gosditch, Josiah Gosditch Esq.'

'Ah. All the men were calling you Mr Gosditch, sir, so I assumed your name was Gosditch Sir.'

'I see. That's logical in a way, if bloody daft. Now we've got that over, do you have a name?'

'Gisella.' I looked around. I'd need to explore a little to discover what manner of lake I was in, but, looking ashore, I saw a pleasingly Arcadian landscape leading up to a brand-new Palladian-style mansion house (or neo-Palladian if one's going to be pedantic), with a backdrop of spectacular moorland. '*Mon dieu*, all this is yours?'

'Ay. Well, that's my posh house anyway. I also own a coalmine, three cotton mills, a couple of iron foundries, four ships and a canal, which I'm guessing you're already familiar with.'

'*Incroyable*. Are you some kind of lord or something?'

'Er, no, that happens to be a work in progress, I'm a self-made man but I have my eye on the prize. I know how to make brass, and by hook or by crook I'm also going to earn respect too.'

'So you're aiming to join the upper crust?'

'Exactly. And I'm well aware of the irony that the first fish in my lake is a bloody common carp.'

'I don't think you'll find many of us that speak. But talking of fish, what other fish are you planning to put in here?'

'Trout of course. Game fish. Summat classy.'

Huh. Trout. Flitty, silly things that fill their gobs with flies and think they're cute because they look like they've got the measles. I know they're supposed to taste good, but all the same. 'A very pretty fish, yes. But maybe you could go for a little diversity too? A couple more carp? And, of course, some tench. You should never underestimate a—'

'I'll think on't.' He glanced at his pocket watch. 'Time stands still for no man. I'd better get back up to th' cut and make sure that band of loafers aren't skulking off on my shilling.' With that, Mr Gosditch turned and strode purposefully back up towards the canal.

Thinking that Mr G wasn't a man to be trifled with, I set off to explore my new lodgings. It turned out that I was in triangular body of water, which had a dam and sluice gate at its far end. It was a generous size, probably at least three acres, with a small stream tricking into it at the shallow end. I realised this was the course that the torrent had taken to fill the lake, although of course it was now tamed and controlled. At this point the lake was three to four feet deep, but it sloped away to thirty or more at its far, dammed-up end.

Once some marginal reeds had grown, along with a few lily patches, it would be more than comfortable.

A couple of days later three large containers of live fish were emptied into the lake. Bloody trout! I'd already formed the opinion that while Mr Gosditch was quite capable of listening, he was also pretty selective about it. Subsequent events would prove me right, but while I hadn't found him exactly *sympathique* as a person he hadn't bopped me on the head either, and he'd also provided me with some very passable accommodation. Also, I rather hoped he'd reappear for further chinwags from time to time, because being stuck in there with a few hundred trout was bound to be exasperating.

I didn't have to wait long. He reappeared that afternoon and proudly told me that his trout were the finest that money could buy.

Whoop-de-do, I thought. But I knew I should try to be polite. 'Talking of money,' I said, 'I'm guessing you weren't born into wealth.'

'Too bloody right I wasn't,' he said. 'My da was a coalminer, and naturally it was expected that I'd follow suit. And I did for a couple of years, but it was bloody awful. Sheer hell. It was just da and me – my mam and sisters had been carried off by the typhus years before, and we worked all God's hours and ate no better than bloody livestock. Da only stood it because he had a knack of switching off from it all and imagining he was in a garden – a big, lovely garden with all kinds of vegetables and fruit and flowers of every description – that were his great dream. But as for me, I didn't want to dream about what I didn't have, I wanted to grab it. And any chance of getting out of there I was going to seize.

'That's what cropped up when a traveller, on his way back to his old home in Carlisle, stopped for a couple in our local public house. You could tell he had brass, and he told us how he'd got it: a spell out in Bengal with the East India Company. He'd been a soldier, in charge of a company of local sepoys, and yes, he'd seen plenty of action. Mainly it was putting down the local bigwigs and their various armies, or chasing after bandits, but more often than not the EIC – *The Company* – got its own way by playing the locals off against one another. Why risk your neck when you can get the blighters to shoot one another? When they did have to stand and fight it was usually a foregone conclusion: the Company's forces, whilst mainly composed of sepoys, were almost invariably better trained and better armed than the locals' armies, and increasingly more numerous too. The Company's forces now numbered well over 200,000, considerably larger than the entire British army! And the pay? The pay wasn't at all bad, but it wasn't as good as the opportunity for graft. The Company siphoned millions out of India thanks to a heavily weighted import / export trade – backed up by cannons and muskets – but enterprising individuals probably drained off even more.

'I could hardly wait to pack the few clothes that I had. Two weeks later I turned up at the grandiose East India House in Leadenhall Street, East London, and the next day I reported to a dowdy building that looked like a giant shed in London Docks, where my official recruitment took place – with no regard at all to my tender age. Another two days after that I was aboard the East Indiaman, *The Colossus* – a somewhat ironic name for a runty two-decked, three-masted vessel with a single row of gunports, that had been captured from the French off the Egyptian coast in 1798. *The Colossus* had seen better days, and a great many of them.

'At first I was terribly seasick, but we were all expected to help the crew in their daily duties, and having tasks to perform at least took one's mind off how wretched one felt. We were told the voyage usually took around six months; *The Colossus* took nine. I had no idea where we'd land, and the fact that we struck shore at the miserable little port town of Kedgeree, by the Hooghly River, was of no consequence at all for me.

'There was a small garrison at Kedgeree, where I undertook my basic training. God it was boring. Drilling, drilling and more drilling. Loading muskets, cleaning muskets, taking muskets apart and putting them back together again, firing muskets, fixing bayonets, bayoneting straw bales, bashing straw bales over the head. Standing in neat rows firing muskets with whizbangs going off all around you. Marching and more marching. Taking orders and giving orders; even although I was bottom of the European pile I was still ranked higher than any of the local soldiers.

'I was a corporal and my immediate superior, Sergeant Geraint Watkins, was a very odd fellow indeed. His face was exceedingly hairy so it was hard to estimate his age, and he was so softly spoken I had to listen very hard to hear his orders before relaying them to the sepoys under our command. His chief pleasure in life seemed to be searching and destroying the lice and bedbugs that infested our barracks. It wasn't so much that he was bothered by all the itching, he liked the pop they made when he squished them.

'As for dealing with the sepoys, we had to learn a certain amount of Bengali – just some basics, such as fire, reload, charge, stick the bloody bayonet in him, run away – although to be fair a number of them actually picked up very decent English. We'd been told the Bengalis weren't very bright, but I'd contest that; they could look after themselves, follow orders, were courageous, disciplined, and of course far better able than us to deal with the insufferable bloody climate. If I had Bengalis working in my manufactories I'd be considerably richer, I can tell you – but I digress.

'The sarge and I were usually given the bum-hole jobs, while the more elite soldiers – every white man except for us in other words – invariably saw the more serious action. Was I happy about that? Well, no, because overseeing latrine duty and taking the colonel's son fishing weren't very likely to make me rich in a hurry. However, after nine months of utter tedium all that changed.

'The main garrison had marched to Calcutta to reinforce the city's defences, because most of the Governor General's army was in the west of India giving the Marathi forces a right good seeing to. That's how the sarge and I were left with what appeared to be the routine task of travelling inland to a minor client state no one had ever heard of to escort a certain Prince Muzrudhin – a pretty insignificant scion in the Mughal dynasty – to his hunting palace for his annual tiger hunt. Having resisted the East India Company in the past his own militia had been disbanded, but there hadn't been any recent reports of banditry in the region so it was reckoned that me, the sarge and thirty sepoys would be plenty for the job.

'After a three-week trek through jungle that appeared to grow ever lusher, we met with the prince and his hangers-on at his main palace at Padharpur, and commenced the journey to join his hunting party. Apart from the heat and the damp and the insects and the smells, the task was dead easy: a three-day stroll along a jungle track. A team of bearers carried his Idleship, who resembled an overdressed, bejewelled walrus, on a vast and splendid palanquin, which was followed by a coterie of court sycophants and servants. We trudged alongside, keeping at least half an eye out for any potential trouble. Apart from the fact we were unfamiliar with the local lingo, all seemed tickety-boo.

'It was in the middle of the second day that all went not quite so tickety-boo. A prolonged burst of gunfire peppered us from the cover of the impenetrable-looking vegetation, sounding like hundreds of firecrackers going off, and those sepoys not felled by the first few dozen rounds could see no targets to fire back at. Within a few seconds they too were casualties. As for me, I felt a searing jolt to the side of my head and knew no more.

'I came to almost crushed by the sarge's weight; unsurprisingly he was dead as a Bombay duck. I was soaked with blood from his multiple gunshots, as well as the nasty wound I'd taken to the head, which is probably what had saved me up until that point. I had no clear idea of what had happened, but dared not move a whisker for fear of giving myself away. I could hear alarmed, excited voices, however, and oddly enough those voices were speaking Bengali. The cause of their alarm, as I understood it, was that one of their number had spotted a tiger, and they'd all of them heard it. Within a few seconds all was silence, and I was reasonably sure I'd been left alone.

'Very gingerly I got to my feet. My head spun and hurt like hell, but I didn't think my wound was critical. Looking around all I could see was death: the prince's entourage were all dead, the sepoys were all dead, and the sarge was very dead indeed. I turned away from the carnage and was about to slip away into the undergrowth when a heavily accented voice implored me in English to come to his aid. It was Prince Muzrudhin, who'd been trussed up like a giant capon and dropped in the margins of the thicker vegetation. For the very first time he deigned to acknowledge my existence, and my first thought was to leave the idle hog to rot – but then he promised to make me rich if I helped him. *That* was different.

'Before I could even find a knife to cut the prince's ropes, however, one of our assailants returned, evidently having heard our voices. He grinned malevolently, raised his musket and fired at me. The shot punched a hole in my shoulder, but despite the terrible pain this time I didn't pass out. The attacker then nonchalantly started to fix a bayonet to finish me off, while I desperately looked for some means to defend myself. The sarge's blood-soaked pistol lay close by on the jungle floor, and although there was little chance of it firing I knelt down and grabbed it. Seeing me armed, the brigand instinctively turned his back on me. I was shaking like a leaf, plus the pistol was covered in gore and really slippery, but somehow I pulled the trigger, and, after fizzing for a full, agonising, almost eternal second, the weapon discharged – and hit the fellow low down in the middle of his back.

'His legs now useless, the attacker begged to be put out of his misery; lying there as tiger bait was a dreadful end for anyone. The prince extracted from him that he was part a group of Bengali bandits hired by his younger brother to assassinate him. They weren't actually Thuggees,[2] but were notorious Hindi riffraff all the same. They'd kept the prince alive to see if they could get a better pay-out from him and bump off his brother instead – before a lurking tiger spoilt the party.

'As promised we despatched the brigand quickly, and, once we'd struggled back to the palace at Padharpur, where the prince's younger brother had already taken up residence, it was obvious the brigand had told us the truth. The look on the younger man's face instantly revealed all we needed to know. His shock was still plain to see, even after a pistol ball had drilled him a third eye.

'I was patched up at the palace and then, rather ironically, put on a palanquin and given an escort to take me to Calcutta, where I'd receive the medical treatment I needed. Another irony was that following my departure Prince Muzrudhin resumed his interrupted hunting trip, fell off his elephant and was eaten by a tiger. A shame really, because in the end I'd rather warmed to the fellow.

'The reason he'd got into my good books was that concealed under my garments there were two body belts stuffed with precious stones.

I'd worried that he might save all the expense and have me assassinated, but not only had he turned out to be a man of honour, he was fantastically rich too. It was then I discovered the real currency of British India: bribery and corruption. Money was able to open doors that previously I never knew existed. In Calcutta I was able to pay for the best medical care available, and, once I'd recovered from my wounds, I bribed my way out of the EIC army and onto a far more salubrious East Indiaman than the poor old *Colossus.* I wouldn't say *The Quicksilver* was as speedy as a galloping thoroughbred, but it was no slouch either, and brought me back to London in just over five months.

'At Hatton Garden, London's jewellery trading district, a certain Mr Schroeder arranged for the sale of my gems. They were worth so much it took a consortium of three traders to purchase them all, but although I was then rich – very rich – I was given some welcome advice: not to simply live on my wealth. That way a person could easily slip into indolence, waste their life away, and very likely drink themselves to an early grave. Ha! That was never going to happen with yours truly. I've been back some five years, and thanks to all my business ventures I've already nearly doubled my wealth – and there's no way I'm slowing down for the foreseeable!'

'*Sacré bleu,*' I said.

Life passed pleasantly enough in the Gosditch estate lake. Josiah was a frequent visitor, albeit usually to boast of his latest business success or flick an artificial fly at some unsuspecting trout. God they were unsuspecting.

The estate gardener, a rather bent old chap in his sixties called Sam, quickly cottoned on that there was a talking carp in the lake, and fell into the habit of stopping by for a natter at the end of every afternoon. He was far more down-to-earth company than Josiah, and generally turned up with a tasty scrap or two kept from his lunch. Every Saturday he brought along a jug of beer for him to drink, and, on special occasions, a bottle of something stronger from which he always poured me a nip. He was quite funny about his master, amused by his efforts to climb the social ladder, which evidently wasn't being made easy for someone with his background, despite his ever-growing business empire. It was hard to know which was stronger in the man: his contempt for the idle aristocracy, or his desire to join it.

It was during one of our chats that Josiah approached us, clutching his pocket watch, his face like stone. 'I pay you a fair day's wage for a fair day's work,' he said. 'Not to stand around gossiping with a bone-bloody-idle fish.'

'Sorry sir, I had no idea. I thought it had to be gone six.'

'It's three minutes to. Three minutes I'm supposed to be paying you for. I won't bloody be having it.'

'I'll make up the time, I promise. It won't happen again.'

'It'd better not. There's plenty of other folk who'd like your job, you just bear that in mind.'

'I will, son,' said Sam as Josiah huffed and walked away. 'That's a promise.'

I stared at Sam in amazement. 'Did I hear you right? Did you just call him—?'

Sam nodded. 'He's my son. He can't help it. That's just the way he is.'

I remained speechless. I knew fish weren't very well known for close family ties, but humans surely?

'What can I say? I always wanted to look after a big garden, and now I'm in charge of a vast one. And Josiah wouldn't really give me the boot, I don't think.'

As Josiah had found out back in India, money inevitably opens doors. The landed gentry thereabouts might have sniggered at his new money and coarse manners, but brass is not only brass, it's a mighty effective social lubricant as well. Josiah married Dorothy Humbernolt, of the Humbernolts of Northumberland, who had the title and connections he desperately sought, while he possessed the kind of wealth her family coveted, having squandered theirs over several generations.

Dorothy was a kindly soul but never really understood the cut and thrust of her husband's world, and was frequently embarrassed by his poor grasp of etiquette. She quickly became another visitor to the lake, and would confide her frustrations to me. He growled at the dogs, tucked his shirts in his drawers, and teatimes were a nightmare. After all, there was a right and a wrong way to slurp Earl Grey from one's saucer, everyone should know that.

Offspring soon ensued. Over the space of four years three daughters appeared on the scene: Anne, Emily and Charlotte. After that Dorothy appeared to have called a halt to things, which coincided with Josiah's absences from Gosditch Manor – business trips naturally – becoming rather more frequent.

The girls loved to come down to the lakeside to play, and Dorothy charged me with keeping a watchful eye on them to prevent any mishaps. She needn't have worried, though, because they soon grew up into such prim and dainty little madams they made Marie-Antoinette look like a tomboy. They'd no sooner have taken a dip in the lake than roll about in a pigsty; a speck of mud on a pretty frock or a sparrow dropping on a bonnet necessitated a trip back to the house and a complete change of outfit. Unfortunately, they were little snobs to boot, and although they'd been told to treat Sam – their grandpapa – with respect, they were quite aloof towards him, and beyond wishing him a curt good day wanted little to do with him.

Sam died when Anne, the eldest of the girls, was ten, during a very hard winter, which took quite a crop of Marsborough's elderly. Trapped under the lake's ice I missed the event, and found out only ten days later when at last a thaw set in. Apart from me, the one who really missed him was Dorothy, who'd grown genuinely fond of him. The girls seem to have been pretty much unaffected and as for Josiah, he'd been away in Crewe attending to *problems in one of his ironworks* at the time, and hadn't exactly hurried home. He did pay for quite a nice gravestone at St Humbert's, though.

The Gosditch empire continued to grow. The country's rapidly expanding railway network was making canals yesterday's news, and Josiah was at the forefront of the revolution. By now he was a highly respected figure, not just in industry but in *society*, among the people that counted. Perhaps he was even more feared than respected, because Mr *Fair Day's Pay for a Fair Day's Work* held the livelihoods, and often even the existence, of thousands in the palm of his hand, from humble workers to retailers to bankers, even although his definition of *a fair day's pay* failed to tally with most other's – even among his competitors.

He now had his most cherished prize in sight: a knighthood. A knighthood bestowed by Queen Victoria herself. He reckoned the clincher would be the inauguration of the new railway line he'd had built, from York to Carlisle, which incidentally passed underneath his own canal's aqueduct as it snaked its way along the River Ure Valley. The ceremonial opening train journey was scheduled to take place on an early August day, and if the weather was fair the Queen herself would be the passenger of honour, riding in a specially constructed open-top carriage from which she'd be able to wave at her adoring subjects. As the date approached, the hot summer weather showed no sign of relenting, and all augured well for the event. *Sir* Josiah, what a grand ring it had about it.

Sam's replacement was an amiable ex-sailor named Seth, who'd lost most of his toes on a fruitless voyage to discover the Northwest Passage, but he was quite capable of carrying out his gardening duties. *Mostly* capable that should read, actually, because any time after the end of the afternoon it wasn't a lack of toes that made him find walking difficult. In his cups he told me tales of his voyages to the Americas, both north and south, to Africa and the Far East and the Antipodes – making me feel like a parochial stick-in-the-mud. I'd travelled widely in Europe, but this chap had been all over the world it appeared. I made up my mind I had to travel further afield in the future, but then I remembered about sharks and killer whales and giant squid and the like, and changed my mind again. Seth was easy company though, and when he was tiddled he tended to get over-friendly rather than bellicose. If he did lose his temper, it was invariably with inanimate objects.

In the lead-up to the grand railway opening, Mr Gosditch was seldom in residence at his estate. I knew he was worried about a break in the weather spoiling the party, but I could've told him the heatwave was going to continue well past the all-important date. In fact the weather was becoming a very major problem.

Mr G was so bound up in his new projects that he tended to neglect his old ones, particularly those close to home. Seth constantly moaned about being stuck with shabby old tools, and was particularly aggrieved at being expected to put up with a twenty-year-old gardening shed that was falling down. He was going to quit, his cottage wasn't fit for a dog, that scurvy young skinflint expected him to live on the sniff of an oily rag. He was still there, though, and the sniff of an oily rag provided just enough moolah to keep him soused in rough cider and rot-gut rum.

Of immediate concern to me was the fact that the lake's sluice mechanisms were corroded and jammed up. They hadn't been maintained properly since the lake was constructed, which was more serious than it sounds. With the sluices useless there was no circulation of water, and three weeks of very high temperatures had led to a toxic blue-green algal bloom[3] spreading over the water, which was starving it of oxygen. I was starting to feel somewhat uncomfortable, but many of the resident trout – which it should be remembered are really stream-dwellers that need high oxygen levels – were looking as if they'd shortly expire.

Things rather came to a head on the big day. To set the scene, the royal train was puffing its way along the new track beside the River Ure, with Queen Victoria, in a pretty bonnet and a sumptuous summer crinoline dress, riding in a very luxurious, open-top carriage, protected by a lightweight canopy. With her sat the Prince Consort, the beaming and fawning Josiah Gosditch, the Lord High Chamberlain, the mayors of York and Carlisle, and an assortment of hangers-on. One hundred and twenty feet above them, a barge loaded with coal was being drawn downstream by its pair of shire horses towards the aqueduct, which still lay a hundred or so yards in front of them. At the same time, an iron-ore-laden barge had just started crossing the aqueduct from the opposite direction. So far, so good.

All of a sudden the locomotive let out a shrill whistle, which spooked one of the horses towing the barge that was already on the aqueduct. The bargee quickly moored the barge to a section of balustrade to prevent it from being carried back downstream, then he unfastened its towing rope, turned his horses around, and led them back down the towpath to keep them calm until the train had passed. So far so good.

Up at the lake, meanwhile, I'd made it known to Seth that if nothing was done about the poisonous algal bloom I'd very quickly become a casualty just like all the poor suffocating trout. Many were now dead;

more dying. He, well aware that his master was absent for the day, had already embarked on a serious bender, and had kindly given me one tot of nasty rum too many – to help quell my upset tummy it should be understood.

In a flash of inspiration, we decided that by opening the grotted-up sluice in the dam wall we'd be able to drain away the surface layer of lake water with all the blue-green scum, and to do that we'd need a sledgehammer. Seith lurched off to fetch one.

One thwack with the sledgehammer: nothing. It was still stuck solid. A second thwack: nothing. A third thwack and the whole rotten structure just fell apart, and water gushed through the gap. In fact it was rather more of a gush than we'd anticipated, and we realised that entire jerry-built dam was starting to disintegrate. For a man missing most of his toes Seth disappeared astonishingly quickly, while I, along with hundreds of dead and dying trout, was swept in a torrent of putrid blue-green water through the ever-widening breach.

The flash flood wasted little time in finding its way back into the canal, whereupon it roared like a pocket tsunami down towards the aqueduct. Hearing its approach, the man in charge of the coal barge had just enough time to unhitch his horses and lead them up the canal bank to safety before the gush of water carried the vessel away.

At this point, the train was just about to pass under the aqueduct, with no one on board remotely aware of the drama unfolding above.

It all happened at high speed. The speeding coal barge smashed into the moored iron-ore barge on the aqueduct, causing the prow of the coal barge to slew into the canal's plate-metal side. Something had to give, and what gave was the aqueduct. Its iron construction, not of the highest quality to begin with, had suffered twenty years' corrosion from the acidic moorland canal water without any maintenance, and with a loud popping of rivets it simply tore apart.

Two barges, a vast tonnage of coal and iron ore, plus a lake full of putrid water, many hundreds of dead trout and a horrified carp, all plummeted into the void. What on earth was it about me and bridges?

Fortunately, the two stricken barges missed the train completely and landed harmlessly on the grassy trackside, but the accompanying deluge of iron ore, coal, filthy water and expired trout derailed the locomotive, whose crew just about managed to leap to safety, and flipped all the grinding, screeching carriages onto their sides, flinging their occupants into the river.

What of me? The deity that keeps an eye on sozzled carp put in a double shift that day. After being swept into the void and definitely not making my peace with powers beyond my control, I somehow overshot the train wreckage and landed on something soft, wet and very squidgy that was slowly starting to sink in the middle of the river. Apparently the Queen's magnificent crinoline was made of the finest whalebone, tulle, satin and silk, all of which were very soft indeed when soaked. Even after falling more than a hundred feet the impact hardly hurt at all; it was a one-million-to-one chance against, but I'd lucked out again.

The Queen, several horrified dignitaries yelled: had anyone seen the Queen? Having been pulled ashore, Prince Albert was frantic. Bloodied railway workers, flunkies and aristocrats ran hither and thither in a panic, but seemed incapable of taking any useful action at all. Josiah Gosditch sat on the buckled railway track, head in hands, unable to speak.

Having been dragged deep down in the pool that lay just downstream from the aqueduct, an unfortunate lady – let's not play games, it was Queen Vic – was entangled in a mass of sodden fabric, so I did what I could to help her struggle free from it. At last we pulled it away, leaving her dressed in no more than some rather immodest silken undergarments. By this time she was panicking and thrashing out wildly, so I told her to shut the fuck up and pissing well hang on to me, and somehow I manoeuvred her to the riverbank.

A quick glance told me that the disaster was every bit as bad as I'd feared. Wreckage everywhere, a severely breached aqueduct with water still cascading from it, and rather a lot of injured, shocked and angry people. Were there any fatalities? Coward that I am, I decided that a retreat back into deeper water before anyone spotted me was the prudent thing to do.

Prince Albert and the rest of the cronies exchanged knowing looks, and the odd meaningful finger tap on the side of the head, when the Queen, her modesty hastily restored with a blanket, swore she'd been rescued by a large, potty-mouthed French fish. She had not found the episode remotely amusing, and furthermore it was never to be reported upon, talked of or even whispered about, on pain of being charged with treason.[4] And as for that traitor, that blackguard, that would-be assassin, Josiah bloody Gosditch… Incidentally, where was Josiah Gosditch? No one could see him.

The aqueduct was never repaired, and the canal abandoned. Modern-day ramblers find its old course, no more than a slight depression in the ground nowadays, very handy however. The railway line suffered a similar fate, for in Mr Gosditch's haste to have it completed on schedule too many corners had been cut in its construction, and it failed even Victorian health and safety standards. A road eventually took its place.

As for Mr Gosditch and his family, they simply disappeared. It had been hoped that Anne, Emily and Charlotte would make very advantageous matches, for they were by then of marriageable age and came with a most attractive financial package, but of course that prospect disappeared like a puff of smoke. It may have been no more than coincidence, but within five years shops up and down the country were selling packets of Gosditch's Superior Ceylon Tea, but who knows, eh?

Me? I thought it would be advisable to seek adventures new, preferably ones that didn't involve bridges of any description, or put me at any other kind of risk. Once I'd left the barge debris, tainted canal water and late lamented trout behind me, I had a pleasant swim down the Ure, which led into the Yorkshire Ouse, and eventually out into the North Sea.

Notes

[1]Wealth acquired generations ago – good, wealth acquired recently – bad… according to posh people back then.

[2]Thuggees. Back in the days of the East India Company and then the Raj, there was ongoing conflict between the Muslim Mughals (usually top dogs) and the Hindu population (more often hoi-polloi). The Thuggees were supposedly a sect of Hindu bandits with a sadistic streak, but there's evidence that the first Thuggee bands were actually from a Mughal background. A rotten lot, anyway.

[3]Blue-green algae, which tends to proliferate in hot, dry weather, can be a major problem on still and slow-moving waters. Dogs should be kept away from it because it's highly toxic, and as for fish…

[4]The Queen's threat was evidently taken seriously. This incident isn't mentioned in any history books, apart from this one.

Chapter Twenty

La belle epoque. In which Gisella joins a very bohemian set

I led a pretty nomadic existence over the next few years, adding considerably to my collection of languages. I revisited the Baltic, having only hurried through the region a couple of hundred years earlier, and found Stockholm a very pleasant city indeed. Lots of canals – it was yet another Venice of the North apparently – interesting buildings visible from the water, not bad cakes and, as far as I could make out from the remnants that ended up in the waterways, large, incomplete but generously piled-up sandwiches. Sweden appeared to be a very civilised place, but I wasn't overkeen on the winters and failed to settle. Helsinki, Tallinn, and Riga were similar, and I bloody nearly froze when I swam up the Vistula and visited Warsaw.

Copenhagen was another lovely city, but news on the waterfront was that Denmark was at war with Prussia, so I decided to move on, just in case the fighting ever got uncomfortably close.

Heading northwest I found myself at Oslo. Nice place. Bloody cold. I headed back south.

I meandered around the rest of Denmark and took my time revisiting Hamburg, Amsterdam and the Hague, plus Rotterdam, Ostend and Dunkirk for some reason (God knows why), until one day I found myself at le Havre. The idea of another trip up the Seine to reacquaint myself with my old haunts in Paris appealed greatly, but news of war between France and Prussia (at it again – those Prussians!) halted me for several months until peace had been restored. France was once more a republic, the Paris Commune had fallen (shame – I'd quite fancied being a Communarde) and, very importantly, the pâtisseries were open again.

The city had grown considerably since my last visit during the Revolution, with a skyline that impressed even from the waters of the Seine. En route I'd seen no sign of the old wigmakers' atelier. It was all newer buildings, but in the centre of Paris most of the older buildings remained – with the Cathedral of Notre-Dame still bossing them all.

A little way upstream from the Île Saint-Louis I was surprised to find a lock gate on the Rive Droite, which of course was begging to be entered. I slipped into it after a river taxi and soon found myself in a wide, elegant canal. I'd discovered the Canal Saint-Martin, although I suppose you could say I hadn't discovered it because it was already there – but it was new to me.

The canal soon entered a wide tunnel – again a discovery for me – that apparently passed beneath boulevards and parks, before re-emerging into daylight near the Place du Château d'Eau (it sounds so much better than Water-Tower Square), later renamed Place de la République. It then passed close to the prosaic, working-class district of Belleville before bypassing Montmartre completely (which to be fair is on a big hill), before making its way to its confluence with the Canal de l'Ourcq, near La Porte de la Villette. By that time, I'd pretty much left Paris (and according to Parisians that was like dropping off the edge of the known world) so I turned around and made my way back to the Belleville stretch, which I decided had a decent, down-to-earth feel about it – not to mention a rather good *boulangerie.*

The Canal Saint-Martin became my haunt, a pretty good window on the Parisian world for a fish. I started to notice a kiosk by the lock gates at Porte de la Villette, because it was occupied by a splendidly moustachioed official in a neat uniform and cap, who appeared to spend most of his time doodling in a sketchpad. It appeared that he was some sort of tax collector, or customs official, for his main task seemed to be inspecting the barges coming into Paris, collecting fees and rubber-stamping documents. That and the fact that everyone called him *le douanier* – the customs officer.

The more I observed him the less I thought him suitable for his job. If a bargee stopped at his kiosk and said he was carrying a cargo of bottled beer, on which the duty should be twenty-five francs, *le douanier* would say that Parisians were thirsty and charge him five. And everyone had a right to eat fresh food, so barges laden with produce from the countryside were charged at one centime on the franc. When a barge stopped at the kiosk with a cat sunning itself on the cabin roof, *le douanier* said he wouldn't make any charge at all if he could just sketch the creature.

At midday sharp every day *le douanier* put up a sign saying closed for lunch and tucked into a beetroot and anchovy-paste sandwich. Unfailingly the same sandwich every day. And then he'd flick the knobbly end of it (his sandwich was always made from a *ficelle*, a small, thin baguette) into the water – where naturally I'd be waiting for it. The beetroot and anchovy paste I could take or leave, but the bread was very acceptable.

'Bon appetit,' he said one day as I wolfed down the bread.

'*Merci, monsieur.*' There was no point in hiding, *le douanier* could obviously see me.

'The name's Henri, Henri Rousseau. People will insist on calling me *le douanier*, but I don't really like to be defined by such a tedious occupation. I'd far prefer to be called *le peintre*.'

'So you're a painter. I've seen you with your sketchpad.'

'*Le peintre*. It has a nice ring about it. *L'artiste*.'

'I don't suppose you could show me any of your paintings? I really like art – not that I'm an expert or anything.'

'Oh I've never actually done any painting. Not yet, anyway. But I'm still a painter – I've done masses of preliminary sketches, I've got reams of them.'

'So maybe you need to take the next step? Dab some paint on canvas, so to speak? Then maybe people'll stop calling you *le douanier*.'

'*Génial!* But of course! That is *exactly* what I will do! To celebrate this momentous decision, will you do me the honour of sitting for my first painting?'

'Most certainly not, when did you ever see a fish sitting? I'd be quite happy for you to paint me, but I'll be staying right here in the water, thank you very much.'

We agreed that on the next fine, sunny day – that would show me off to my best advantage – Henri would make a few watercolour studies of me, and then afterwards he'd produce the finished work of art in oils at his atelier, or rather his modest house. Once he'd bought all the materials, that was, and learnt the art of mixing paints, etc. First things first, eh?

Henri was able to make a few rough watercolours of me during the next month or so, but then the actual execution of the oil painting seemed to take forever. Whenever I made a tentative enquiry about it Henri told me to be patient, you can't hurry art. I was beginning to think this fabled painting was all in his head.

In the meanwhile, I'd been intrigued by the ongoing renovation of a tumbledown, seedy old bar on the edge of Belleville, that stood by a pleasant, tree-lined canal-side *quai*, two doors along from the Hôtel du Nord. Over the course of six weeks Les Deux Langoustines (named presumably after all the crayfish traps the locals set in the canal) was replaced by Les Deux Anguilles (named presumably after all the eel traps the locals also set in the canal), which to my eye didn't look a great deal less tumbledown and seedy than its predecessor.

At the same time, I couldn't help noticing a rotund and hairy *clochard*, a tramp, who frequently passed through the area and was often so sozzled he'd fall into the canal. I'd keep an eye on him to make sure he got out again all right, because from time to time it was obvious he needed a helping nudge. I learnt that people called him Boudin because he was so partial to those succulent blood sausages, when he wasn't too inebriated to think of eating. His petty thieving, his loud snoring, his drunken rambling, his habit of urinating in a variety of inappropriate spots, in fact his distinct lack of personal fragrance, were all tolerated in the neighbourhood: Boudin was part of the local fabric.

To my great surprise the new bar attracted a lively clientele of labourers, shopgirls, street vendors, prostitutes, ruffians, writers, musicians and artists who fancied a change of scene from up the hill in Montmartre. By day it still looked somewhat down-at-heel, but paradoxically at night it became vibrant, colourful, full of life. Naturally I was very drawn to it.

I liked the chatter and the music and all the dancing that spilled out onto the pavement, but especially I liked the *pommes frites.* Chips had been the new culinary thing for more than a decade, and Lise and Gilles, the proprietors, quickly realised they'd have to serve some sort of food to help the customers mop up all the booze. There were two dishes on the menu: *steak frites* and *tarte aux pommes.* They proved immensely popular with all except for one sole customer, a Belgian named Hughes, who maintained that Belgian chips were vastly superior to French, and that chips had been invented in Belgium anyway. This led to fisticuffs between him and a very irate Gilles, which in turn led to Hughes ending up with two black eyes and a dip in the canal. I made sure he reached a set of iron steps safely, and within a quarter of an hour a few placatory words and a complimentary

drink or three quite restored the Belgian's good humour. Of course quite a few *pommes frites* would end up in the water, and I made sure I was first in line for them.

Little by little *Les Deux Anguilles* became a home from home for alternative painters. It started with a well-built, gruff old chap who'd been kicked out of most of the bars in Montmartre and Montparnasse for getting into arguments with other artists. His constant gripe was that his work was never accepted by *Le Salon*, the annual exhibition of the *Académie des Beaux-Arts*, who were all complete *connards*, which translates loosely as arseholes. Édouard Manet was soon joined by a thin, frail, bearded chap called Edgar Degas, whose work had been rejected by the Académie ever since he'd got a thing about painting lady ballet dancers and call girls – mainly without their clothes. Apparently it was all right to paint naked ladies if they were in a classical setting, but if you put them in a natural, everyday situation then you were creating scandalous obscenity. Édouard had painted a picture of a couple of ladies in birthday suits enjoying a picnic with two clothed gentlemen, which had outraged polite society, presumably because of what the work said about sexual politics and gender imbalance. Bravo, said Edgar.

Lurking near the café's canalside tables I enjoyed the artists' chats enormously. The circle was soon widened as other painters, such as Vincent van Gogh, Gustave Courbet, Berthe Morisot, Henri de Toulouse-Lautrec, Paul Cézanne, Camille Pissarro, Pierre-Auguste Renoir, Alfred Sisley, and Claude Monet took to dropping by.[1] Even the demure Mary Cassatt would lend her presence from time to time, to sip a *vin blanc cassis*.

They shared one thing in common: a lack of acceptance by the artistic establishment. Failure to be recognised by the Académie wasn't the end of the world for them, because an alternative exhibition for more adventurous artists had been created, called Le Salon des Refusés, which attracted quite a few of the more progressive Parisian art collectors. One day, however, the furious Gustave Courbet turned up at Les Deux Aiguilles, clutching a hessian-wrapped painting under his arm.

'*Qu'est-ce qu'il se passe?*' asked Edgar Degas.

'They bloody refused it,' said Gustave. 'Le Salon des Refusés bloody refused my latest painting! They said it was obscene!'

I looked on fascinated as several regulars gathered to commiserate with M. Courbet.

'Well don't keep us hanging about,' said Gilles, *le patron*. 'Let's have an eyeful.'

Gustave removed the hessian cover with a flourish and held his canvas up for everyone to see.

'Egad,' said Renoir. 'A bit revealing or what!'

'You're a very mucky man,' said Lise, *la patronne*.

'*Très belle*,' grinned Alain, a water-taxi owner who'd popped in for his regular *demi* of beer. 'Though I wouldn't say no to seeing her face too.'

'Who on earth agreed to model for *that?*' said Berthe Morisot.

'I like it,' said Suzanne Valadon, a young artists' model who was seldom seen without a sketchpad. 'It's honest – what we're really like.'

'It's what certain parts of us are like,' said Mistinguett, an aspiring young singer who'd recently auditioned at le Moulin Rouge. 'The parts men are interested in.'

Nom d'un chien, I muttered to myself. From where I was swimming I couldn't get a look at the painting to judge for myself.

'I have an idea,' said Gustav. 'A new salon. Le Salon des Refusés par le Salon des Refusés.' The Rejected Rejects' Exhibition.

Le Salon des Refusés par le Salon des Refusés turned out to be one of those ideas whose time had not quite arrived. This was because staging art exhibitions required a high degree of organisation and venues cost money – two things that most struggling artists didn't have very much of. Occasional open-air shows took place along the banks of the canal, but they tended to be patronised only by other artists.

The good thing about Le Salon des Refusés par le Salon des Refusés was that an artist was virtually guaranteed to have his or her painting accepted. In all its history there was only ever one refusal: a creepy young chap called Victor de la Homps, all tweeds and wispy whiskers that failed to hide his weak chin, who'd painted a very bucolic scene of lambs and nymphs and satyrs and classical ruins – a syrupy pastoral pastiche. There was a scrolled inscription at the top of the work, *Et in Arcadia Ego*,[2] which failed to detract from the picture's dire pretentiousness. But its biggest problem was that it was simply crap, really badly painted, the product of a bad weekend dauber on an off weekend. He proudly announced himself as a member of the Brotherhood of Pre-Poussainites, who held that painting had badly lost its way ever since the days of Nicolas Poussin nearly 300 years earlier, and demanded that his *oeuvre* take pride of place at the next exhibition. When *Arcadia* was politely declined, he became quite abusive and assured all present that they'd rue the day they crossed a member of the Brotherhood. They were all vile modernists, purveyors of crudity, pornographers and iconoclasts. 'Oh dear,' said Lise. 'Monsieur de la Homps has got the hump.'

What of my old friend Henri Rousseau during this time? I still made occasional trips to La Porte de Villette, although I'd pretty much given up on Henri ever producing the painting of me that he'd promised. Then, one day, he confided in me that he'd actually finished it, but outrageously it had been refused by Le Salon. Worse, it had been refused by Le Salon des Refusés, the imbeciles! I asked if he'd show it to me, and he fetched the picture from his kiosk.

It was like nothing I'd ever seen. A highly stylised version of me, all burnished reds and golds and emerald greens, luxuriating in a waterscape that resembled a tropical rainforest more than an urban canal. The colours were stunning, it exuded life. I loved it, and told him he ought to take it along to Les Deux Anguilles.

Opinions about *Carpe équatoriale* were divided.

'A question,' said Paul Cézanne. 'Why is the fish, clearly a common carp, swimming in a jungle? Surely rusty old bedsteads and dead cats are a more typical background in the waters around here.'

'Ah,' Henri smiled. 'The rainforest represents the wonders of nature. This reflects what I saw when I travelled extensively in tropical Central America.' (I later discovered that he'd never travelled any further afield than Poitiers, but why let the truth stand in the way of a good yarn?)

Berthe Morisot found the painting childlike. Toulouse-Lautrec liked the composition. Degas, looking iller and more dishevelled than ever, said the perspective was too flat. Van Gogh loved its colours and *joie de vivre.* Young Suzanne Valadon, never short of an opinion, declared it showed amazingly strong design. Édouard Manet suggested that Rousseau maybe shouldn't give up his day job quite yet.

'I already have,' said Henri. 'I'm sure my genius will be recognised in time, and the world should not be denied the opportunity to feast upon my works.'

Lise gave a wry smile and tapped the side of her head. 'Pompous or what,' she muttered under her breath.

'I see a public divided,' said Henri. 'Perhaps we should allow the subject of my painting to be its final arbiter. Gisella?' He pointed down at the canal, straight at me. Everyone stared; I could easily have swum off, but I felt some loyalty towards my friend and didn't want everyone to think him even more eccentric than he actually was.

'I like it,' I said. The collected onlookers all started; I was definitely an oddity, even in their bohemian world. 'The jungle setting is the fruit of a truly fecund imagination, canal or no canal, and as for the exaggerated colours, my colours, they reflect the vivid and endless variety of—'

'Good God,' said Lise. 'The fish speaks complete bollocks too.'

'All right,' I said. 'I like the painting, okay?'

'And we like M. Rousseau,' said Mary Cassatt. 'It's a good thing for artists to be confident, right?'

'I'm sure the work will find a home in Le Salon des Refusés par le Salon des Refusés,' said Alfred Sisley, not as a rule the most effusive of men. 'Wear it as a badge of honour, *mon ami.*'

'My unique talent will shine through, said Henri. 'But enough chitchat *messieurs-dames*, I have a thirst and would gladly sip a little *tisane*.

'Splendid idea,' said Toulouse-Lautrec. 'I'll have something green and sticky!'

'A round for everyone,' said Gilles, who'd been swept up in the convivial mood. 'And that includes Gisella. Unless you have any objections, *mademoiselle*?'

Lise reappeared with a tray of glasses filled with some viscous green liquid, knelt by the water and proffered one of them to me. 'What is it?' I asked. 'I sometimes don't do too well with strong liquor.'

'It's just absinthe, honey,' said Lise. 'Totally harmless, it'll do you a world of good.'

Oh, my word.

Over the course of the evening more people joined the gathering, someone wheeled an upright piano out of the bar and started thrashing the ivories, and people danced on the *quai*. Having knocked off early from le Moulin Rouge two young *danseuses*, Jane Avril and a drink-snatching extrovert known as La Goulue, twirled and cavorted with abandon. Then everyone called for Mistinguett to sing for them, some of the old Parisian favourites. She thought for a moment and then walked over to the side of the canal. 'Come on, Gisella,' she said. 'What say we give them a double act?'

'Me? Sing with you? *T'es folle*?'

'Listen to you. You have that sultry, smoky voice that's pure street Parisienne, it'll complement mine perfectly.'

'I'd say it was more canal Parisienne.'

'Come on, Gisella.'

'Come on, Gisella,' everyone echoed. 'Sing, sing, sing!'

'I don't know any songs.'

'I'll sing the first few bars, then you join in. *Allez! Un, deux, trois….*'

So that's how I ended up singing *Ça, c'est Paris* with the immortal Mistinguett. I can still remember most of the lyrics: '*Paris, reine du monde, Paris, c'est une blonde, le nez retroussé, l'air moqueur, les yeux toujours rieurs....*' Which was some achievement considering I was very drunk indeed on absinthe.

I was still just about functioning when I heard a loud splash and had to help poor old Boudin back to the canal bank, where several willing hands pulled him to safety. Having surreptitiously nicked several people's drinks, he was even more plastered than usual. 'What happened?' Lise called from the bar.

'Nothing much,' said Auguste Renoir. 'Gisella just saved Boudin from drowning.'[3]

The rest of the evening was a complete blur, and the next morning I had a hangover that could've been spotted from outer space. Did I learn my lesson about absinthe? Absolutely. For about a fortnight. Until I started to forget just how ghastly it had made me feel. Had I made an utter tit of myself? No, my new friends assured me, they were all feeling rather green about the gills too, and outrageous behaviour was the rule rather than the exception amongst them.

I soon became a fixture at Les Deux Anguilles, and if I don't appear in any of the accounts from the period it's because my presence was only known to a tightknit bohemian circle of around 500 people. And when people say my voice is like that of a Rive Gauche nightclub singer with a forty-Gitanes-a-day habit they're not far wrong – except I was on the *rive droite* and would've found it very difficult to smoke underwater. Mistinguett et Gisella, we formed an informal double act for many years.

All the while Paris was shedding the nineteenth century and preparing to embrace the modernity of the twentieth. Electric streetlamps had replaced gas, the first Metro lines were opening, the *Tour Eiffel* now dominated the Parisian skyline, and to everyone's utter shock Alain the boat taximan had thrown away his oars and had installed a new-fangled diesel engine in his craft. Passengers were a little wary in case it blew up, but appreciated its speed.

The Great Paris Exposition of 1900 was a momentous occasion, a celebration of a brave new age and France's exalted position in the world. Achievements of all descriptions were on show, featuring the latest in science, manufacture, literature, painting, music and even the Lumière brothers' sensational moving pictures. Art Nouveau was absolutely the thing, and even some of the painters who'd struggled over the past thirty years now found themselves in vogue and desirable. It was a wonderful new world.

But life at Les Deux Anguilles continued pretty much as it had done for decades. The Exposition had made no difference to trade, because while some of its more adventurous visitors had been happy to gawk at the bohemians in Montmartre and Montparnasse, and thrilled to the high-kicking *danseuses* in Pigalle, the modest canal-side café was far too old world for them.

Which was a mistake, because the clientele included some of the most forward-thinking minds in the country. While public taste had moved on and the Impressionists had belatedly gained public favour, fresh ideas and a brand-new avant-garde was emerging and, in its turn, outraging the old established order. A stream of new faces such as Pablo Picasso, Georges Braque, Henri Matisse and Raoul Dufy became regulars; and in addition to painters, literary figures and musicians including Emile Zola, Alfred Jarry, Marcel Proust, Guillaume Apollinaire, Maurice Ravel and Erik Satie made a habit of dropping in. And many of the surviving long-time locals continued to frequent the bar. My old chum Rousseau still painted and pontificated, Monet still dropped in on visits to the city, Suzanne Valadon had graduated from sitting for paintings to painting them, and a few of my old friends from Pigalle still showed up from time to time. The years hadn't been kind to La Goulue, who'd expanded sideways to an alarming degree, but Mistinguett had become a national superstar. She never forgot her roots, though, and she wasn't too posh to sing the odd duet with me still.

Just like their predecessors, the younger artists found it hard to get their work exhibited and even harder to sell any of it, even in some of the more modern salons, such as the Salon d'Automne. It had been years since a Salon des Refusés par le Salon des Refusés – now better known as les Double Refusés – had been held, and now that another winter was starting to bite no one had the stomach to mount another outdoor exhibition.

Which probably explains why Pablo, Georges, Raoul and others were so enthusiastic when a tall, gaunt middle-aged man, dressed in a very smart three-piece tweed suit, made them a proposal they couldn't refuse. Monsieur X – he insisted upon anonymity – had missed visiting the Double Refusés exhibitions in recent years and proposed staging one in an appropriate setting. He was willing to hire the Orangerie[4] in the Jardin des Tuileries, Napoleon III's old hothouse, as a venue, as well as publicising the event and hanging all the paintings. All they had to do was choose a bunch of their favourite paintings, as many as they wished, and bring them over to the Orangerie. '*Est-ce que les ourses chient dans les bois*,' said Pablo, which translates into something about bears' sanitary habits.

Most of this exchange took place inside the bar at Les Deux Anguilles, but I did catch sight of the man shaking hands with several of the artists outside on the *quai* immediately afterwards. A warning tingle in my lateral line made me cautious. I didn't like the way the gaunt man nervously tugged at his beard, nor the way his eyes flickered from side to side, gauging reactions all the time. I instantly didn't like him.

When Raoul and Pablo filled me in about the offer I was still dubious. My feeling was that if something appeared too good to be true it probably was. Lise, Gilles, Suzanne and Alfred Jarry tried to remonstrate with me, how could one turn down such an offer, the guy was obviously an art-lover with a discerning eye? Suzanne said I should really try to stop being so suspicious, and Henri crossed his arms and declared I was out of my mind.

Monsieur X had departed in a water taxi – unfortunately not Alain's – so, refusing to let go of my misgivings, I set off downstream to look for it. I caught up with it as it left the canal tunnel near l'Arsenal, but instead of carrying on to the Seine it veered off to the left, entered a lock, and chugged into a maze-like network of now disused channels and loading bays and tumbledown warehouses behind the Gare de Lyon. Sixty years earlier the area would've been filled with barges and goods and dockers, but the railways had killed all that. Now it was open spaces, straggly buddleia bushes and crumbling walls.

At length the boat stopped, and I saw Monsieur X disembark and meet with a fellow in a cap and long coat in what once had been a vast goods repository. Its roof was long gone, but two of its walls remained, with several rows of wooden benches arranged along one of them. Monsieur X was handing the man a wad of bank notes, but as I moved closer to listen to what they were saying the boatman caught sight of me. 'Jesus, what a whopper!' he exclaimed. I was off.

In my panic to get away I lost my bearings completely, but by following an almost infinitesimally slight downstream current I eventually found my way back to the Canal Saint-Martin proper.

Back at les Deux Anguilles I tried to tell anyone who'd listen that Monsieur X was a wrong 'un, bent as a nine franc note, but the lure of fame and public acclaim had deafened them all. I was pooh-pooed, accused of having a suspicious mind, told by young Alain Derain that I was paranoid and needed my head examining. 'Come to think of it,' chuckled Alfred Jarry, 'there's someone back at the bar who's an expert on paranoia and the like.'

I was wary. Alfred had a mischievous streak, and many people tended to think that *he* should get his head examined. His writing was, er, highly original (although we all absolutely loved his absurdist play

Ubu roi), and his theories, such as *pataphysics*,[5] left me frankly baffled. Maybe such complexities are beyond a humble common carp.

After disappearing into the bar for a couple of minutes he came back out with a smartly attired gentleman who sported a greying beard. This apparently was Doktor Sigmund Freud, part of a delegation from Vienna visiting Paris for a conference on psychology (the term psychiatry wasn't yet in general use), who'd wanted to sample a little of the flavour of Paris street life. He was very intrigued at the prospect of interacting with a paranoid talking carp, and after a swift introduction told me to relax, I'd be able to speak freely.

'First Gisella – I can call you Gisella, *ja*? – I'm told you have trust issues. You're suspicious of people.'

'That's a bunch of *conneries*, I'm suspicious of one person in particular and that's because he's obviously an arsehole.'

'I'm wondering where this evident paranoia comes from. Do you have trust issues through poor family bonding? All girls love their fathers after all.'

'I never knew my father.'

'Poor you, that explains a lot. And did you have to fight with your siblings for your mother's attention?'

'You could say that, seeing there were approximately 300,000 of us.'

'*Gott in Himmel!*'

'We can speak in German if you prefer.'

'*Das würde mir sehr gefallen, danke*,[6] my French is not so good. So you speak more than one language. Is that due to some sort of urge to be liked?'

'I tend to travel a lot, and speaking people's languages generally helps when you don't want to be eaten.'

'Really, and would you relate that to a crude survival instinct or rational thought?'

'Would you like to be eaten? What is it that makes you ask a bunch of dumb questions?'

'Well, I suppose I need to make sense of people. Find out what makes them tick.'

'So, you're nosy. Have you always been like that?'

'Probably, yes, now I think of it. Maybe it comes from a form of nervousness. I don't know. If I can suss folk out then there are no nasty surprises.'

'So you're an anxious type. Childhood bullying perhaps?'

'Not that I recall. But when I was little *Mami und Papi* used to go away quite frequently, and my *Kindermädchen*, my nanny, used to comfort me.'

'And you feel there was something wrong about that?'

'Hmm, she had a very *particular* way of comforting me that wasn't in any of the childcare books, and I'm pretty sure she wasn't supposed to do it.'

'And do you have issues with women now?'

'To be honest I really like big, powerful women. Always have. Nanny Traudl was rather generously proportioned and I suppose it's stuck. And, while I'm being frank, I guess I like getting to hear about other people's sex lives. It's a bit of a turn-on.'

'Doesn't sound that unusual to me. But while we're together, is there anything else that's bothering you? Unburden yourself.'

'Only that Jung. Freudianism is just about getting off the ground and then along comes that charlatan Carl Jung with all his collective unconscious bollocks, and suddenly I'm old hat. I bloody hate him.'

At that point two of Herr Freud's colleagues, who'd been enjoying the sights up at the Folies Bergère, arrived on the scene and led him away to their waiting cab. Alfred Jarry eagerly asked me if I'd learnt anything, and I told him that as far as I was concerned the eminent head-shrinker had sex on the brain, and compared to him I had no issues whatsoever. My opinion about Monsieur X and the Orangerie offer still stood: I was still as suspicious as hell.

Two days before the exhibition an assortment of painters delivered the cream of their work to the Orangerie. Amongst the artworks were: Renoir's *Bal du Moulin de la Galette*, *Les Demoiselles d'Avignon*, by Picasso, Degas' *Absinthe Drinker*, the first in a projected series of water-lily paintings by Monet, *Flood at Port Marly* by Sisley, *Goldfish* by Matisse....[7] Pretty well all the *premier cru* of progressive painters had contributed, the older hands who already had a reputation, and the young hopefuls who were striving to earn one. Deliveries done, most of the crowd retired to Les Deux Anguilles for a night of jollity, inebriation and eager anticipation: the next day their works would be hung and the following one, their long-awaited breakthrough and no doubt rich buyers galore! As for me, I lurked by the *quai* having a bit of a sulk because no one had listened to me.

At about four the next morning I heard Boudin calling for me. He was upset and babbling a little bit, but when I'd calmed him down he explained that late the previous afternoon he'd sneaked into l'Orangerie because it had a really good central heating furnace and was a good place to kip for the night. At his age sleeping rough had become almost impossible and he had a long list of warm boltholes. Anyway, he'd been awoken at some point by a chain of people picking up the paintings, carrying them out to the Seine, and loading them all onto a couple of barges. What was he telling me for, I exclaimed, he needed to rouse Gilles and Lise. I hesitated to say 'told you so' right away, but I was going to as soon as anyone listened.

Lise said they had to call the gendarmes immediately, but Boudin told her there was no point: they'd already been got at. A couple of gendarmes had helped to load the paintings onto the barges. Then they had to get everyone together, said Gilles, this was something they'd have to see to themselves. Boudin suggested maybe a little tincture of absinthe first, it may have been first light now, but it was still bloody cold.

Gathering together a group of very hungover bohemians proved far easier said than done. For a start, very few of them lived on the fringes of Belleville and Goncourt. Gilles, Lise and Boudin found themselves trogging from garret to garret, from Montparnasse to Pigalle to Montmartre to the Rue Saint-Denis. It was getting on in the afternoon by the time a decent crowd had assembled on the *quai* outside the café, and I was able to get in my first *Told you so*.

'And what makes anyone think Monsieur X is to blame?' said Georges Braque.

'Georges, seriously,' said Pablo, eyebrows raised. 'I think it's time to admit Gisella called this one right.'

'Bravo, Gisella, you were right and we were all wrong,' said La Goulue rather sourly. She looked as if she hadn't wanted to rouse herself even at that time of the afternoon, a mass of wrinkles and eyebags in spite of her considerable bulk, but in the end she was a real trouper and not one to let her comrades down. 'If you're so bloody smart perhaps you can tell us what Monsieur X has done with all the piccies.'

'I think I can, actually. You're going need boats, because you're going on a little canal trip. And, by the way, I told you so.'

'*Ferme-La*, Gisella!' several voices chorused, shut the hell up.

The light was beginning to fade as I led a small armada of water taxis and pleasure craft along the canal to the lock leading into the old docks area behind the Gare de Lyon. It was impossible to remember the maze of water channels properly, but fortunately the passage of several boats the previous night had stirred up so much sediment from the bottom that I had a very easy trail to follow.

In the disused goods repository a little way distant, Monsieur X stood in front of an enormous pile of framed paintings, in amongst which several very serious-looking fireworks had been arranged. He was addressing a large group of gentlemen (there wasn't a single woman present), whose fashion sense was at least sixty years out of date. To their side, completing the ensemble, an ancient-looking string quartet was playing airs from Handel's *Music for the Royal Fireworks*. He welcomed his esteemed colleagues from the Brotherhood of Pre-Poussainites to their special *son et lumière*, where the cream of modernistic filth was about to be consumed by a massive display of *feux d'artifices*. Bravo! Cheered the venerable Brotherhood.

'Not if we can help it!' roared Pablo Picasso, leading a stampede of enraged arty-farties across the waste ground.

Fisticuffs ensued, but a bunch of doddery old fogies was no match for an irate avant-garde mob of artists, writers, singers and their comrades. In the melee Lise spotted Monsieur X and exclaimed that now she recognised him: he was the odious Victor de la Homps. The same, he cackled, and they were too late, he'd already lit the fuse to all the fireworks – modern art was about to become history! The next instant he crumpled under the weight of a straight right from La Goulue. To be fair, few professional boxers would've fared much better.

The fireworks' fuse could be seen fizzing along the ground, zipping towards the pile of irreplaceable masterpieces. Then, with a fizzle and a splutter it went out. 'Sorry about that,' chuckled Boudin. 'Just can't trust the old bladder nowadays.'

Of course the details of the evening's fun and games were recounted to me once everyone returned to the boats, but it hadn't been too hard to follow what had gone on even from the water. It was now a race to gather up all the paintings, get them back to l'Orangerie, and set up the exhibition for the grand opening the next day. It would involve working through the night, but the prize was immortality. Nearly all the Brotherhood had dispersed into the night, but Pablo Picasso and Alfred Jarry kept a firm grip on Homps, who was to have the honour of welcoming the public to the grand exposition the next day. 'Could I blease bisit a hosbital first?' he mumbled. 'By dose needs fixing.'

It would be nice to report that the exhibition was a roaring success, but it wasn't. Firstly, Homps had done nothing to promote it, so the attendance was mostly limited to family, friends and a handful of curious passers-by, secondly, that the established artists didn't sell any work because they'd priced their paintings too high, and thirdly, the new artists didn't sell any work because their art was too outlandish and way ahead of public taste. All that would of course change, but at the time it was truly disappointing. The only glimmer of satisfaction was from Monsieur de la Homps' acute discomfort at being forced to wax lyrical about avant-garde art, and suffering from an as yet un-mended broken nose. Thanks to La Goulue's glowering presence there was no question of his slipping away.

Life drifted back to normal along the *quai* and inevitably changes took place. Many members of the Deux Anguille's avant-garde clientele became respectable and moved on, while others fell on hard times and disappeared in a cloud of absinthe. One notable loss was Boudin. No one knew how old he was, in fact he looked pretty shop-worn when I first encountered him, so for a gentleman of the road he'd proved remarkably resilient, but one winter's morning he was found under the Pont Neuf, as stiff as a board.

The final straw for that little bohemian community was when *les patrons*, Gilles and Lise, decided they were too long in the tooth to run a counter-culture institution and called it a day. Their successors, a vanilla young couple called Gregoire and Charlotte, stopped serving absinthe and started serving coffee with milk. The café was on its knees within a fortnight.

Meanwhile, all over town there was talk of the worsening international situation. In hushed tones people agreed that the continent was lurching towards war. As the cliché goes, storm clouds were gathering over Europe, but I find using a meteorological analogy for something as catastrophic as a protracted bloody war that slaughtered upwards of 20,000,000 humans insulting, fatuous and bloody lazy.

Many people didn't even know who the war would be against, some suggested the Rosbifs and others the Russians, but the better informed all spoke knowingly of the inevitable showdown between the Entente and the Central Powers. Something that had been fermenting for years. And events in Sarajevo proved them right.

As for me, I wanted no part of it. While I'd spent the majority of my life in France and England, I bore no grudge against Germany or any of the other Central Powers either. I decided it was time to leave again, especially as rumour had it that the impregnable Maginot Line might not prove to be so impregnable after all. I made up my mind to head south – as far away from the war zone as my fins could propel me.

Notes

[1]The artists who started frequenting *Les Deux Anguilles* represented the cream of French avant-garde painters before they became establishment figures. Gisella wanted to include paintings by all of them in this book, but it had to be explained to her that the printing costs would've been outrageous.

[2]*Et In Arcadia Ego* was a refrain much repeated by Seventeenth Century artists churning out idyllic pastoral scenes. A literal

translation of the phrase makes little sense and academics who argue about it are just being pains in the backside.

[3]If anyone wonders where Jean Renoir, the film director son of the painter, got the idea for his 1932 picture *'Boudu Sauvé des Eaux'* (Boudu Saved from Drowning), this incident gives a clue.

[4]The Orangerie is still used as an art gallery and exhibits all sorts of the works that Gisella is partial to.

[5]Pataphysics is to science what this book is to history.

[6]*Das würde mir sehr gefallen danke.* Yes please.

[7]Again, again, if it were up to Gisella every painting her friends created would be in this book.

Chapter Twenty One

The lost generation. How Gisella survives a war and falls in with a new set of bohos on the French riviera

From the mouth of the River Seine I took a well-worn path, down the coast of western France, through the Canal du Midi into the Mediterranean, around Italy and on to the Balkans. Although this trip took the best part of a year I didn't feel like stopping anywhere for very long because all the talk I overheard in every port that I visited was of war. I did manage to pick up a handful of bonus new languages, however.

Great guns guarded every port approach, naval boats patrolled every mile of coastline and increasingly I saw strange but flimsy contraptions flying overhead. They weren't as elegant as Leonardo da Vinci's had been, but they seemed to stay up in the air rather longer. If they became involved in the fighting then my old friend the maestro would be proved right, his vision of hellfire raining down from the sky would come to pass. It appeared that my grand idea of keeping clear of the conflict had been hopelessly optimistic.

There didn't appear to be any fighting in Greece, but passing the naval docks at Piraeus I saw countless warships at anchor, so I just carried on. I was weary and it occurred to me that age was catching up with me, but with every country I passed either at war or preparing to go to war, I had no desire to stick around.

The heights on either side of the Dardanelles Straits were impressively defended, studded with gun emplacements like spots on a trout's back, but whatever they were waiting for it wasn't a carp, so I carried on swimming. I reasoned that I'd soon be in the Bosphorus, and soon after that I'd be in the Black Sea. Surely no one would be fighting as far away as that.

It was then that I felt the vibrations of distant engines, engines that were getting closer. Ships. A great many ships. I kept swimming and soon found myself facing a large spherical iron object, studded with truncheon-like metal protuberances, lurking just under the surface, which appeared to be attached to a vast chain of similar orbs. In fact there were multiple chains of them, running right across the strait. Intrigued, I swiped the object with my tail. It just made a dull clang. Then I tried biting one of its protuberances, but of course carp have no teeth. Naturally I made no impact on it, but the device did start to make a disconcerting ticking sound, so I backed away from it. Whatever these things were, every instinct told me to keep well away from them.

The ships that had been catching up with me were of course warships, great hulking metal things, bristling with gun turrets. As the first of them caught up with me I turned tail and, doing my best to keep well clear of the vessels following it, tried to head back out into the open sea. Then there was the most shattering explosion: the first ship had collided with one of the spherical objects.

In trying to escape the hell of war I'd swum right into the middle of it. The stricken ship was engulfed in fire and smoke, while its companions opened fire on the shore defences and the shore defences opened fire on them.

For those of you who've never swum close to a blazing ship going down with most hands still on board, I wouldn't advise it. It's ghastly, harrowing and indescribably horrifying, and it's something that'll never leave me. I don't know what sort of damage was being sustained on the Gallipoli heights, but out in the sea channel it was slaughter. Two more ships succumbed to mines while a further two were quickly sunk by the onshore gun batteries. The rest of the fleet quickly abandoned the attempt to sail up to the Bosphorus and attack Istanbul, and turned back to the open sea.

I was shattered and disorientated, it was hard to see and my lateral line felt as if it had been trampled on and then tied in knots. In addition, my swim bladder had obviously been affected by all the violent pressure changes caused by the shelling and it made it painful for me to descend to any depth, so I was forced to swim among all the floating wreckage, burning patches of oil and dead and dying sailors. At length the firing died down and then stopped, probably because there was nothing left to shoot at.

Death inevitably attracts scavengers, and to my alarm I saw some very large, blue hued fish homing in on all the gore. They obviously weren't tuna so the only suspects I could think of were sharks – blue sharks probably. It was a reasonable bet that they were there for an easy meal rather than chasing live prey, but I'm not a gambling fish so I headed as close inshore as I dared in order to stay out of their way.

Little by little I backtracked all the way to the Greek coast. I felt truly grim, every one of my near nineteen hundred years was weighing on me. I decided to hole up and get a proper rest when I eventually reached Thessaloníki, which appeared to be a very pleasant, relaxed kind of place. I liked the food too. I hadn't sampled a decent baklava in centuries, and they made very, very good ones there. People relaxed by the harbour, the sunshine was pleasant. Grey mullet and sea bream milled around the moored boats, bothering no one, and there were no sharks. Why on earth hadn't I stopped there to begin with, instead of steaming ahead to the Dardanelles and ending up in a marine inferno?

Real life caught up with me with revolting speed. On day three of my stay word spread like wildfire along the quayside that Greece had thrown in its lot with the Entente and declared war on the Central Powers. Flags were waved, oaths were sworn, rifles fired into the air, ouzo was swilled, girls were kissed, and death was sworn to every bastard Turk and anyone else who sided with them. Why is it that otherwise sane humans can be so enthusiastic to rush off and get themselves killed? Fish might not be the brightest sparks on God's earth, but not many deliberately set out to swim straight into nets.

I'd heard that Spain was actually neutral and decided that that would be my next destination, but from Greece it was a hell of a swim for a fish no longer feeling in the first flush of youth. I plodded along into the Adriatic Sea, around the toe of Italy and onward into French coastal waters. By the time I wafted into the harbour at Antibes I'd had it, and decided that come what may I wasn't going to swim any further. It was the Côte d'Azur for me, and if the war caught up with me then bollocks to it, *tant pis*. I soon found that I'd made a pretty good choice, however. I'd expected Antibes to be a quiet little fishing town but it was rather more than that: a viable fleet of small fishing boats still operated from it, but it was also a resort for bohemians, the idle rich, and their various parasites. You really wouldn't know that a war was still taking place far to the north, but rumour had it that the Americans were about to throw their hats into the ring, which certainly spelt the beginning of the end for the Boche.

The rich had their faults and an awful lot of them, but they dressed their children very nicely (or rather had their servants dress them very nicely) and above all they knew how to eat well. That, and they were very wasteful. All of which was very good news for a discerning carp in need of sustenance and recuperation.

All I had to do was hang about below the terraces of rich people's seaside villas, or by harbourside restaurants, and I could feast on scraps of lobster, *filet mignon* and *baba au rhum* (it was considered quite posh back then). And if I felt more like showing a bit of proletarian solidarity, I'd scoot over to the working side of the harbour where the fishermen and dockers ate, and scoff some *frites*. The grey mullet were sometimes a bit shirty about me muscling in on their patch, but I pointed out there was plenty for everybody – and I was much bigger than them.

I saw out the rest of the Great War in Antibes, and then I stayed some more. The climate was agreeable, I had nothing to fear from the fishermen, and I was enjoying a varied and interesting diet. I was starting to miss intelligent company again, though, and there was no one to slip me the odd tipple. But, on reflection, having a few years off the juice was no bad thing.

Frequently I started to notice a very suave chap, middle-aged and with a most dashing moustache, stop and exchange greetings with a variety of people around the harbour, so when one afternoon I found him standing on the quayside, inviting a very posh couple, who were lounging on the deck of a swish yacht, to a party at his villa that evening, I naturally stopped to listen.

He then turned and looked down towards me. 'Ah, Mademoiselle Gisella, so delighted to make your acquaintance.'

'Likewise. Er, do I know you? How did you know I'm – me?'

'You were obviously listening to us, and how many fish are able to listen in on conversations? Good old Henri Matisse told me about this talking carp that used to hang about in the Canal Saint-Martin, but I always thought that if I ever did run into you it would be in Paris.'

'I left to escape from the war. One of my stupider decisions; I would've been far better off staying put.'

'You certainly sound Parisienne. Little wonder you made such a good double act with Mistinguett.'

'You've got a bit of an accent too, Monsieur, if you don't mind my saying. Hungarian?'

'Spot on. Count Andras Tibor Attila Ferenc Wisterhazy at your service.' He executed a perfect, clipped bow.

'*Örülök, hogy megismerkedhet, uram.*'[1]

'*Hát átkozott leszek!* Good bloody grief! A Hungarian-speaking fish. I'd heard you were a phenomenon, but this leaves me speechless.' I'd find out that nothing, absolutely nothing left the count speechless.

'I'm afraid my Hungarian is a bit ropey, it's the one language that's always been a bit of a problem for me.'

'Shush, dear fish, no self-denigration from you or I'll think you're fishing for compliments. You must come to my party, I absolutely insist. Turn right when you leave the harbour, mine's the third villa as you make your way down the Cap d'Antibes. There'll be oodles of interesting people – I'd particularly like you to meet Frankie and Zelda Fitzgerald. There's still a whiff of the Midwest about them, but they show promise, great promise.'

I'd passed Count Andras's villa many times. It was one of the grander properties on the Cap, set discreetly back from the rocky shoreline, with tumbling cactus and flowering shrub-filled gardens that led down to a winding set of steps, that in turn descended to a wide landing stage. The sun had just set as I approached it, and the entire area was illuminated by lanterns, giving the setting an enchanted, fairy-glen-type feel. How the other half live, I thought.

I was early. An unforgivable *faux pas* among the sophisticates of the Côte d'Azur, but considering I'm a carp I was permitted a certain amount of leeway. On the landing stage a couple of young men, who managed to look the picture of elegance despite only wearing short-sleeve shirts, baggy linen trousers and espadrilles, were setting out numerous plates of hors d'oeuvres on two long trestle tables, while a bewildering array of bottles, jugs and cocktail shakers stood on a third.

At the sound of a roaring engine I quickly swam to one side to avoid a sleek motorboat as it made a hectic emergency stop at the landing, and then disgorged the most unlikely of couples: an intense, squat man with thick, round glasses, attired in the most ill-fitting clothes, accompanied by a most attractive young woman in a daringly short, black cocktail dress, with fashionably short, dark, bobbed hair. She looked fun. As if by magic Andras appeared at the bottom of the steps, arms out wide. 'Man, Kiki,' he beamed. *Bise-bise*, embraces were exchanged. 'Wonderful you could make it – the party starts *now!*'

Kiki eyed the two young men approvingly. 'Nice,' she said to Andras. 'Your taste is immaculate, as ever.'

'One should be surrounded by beauty,' said Andras, who then turned to the taciturn fellow. 'Wouldn't you agree, Man?'

'Sure,' said Man, with a slight nod.

Kiki, meanwhile, demanded a drink from one of the young men, who poured her a glass from a cocktail shaker. She necked it in one, and seconds later another went the same way.

'On you go up, my dears,' said Andras. 'There's a jazz band, fresh from New Orleans, King Malcolm and his Manic Melodians, I just know you're going to love them.'

'That's just the kind of thing I left the States to escape from,' said Man.

'Ooh, my cute little curmudgeon,' grinned Kiki, pinching him on the cheek. When he scowled he looked even less cute than before.

'Go,' said Andras. 'There's someone I want to talk to.' He turned and looked down into the water.

'I didn't think you'd seen me.'

'I always notice people. It's an essential gift for a socialite. I'm so glad you're here, we're going to have fun.'

It was then that I saw the speedboat was drifting away from the landing stage, the couple had neglected to moor it.

'Just as well,' said Andras philosophically. 'I fear to think what would've happened if they tried to drive back after tonight.'

'And they are?'

'Man Ray, the latest thing on the Paris arts scene, and Kiki, Kiki de Montparnasse, artist's model, singer, painter and *enfant terrible*. And now I'm afraid she's going to spend all night trying to *turn* Georges and Philipe, just to prove a point.' He nodded meaningfully towards the two young men.

'Ah, I thought she and Man Ray were a couple.'

'And so they are, my dear, but they do like to stretch the boundaries of what being a couple means. They both love their little conquests, and then prove their undying commitment to one another by returning to each other.'

'And do you think the boys will be tempted?'

'I shouldn't have thought so but it'll be delicious to see, won't it? Now, I'd promised to introduce you to this charming young couple from the States so I'll pop up and see if they can be roused, but first can I offer you something to drink? I remember Henri saying something about your taste for absinthe?'

'Better make it a *pastis*. Me and absinthe – not a good combination.'

Enjoying the warm aniseed glow in my tummy I looked on as several more craft deposited guests at the landing stage. The rich, the beautiful, and their appendages, and more ostrich feathers than you could shake a kipper at. Okay – that was a very large drink Georges had poured into my mouth.

'An' you gotta be Gisella,' said a stolidly built, sandy-haired fellow in an accent I soon learnt was American. 'The name's Frankie Fitzgerald, and this here's Zelda, my gorgeous wife.'

'I'll be the judge of that.' Actually, I didn't say that but it's what I thought. I'm afraid the *pastis* was already taking charge. Mrs Fitzgerald seemed to me far too cornfed to be a Zelda, despite her rather stunning Art Deco dress and feather boa.

'I'm a writer,' said Frankie, 'or rather Andras is grooming me to be a writer. You need to get some real-life experience to write, he says, and he *also* says that everything worthwhile in life comes out of a cocktail shaker. So here we are, living life.'

He and Zelda were both making short work of their cocktails. 'You look like you're A-plus students,' I said.

'I did some articles an' magazine stuff back home,' Frankie continued. 'A basketball column in the *Buffalo Bugle* and a loada pieces for *Philatelists' Monthly*, but Zelda here pointed out I was going nowhere stuck out there in upstate New York. Said we had to come out to Yurr-up to soak up some of that sophistication, so here we are.'

'Gawrsh, when I think back just a few months,' said Zelda. 'What a coupla innocent hayseeds we were.'

'But that was before we hooked up with Andras,' said Frankie. 'He introduced us to a whole bunch of interesting people. Expanded our horizons so to speak.'

'An' now we're pals with a talking fish,' said Zelda.

'I think we could use a refuel,' said Frankie. 'Enlightenment with a cocktail olive. What happens to be your poison, Gisella?'

At some point during the evening I must've switched to absinthe because you don't get a hangover like that from *pastis* alone. The next morning I felt like death, and if I'd had the energy I would've swum out to the nearest fishing boat and got myself caught just to put me out of my misery. The few folks milling about the garden and down by the water looked like the barely living dead, and for some reason I didn't care to discover Man Ray was wandering about in Zelda's dress. The only two who'd survived unscathed were Georges and Philipe, who to my disgust still looked as fresh as daisies. I guessed they'd managed to avoid Kiki de Montparnasse, because King Malcolm most definitely had not. Not that he appeared put out by the experience, in fact he gave every impression of having had a grand time.

These parties, and others like them, were a regular thing, and I was a regular guest. I made it a rule, however, not to drink absinthe anymore, and I managed to stick to it nearly all of the time. Central to the scene was Count Andras, who was what one would term a catalyst. He made things happen, he was an enabler, a fixer, someone who effected change without changing. It was widely believed that he was homosexual, but those who'd been in his circle a long time (because in all probability no one *really* knew him) said he loved young men in the way a connoisseur loves fine porcelain. He loved scandal and affairs, but it was always other people's scandals and affairs. As a host, however, he was absolutely *sans pareil.*

The *lost generation*, they were called. Maybe they were, maybe those who'd come through The Great War had lost something very fundamental and were trying to replace it with hedonism – survivors tempting fate once again. Of course, those living it up on the Côte d'Azur were largely the rich and the idle, and many of them had avoided the war altogether, but the term was still very apt. As for those who'd survived the trenches and come home to unemployment, sickness, shellshock and poverty, they were most emphatically a lost generation. But who am I to speak? I was having a great time amongst all the wasters and parasites.

One day I was sunning myself in a corner of Antibes harbour when Andras approached me in a state of great excitement. He was expecting a guest. Well, Andras was always having guests, but apparently this wasn't just any guest. Ernest Hemingway was an exciting emerging novelist, and by all accounts a bit of a hellraiser. In other words a real addition to Andras's collection, I thought. He'd written stories about frontier living and wild women and big-game fishing that would make the hairs on your neck stand up, Andras enthused. Their little community could do with a bit of shaking up, and Ernest was going to be the one to do it. In amongst his stream of words one thing about the writer had stuck with me: he evidently liked big-game fishing. Worry not, my dear, Andras smiled, you are most definitely off limits.

I didn't witness Mr Hemingway's arrival at the villa because he came by limousine, but early that evening he was led down to the landing stage to meet me and enjoy a pre-party cocktail. Of course there was going to be a party; this was Andras Wisterhazy entertaining.

'You've been holding out on me, Ernest,' said Andras. 'Surely you'll have a proper drink *now*.'

'Another lapsang souchong will do me just fine,' said Ernest Hemingway.

'Georges,' said Andras, his patience wearing a little thin, 'pour the man a *real* drink.'

'Well, if you really insist, I think I'll risk a small sherry,' said Ernest.

'*Isten adjon türelmet*,' said Andras under his breath. 'God preserve us.' Then he turned to me. 'You'll have something sensible, Gisella.' It wasn't a question.

'*Pastis Cinquante et Un?*' said Philipe.

'The elixir of the Midi,' I answered. 'How well you know me.'

'This is the remarkable fish I was telling you about, Ernest,' said Andras. 'She speaks thirty languages, if not more.'

'Pleased to meet you,' said Ernest. 'I guess Andras must be exaggerating a tad – I've heard Hungarians are famous for it. Thirty languages indeed – that really is most droll!'

'He's not bullshitting you, I reckon I must speak getting on for fifty or so,' I said.

'Well, I'll be diddly-dashed.'

'There's a real treat for you tomorrow,' said Andras, 'knowing how keen you are on fishing. We have a boat lined up for you, I've hired some tackle and arranged for bait to be dropped off. You're going tuna fishing; there are meant to be some really big specimens hereabouts.'

'Whoopee,' said Ernest. So quietly only I could hear him.

'And don't you go fishing for Gisella, she's out of season.'

'I wouldn't dream of it,' said Ernest. 'Really I wouldn't.'

The next morning Ernest insisted on going out fishing alone. He maintained that for him, big-game fishing was all about a young man and the sea – a solitary experience. Georges and Philip carried a picnic basket, several bottles, a couple of cocktail flasks and a cool box of bait onto the fishing boat, and Andras bade the intrepid angler farewell. Rather than relishing the trip, however, Ernest looked more like an eighteenth-century French aristocrat being manhandled onto a tumbril.

Normally a deep-sea fishing trip wouldn't be high on my list of fun days out, but this was different. The prospect of seeing how this foul-mouthed roisterer – who in reality had the crusts removed from his cucumber sandwiches and wouldn't say boo to a gosling – would fare was too intriguing to pass up. I swam along after the chugging fishing boat as it headed away from the villa.

Shortly after passing the rocky Cap, Ernest leant over the side of the boat and threw up violently. There was no swell to speak of, just very small, lapping waves, like the Tuileries ponds on a summer's day, but there was no doubt about it, Ernest was suffering from a severe bout of seasickness.

'Is there anything I can do to help?' I called up to him.

'I don't think so. I just want to die.'

'I thought you were this big-game fisherman.'

'That's half true. I used to fish a little bit in the pond at the end of my Aunt Dorothy's garden. God, I feel ill.'

'Try having a drink, that might help.'

'But I don't drink, not really. It makes my head go all spinny.'

'Good God, man, do you want to spend all day spewing your guts out? Open a bottle of cognac, have a really good pull at it, and while you're at it give me a shot too.'

He followed my advice and almost instantly felt a bit better. Then came the ordeal of fishing, which Ernest felt dutybound to try. What bait, he wondered, squid or mackerel?

'Try squid,' I said wearily. 'I believe tuna are supposed to like squid.'

'Ee-ew! It's all slimy and yucky!'

'Then shut your eyes, but try not to stick the hook in your hand.'

Ernest took another big pull of cognac and just about succeeded in baiting his hook. Then, after another slug, and another one for me too, he managed to cast his line out. Another slug.

A little later we were singing a rousing duet of Mademoiselle d'Armentières when, without warning, Ernest's fishing rod buckled over crazily. He grabbed it and hung on for dear life as he was pulled overboard then towed away at high speed by a giant, unseen fish, leaving a frothy white wake behind him. I'm not sure that Ernest was the world's first water skier, but I'm pretty certain he was the first on the Côte d'Azur. How he remained upright was a complete mystery to me, but after a hundred yards or so he lost his footing and continued to whiz along on his stomach. 'Let go of the rod, you bloody idiot!' I yelled after him, but he was already well out of earshot. And actually, amazingly, he appeared to be having the time of his life. With a deep sigh I set off after him. I didn't know what he'd hooked, in fact there was no way I wanted to know what he'd hooked, but I guessed he might be in need of help in the very near future, so I did my best to put it out of my mind.

Inevitably the line ended up snapping, and then I was able to help the half-drowned but ecstatic Ernest back to the boat. What a life-changing moment, he babbled, to think people live their entire lives without experiencing that crazy rush. He'd had an epiphany: booze was great, fishing was great, living life on the edge was great. For him things would never be the same.

Over the next few years a succession of new faces and old friends graced the Villa Wisterhazy. One young man Andras took a particular shine to was one of those fresh-faced, wispy English chaps called Christopher Isherwood. He'd landed up escorting an aunt to a sanatorium near Cannes (strange how young Englishmen of a certain class have such a plethora of aunts), and had time to kill before returning for the new term at Cambridge University. Andras had found him wandering about aimlessly near the harbour at Antibes, stood him a drink and naturally an invitation to the villa had ensued.

Doesn't even know he's queer yet, Andras smiled at me. Of course he went to an English public school, but for some reason most of them don't count what they do there as queer. The Nelson blind eye, he supposed, a particularly English talent. I asked what plans Andras had for him. Just to ease him on a voyage of discovery, Andras said, find out who he is, help him unlock his potential. There's a writer somewhere in there, but it won't emerge if he remains all stiff-upper-lip and M&S string vests.

It didn't take long for the real Christopher to emerge. A history degree at Cambridge quickly lost its appeal and, yes, he wanted to write. Another thing he wanted to explore further was boy bars, which he'd heard about from various of Andras's friends, but were in short supply along the Mediterranean coast. Attitudes amongst their own bohemian circle were very relaxed for the time, but for Chris to find what he was looking for he needed to head north. Everybody said it, the Mecca for boy bars was Berlin, and Andras, ever generous-spirited, told him to go there with his blessing.

I asked very tentatively if there were any worthwhile rivers in Berlin. There's the Spree, Andras told me, it passes right through the city, and right by it is the famous Tiergarten, a magnificent sort of Tivoli pleasure garden, which is frequented by the great and the good and the very, very bad. I was going to love it. The truth was, I needed to move on. Even a carp can have an excess of hedonism, and I thought that a new major city might breathe fresh life into my jaded old gills.

I'd hoped there might be an inland waterway route to Berlin, but if it existed no one I talked to knew about it, and I was forced to take the long route. Canal du Midi, Brittany, Pas-de-Calais, the Low Countries and then a month's recuperation in Hamburg, not that I'd been breaking any records en route. I found it hard work, even proceeding at a flounder's pace.

Somewhat refreshed, I retraced old steps ascending the River Elbe, then broke new water by entering the Havel, and after that passed through a succession of large lakes before at last finding my way into the Spree. More lakes, more plodding, God I was weary again. But eventually I reached what could only be Berlin. A grand and splendid city – from what I could see of it from the river – and then, on my right-fin side a vast park: the Tiergarten. I took a small side channel from the river and found myself in a network of watercourses and ponds that crisscrossed the park, which turned out to contain woods, gardens, cafés, lawns, bandstands, statuary, open-air stages and what looked like a Baroque orangerie. Just as I reached a food stall, a passer-by tossed a generous three-inch-end of a sausage into the water. It was smoky, aromatic and succulent, and I took it as an omen that I'd reached a very good place.

The Tiergarten was a wonderful place to spend a summer, with an incredible variety of human beings parading along its myriad paths and tracks. There was entertainment, in the form of live music of all kinds, open-air theatre, and, naturally, loads of gossip. People were starting to talk about a new political party, more a collection of thugs really, and its weaselly leader, with his ridiculous pumped-up rhetoric and silly toothbrush moustache. The *Nationalsozialistische Deutsche Arbeiterpartei* was widely regarded as a bunch of *Arschlöcher*, which in English translates pretty much as it sounds, but mainly people came to the Tiergarten to forget about such things.

In one of the open-air theatres *The Threepenny Opera* was being staged – *a play with music* according to its author. As *an example of expressionist theatre, showing a highly mannered yet socially aware view of street life* (apparently), it was resoundingly successful. Actually, in my book it was jolly good fun and I loved the music. In fact I loved it so much I ended up watching it three times in a row (one of the watercourses ran quite close to the theatre giving me a restricted but passable view of the stage), and afterwards found the music well and truly lodged in my head to the extent that I couldn't stop singing 'Die Moritat von Mackie Messer', in other words 'Mack the Knife', for several days afterwards.

It was while I was warbling 'Mack' to myself, or I thought to myself, that a voice rang out. 'Is that you, Gisella? It's got to be you!' A chuckling Christopher Isherwood knelt down by the water's edge. 'Did anyone ever tell you you've got a perfect voice for cabaret?'

'Christopher! I'm so embarrassed – I didn't realise I was so loud.'

'Now that I think of it, I remember hearing about you singing with Mistinguett, but that was a long, long time ago.' I didn't comment, but it wasn't such a long time ago for a near millennium-old carp. Instead I said, 'It's good to see you, Christopher. How has Berlin treated you? Did you find your boy bars?'

The Christopher Isherwood I remembered from Antibes would've turned as red as a beet, but not this cosmopolitan young man. Andras had definitely been right about the benefits of a change of scene. 'Loads of them, sweetheart,' he beamed. 'I've made all sorts of new friends, and not all of them queer either. In fact I'd love you to meet them, they're all frightfully fascinating and I do have a bit of an ulterior motive: I may just have inadvertently boasted about being chums with a talking carp, and of course they all think I'm a *monstrous fibber*. We can set them right.'

I hesitated. Did I really want to get into another boozy, devil-may-care circle of bohemians?

'I'll ask Kurt Weill to come along, the chap who composed "Mack the Knife". And Bertold Brecht, the *Threepenny Opera* playwright. I know they'll be thrilled to meet you.'

I could feel myself weakening. What harm could it do just to meet them? Was there any rule that said I had to imbibe alcoholic beverages just to lubricate social interaction?

Five days later we found a secluded corner of one the many interconnected ponds, partially screened by willows, just a stone's throw from a drinks stand. Christopher had arranged for a select little gathering and made the introductions. 'Gisella, please meet Jean Ross, with whom I bunk, but not in the biblical sense…' (Jean gave him a gentle slap), 'Kurt Weill and Bertold Brecht, whose work you already admire, George Grosz, whose artwork is far too good for the authorities to stomach, Fritz Lang, filmmaker extraordinaire, Brigitte Helm, a most gifted actress, Peter Lorre, a star of the silver screen, Gerry Hamilton, who has a finger in every pie and is quite the *worst* man in Europe, Gretchen, everybody's favourite hooker, and last but not least Heinz, a rather special chum of mine.'

'*Ich freue mich sehr, Sie alle kennenzulernen…*[2] er, *enchantée…*.' I was stalling. Everyone was looking at me expectantly, but I really had no idea what to say next. 'I know what, does anyone fancy a drink? I could murder a Schnapps.'

What had I been worrying about? For a start everyone was thrilled at meeting a talking fish and discovering that Christopher hadn't been talking bollocks after all, and my suggestion about a little drink turned out to be a stroke of genius. Tongues were oiled, inhibitions were shed and confidences shared – mainly by me I'm afraid. It appeared that all my new friends took delight in pouring shots of firewater into a carp's mouth, and consequently my new friends learnt all about the real history of the Hundred Years War, Shakespeare's plays and the sad tale of Marie-Antoinette, and if they thought I was telling a load of *mensonges*, whoppers, they were too kind to say so.

While it was fascinating to learn about what was new in the world of literature, music, painting and theatre, what really captured my imagination was hearing about films – something I knew about but had never seen.

'It's the art form of the twentieth century,' said Brigitte Helm. 'The drawing together of all other disciplines.'

'Harumph,' said George Grosz. 'I wouldn't want artists to be relegated to painting film sets.'

'We all know she's right,' said Kurt Weill.

'But don't worry. I'm sure people will still be looking at your paintings in a hundred years' time,' Bertold Brecht added.

'I wouldn't mind seeing a film someday,' I said.

'Good luck with that,' said Christopher. 'They don't have cinemas in public parks.'

'But they do, Herr Issyvoo.' Heinz loved to tease Christopher by hamming up his German accent. 'Have you been hiding under a rock or something? The Open-Air-Kino opened last month in the east of the park, and I'm pretty sure one of the *kleine Flüsse*, little rivers, runs close enough to the screen for Gisella to get a look at it.'

'Does anyone know what's showing?' asked Jean Ross.

'It's Fritz's latest,' said Peter Lorre. '*M*.... I happen to play a rather charismatic child-killer.'

Brigitte turned to Fritz Lang. 'I'm still pissed off you never found a part for me in it, Fritzi.'

'You're too glam and not sinister enough,' said Fritz.

'Sinister? *Wer? Ich?*' said Peter. 'I'd hate to end up getting typecast all my career.'[3]

The open-air cinema was in a part of the park I wasn't familiar with, but once I'd found it I became a regular. It was just a shame it was open only during the summer months. I found *M* chilling but addictive viewing – especially Peter's performance, with his compulsive whistling of 'In the Hall of the Mountain King' – and ended up seeing it four times in a row. Which is how Edvard Grieg finally evicted 'Mack the Knife' from my head.

I became a connoisseur of late German expressionist cinema, and also enjoyed some of the handful of American talkies that were screened. These became fewer and fewer as the county's political mood darkened, and foreign influences were frowned upon.

But in the meantime I saw my friends on a pretty regular basis, even during the winter, when they'd break the ice to make sure I had my fix of calorific treats and occasional snifters to keep out the chill. Gretchen the hooker would stop every afternoon to make sure I was okay, and Jean Ross in particular used to take the time for long chats, even in the snow. She'd tell me all about her latest nightclub performances, her failed auditions for the movies, who was shagging who and, of course, her own bewildering array of conquests. She'd get quite irritated with Christopher, especially when he included a character called Sally Bowles in his short stories – a highly liberated, extrovert, crazy-girl character – supposedly modelled on *her*. How simply outrageous, I commiserated, barely concealing a laugh. But Jean wasn't simply a flighty flibbertigibbet, she had a serious side to her too. For a start she was a member of the Communist Party – much to Christopher's amusement. He told her that in his opinion it was far better to be a communist in a capitalist country than a capitalist in a communist one, and if she was so keen on Bolshevism why didn't she hightail it to Moscow. She reckoned the jury was still out on Uncle Joe – he was showing some disturbingly dictatorial tendencies – but as for being a communist in Germany, that was becoming a risky business. Her faith was still unshakeable, however.

The rise of the Brownshirts was visible everywhere, and the Tiergarten was becoming a popular location for both fascist rallies and bouts of queer-bashing, Jew-baiting or just general intimidation, violence and frequent murders. But once the Nazis moved on from simply occupying the streets to actually ruling the country, there was a dramatic shift in mood. Thuggery was rubber-stamped and, by and large, the nation went along with it. True, Germans had lived through hyperinflation and a worldwide economic slump, but the fact that a nation chose to turn a blind eye – at best – to the inhumanity of the New Order doesn't speak well of the human race. I won't go on about this at length because anyone ignorant about Nazism in Germany at this time probably can't read.

It was a good time for those who'd incurred the wrath of the Nazis to get the hell out of Germany, and increasingly those who could, did. For the past two or three years there had been a trickle of people leaving the country, and that trickle was increasing month on month. Artists, scientists, writers, filmmakers: the country was no longer safe for them. Albert Einstein had already departed, Marc Chagall left, and Max Beckmann, Max Ernst, Gustav Born, Billy Wilder: thousands fled; but for many millions of others, finding sanctuary from the barbarism was an impossible dream. If you were Jewish, Gypsy, left wing, homosexual, a dissident, had mental problems, or perhaps had just fallen out with a neighbour and been denounced, your right to exist had been revoked.

Our happy little circle of friends followed suit. Christopher left and Heinz made every effort to – although he was ultimately and tragically unsuccessful. Kurt Weill, Bertold Brecht, Fritz Lang and Peter Lorre all made their way to the United States and Brigitte Helm didn't leave it too long before hopping it to Switzerland. Jean Ross had a serious word with me and advised me to go too: the Nazis hadn't yet proscribed talking fish, but she had no doubt I wouldn't last long if they ever found out about me. She was going to go as well. She told me being a communist it wasn't healthy for her in Germany, and that doubtless she was on some list or other. I assured her that as soon as the weather improved the next spring I'd be off, but I didn't fancy a long swim through the German winter. After Jean's departure the only friend who remained was Gretchen. She also hated what had become of Germany, but she had nowhere and no one to run to.

At long last the willows were coming into leaf, water lily leaves were breaking the water's surface and the reedmace was growing an inch a day. Spring was bursting out and with the rise in water temperature I was feeling a little less like an ancient curmudgeon.

In fact, I had to admit it, it felt very pleasant in the spring warmth, and I might've been tempted to linger in the Tiergarten a little longer if only the political climate had been as benign as the meteorological one, but there was an all-pervasive atmosphere of fear and brutishness that one could almost smell. Even the individual Brownshirts walking hand-in-hand in the park with their sweethearts gave me the creeps, but just as often they went around in carnivorous groups, swilling beer at the drinks stalls, singing their obnoxious *Horst Wessel Lied*,[4] on the lookout for any unfortunates to stomp the shit out of. It was time to go.

On the morning I'd decided to leave I was alarmed to hear a distant cacophony of shouting, dogs barking, and the odd crack of a pistol shot. I knew I shouldn't have dawdled. Then a breathless Gretchen staggered across to our secluded meeting spot with an even more breathless man in tow. He was a slight figure, with an unruly shock of hair and a bushy moustache, the archetypal nutty professor type if ever there was one. This was Albert Einstein, Gretchen panted, the Brownshirts were after him and he needed to hide. Could I help?

We agreed that Gretchen would make herself scarce and return that night, once the furore had died down, meanwhile I was expected to come up with some brilliant hiding place for the renowned savant. Fortunately I knew just the spot, but unfortunately it was a little way off, and, with the sound of Einstein's pursuers getting louder by the second, they were odds on to catch up with us before we reached it. We needed to buy time with a diversion. Telling Albert to get in the water and duck behind some willow branches, I shot off.

The leading Brownshirts heard a loud splashing sound from one of the river channels, then a siren-like voice rang out. It had a husky French lilt to it, but it was as sexy as hell. 'Yoo-hoo, *Kerle*…fellas…I've been skinny-dipping but some *schweinhund* has swiped my clothes! I'm all helpless here, and I'm not wearing a stitch!' Predictably the first of the pursuers screeched to a halt, looking for a naked lady, while their companions, who hadn't heard me so well, thundered into their backs. 'Oh boys, I'm over here, and you wouldn't believe what the cold water has done to my—' Men can be so gullible, especially those with the intelligence of wallpaper paste.

The Brownshirts were one problem, but the Gestapo, who were bringing up the rear, were another. They had brought a couple of tracker dogs with them, and the dogs had found a scent.

We, however, had now succeeded in reaching my hiding place, a culvert that led from a neglected, silty, debris-strewn arm of the watercourse, under a bandstand, and away to somewhere unknown. I urged Albert into the narrow, concrete-covered water channel, and nosed a mound of filthy flotsam and foul black mud into its entrance after him, leaving just enough of a gap in it for me to get in and out. It wasn't pleasant, but the smell was so strong the bloodhounds wouldn't have been able to detect a sack of *Bratwurst* in there. I followed him into the gloom and waited while all the thugs steered well clear of our malodorous bolthole.

Of course I knew who Albert Einstein was, everybody did, but I'd thought he'd emigrated a couple of years ago. The Nazis had been after him then, accusing him of conducting anti-German research and spouting treasonous Jewish theories, so what on earth had possessed him to come back?

'I fell into an elaborate trap. I received a letter from my dear old friend Professor Sigmund Wanowsky, something along the lines of discovering a brand-new theory that disproved all my work on relativity, so how could I resist? This was something we had to discuss and it could only be done face to face, plus, at his age, the prof was very averse to leaving his apartment. I knew it would be a massive risk returning to Berlin, but then Siggi sent me some documents that supposedly guaranteed me safe passage, signed by Joseph Goebbels no less, letters of transit in fact, so I'm afraid I rose to the bait.'

'Letters of transit? Sounds like phony baloney to me.'

'I know that now. I'm supposed to be this top-notch genius, but at times I'm the world's biggest klutz.'

'So what happened?'

'I knew something was wrong when I arrived at Siggi's apartment block. Instead of greeting me with a big hug as usual Frau Stern, the concierge, had lost all the colour from her face, couldn't look me in the eye, and was actually shaking. I turned and fled, but several Gestapo officers, who'd been waiting for me in her lounge, were quickly on my tail.

'A man and woman hurriedly pulled me into an alleyway. It turned out I'd been recognised by friends as well as enemies, and these two were part of an anti-fascist cell who'd been keeping an eye on me. Long story short, the man was unfortunately shot as we made a run for it, but the woman, who you appear to know—'

'Gretchen.'

'Yes, Gretchen, managed to lead me here. You know, I'd rather die than let the Gestapo get their hands on me.'

'I thought that was the object of the exercise.'

'Ha. The more able brains of the Gestapo want me very much alive. If they knew the intricacies of my latest work they'd eventually figure out how to use it to develop the most horrifying weapons of mass destruction – capable of killing tens of thousands at a time – and I know that under torture I'd spill the beans. That kind of knowledge must never fall into the wrong hands, or I dread to think of the consequences. I'd rather be shot in the head.'

It took thirty-six hours for the Nazis to take their search elsewhere, by which time Albert was freezing cold and badly dehydrated, but alive. When they finally showed up, Gretchen and two men from her group told me there was a car waiting for them and led him away, teeth chattering, swaddled in a blanket. As for me, my exit was well overdue. I'd have ample time to think about my next destination while I made the long trip back down to the North Sea.

Notes

[1]'*Örülök, hogy megismerkedhet, uram.*' Delighted to make your acquaintance, sir.
[2]'*Ich freue mich sehr, Sie alle kennenzulernen.*' Pleased to meet you all.
[3]Peter Lorre almost cornered the market in playing sinister roles, but he made a damn good job of it.
[4]*Horst Wessel Lied.* The Nazis' favourite drinking song. You've heard it in countless films.

Chapter Twenty Two

The Duration. Gisella breaks her rule about remaining impartial in the affairs of humans, helps a bunch of boffins, goes on a hush-hush mission, and plays a small role in altering the course of history

I stopped briefly in Hamburg, but when I swam through one of the canals that bisected the Jewish Quarter, hoping for the odd end of a *challah* maybe, and saw what was going on, I terminated my visit immediately. That was it. All of a sudden jellied eels and sausage rolls had become incredibly appealing, and I braced myself for a most unappealing swim across the North Sea.

London stank. It reeked. I don't mean I didn't like the city, I've always had a soft spot for London, I mean the Thames wasn't very nice at all. The water was breathable, sort of, mainly due to the fact that a number of sewage plants had been built to deal with the capital's human waste – but there was still an unwholesome amount of manufacturing effluent being poured into it. I didn't even want to think about that.

Most of the native fish had done the sensible thing and cleared out, but I found the river water was slightly more bearable above Battersea Bridge, and discovered a nice area of slack water, no matter the state of the tide, by the slipway at the side of the Ship Inn at Wandsworth. The pub appeared to have a superior calibre of drinkers because those enjoying a pint at the outside tables often threw pork scratchings into the water. There's something about pork scratchings that not even polluted river water can spoil, a bit like *andouillettes.*

Naturally I was able to follow foreign affairs by listening in on conversations, and what was happening on the world stage gave me *la trouille* – the willies. I didn't know all that much about East Asia, but it appeared that countless millions were swapping one bunch of colonial masters for another, which gave every sign of being even worse – not that they had any choice in the matter.

Meanwhile Italy had been attacking Abyssinia, the Balkans were in turmoil (as per), two irreconcilable factions faced each other in Spain, and Hitler's *Lebensraum*[1] ideology was sending shivers throughout Europe. Germany signed non-aggression pacts here and there, but it took a peculiar brand of optimism to believe they had any solidity. People were divided into three camps: those who remembered 1914–18 and wanted to avoid war at any cost, those who thought Mr Hitler had to be stopped, and the sooner the better, and those who kept ordering drinks and hoped it would all go away.

In the end I sympathised with the third group, although I was unable to order any drinks. Deep inside I suppose I knew another war would soon break out, but I wanted no part of it. I'd made a big mistake leaving Paris during the Great War so this time I was going to stick around in London, where I was one hundred per cent certain I'd be quite safe. Far, far away from any danger.

I say I couldn't order any drinks, but that's not completely true. One of the barmaids, Brenda, who embodied nearly all the qualities valued by pub customers, eventually caught on that a large shape in the murky water appeared to be listening to conversations (and audibly muttering to itself), and casually spoke to me one evening. She took befriending a large, lopsided, French-sounding carp completely in her stride, telling me that during her years as a barmaid she'd seen and heard a great many of the oddest things. She never gave me anything from the bottles behind the bar, but often punters left half-finished drinks and I seldom missed out on a little tot of Scotch after chucking-out time.

As the months rolled past the atmosphere continued to darken. Arguments would sometimes break out between the *give Hitler a bloody nose* faction and the *we mustn't go down this hellish path again* lot. This was when the one or two neutrals would step outside to enjoy their drinks in peace. I noticed one chap in particular who stood out from the crowd, who seemed to turn up for a couple of pints every fortnight: it wasn't because he looked in any way exceptional, it was rather his air of preoccupied detachment. He was tall, had sandy hair, wore extra-baggy trousers, a knitted tie and a tatty tweed jacket with patched elbows. I deduced that someone dressed that badly could only be a mathematician.

When Mr Chamberlain returned from a third meeting with Mr Hitler declaring *peace for our time* (so often misquoted), one could probably have heard the jubilation and relief inside the pub right down at Gravesend. From my spot by the slipway it was almost deafening, in spite of the ebbing tide, and in order to escape the hubbub the mathematician had decided to ignore the late September chill and enjoy his pint outside.

All for a sudden extra loud shouting broke out, along the lines of *get the Kraut*, with a brief sound of something being smashed, and a middle-aged, balding fellow staggered out of the saloon bar and collapsed at the top of the slipway. '*Dļl gailesĶio padļk man*,' he gasped.

Alarmed, the mathematician dropped to his knees by his side. 'Gosh, what's the matter, old chap? Can I help you?'

'*Negaliu kvļpuoti!*' the stricken man spluttered.

'I don't understand,' said the mathematician. 'Are you German? No, I don't think you're German.'

I popped my head above the surface. 'He's Lithuanian,' I said. 'He's saying he can't breathe.'

'Golly, a talking fish! You understand Lithuanian, and evidently you speak English too. Extraordinary!'

'Actually I speak several languages, it's a bit of a hobby.'

'Fascinating! And which languages would they be?'

'Oh, all the main European ones, plus several dialects.'

'*Gak*,' the Lithuanian gentleman wheezed.

'What a gift,' said the mathematician. 'Could you put a number to it?'

'I guess around fifty or so, not that I've counted.'

'But you sound a little bit French, would that be correct?'

'Hey, you two!' cried Brenda, storming out of the saloon. 'What are you doing yakking away while this poor gentleman's choking to death!' Without more ado she hiked up her skirt, straddled the Lithuanian, and clamped her lips to his, which by this time had turned a bluish colour.

'I say, Brenda,' said the mathematician, 'you don't even know the fellow!'

Brenda continued to breathe air into the stricken man's mouth, then she pummelled him on the chest. With a loud gasp, he started breathing again.

It turned out that the Lithuanian was a minor official from a diplomatic mission, and he'd made the mistake of postponing his English lessons until after his arrival. After an ambulance had taken him away Brenda had singled out the fellow who'd attacked him, a brain-dead, twenty-stone troublemaker called Nedwyn (which explains a lot), and kept him in an armlock until the police had arrived. To her disgust the officers had laughed that if they arrested everyone who attacked German-sounding foreigners they'd have no time for real crime, and Nedwyn suffered no worse an outcome than being barred from the Ship. That went for the officers too, Brenda had fumed.

Thereafter the mathematician, whose name was Alan Turing, always looked me up on his regular visits to London. He told me that only an idiot would believe there wasn't going to be a war, that he was involved with something rather hush-hush to do with it, and that I'd be a real asset if I came and joined him. I always told him that in the affairs of men I had no nationality or affiliation, and would always remain a neutral. Alan always took my refusals in good heart, and would still stand me my preferred Glenlivet. He seemed to have a quiet confidence that at some point I'd change my mind – the fool.

Over the next several months little changed, but then, one dismal day, it was announced that Britain had declared war on Germany. All of a sudden there were sandbag walls everywhere, ack-ack gun emplacements sprang up like mushrooms, and great marrow-like balloons occupied the city's skyline. Still, I thought, there was no sign of any fighting taking place anywhere close by, I was quite safe in my little inlet by the good old Ship Inn. Brenda told me that in my place she'd be off with Alan in a heartbeat. Then why was she still there, I asked? That was different, she was part of the pub's fabric and foundations, if it went up in smoke then so did she.

While Alan and I were enjoying our habitual fine single malt one late morning, an air-raid siren started to sound. That was nothing unusual, there had been plenty of drills over the past few weeks. This time we could see an aeroplane that would shortly be flying over us. Again, nothing unusual, it was normal for planes to fly over. What was unusual was that all the anti-aircraft guns started firing at the aircraft, creating little puffs of smoke all around it. All the shots missed, the plane banked widely and appeared to be heading off in the direction it had come from. At it disappeared from sight two more smaller planes appeared, evidently in hot pursuit. This time, rather than firing, the ack-ack gunners all cheered.

'This work you're doing,' I said to Alan. 'If it's hush-hush can I assume the Germans don't know its location?'

'Affirmative,' said Alan.

'And if, hypothetically, I joined you, what would I be doing? You do understand I'm strictly a non-combatant.'

'Absolutely. Listen, Gisella, we need a translator, someone good with languages. It'll just be routine stuff, nothing to do with the war effort.'

'You promise?'

'Scout's honour.'

'And where is this place? I'm not exactly built for working in an office.'

'We're way out in the country, and you'd have a rather lovely one-acre lake, complete with lilies, reeds and willows. You'll love it, and more importantly, you'll be absolutely safe there.'

Things then moved at great speed. The next day an anonymous-looking truck turned up at the pub. I was allowed to say a brief farewell to a damp-eyed Brenda before being heaved into a large tank, requisitioned from the already closed London Zoo, and driven at high speed by three mackintosh and trilby-wearing spooks – obvious from their uniform – through the streets of London and the Home Counties. So much for my cherished vision of another scenic meander through the picturesque English countryside, as during my travels with Surprendo's Fair during the seventeenth century, I was whisked incognito to Bletchley Park as quickly and quietly as possible.

The lake was everything Alan had promised, although an acre might've been a bit of an exaggeration. I shared it with some roach, rudd, perch and a few tench; they didn't bother me and I didn't bother them. A bankside hut was quickly erected for me, containing a power supply, a telephone, a film projector and screen, and a table and chair for my assistant. Well, I couldn't manage those things myself and Katy was a wonderful helper – once she got used to the idea of being a carp's general factotum. I was given pretty well anything I asked for to help in my work, which generally involved being shown pages of text in various languages and dictating the English translations. I was also was given rations that most of the other inmates at Bletchley were understandably very jealous of. Who else was spoilt with real butter brioche and single malt whisky?

Of course the penny quickly dropped that the translation work I was undertaking did have something to do with the war effort – rather a lot in fact. Stuff about targets in the Low Countries, plans for the occupation of Norway, correspondence with resistance movements in a number of occupied countries. I decided to have this out with Alan.

'Ah, yes.' He scratched his chin thoughtfully. 'The long and the short of it is I lied. Anyway, London is being bombed to hell pretty much every night – you're well out of it.'

'That's beside the point. You told me I wouldn't be doing war work and I am. Why me, anyway? Anyone with modest language skills could do these translations.'

'Bear with me and I'll show you what's really at stake. At the start of the war the Poles gave us a German encrypting machine[2] they'd swiped, and we figured out how to decode their messages, even their top-secret ones. It's a sobering experience.'

Alan proceeded to show me transcripts of documents detailing plans for a surprise invasion of Russia, of Fifth Column activities in the remaining allied countries, film clips of mass killings in the Balkans, of the rounding-up and murder of thousands of Jews, Gypsies and undesirables of dozens of descriptions, in Germany and in all the territories the Nazis had occupied, of Stukas dive-bombing and strafing refugees. He knew I'd been in Germany at the time Hitler assumed power. I had to imagine a situation that had become a hundred, no, a thousand times worse. And then he produced the *coup de grâce*, a top secret report suggesting a possible *Final Solution* to the *Jewish Problem*, along with sketches of what looked like vast internment camps and factory-type buildings with tall chimneys. He asked if I was still prepared to stick in the neutral camp.

'*Touché*, all right, I read you loud and clear. But I still don't understand what I can bring you that any other translator can't.'

'Up until now all the messages we intercepted, once we'd decoded them, were in German. We had no problem with that. But, as we'd feared all along, they're now encrypting other languages, and jumbling them up, which is another kettle of fish completely. What we need is someone with an incredible head for languages.' I said nothing. 'Now, unless I'm mistaken, you can translate from one language to another in the blink of an eye, no? And you speak about fifty languages, give or take. And in each language you probably have a better than average vocabulary – say about 40,000 words? That gives you a basic lexicon of about 2,000,000 words, but when you throw in all the permutations of jumping back and forth between all those languages, your fishy little brain is running through about 4,000,000,000,000 possible connections – almost instantly. I'm trying to construct machines that make complex mathematical calculations, but to match your computing power I'd have to build one the size of St Paul's Cathedral. What do you say to that?'

'Can I have a chocolate biscuit, please?'

'Yes, of course... But back to the matter in hand. What if, for instance, we receive a message that turns out to be in Finnish, but the Finnish contains several of those annoying multiple-meaning words that on the face of it are gobbledegook? What if we can only find their meaning by trawling through dozens of other languages? The permutations are almost infinite, and only a mind with a detailed knowledge of all those languages stands a chance of making the right connections. Mathematics can take us so far, but it can't unravel context. What could well see us bogged down for weeks – weeks that we don't have – we believe you could unravel at high speed. Is that correct?'

'You do the maths and I'll do the context. Easy peasy lemon squeezy.'

'Gisella, you have a beautiful mind.'

'And now, that chocolate biscuit?'

So I was set to work using my language skills to help decipher German messages. Actually, at first some of them were somewhat challenging, because after leaping from, say, Bulgarian to Greek to Latvian, I sometimes got results such as a convoy of profiteroles heading for Lvov, or a squadron of Junkers bombers grounded at Beauvais due to chronic constipation. But I soon got the hang of it.

Katy was a godsend, a native of Liverpool with a lightning sense of humour and a heartening lack of deference for those from *better-class* families, or posh university graduates, but, considering the stodgy makeup of the society they were recruited from, the boffins at Bletchley Park knew a thing or two about recognising a person's abilities, regardless of their background. Katy had an incredible knack for anticipating my needs, often before I did.

At Bletchley we shared triumphs and we shared disasters, we shared almost everything (except I was pretty rubbish at sharing brioche). It was deeply upsetting having purposely to ignore information that could've saved Allied lives, but if we appeared too prescient about German operations we'd give the game away about cracking their codes. For instance, knowing a wolfpack of submarines was about to hit an Atlantic convoy and doing nothing to warn it was harrowing, but such things were judged to be necessary.

It was especially awful when Katy's fiancé was declared missing in action, presumed killed. He was Royal Navy, part of the crew of a convoy escort destroyer. It had been close to home, moored just off the Mersey estuary prior to docking the next day, when disaster struck. There had been a night-time air raid on Liverpool, scores of bombers, ack-ack, searchlights, explosions, fires, smoke. A plane was hit and began a rapid descent, leaving a fiery, comet-like tail behind it. The jubilation of the anti-aircraft gunners turned to horror as the doomed Heinkel smashed right into the destroyer, hitting it amidships. The plane hadn't yet dropped its bombs and the vessel was obliterated almost instantaneously; anyone succeeding in leaping into the water was still engulfed by the fireball.

Katy was given a five-day compassionate leave, but when she returned from Liverpool she still looked like she'd aged a decade. The war was doing that to a lot of people. We had to remind ourselves that what we were doing was of immense value – and we had the added advantage that we were as far from danger as could be hoped for in southern England, away from all the usual bomber flightpaths.

Sometimes there were setbacks, the raid in Dieppe was a bloody shambles, literally, and sometimes great successes, such as the Battle of El Alamein. But, little by little, the Axis advances were grinding to a halt and being reversed. The U-boat packs had taken a terrible toll of Allied shipping, but now the Atlantic was becoming a most perilous place for German submarines. The hunters had become the hunted. The Russians were turning the tide in their homeland; in spite of his strategic nous Rommel was losing in North Africa; the Japanese juggernaut looked as if it was grinding to a halt in East Asia. There was cause for optimism.

Alan Turing and I were in the habit of sharing a single malt in the evenings and we were usually joined by Katy, although she preferred beer. In pints. She was now seeing an Air Force chap, a mechanic, which at first sight was a safer choice than the blokes who went up in the air. Alan told her she should look out for a nice army major next, get the full set so to speak. You never know, she said, smiling enigmatically at him, she could go for something completely different – such as a back-room brainbox sort of fellow… or maybe not? Alan coloured up like a beetroot and Katie let out a loud snort of laughter. As I said, she was both astute and discreet.

More Allied successes. Goering had acknowledged that mass bombing of the UK was unsustainable – the Luftwaffe was being eviscerated. A toehold was gained in Italy at Sicily. The Russians resisted at Leningrad, forced the Germans back at Stalingrad, and won a decisive victory at Kursk. Further east the Imperial Japanese Army was now becoming accustomed to setbacks, and had lost its aura of invincibility.

While the war was now being won, the news from Germany, and what they referred to as the Greater Reich, went from sinister to deeply alarming. At that point we had no photographic proof, but from the communications we were intercepting we knew that the *Final Solution* was probably already in motion – although many of the details were far from exact. As if that weren't bad enough, there was little we could do with the information without seriously jeopardising the war effort: our only recourse was to do everything in our power to bring the war to a conclusion as quickly as possible. We knew an Allied invasion of northern France was imminent – as did the Nazis. It was up to us to ensure that it was successful.

One late spring day – the weather was filthy – Alan and I received two visitors at the lake. They were both dressed in mackintoshes and trilby hats so I surmised they were Intelligence, and indeed they told us that they were from the SOE, Special Operations Executive, and they had a very delicate mission for me.

The brief was to keep the Germans believing that the most likely area for the forthcoming Allied invasion was the Pas de Calais, right up in the north of France. Up until now German High Command had bought into the bluff and double bluff about the Allies favouring the northern site, and to help matters the German Commander-in-Chief in the West, General Gerd von Rundstedt, had adhered to a policy of keeping most of his armoured divisions well back from the coast, in order to plug any gaps when the Allies made landfall. What they needed was someone who had von Rundstedt's complete confidence to reassure him that that was the correct strategy – and keep the Panzers well away from the coasts. And that someone was Generalfeldmarschall Erwin Rommel – the Desert Fox.

Rommel was Wehrmacht, an army man, through and through, and it was suspected that while he was a devoted patriot he wasn't one hundred per cent besotted with the Nazi Party. Intercepted secret correspondence between him and his wife showed he was very well aware of the fact that the war was by now unwinnable for Germany, that the Nazis were engaged in some deeply dishonourable actions, and if a way was found to extricate the fatherland from the conflict before it was wiped from the map it might be worth considering.

'That's fascinating,' I said. 'What's making me slightly uneasy is what any of that can possibly be to do with me.'

'We're coming to that,' said *Mr Smith.*

'We need an emissary to negotiate with Rommel, someone fluent in German who can get to see him without arousing any suspicion,' said *Mr Jones.*

'And with all the myriad resources at your disposal you appear to be choosing – a fish,' I said.

'Didn't we say she was as bright as a newly minted florin?' beamed Mr Smith.

'We think it might be possible to get him to see the bigger picture,' said Mr Jones, 'and to soft-pedal on their coastal defences. Not to betray the Reich, not tarnish the uniform.'

'It's all insane. How the hell am I supposed to get to the man? It's not as if we'd be able to meet incognito at some boulevard café, and for a start I'll bet he has minders who don't let him out of their sight.'

'As a matter of fact he's about to spend a quiet weekend with his old military academy chum Werner von Traur, at a quiet mansion house near Montreuil,' said Mr Smith. 'They're both *potty* about Haydn.'

'You'll have plenty of opportunity for a chinwag with the *Generalfeldmarschall*,' said Mr Jones.

'But time is of the essence, Gisella,' said Mr Smith. 'We aim to get this show on the road as soon as this rotten spell of weather breaks.'

Alan gave an apologetic shrug, as if to say he didn't have any choice in the matter. I believed him.

That's how thirty-six hours later I found myself in a large zoo aquarium crammed onto the back of a speedy MTB,[3] which took me most of the way to the mouth of the River Canche, cutting its engines to a mere hum as the silhouetted French coastline came into view. Normally one would've had a fine view of the lights of le Touquet, but of course the resort was now drenched in shadows due to the blackout. Our intelligence was good, we avoided all the mined areas, then I was released and made my way into the Canche and towards my rendezvous spot just upstream from Etaples.

My contacts were Yves and Yvette. I had an inkling those names were no more kosher than Mr Smith and Mr Jones had been. They were clad from head to foot in black, and their faces were blackened too. I felt a bit silly giving them the password, *ceviche*, a, because using a fish dish for it was in poor taste and b, they probably didn't come across that many talking carp anyway, so why the hell did we need a password? Hushed introductions over, they boarded a small rubber dinghy and led the way cautiously upstream.

The weather was still appalling, which may not have made it pleasant for my friends from la Résistance, but it also meant that the few German patrols that were out and about were more concerned with keeping dry than with spotting Maquis. We proceeded unhindered.

With the squat tower of the Church of Saint Pierre and Saint Paul just peeking above a wooded rise, signalling that we were approaching Montreuil, Yves announced that we'd arrived. I did a double take; we were still in the middle of nowhere as far as I could see. He promptly took a set of steel cutters from the bottom of the dinghy and started snipping away at the wire grille covering the gushing outlet of a three-quarters submerged, moss-covered pipe, which I hadn't spotted before. Once it had been removed he handed the cutters to Yvette, who told me to follow her as she crawled into it. It was just as well she was very petite, I didn't exactly find the pipe roomy myself and hoped I wouldn't suffer a bout of claustrophobia, but I needn't have worried. The pipe led under a road – I could feel the vibrations of a couple of vehicles passing overhead – and not long after there was daylight again. Yvette had to snip through a second wire grille, but then we were in the open again, where a small stream emptied into the pipe. Then, to my surprise, she picked me up in her arms and hurried across an overgrown lawn, and then a circular gravelled area, before depositing me in a large, raised, ornamental pond. Because the weather had been so wet the water had reached the pond's rim, and by sticking my head just above the surface I was able to take in a panoramic view of my surroundings. The pond was circular, with a Rococo stone statue of a mermaid in the middle; water should've been spouting from her mouth and breasts, but you had the impression her tubes had furred up long ago. The surrounding gardens must've been sumptuous at some point but had obviously suffered from years of neglect, as had the nearby large, pleasantly proportioned eighteenth-century mansion house itself. From what I could see it was still quite habitable, even if the rampant wisteria smothering its walls was also blocking some of its windows. We appeared to be quite alone out there, although just beyond the manor's driveway there was a metal double gate with a sentry box just outside it – which one assumed was manned.

Yvette wished me luck collaring Rommel, told me she'd return to see how I was getting on that evening, and left me to my own devices. First off I reckoned I'd have to wait for the rain to stop before there was any chance of Rommel appearing. Then I realised with immense annoyance that no one had thought to provide me with a packed lunch. Talk about taking advantage of a fish. Still, music was being played in one of the mansion's ground-floor rooms, which made the wait a little less tedious. I slurped down a couple of half-drowned mayflies that only made me feel more hungry, and waited.

Halfway through the afternoon a tall figure, shrouded in waterproofs, burst out of the mansion's front door, almost being towed by two large, slobbering Dobermans. This was undoubtedly Rommel, for I'd been briefed that von Traur was short with a waistline like a *Bierfass*, beer barrel, but he was being pulled so fast he'd gone before I thought to call out to him. That served Rommel right for getting involved in a such a ridiculous task, I thought sagely. Then I remembered I was there only because I'd been volunteered for that insane mission myself, and was a little more forgiving towards the *Generalfeldmarschall.* A couple of bedraggled guards let him out of the front gates, and I settled down to wait for his return.

After an hour he was back – trudging, muddied and weary. 'You were listening to the Bach Double Violin Concerto in D Minor,' I called out to him. 'I thought you were supposed to be a Haydn man.'

'Variety is the spice of life,' he answered. '*Himmel*, you're a carp!'

The dogs were rather astounded by me too, but their reaction was to charge towards me, snarling and slobbering. '*Anhalten!*' I cried, more by instinct than anything. '*Setzen Sie sich hin und halten Sie die Klappe!*' Stop! Sit down and belt up! To my great relief they did so; on this occasion I was most grateful for the Teutonic habit of blindly obeying orders.

'Don't tell me,' said Rommel, who'd recovered his composure with admirable speed, 'you're here with a message from the Allies.'

I nodded.

'I've been expecting contact in some form or another, but using a trained carp – what an amazing level of ingenuity.'

'Less of the trained, please, I'm here of my own free will – sort of.'

'And what is it you want?'

'Well, you must realise Germany can no longer—'

'Wait! Let me stop you right there. We can't win, you're absolutely preaching to the converted here *mein lieber Karpfen*, we've lost access to most of our raw materials, the Luftwaffe is a skeleton of what it once was, and we're retreating on nearly every front. It's a just matter of time.'

'And lives, *Generalfeldmar*—'

'It's just *General* now. It appears I'm no longer flavour of the month. Listen – we all know the invasion is imminent. The difference between von Rundstedt and der Führer and me is that they believe the Allies can be thrown back into the sea, while I know their success is inevitable. It appears I'm suspected of being a waverer, and my influence is no longer what it was. I believe that with the Allies in France, Germany will have to sue for peace with honour, but even to breathe those words right now is enough to put you in front of a firing squad.'

'Your lot have already blown the honour part of it, but the sooner the Allies retake France the sooner the killing comes to an end. The landings must succeed, and the key to that is where all the reserve Panzer divisions are stationed.'

'Here's the bad news,' said Rommel sadly. 'Even that Dummkopf von Rundstedt has twigged that having most of our tanks held up in parking lots to the north of Rouen won't help repel anyone, so he's sending one third of the Panzers up to the Pas de Calais and two thirds down to Normandy, where the front will potentially be much wider. All they're waiting for are rail deliveries of fuel and ammunition.'

'*Merde.*'

'As you say, *Scheiße.*'

'It's been a pleasure, General Rommel, but sometimes it's best to keep these visits short and sweet. I don't suppose you could help me over to the stream back there?'

At their riverside hideout near Etaples Yves and Yvette unearthed concealed a radio set, called up their contacts in England and shoved a microphone in front of my face. There was always the chance the Gestapo or similar would be listening in to our communication, but matters were extremely urgent and that was a chance we had to take. '*Bonjour, Angleterre*, hullo Blighty.' I had the jargon off pat. 'Fritz wants to gate-crash the tea party, I repeat, Fritz wants to gate-crash the tea party.'

'What are you talking about? Stop speaking gibberish, you stupid Frog tart.'

'Oh for fuck's sake. They're going to move all the reserve Panzer divisions down to the coast so you're going to have to get your skates on. There's no time to lose.'

'Oh, golly!'

'Do you understand me? Dither about and the whole thing will be a catastrophe!'

'The invasion fleet's on standby, but we can't move until the weather clears, and the forecast is really crappy for the next fortnight.'

'Listen, there'll be a brief window in the bad weather on the morning of the day after tomorrow. That's the sixth of June. Yes, the sixth. Ask Alan Turing, he knows my forecasts are much better than the Ministry's. That should give you a head start on the Panzers, they're still waiting for re-provisioning, but you can't dilly-dally any longer.'

'Roger wilco. That means will comply. I think.'

'I kind of got that.'

In spite of the fact that the Gaullist and Communist factions of the Resistance weren't really on speaking terms, and both were a bit dubious about the Rosbifs, several attacks on the northern French rail network were carried out successfully, which delayed the Panzers' mobilisation until the Allies had landed at the Normandy beaches and struck well inland. Even once the tanks got moving their progress was continually hampered by RAF raids, which took a considerable toll.

As for me, it was decided that with a breakout from the Cotentin Peninsula imminent, the fighting would probably spread rapidly northward, and I should be evacuated. Of course I could've swum back to the UK, but I was considered too valuable an asset to risk in a watery war zone so transport would be arranged for me. Thus one early August night my two Resistance friends (communists, as they'd lectured me daily) led me out into the Canche estuary, where a Royal Navy submarine suddenly broke surface and a large pannier was lowered over the side for me. That was a relief, because I'd had a sudden vision of having to swim aboard via one of the torpedo tubes.

After being put ashore at Felixstowe I was whisked into the back of a lorry and several bumpy hours later found myself back in my little lake at Bletchley Park. Alan, Katy and all the rest were waiting for me, all jubilant at the success of my mission, and we celebrated my return from France with very rich brioche, fine cognac, and someone had even sourced some *andouillette* from somewhere. I like it; I'm a carp. No one else did.

The war continued, and although we were all frustrated by the length of time it was taking to force the Axis to its knees the eventual outcome was in no doubt at all. Following a failed attempt on Hitler's life we heard about Rommel's supposed involvement in the plot and his subsequent suicide, even although the official version was that he'd been strafed by Allied aircraft. Was he part of the conspiracy? Quite possibly. I believe he did have a code of honour, and I'm pretty sure what he already knew about Nazi war crimes would've been more than enough to push him over the edge.

As the war's conclusion neared, the discovery of the full extent to the Nazis' horrific extermination programme cast a pall over all of us. At the same time the Allies, with whom I'd thrown in my lot, had developed a strategy of carpet-bombing enemy cities, except of course they weren't really *enemy cities* because they were largely inhabited by non-combatants. Civilians. All caught up as firestorms engulfed entire communities and killed people in their tens of thousands. Dresden, Hamburg, Kobo, Tokyo. And then there was the *coup de grâce*, Hiroshima and Nagasaki. It was true that more people had died in the firestorms caused by the carpet bombing of, say, Tokyo, than the two nuclear blasts put together, but to unleash a single device capable of wiping out an entire city? All those kindly boffins, with spouses, children, sweet little grannies, what the hell had they been thinking of when they devised a technology that could scourge large areas of the planet?

Alan and Katy tried to lift my spirits, but they knew better than to repeat the official waffle the great and the good were spouting to justify all the carnage. And I was partially to blame. I'd aided and abetted arguably the two greatest minds of the age – Einstein and Turing – who'd used their genius to supercharge the war effort. Katy pointed out that it would've been far worse if the other side had won, but I wouldn't be consoled. The Great War had been the War to End all Wars, yet we'd just had another one, and now the global pack of cards was being shuffled yet again, and a new set of enmities was being dealt out. Whoopee.

Notes

[1]Lebensraum literally means living space. More to the point, it involves nicking living space – often with extreme brutality.
[2]The codebreaking gizmo was nicknamed the Enigma machine. Generations of filmgoers have grown up believing the English or Americans nabbed one first. It was the Poles. But the clever folk at Bletchley Park deciphered it.
[3]MTB, Motor Torpedo Boat. Horrible things – so fast they're on top of a fish before it knows it.
[4]As we know, Gisella's weather forecasts were far better than the official ones, and still are for that matter.

Chapter Twenty Three

You've never had it so good. In which Gisella battles austerity, depression and a flood

A depressed carp was of little use to the British Intelligence services and the staff of Bletchley Park were all going their own way anyway, so I was demobbed. Given the choice of where I wanted to be, my first choice was back at the Ship Inn at Wandsworth. However, I was told that the lower Thames pollution had become so bad that a dip in the river anywhere downstream from Slough meant instant death. My second choice was Oxford. That wasn't a quest for enlightenment or erudition; one of the colleges, Magdalen if I recalled correctly, had a tradition of fine eating, and I felt a quiet sojourn in the lee of that venerable seat of gastronomy would suit me just fine. I recalled the four old dons and their spread of sandwiches, pies, cakes and vintage port, and looked forward to assuaging my gloom and guilt in a sea of calories. Apparently depressed humans are usually disinclined to eat very much; we carp are different.

The best laid plans frequently come to naught, and this was no exception. Even Oxford University was subject to post-war rationing, and while the dons and students all talked endlessly about what they'd like to be eating, they weren't actually doing very much of it. What they did get to eat was pretty bland, and waste was still a sin anyway, so I had next to precious nothing to mop up. All that ended up in the water were remnants of the abhorred tinned *snoek*, a very, very poor relation of the bass, from southern climes, and even I turned up my nose at that.

Still, I hung around for a while. Not that I was that interested in the affairs of humans anymore, but I couldn't help overhearing learned conversations about the state of the world, post-war rebuilding, and plans for a Welfare State, which involved homes for everyone, and universal healthcare and education, free at the point of use. *Mon dieu,*

I thought, someone's got their head screwed on at last. Not that I cared, of course. I had to remember I was beyond all that.

Strangely enough, nearly all the dons and most of the students took a very dim view of the Welfare State. Apparently it could well bring about a mixing of classes, an erosion of traditional values, a dilution of wealth. What if a chap at uni found himself studying alongside the son – or, God forbid, daughter – of a family servant? Things had worked better before the war, although admittedly Hitler needed to be dealt with (the plebeian little upstart). What the country was facing now was no less than a rapid descent into communism.

If these were the cream of the nation's intelligentsia then heaven help us all, but I had a suspicion that they were just highly entitled *connards*, fuckwits, with a veneer of classical education. I decided I'd had it with Oxford, so I headed back into the Thames and made up my mind to swim upstream, just for a change.

I'd passed through Lechlade some 400 or so years earlier, but to be honest I couldn't remember it very well. It seemed a pleasant enough place, and with the Trout Inn bordering the river I didn't see any reason not to stay put for a while. On summer days people often ate out in the pub garden, and naturally all sorts of bits and pieces of food ended up in the water. A great favourite at the inn was the ploughman's lunch, which meant I enjoyed plenty of doorstep-like bread crusts, ends of crumbly Cheddar cheese, and sometimes bits of ham rind. All good, but the one thing I never warmed to was pickled onions. To me they're one of life's great mysteries. Sundays, though, I liked especially – Sunday roast with all the trimmings. With austerity still in full force there was far less roast and far more stodgy trimmings, lots of glue-like stuffing and overcooked cauliflower, which frequently found their way into the willing mouth of an impressive carp.

In spite of the inn's name there weren't all that many trout in the upper Thames. There were some, and they grew big, and were much prized by anglers, but mainly the river was occupied by us coarse fish. Roach, rudd, dace, pike, perch, bream, chub – a few barbel had made their way that far up the river, not many – and me. I was the only carp and I was big so they gave me a wide berth, which suited me just fine. As for salmon, they'd long since disappeared from the river, victims of all the pollution downstream, which would get even worse before it got better.

Naturally, I picked up loads of gossip from the pub's clientele, and couldn't escape the mounting excitement about the forthcoming coronation of Queen Elizabeth II. There was to be a grand open-air party in the big meadow beside the river, a little way upstream from the pub. All were invited, and I assumed that included me.

The second of June dawned grey, drizzly and chilly, and the weather didn't improve throughout the day. Did that dampen spirits? No, not a bit of it, unless you count a few of the younger children who'd refused to wear their waterproofs and ended cold and wet. Bunting fluttered, fires spluttered and smoked, flags were waved, a brass band oompahed, mountains of fish-paste sandwiches and meat-free sausage rolls were scoffed, squash and ale were quaffed, people danced and the odd fight broke out – in short people had a really great time.

The mood was quite infectious, and completely overcame my determination to be miserable about it all. As for the issue of the monarchy itself I rather tended to my old *copain* George III's view, that it was all somewhat absurd, but everyone was having such a good time that I just went along with it, and of course helped myself to all the alimentary debris that ended up in the drink. Let them all have fun, I thought, some relief from the unrelenting post-war grimness. Patronising? *Qui, moi?*

Gradually austerity loosened its grip, and with more homes built and jobs created people's lives grew easier. Looking up at the pub garden I couldn't help noticing changes in the fashions being worn and the music people listened to; there was even a plethora of new words entering the English language. All these changes were being imported from the United States apparently, which most of the pub's customers regarded as a shining beacon for the world, twenty years ahead of Britain and light years ahead of everybody else. I tried some bubble gum that someone threw in the river, which kind of convinced me that not everything that was crossing the Atlantic was all that marvellous.

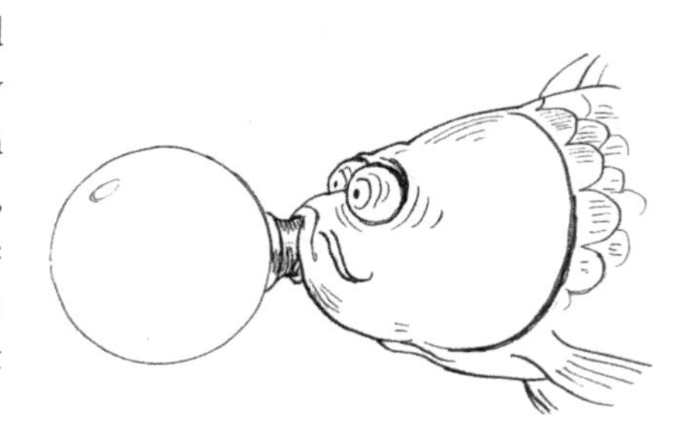

I also heard about all the wars that were taking place all over the world. The USA and the UK seemed to be mixed up in an awful lot of them, although at the same time politicians were convincing folk that this long period of peace was bringing amazing prosperity and we'd never had it so good.

I was still puzzling over the worldwide period of peace we were all enjoying when all of a sudden all the talk at the Trout Inn turned to a Russian convoy, which was carrying nuclear weapons to Cuba, and the Americans' determination to stop them. A breathless stand-off was developing; would a nuclear holocaust ensue?[1] Given that a single atomic bomb could take out an entire city, and there were now thousands of such weapons on either side, and much bigger ones too, a four-minute warning to hide under your kitchen table, protected by milk-soaked sheets, seemed less than adequate. All the gloom I'd felt fifteen years earlier returned with a vengeance and I simply sank to the bottom of the river, determined once more to sever all ties with the terminally self-destructive human race.

That winter was the most uncomfortable I can recall, and I'd over-wintered in Russia not so many centuries before. What made the experience so bad was being in a river rather than a deep lake, where the temperature remains a constant four degrees. The shallower, faster stretches of the Thames remained ice-free, in spite of below-freezing-point water temperatures, while the slower sections acquired a covering of thick ice. I found the deepest water I could, but it was still bloody perishing. Countless thousands of fish perished, and, semi-comatose myself, I survived only because I'd built up a great store of body fat over the warmer months. Somewhere in the dim recesses of my befogged mind I thought: this is what it must be like to be a mullet.

It wasn't until March that a thaw set in, and with it came several atmospheric depressions, along with front after front of rain – and floods. These floods weren't the worst I'd experienced by any stretch, and we fish usually find ways to find shelter, and not get left high and dry when they recede, but this time around all my strength had long since vanished, and when the river burst its banks I was carried helplessly over fields and roads and through woods until I finally found myself in deep, still water. Wherever I was, that was where I was going to stay for the foreseeable.

Gradually I became aware that I was in a lake, so I'd dodged the bullet of being left stranded in a field. It was a pretty barren place, evidently newly excavated, and when the floodwaters had vanished the heavy plant machinery situated at one end of it started – or resumed more like – scooping up gravel from the lakebed.[2]

Even in a new lake there's a certain amount of natural food, hatching insects, beetles, frogs, snails etc., and if it wasn't yet particularly plentiful, at least I wasn't having to share it with many other fish. A few roach and perch had also found their way into the gravel pit, but they weren't going to stand in the way of a specimen-size carp with several months' feeding to catch up on.

As the pit matured the amount of food increased. Weed proliferated, water lilies appeared, there was a profusion of insects, and bankside vegetation rapidly spread over the naked gravel landscape. After a couple of years the gravel extraction ceased and the plant machinery was dismantled. Peace, perfect peace.

Then, a few years later, a couple of lorries rolled up and dumped tanks of roach, rudd and tench into the water, to add to the small population of fish already present. Signs saying Springhampton and District Angling Club were erected, and I knew I'd soon have human company again.

Actually, I wasn't too bothered by the chitter-chatter of the handful of anglers who frequented the lake. They were harmless enough, contented themselves float fishing for roach and rudd, and kept me sort of abreast of what was happening in the world. Not that I was remotely interested of course, but I did hear snippets about *the pound in your pocket*, *The Who*, *the three-day week*, *Watergate*, *On the Buses, Maggie Thatcher Milk Snatcher*, *Blondie*, *The Miners' Strike*, *The Fall of the Soviet Empire*....

At the same time, I was fascinated by the evolution of fishing techniques and equipment. To begin with, nearly everyone float fished and baits were strictly bread, maggots or worms, but with the passage of time the fishing tackle improved beyond all recognition, methods were refined, and wonderful new baits appeared season after season. When carp fishing came into vogue a few of my mirror carp cousins were surreptitiously slipped into the lake, in spite of the club wishing to keep Coote Lake as a tench and roach venue, and thereafter a small number of carp aficionados would come and set up shop every weekend. I was amused by the intricate rigs they launched into the water to snare my unwitting kin, and tutted when one or other of them made a boo-boo and picked up a bait attached to someone's line. The lines in the water didn't bother me, but I took exception to the use of remote-control model boats to place an angler's bait. As the saying goes, it's simply not cricket. It was surprising how many of those silly little craft met with unexplained accidents.

Sometimes the carp anglers got lucky, more often not. On warm days with good visibility, some anglers reckoned they sighted an outsized common carp that looked a bit lopsided, although how they determined it weighed thirty-seven pounds is anyone's guess. It was just a rumour, however. All the while thousands of boilies were being fired into the water, along with fish pellets, maize, dog biscuits, chunks of peperami, and any other bait that was in fashion, and I always had an ample selection to choose from. However…. However…. I've eaten scraps from some of the top tables in Europe, but I have to say that nothing, just nothing, had proved more appealing to me than a fragrant Vor-Tex boilie. That magic maple syrup and fenugreek mélange, it's pure heaven, even better than the finest brioche, amazing to say. I was heartbroken when all of a sudden people stopped using them a few years back, and that perhaps explains why one fateful day I completely let my guard down when I chanced upon a single, lonesome Vor-Tex boilie sitting on the lakebed. It was just so *fenugreeky*.

Notes

[1]People were truly terrified of a nuclear armageddon during the Cuban Missile Crisis. With good reason.

[2]The 1960s was a time of massive construction, especially motorways, all of which necessitated vast quantities of gravel. The excavations then filled with water, creating hundreds of lakes.

Chapter Twenty Four

La grande évasion. How Mike and Gisella plot their great escape, embark on a grand road trip, and make a new home

Gisella and I had long talks every time I made it over to the lake, mainly about how to confront the problems we each faced. First and foremost, Gisella needed to find a new

home before Coote Lake was filled in. It's true that the fishing club had struck a deal to sell all the resident fish to a big commercial fishery, but she would've found that kind of place a nightmare. Noisy, overcrowded and overfished – no thank you. She could've pleaded that she was a special case, given the game away that she was a highly intelligent talking carp, but she considered the consequences of doing that would be several times worse. As for me, rumours I'd been hearing about redundancies at the firm I worked for were becoming fact, and my name was right there on the list. It was a bittersweet pill: it's true that I detested my job, but what in God's name was I going to do? The silver lining was that we'd been swallowed up by one of the multinational big-tech firms, plus I'd been in that job since I left college, so my redundancy package was large enough for me to put that decision off for quite some time.

A few quid extra would help increase our options of course, and Gisella's reminiscences gave me a bit of an idea (and it was *my* idea, no matter what Gisella says). Any history nerd would be fascinated by her alternative accounts of our turbulent European past, so why not try to cash in on them? It was simple enough to bring along a laptop and document her account of the Norman Invasion using a pirated version of Autojot © – in fact the speed at which she familiarised herself with the technology was frightening. Then off it went to *The New Polymath*, and of course that led to the book deal. And to our surprise and delight we had a tiny bit of a hit on our hands.

We still had to figure out our future, and we were acutely aware that Coote Lake's days were numbered. Gisella complained about her old-age aches and pains (with every justification, given her advanced years) and griped that she didn't want to see out her last days on a cold, damp island, where only the most upmarket supermarkets sold decent brioche. For my part, I wondered what was holding me in the UK. I was renting a nondescript flat in a nondescript town and had been fired from a nondescript job, what's more I had my redundancy money and what I'd saved from when Anne and I had divorced and we'd sold our house. Then, hey presto, there was a book deal and the tantalising prospect of royalties. We started looking at online French estate agent ads; down in the Midi, Gisella insisted. She'd be able to retire in comfort, and I'd live the dream of every bourgeois Brit and have my own gaff in the South of France.

Finding a modest property with river or lake frontage at a price that we could afford was never going to be easy, and all the estate agents' fanciful bullshit, as hallucinatory in France as anywhere else, made the task still harder. I'd given my notice at my flat, contractors were starting to construct a fence at the far end of the lake, we needed a breakthrough. Then, scrolling through yet another succession of swish villas and cramped pieds-a-terre Gisella barked at me to stop. *Ancienne propriété en pierre avec colombages, à restaurer.* Old stone property with beams, to restore. We'd found the one. *The* one.

Our bid for the property was accepted so quickly we realised we'd probably been ripped off, but this was the place we wanted. We were able to select a local *notaire* online, and when Gisella spoke to her on the phone of course she had no idea she was dealing with a carp. A deposit was wired, the notary, Mlle Marie Dulac, assured us we'd be able to complete within a matter of days... The property had been empty for a considerable time.

The next problem to surmount was logistical: how to transport the few belongings I wished to hang on to – plus a large carp – into France. I traded my Skoda Yeti in for a six-year-old Renault Trafic van, and bought an outsize fish tank along with an aerator, but that didn't solve the problem of crossing the Channel. All vehicles leaving UK ports are routinely checked, and explaining away a live, thirty-something-pound carp would be an impossibility. Much to her disgust, Gisella was going to have to go for another long-distance swim.

On the morning I came to scoop Gisella out of Coote Lake, I found the entire area fenced off. The work had evidently already begun. Fortunately it was a Sunday and nothing was happening, so after a quick run to B&Q for some wire-cutters, and then a spot of very satisfying vandalism, I popped my friend in the fish tank and set off. In with my luggage was a quantity of fishing tackle, quite a bit of fishing tackle in fact, but if Gisella was unhappy about sharing a van with it she managed to keep shtum.

It's a wretched drive all the way across southern England to Folkestone, but for Gisella to undertake the more direct Channel crossing, from Portsmouth to St Malo, was expecting a bit much of a thousand-year-old carp. I released her in the sea at Folkestone Beach and we agreed to meet up again at the beach at Wissant. The Channel was calm enough for a human to swim across but she still grumbled. I then had the simple business of taking a Dover-Calais ferry – so much cheaper than the train – and making the short journey down to our meeting point.

It was while I was waiting for Gisella at Wissant Plage, after having refilled the fish tank with water, that a vanload of police – they looked rather more psychotic than normal gendarmes – pulled up, demanded that I open the back of my van, and started haranguing me so vehemently I couldn't figure out what they were on about. I'm not a great linguist anyway. But then I picked out the word *trafiquant* and the centime dropped.

'I'm not a trafficker,' I blathered. '*Je ne suis pas trafiquant….*'

'*Alors*,' rumbled one of the brutes. '*Qu'est-ce que tu fous là?*'[1]

'Pardon? *Quoi?*'

'Why you 'ere, *mecton?*'

I hurriedly took out one of my fishing rods and assembled the two sections. 'I'm going fishing. Je suis…*pêcheur!*'

The police evidently thought I was barking mad choosing to fish there, or maybe one of them actually realised my carp gear was less than suitable for beach fishing, but they abruptly lost interest in me and drove off.

'*Bon vent, sales flics*,' said a raspy feminine voice from the seashore. 'Are you going to get me out of here? I'm bloody knackered.'

I lifted Gisella from the surf and placed her in the fish tank. '*Je crève de soif.* I'm bloody starving too.'

'It's just as well I stopped off at the Carrefour then. I've got bread, ham, cheese, fizzy water, brioche….'

'And? And?'

'A bottle of Calvados.'

'*Hors d'âge?*'[2]

'*Hors d'âge….* It was bloody expensive.'

We opted to stick to the *routes nationales* rather than take the *autoroutes*; we were in no hurry and I didn't fancy paying all the tolls anyway. We'd decided to avoid Paris, mindful that I wasn't a natural van-driver, and the survival rate for dithering Brits on the *Périphérique* is on the low side. It made sense to pass to the left-hand side of the capital, so for our first night in France we stopped at a Formule 1 hotel near Reims. It was cheap and not very cheerful.

I ate in a Restaurant Léon, which is apparently a chain of Belgian-style eateries, and was made to feel quite uncomfortable by my fellow diners. That could've been because I ordered two portions of *moules frites*,[3] one of which I took away with me when I left. Gisella appreciated it greatly, and said that maybe the Belgians were good for more than just producing comic books after all.

Our next stop off was a Hotel Ibis just outside Dijon. What a wonderful place Dijon is, with all its gloriously colourful, patterned medieval roof tiles cheering up the entire city. It also had a reputation for really good restaurants too, but I dined at the hotel. It had a twenty-euro *menu touristique* with an all-you-can-eat buffet as *entrée*. I was reasonably sure no one saw me scooping all sorts of *charcuterie* and shellfish and mayonnaisy things into a bag for Gisella.

It wasn't until we reached Lyon that we ran into any trouble. Finding a hotel was tough because there was a Europa League football match that night between the home team and Olympiakos, but in spite of all the red- and white-shirted Cro-Magnons pacing the streets, I managed to get a room in a…Formule 1. That wasn't the problem I encountered, however, nor were the football fans, in spite of their rowdiness. I was set upon by fellow anglers!

A group of four chaps in *camou* jackets, *carpistes*, carp-fishers evidently, caught sight of me dropping some pieces of *paupiette de veau*[4] into Gisella's tank in the back of the van and laid into me.

'*Voleur! Braconnier de poisson! Escroc! Bâtard Rosbif!*' they yelled. I decline to translate such insults, but I'm certainly *not* a poacher.

'What the fuck,' I winced as another boot thudded into my ribs.

'*Assez!*' bellowed a female but hardly feminine voice. '*Imbéciles! Crétins! Arrêtez cet instant!*'

Realising it was the large carp in the fish tank shouting at them, the four irate idiots did stop that instant. They'd been drinking, but were still aware that they couldn't all be sharing the same hallucination. That left them two options: engage with the bizarre creature who was evidently very ticked-off with them, or simply leg it. They chose the latter.

In spite of the shock and the pain I was in, I was able to offer Gisella more of an explanation for the attack than she could come up with. Many Brits own lakes in France and are notorious for nicking French carp to help stock them. Those guys probably thought I was doing the same with Gisella and decided to teach me a lesson. If I hadn't been hurting so badly I might actually have had a bit of sympathy for them.

The next day we agreed that our road trip wasn't proving as much fun as we'd anticipated, and Gisella was getting mightily fed up with living in a fish tank. We headed south, destination Provence. It was a long haul, made even more frustrating when we ground to a halt in appalling traffic as we approached Avignon.

Eventually we found ourselves on a D road, following a tributary of La Durance called le Vairon, passing through a charming little village called Vairon-la-Romaine, and then following what was no more than a dusty track to an ancient stone-built mill on a side stream from the river. Le Moulin de la Herse. We'd bought, or rather were buying, the mill where Gisella had spent several happy years with Esteve, Beatris and Manon, around the time of the Napoleonic Wars. I was still hurting from my going-over from my fellow carp anglers, and completely knackered to boot. I lifted Gisella from the fish tank and placed her gently in the cooling, soothing mill pool, then I fumbled together my fishing bivvy, dragged out my bed chair, crawled into my sleeping bag, and fell into deep sleep.

The next morning I realised how accurate Gisella's description of the old mill had been. Set in perfect Provençal countryside, the ancient stone building, with an adjoining boathouse, stood above a delightful, eddying pool. The millwheel was now no more than a skeleton, but we weren't planning on grinding any flour, so that was fine by us. The whole place needed serious restoration, but we'd understood that when we'd seen the photos. We were both seriously hungry, so before all else I drove back into Vairon-la-Romaine where I'd spotted a Huit-à-Huit convenience store, and stocked up on a few basics. When I returned I found a sporty little Peugeot parked by the mill house and a smartly dressed lady taking an interest in my bivvy, and, when I pulled up, me. I couldn't help noticing how attractive she was: mid-thirties or thereabouts, shortish but elegantly cut black hair, and a noticeable mole on her cheek that only accentuated her good looks. What she saw in me was probably a very rumpled tourist with purple bags under his eyes and in desperate need of a shower.

'*Et vous êtes…?*' she said as I climbed down from the van.

'*Je m'appelle Mike Apperley. J'— J'achète cette maison.*'

'Ah, the Englishman. I presume I spoke to your wife before? Or your secretary? My name is Marie Dulac, *notaire….*'

'Ah, delighted to meet you. You spoke to my, er, *associate* before.'

'Her French was immaculate.'

'So I believe.'

'Someone told me they saw a van here yesterday evening so I thought I'd take a look.'

'I hope it's okay stopping here. But I am buying the place, and I could hardly have myself arrested for trespassing on what's about to be my own property.'

'Of course not. *Ben alors*. You have some work to do here, no?'

'Just a bit. I understand the house was last lived in seven years ago and everything needs redoing. Looking at it, that's an understatement. But my God, look where we are. The hills, the lavender fields, the sunflowers, the river. It's paradise, or it's going to be.'

Marie handed me her card. 'Come and see me in Vairon tomorrow morning, we can clear up all the paperwork then and it'll all go far quicker for you. I can also give you the details of some really good local contractors – in a few months you won't know the place.' We shook hands.

'You like her,' said a husky voice from the mill pool as soon as the Peugeot had scrunched away down the track.

'What do you mean? I don't know her.'

'Ah, you *do* like her,' Gisella chuckled.

'So she's attractive. I can't go around fancying every attractive woman I meet.'

'That's odd, I thought all men did that. Anyway, you're probably right. She'd probably chew you up for breakfast and spit you out again.'

'Thank you, Gisella.'

The documents were signed the following day, but Marie's estimate that the work on our house would take only a few months was pure imagination. We were in the Midi, where the laws of time operate totally differently. But over the next three years the roof was fixed, the electrics redone, a new kitchen and bathroom fitted, a new septic tank installed (the salesman *was* bald and I wondered if he was a French cousin of the creature my ex-wife had run off with), and a doorway was knocked through from the kitchen to the adjoining boathouse, which was converted into Gisella's den. I'd managed to rig up a large-scale waterproof keypad and remote control, which could be operated with taps of a fish's nose, so Gisella had full internet and TV access.

I attended weekly French classes at Cavaillon, but my progress was painfully slow. I made a few friends locally – one or two even close enough to be trusted meeting Gisella and keeping her presence secret – but I steered pretty much clear of the British ex-pat community – those who remained that was. Pink gin really wasn't my thing, and their urge to prove who'd been in the area the longest, as if it afforded them some kind of kudos, was intensely irritating. It was the Raj revisited. As for the fragrant Marie Dulac, she soon left to join a bigger practice in Nîmes, but really and truly big city life (in the grand metropolis of Nîmes!) never suited her very much and she recently returned to Vairon.

Our pleasant life continued on an even keel until a week ago I received a call from the people at *La Dépêche* requesting an interview. Some English family had dobbed me in, telling them about an eccentric English writer living at an old mill who'd written a mad history book some years back. Probably revenge for me not turning up to one of their insufferable long lunches, where everyone bitches about the bloody French but still shows off their immaculate French accents. With a heavy heart I agreed to meet their reporter, as a refusal almost always makes those people even more painful.

Notes

[1]These uncouth police thugs used the 'Tu – toi' familiar form of 'you' rather than the more formal 'vous', simply to be intimidating. It was quite lost on Mike.
[2]Hors d'age, as we know, beyond age. Important if you want a really good Calvados.
[3]*Moules frites.* Mussels and chips. Simple, delicious, and one of the most underrated dishes in the world.
[4]*Paupiettes de veau.* Veal rissoles. Honestly.

Epilogue

'He's gone.'

'*Bon vent.* Good riddance. Now I'm looking at *Tías y Otros Amantes*, so a bit of hush please.'

'Those Spanish soaps'll turn your brain to Roquefort, Gisella. Buying you a TV was the worst decision I ever made.'

'Do you think if Rodrigo sleeps with his step-mum's sister it's really incest, or does the fact they're not blood relatives make it okay?'

'I don't care who's bloody sleeping with who. Those programmes are brain-dead.'

'But is Consuela Inez's mother or daughter?'

'Gisella!'

'*Bien, bien.* I'll pause it. So you met the journo. And you told him the unblemished truth, yes?'

'Yes, or near as dammit. But maybe I let him think the book paid for everything here. Forgot to mention the, um, lottery thing.'

'Telling complete strangers I'm actually real gives me the willies, Mike. Someday someone's going to call your bluff.'

'But it works, doesn't it? It's known as hiding in plain sight – everyone thinks I'm nutty as a fruitcake and leaves us in peace.'

'But did you have to give that *mec* the full treatment? You bent his ear for the better part of a day, I'm surprised he didn't fall asleep on you.'

'I think he did a few times.'

'Couldn't you just have rolled your eyes a little and drooled on your sleeve?'

'It was fun. It's quiet around here. And *La Dépêche* certainly won't be bothering us again for a very long time.'

'He didn't even ask to see me?'

'As a matter of fact he did. I led him up and down the millrace calling out for you, then I told him you'd probably swum down to Vairon to see what people were throwing in from the bridge. He just took it as added proof that I was round the twist and couldn't wait to leave.'

'Letting him believe the book royalties paid for all this though, not a word about our little windfall, that was *vilain*...naughty.'

'The devil made me do it. Anyway, if he's naïve enough to believe that anyone makes money from writing books let him carry on. The *Rights of Man and Fish* makes us enough for my trips to Intermarché, otherwise we're living on ill-gotten gains.'

'Mike Apperley, long-suffering moralist. So you found a lottery ticket in a supermarket trolley and it won us nearly 2,000,000. Get over yourself.'

'It could've been lost by a single mum on benefits.'

'It could've been lost by a demented racist who bricked up his gran in a chimney. You can always donate the money to charity – but I'll kill you if you do.'

'You know maybe it would've been better if that journo *had* believed it all. You'd become famous.'

'*Assez*. Letting everyone believe you're a crazy fantasist has worked fine so far, let's not ruin it.'

'But imagine it: *Gisella the amazing thousand-year-old talking fish*. You'd be a sensation, and we'd make an absolute fortune!'

'*Oui*, I can just imagine it. Talk show appearances, TV panel games, discussion programmes, the celebrity treadmill, greed-crazed agents, paparazzi on our case twenty-four-seven, book deals, film rights, lawyers, defamation cases, endless transatlantic trips, religious nut groups, armies of hangers-on and parasites that would make Cesare

Borgia's killer lampreys look cuddly. What a complete bloody *cauchemar*...a nightmare!'

'You didn't mind being a celebrity a hundred or so years ago.'

'That was different. I was a secret celebrity. Anyway, people had more decorum back then.'

'Okay, calm down. You know I'm pulling your fin. I'd hate that just as much as you.'

'Just don't say that sort of thing. I'm an old fish and I don't need the aggravation.'

'Very well, grandma. Changing the subject, you haven't forgotten Marie is coming round for dinner tomorrow evening?'

'No, I haven't forgotten.'

'And I hope you won't be as rude to her as you were last time. I'm surprised she's coming back here even.'

'Judging by the noises coming from upstairs I think you'd have a problem keeping her away.'

'I must get those floorboards seen to. I'd forgotten about you and your super-sensitive lateral line. Why can't you just go deaf like normal old people? And anyway, what have you got against Marie? You obviously don't like her.'

'She's got a mole.'

'Seriously? You don't like her because she's got a mole?'

'*Exactement*.'

'Oh blimey, she's got a mole on her cheek, and apparently I shouldn't wear shorts because they make me look like Toulouse-Lautrec. Even although I'm nearly six foot.'

'It's a matter of proportion. Long trunk, short legs. It's not a good look.'

'You know Marie still thinks there's something very slightly odd about us two.'

'Ha, Gisella and Mike, the great romance for the ages. You should be so lucky.'

'It was doomed to failure from the word go. The age difference was just too great.'

'Idiot.'

'And with that I'm going to go—'

'Before you do anything I need my *pastis*.'

'Right away, madame.'

'And I hope you didn't get that supermarket muck.'

'Pastis Cinquante et Un, as always. And now I'm off down to the main river for an evening's fishing.'

'If you catch one of those obnoxious catfish bonk it on the head.'

'I won't.'

'And I hope you fall in.'

'Fuck you too.'

'And you.'

'I love you, Gisella. And try not to stay glued to that TV all night.'

COGNA
HOR'S
D'AGE

Other AN Editions Titles

We are a small, independent publishing partnership that promotes the values of Humane Socialism, Humanism, a wide spectrum of independent thinking and art for art's sake. Our aim is to publish works that are original and worthy of note, rather than follow trends and merge into the mainstream.

Oscar: The Second Coming, by Dan Pearce

"It's delightful! Very very funny ... anyone with a true sense of him should find it wholly engaging!" — Stephen Fry

This beautifully illustrated graphic novel from cartoonist and artist Dan Pearce brings the celebrated and notorious Victorian a hundred years into the future. With humour and a Wildean sense of mischief in his own right, Dan recounts that the idea for the book came to him several years ago during a meeting with the editor of the famous humour magazine Punch. The editor had seen a few pages of a pictorial biography of Oscar Wilde that Dan had been working on. When he asked if there was a way of making it more contemporary, Dan had the brainwave of having Wilde abducted from Reading Goal by aliens and transported a century into the future.

That Was Hugo Blythe MP, by Peter Cowlam

Seasoned literary craftsman Peter Cowlam presents us with the unexpurgated diary of Alaric Casteele. Casteele, an acid, aloof intellectual at odds with his teaching job, has as a 'last ditch' agreed to work as researcher for Hugo Blythe, who heads up New Labour's so-called 'Ministry of Cult'. Through the whisperings of Westminster, Alaric discovers something is afoot. People in the department are briefing against Hugo, but Hugo begins to think that Alaric is the culprit. Casteele turns to electronic skulduggery in order to find out who really is behind the attacks, drip-fed to the press. He writes his diary in a concentrated aestheticised style, as we pay close attention and read between the lines. Love him or hate him, Alaric – in reality a small-c conservative, a sort of enemy within – reinvigorates a forgotten Zeitgeist, and an era pre-dating '#Me Too'. But is Casteele's diary all that is left of Blairite Britain and its milieu as disillusion deepens? Peter Cowlam's magnificent achievement is to create a character whose glancing passage through the 'Ministry of Cult' mirrors a complex world of moral ambiguity and disaffection. That Was Hugo Blythe MP is a compressed, unblinking portrayal of a politics consumed by intrigue, where value placed on celebrity outbids anything else.

Captcha This! by J.W. Wood

"*J.W. Wood's stories evince a gift for the quotidian, employing brilliant conceits and mischievous turns of phrase which enrich the writing at every point. Capturing the frustration of curtailed lives and the grim horrors of the corporate world, Wood presents a meta-fictional universe in which the rich realise their folly and we control computers, not the other way round.*"

– Julian Stannard, award-winning poet, author: The University of Bliss (Sagging Meniscus, 2024)

In 2015, J.W. Wood jacked in his day job and disappeared to homestead acreage on an island in British Columbia, Canada – armed only with an axe, some tools and the determination to free himself. *Captcha This*! spares no-one: pompous investment bankers, vacuous fame-hunters, feudal tech overlords, invasive grammar-nazi software, government by bogus statistic and further denizens of today's digital abyss are all given a not-so-gentle skewering.

www.ingramcontent.com/pod-product-compliance
Ingram Content Group UK Ltd.
Pitfield, Milton Keynes, MK11 3LW, UK
UKHW021834260225
455614UK00021B/204